MW01640226

Scout Squad: Going Native

Scout Squad: Going Native

Mark O. Chapman

To Joy + Michael,
Thanks for your support and
Friendship through the years!
Mark O. Chap

iUniverse, Inc.
New York Bloomington

Scout Squad: Going Native

iUniverse books may be ordered through booksellers or by contacting:

iUniverse
1663 Liberty Drive
Bloomington, IN 47403
www.iuniverse.com
1-800-Authors (1-800-288-4677)

ISBN: 978-0-595-46904-8 (pbk)
ISBN: 978-0-595-71657-9 (cloth)
ISBN: 978-0-595-91193-6 (ebk)

Printed in the United States of America

iUniverse rev. date: 1/26/2009

Dedication

My first novel is dedicated to Mom, Dad, and all those who never laughed.

I also want to give special thanks to the love of my life, my wife, Pilar.

Contents

CHAPTER 1

The two scout ships flanked the science shuttle on the Chief Science Officer's first visit. The symbol of the UWC Orion was emblazoned on the side of each ship. The Council had sent its flagship to the distant world the Council had named Venus Two due to its vast regions of lush green forests. A long distance probe had made contact the year prior to the arrival of the Orion. There were several Brodarian satellites circling the planet and its water covered moon. The people of the planet had been contacted before.

The three ships had circled the water moon, looking at the ample sea-life below before they moved on to the planet. They skirted around the populated areas and slowed to land on a grassy plateau overlooking a vast forest that covered miles of lowland before it struck across the foothills and into the towering mountains.

The two scout ships broke away from the shuttle and circled the landing area twice before settling in beside the shuttle. The front cockpit on each scout ship popped open with a hiss. The pilots climbed out on the wing and down a ladder that extended off the backside. The rear door of the shuttle clicked and lowered down from the top so a vehicle could drive out, but today Conrad Singh walked down the ramp. He was followed by a man and a woman dressed in green fatigues, each carrying portable scanners. Conrad smoothed back his dark hair, just starting to gray at the temples. His green eyes stood out against his dark skin. He glanced across the horizon, with his hands in his pockets.

The pilots walked around behind their ships, and Conrad looked back and forth at them. The two techs, who already had their orders, walked in opposite directions with their heads bent to their scanners.

Conrad looked at Sydni Colton. As she saw him looking at her, she broke into a spontaneous smile, and her dark brown eyes sparkled in the bright sunlight. She flipped her brown hair back over her shoulders and pulled out her scanner. Conrad smiled back before he glanced at Willy Colton, who had stopped and was looking off at the mountain. Even though Conrad was the Chief Science Officer on the UWC's flagship, he had a hard time believing that Willy and Sydni were twins.

Every scientist and science officer throughout the UWC knew about the Coltons although they didn't know their names. Willy and Sydni's parents were settlers on the planet Quadra Three after the scientists had cleared the planet for human habitation. They had missed something. A protein growing in the plants had acted much like radiation and genetically altered one of Cassandra Colton's twins.

As Conrad watched Willy, he shook his head a little. The textbooks and classroom lectures never told about the life that Willy was forced to lead as an outcast of his society. Willy's skin was as dark as Conrad's, but looked more like leather, and his eyes were gold-flecked brown, but shaped more like a cat's than a human's. His nose was shaped much like a regular nose, but only two slits opened with each breath instead of open nostrils. He had let his hair grow long, but tied it back in a ponytail with a piece of green flight suit material.

Sydni stopped next to Conrad and nudged him with her hip, gaining his attention. "So?" she asked.

"The trip was more than you said it would be," Conrad said, his voice accented from growing up and going to school in the New New Delhi Academy on Earth. "The moon of water is spectacular and would provide a great source of food if harvested properly."

Shaking her head, Sydni said, "Always thinking of the project."

"Not always," he said. "Just mostly."

Sydni punched in a code on her scanner, and her scout ship wavered and disappeared. Willy moved over to a compartment on the side of his ship and pressed his hand on a panel and a door slid open. He pulled out a rifle and pack. After slinging each one over a shoulder, he shut the compartment, then punched a code in his scanner, and his ship wavered and disappeared in front of him.

Turning back to Sydni and Conrad, Willy smiled and said, "What do you think, Doc?" Willy's voice was deep and gravelly.

"My friend, it is as you described it to me, although I will feel better when I am safely back to the walls of the Orion."

Willy started walking toward the edge of the plateau facing the mountains. His voice was nearly carried away with the wind, but they heard him as he said, "I can barely bring myself back up to that metal tomb every time I come down here."

"This planet is almost perfect for Willy's plans," Sydni said.

"What plans?" Conrad asked looking down into Sydni's eyes.

"Retirement plans."

Conrad laughed out loud. "What, in another twenty, thirty, or maybe fifty years. It's good and all, but how could you figure out where you want to live so far ahead of time?"

Willy looked over his shoulder. "Contracts. You forget, we are listed as hazardous duty full time. Since we spend our time on planets, we are contracted for it and can retire in half the time." Using his thumb, but looking forward again, Willy motioned to Sydni and said, "We only have ten more years until we can retire."

At the edge of the plateau, Willy crouched down. "This planet is perfect. It is not only big, it is mostly uninhabited." Pointing, Willy almost started talking to himself, "I could go deep in this place. So deep in the forest that no humans would be present for miles."

"So why retire?" Conrad asked looking at the vast land that stretched out from where he stood. "Why not just go now?"

Willy was silent for a moment while Sydni jabbed Conrad in the ribs, whispering, "Don't encourage him. I'm afraid he'll go."

After a while, Willy turned and looked up at Conrad. "Doc, I have to tell you, I have been close." Willy stood up and faced them. "I was close on Quadra Three when I was in third year of the junior Academy. My parents wouldn't have cared. My classmates wouldn't have cared. The neighbors wouldn't have cared. Only one person would have cared. My sister was the only person who gave a damn about me." Spinning around, Willy faced the mountains again. "She knows she is the only link I had to still being human, and I guess I wasn't ready to hide from the human race. Now I want to be where she can find me, and I have found that having a paycheck waiting in a bank could supply me with a few things that the vast forest could not."

A large bird flew out of the trees, his large wings beating against the still afternoon air. Willy watched the bird for a minute and then said, "Now, Conrad, it would seem that there is another person in the known universe, who does not shrink away from my countenance."

The bird turned and circled overhead for several minutes before heading straight for the tallest peak. Conrad stared at Willy and commented, "The way you wear your cloak over your face around the Orion, you are certain to not let anyone near. Surely a people who can stamp out prejudice can overlook a genetic malformation."

Willy laughed out loud, and it echoed back from the hills. "We have stamped out prejudice against race, religion, sex, but I strike a deeper fear in people's hearts."

Shrugging, Conrad asked, "But how? In what way?"

With a finger, Willy touched one of his sharp teeth. Then he pointed to his eyes and the tips of his somewhat pointed ears. Holding up a hand, he extended his claws, which were two inches long, starting at the first knuckle. "Many see me as the image of evil. Even though they read the computers, and see the notes on my condition in the med journals; they fear that which is different."

"I only see skin differences with us, nothing more. Inside you have the heart of a warrior and the soul of an explorer."

Sydni slid her arm inside Conrad's and said, "Now if you could convince billions of others, we'd be okay."

"Out there may be a solitary way of life," Willy said, turning away again. "But I have long since given up on the traditional UWC family living happily ever after, working out of some spaceport." Willy shook his head a little. "That will work for you, Conrad, or maybe for Sydni."

Conrad knew it was true, but he didn't want to admit it. His ideals of life didn't want to admit such a thing could be true in the Twenty-third Century. He was searching for words to try and console his friend when Willy spoke up again. "But I did not bring you all the way down to the planet to listen to me and the stories of my life."

Willy pulled his rifle off his shoulder and started down the hill; he walked slowly, listening for anything different. Sydni pulled her scanner off her belt. She pushed a few buttons before following her brother down the hill with Conrad close on her heels, glancing back and forth.

The laughter from Sydni danced down the slope when she noticed Conrad's uneasy movements. Sydni slowed down and allowed Conrad to come alongside of her. "Don't you worry, Conrad. I will protect you."

Suddenly, like an animal caught in a trap, Conrad looked for his assistants. "It has been a long time since I have landed on a planet without a spaceport."

"I'll wager you never much like landing on planets for research at all."

Conrad caught her eye and raised his eyebrows. "Don't let my staff know. I would never be able to live it down."

"Your secret is safe with me," she said with a wink.

The slope gave way to a creek bed lined with dark gray and black rock. Water trickled along from pool to pool. Willy was crouched down at the edge of a pool sipping water from his hand.

"You should try this water, Doc, it'll kill you to go back to the ship and drink the reconstituted." Willy took a small canteen off his belt and filled it. He reached down and scooped up more water as Sydni helped Conrad down the rocks on the bank. "The most difficult part of taking the long hike across the galaxy every time is going without fresh water for a few weeks."

Sydni crouched down and started drinking. When she noticed that Conrad was hesitating, she said, "Come on, Conrad. You yourself okayed the water here."

Crouching between the two, Conrad mumbled, "I know, I know. Next you're going to make me camp out down here and sample the wild cuisine."

Willy laughed and glanced sideways at Conrad before he said, "After I show you what I found, you're going to want to camp out down here."

Wiping water away from his mouth, Conrad stood up saying, "Not bloody likely."

Taking off right through the stream, Willy said, "It's just down here a few more meters."

Sydni followed Willy's path as Conrad picked his way across the rocks. Once across, Conrad fell into a jog behind the twins. Up over the next bank, there was a short rocky out-cropping. Sitting on top of a rock was a large black bird with a bright red beak and blue tail-feathers. The bird turned and watched the three until Willy was only a few feet away.

With a sharp squawk and a beating of wings against the rocks, the bird took off and quickly ascended far above them. The slits of Willy's nose opened wide and he breathed in. "Can't you smell it yet, Doc?"

Conrad sniffed the air and knew there was a hint of something in the air, but he couldn't decipher it. They walked around the rock, where there was a cleft. Another boulder was wedged down as far as it could go.

"I don't know why we examined it," Sydni said. "It's been sitting here umpteen million years without anyone else disturbing it."

Shoving his nose down close to the rock, Conrad sniffed again, this time jerking his head back. He reeled for a moment, and Willy reached out a hand and grabbed his shoulder, steadying him. "I forget you're probably not used to its raw form."

Sydni grabbed the rock and pulled on it. The rock gave a little, but was wedged in. On her second try, the rock came free with the sound of breaking crystals. The rock was coated with a thick coppery coating. Immediately, Conrad smiled.

"I never dreamed this planet would have Coppertroid Fuel. The UWC will be very pleased with this find." Conrad pulled out his scanner and turned it on, hovering it over the cleft in the rock. "With a source of fuel, the search of the galaxy could be expanded from here to cover this whole sector."

"This would also explain the Jolabwe source of power, without speed or flight." Sydni said.

"Who?" Conrad asked.

Willy smiled and said, "You would call them the City Dwellers."

"Ah," Conrad said, still keeping his eyes on the liquid. "If they have not learned to refine it yet, then that could be very true."

Finally looking up, Conrad turned to Willy and said, "What did you tell me of the Forest People?"

"The Hingandu I have not contacted yet, although I am close, but I have heard that they seem to have powered weapons of some sort. Extremely sharp spears, knives, and bow-like weapons. This land is actually in the Hingandu territory, which is why we have not produced a sample yet. Once they have been contacted and we have approval, then we shall proceed."

Distantly a bird called out. Conrad looked up. His mind swirled at this information. It would be a grand find for the UWC, and he would be the one who reported the scout's findings. Glancing down at his scanner, he spontaneously broke into a smile; the unrefined Coppertroid was the purest he had ever seen. "I will say this much, my friend, your find is a great one that brings me much pleasure, but not even this would make me want to camp out on this planet. I can wait for a sample."

Sydni laughed, but Willy held up a hand and silenced her. She studied her scanner and adjusted the parameters to cover movement. Several blips showed on her screen. Holding up her hand, she gained Willy's attention. "Twelve. From the mountain."

Willy nodded toward the outcropping, and Sydni reached out and grabbed Conrad's arm and began dragging him around the rock. They crouched down and watched as Willy still stood where he had been. Willy pulled out his communicator and said, "This is Willy, get the ship cloaked and stay down."

A quiet voice spoke back, "Affirmative."

Willy turned and walked to where Sydni and Conrad crouched. He crouched down behind Conrad and pointed over Conrad's shoulder. "Look there, they won't be long."

Twelve flying creatures broke onto the horizon, flying faster than Conrad imagined they could have. He squinted to look at them, and Sydni pushed a view recorder in front of him. Conrad took the view recorder and zoomed in on the flying creatures. They were feline-like animals with large wings that spanned at least fifteen feet. Suddenly all their wings held fast and the creatures began to soar before they banked and turned away from them.

Conrad cursed under his breath. He whispered, "I didn't get a look at the riders."

"Actually, only the lead three had riders, the others were without," Willy said.

"Very beautiful creatures."

"Extremely," Sydni said, still looking out toward the specks in the sky. Conrad held the view recorder out to Sydni until she looked his way and took it back. "Their wings are incredibly strong and can carry two or three people. I have seen them soar at higher altitudes rising and falling on the winds."

"Don't be fooled by their beauty. Someone told me that they can pluck a grazing animal off the plain and fly off all the while carrying a rider."

"Incredible." Conrad looked again to the sky, but the creatures were long gone. "That I would like to see."

"Me too," Sydni added.

"Not me," Willy said. They both looked up at him, and he smiled and continued, "I want to be riding on one when it plucks something off the ground and soars away."

"That's my brother. He's always thinking of the hunt."

"Or just new ways to hunt," Willy said.

Conrad stood up and leaned against the rock. "Is that the whole reason you became a scout?"

Willy shrugged. "When I was little, five or six, just after I started taking off into the woods, I was torn between two voices. One was the call of the woods, and the other was Sydni calling out to me to come home. That was when I heard about scouts." Willy slung his rifle across his shoulder. "I thought that they made that job for me so I could live in the real world with Sydni."

"One night, after he learned about scouts, he took me outside and started leading me through the woods. We crept right up behind a Quadra Three Gazelle as it drank from a stream. It never knew we were there." Sydni smiled as she remembered. "Willy looked at me and said they would pay us to do that."

"That was the night we made our pact," Willy said climbing up on the outcropping and sitting down.

"What pact?" Conrad asked.

Willy and Sydni locked eyes for a moment. They had been together since birth, and often didn't need to speak since they knew what the other would be thinking. They both knew that to Conrad, they were more than a living science lesson. He was their friend, and there would be no problem in telling him anything.

Sydni checked her scanner and sat down in the grass. "Even at that young age, Willy knew people didn't accept him." Conrad frowned and Sydni noticed. "Most people didn't accept him. If we wanted to get anywhere, we had to be the best. Not just in any one thing, mind you, we had to be the best at everything. So we started studying like never before, we traveled the forest daily in all conditions, and if we could, we would take our books into the woods and study there." Sydni paused and looked at her brother again. "To get to my point, our pact was to never be separated, and always sign on as a team."

Willy chuckled deep within himself. It had bothered others of Quadra Three to be around him, but when he and Sydni demanded to play on the same team, to be in the same class, and not go if they couldn't, it had frustrated many. He didn't care. The people of Quadra Three had never cared about him; his own parents didn't even seem to care. Willy sighed.

Conrad strained his neck to look at Willy. "Didn't the children you grew up with become...well....used to your appearance."

"No, they were full of their parent's prejudice and fears. It was as if I were diseased and they all could catch it."

Sydni cleared her throat. "Phyllis was awfully used to you."

"Until her father put a stop to it, the..." Willy stopped himself. "I would like to see her again someday. She was one of the only other people in that city who took the time to get to know me."

There was a long pause as they sat watching the day pass. After a few more minutes, Conrad laughed. "Do you think we should tell my assistants that they can move about now?"

Willy pulled out his communicator and said, "All clear. You can resume activities."

"Well, that certainly will keep them on their toes," Conrad said.

"We should not stay here long," Willy said standing up. "This is near the territory of the Hingandu tribe I want to contact. I do not want to endanger my chances of meeting them by scaring them."

Conrad stood up and nodded. "That would be wise. Besides, many things now must be done about the Coppertroid. I need to be in my office." He reached down with a slender hand and offered it to Sydni, who graciously took it. He pulled her up and she thanked him.

Willy started jogging back the way they had come, leaving Conrad and Sydni staring into each other's eyes for a moment. They saw him and turned to follow. Sydni checked her scanner as Willy reached the top of the rise and crouched down. She could tell by the readings that a small group of herd animals had stopped by the stream.

Willy was lying on his stomach at the top of the rise, and Sydni and Conrad crawled up on either side of him. There were twenty creatures, only three feet tall and four feet long, with shaggy brown fur. Each had corkscrew horns that were about two feet long and tails that hung to the ground. One of the largest animals, with horns about three and a half feet long stood on the far side of the herd with its head held high, sniffing into the wind.

Willy whispered in Conrad's direction, "They are very skittish, and if the breeze shifts again and they smell us, they will be gone in a flash."

Conrad nodded and continued to look. Willy knew that Conrad enjoyed the live view of the creatures of the planet, but had no joy of such open spaces. This was often the case with people who grew up in the mega-cities of Earth, who never saw open blue skies or had rooms by themselves growing up. He also knew that for Conrad to make Chief Science Officer, he would have had to go planetside many times before ever achieving the rank.

A gust of air rushed around them, and the animal overlooking the others stamped its foot. They raised their heads in unison at the warning. Another second and the tiny creatures bolted in unison down the creek bottom at full speed. The long tails of the animals bounced in the air as they ran.

"Very impressive show you've put on for me today," Conrad said as he stood up.

"And to think we were just playing it by ear. Willy and I don't often throw such parties."

Willy grunted and said, "To think I just wanted to walk in your office with a picture and tell you."

Conrad held up a hand. "With a find of this nature, I don't care how you tell me as long as you tell me."

Sydni and Conrad started down the hill, and Willy looked around. He wanted to remember what this place looked like before they fouled it with the stink of humans, before buildings that reached the sky cluttered the beautiful horizon, and mostly before they criss-crossed the land with roadways and litter dropped by inconsiderate people.

Laughter caught his attention, and he saw Conrad standing on a rock shaking his leg, which was soaked to the knee. Sydni was standing in the water laughing at him.

Willy started running down the slope and picked up speed. When he reached the bank, he launched himself into the air and vaulted over the stream. Landing on the far side, Willy took a few steps, stopped, and turned. Conrad was staring at him, having paused with one leg still held up in mid-air.

A smile crossed Willy's face, showing his sharp teeth as he crossed his arms. "If you don't want to get wet, you need to learn to jump."

Conrad looked back and forth at the thirty plus feet that Willy had cleared. He continued his way across the rocks and joined Sydni and Willy on the far side. "Sydni, can you jump that far?" Conrad asked.

Sydni shrugged and said, "If I was really pushed, maybe. Probably not on a regular basis, though."

Conrad shook his head, amazed at the agility of both his friends. Willy clasped a hand on Conrad's shoulder as they walked and said, "Doc, you have to remember that we've been practicing this kind of stuff since we were kids. It's how we grew up."

"That does not keep me from being amazed, Willy."

Sydni turned off her scanner and hooked it back on her belt. "Conrad, if we ever stop amazing you, life will get awfully dull."

"Well," Conrad said looking up the hill for the ships. "Let's keep the fun going and have dinner together back on board the Orion."

Willy, who usually kept out of the public dining halls due to most of the talk he could start with his entrance, paused. Sydni loved the idea and immediately responded, "Great. What a way to top off a wonderful day."

Sydni, already thinking that Willy would decline, saw the look in his eyes; to her delight, Conrad was one step ahead of her. "Since the cook owes me a favor, I shall have him prepare the meal and bring it to my quarters."

The two science techs were ahead, looking over a scanner one of them held. Willy reached back with one hand and pulled the hood of his cloak up over his head to help hide his face. He had found most people could live with the mystery more than the real facts, so he kept the hood up while in the company of others. Although the Techs had mostly seen him since they often worked together, it was a habit he kept.

"Sounds good to me too, Doc," Willy said smiling under his cloak. "Just let me know what time."

The two techs snapped to attention when they realized that Conrad had walked within range. Conrad's tone became one of authority and command as he said, "Ready the shuttle for takeoff."

After a quick salute, the techs were gone. Willy uncloaked his ship and walked over and pressed the panel. He placed his rifle and pack in the compartment and pressed his hand again on the panel and the compartment closed. He turned back to Conrad and Sydni when Conrad said, "I will leave you a message and tell you what time dinner will be served."

The cloak hiding the shuttle shuddered for a moment as the whir of the engines began. Bowing just a little, Conrad said, "I better go before they leave me down here."

"See you shipside," Sydni said with a little wave.

Willy just nodded in return.

Both Willy and Sydni began stepping back from the shuttle. The whir of the engines increased to a high pitch. With a burst of warmth, the sound began to recede into the sky.

Sydni stretched her arms back over her head and watched the sky for a moment longer. Willy crouched down, plucked a blade of grass, and looked up at his sister. "I could always just not show up, tonight."

She looked at him and cocked her head to one side. "What are you talking about?"

Willy knew she knew, but she liked to play shy and innocent with him. He played along. "You know, Doc and you." Sydni put a hand on her chest and shook her head a little. "He sure does love you, Syd."

Sydni turned her head and looked at the mountain. "I know."

"Do you love him?"

She paused for almost a minute before she said, "I think so. I don't know. What do you think?"

Shaking his head, Willy said, "I can't tell you what's in your heart, not where it concerns love."

With a smile, Sydni muffled a laugh, "You know what I mean."

"I think Doc Singh is good people. He's honest and fair and has a good heart." Willy paused and smiled at her for a moment. "Would he satisfy your sense of adventure? It's not like he would spend a week in the wild with nothing more than a tent."

Leaning back against Willy's cloaked shuttle, Sydni said, "You know that has nothing to do with love. If the man I marry loves me and is a good man and father, then who cares if he won't traverse unknown planets? That's what I have you for."

Willy put his hand on his ship and looked past Sydni. "It would be the first person you dated who wasn't shaking in his boots when faced with the task of meeting me."

Sydni laughed. Inside her heart ached, wishing that her brother could meet someone who could see past his appearance and see the man within. "A family dinner without sideways glances to make certain you wouldn't pounce on them."

"They always seemed a little on edge." Willy smiled so that his sharp teeth were exposed and continued, "Besides, once I can smell the fear in them, it would just egg me on." He put a hand on his sister's shoulder. "I couldn't stand letting you settle for such a wimpy group."

"Good thing. The last time we were home, almost every one of our classmates was still planetside raising little families and tending to very, very boring jobs."

"Mom and Dad wished and prayed that you had stayed planetside with a man from the community to raise the perfect family of little gremlins running around at their feet."

Sydni patted Willy's hand before she said, "I never understood them."

"They were dumped with a situation that was irreversible, Syd. I was the embarrassment they couldn't stand to admit. I was blamed for all the missed promotions, bad luck, and the reason they were not the popular community hoppers. Deep down, they were really good people who I will always believe loved me, but being so afraid of me, just didn't know how to show it." Willy looked away and withdrew his hand. "They were one of the first family settlers to that place and they ended up shunned. I think they breathed a sigh of relief the day I was accepted to the Academy. Too afraid I would stay forever on the mountain behind their house, lurking in the night."

They paused for a long time and Willy added, "I just hope that someday they are both happy, but afraid they will never attain that with you living so far away from them and so close to me."

"I just hope that you are happy, brother."

"Look around at this beautiful land. How could I not believe in God when I see such a place that was created and is at my disposal for the next, what maybe a year or two? I have you to spend the time with, and a new friend in Conrad when I am forced to spend time on the ship. How could I be anything but happy?"

Sydni knew he just skirted around her true meaning, and she also knew he didn't like discussing his feelings about the future, a family, and life other than some place to roam. "I mean about happiness of the heart, love, sex, passion."

Willy's nostrils flared and he stood straight. Almost laughing, he said, "Jeez, Sydni. Why don't you just get to the point?"

"Come on, Will. With all this talk of Contrad and me, I want to know how you are."

"Love. Nothing there. Sex and passion can be split two ways. My passion for exploring this place is unbound, but as far as my passion with sex, you know that on almost every tour I've been on, there has been some woman very curious about me. Not wanting anyone to know, or no public show of a relationship, yet curious."

Sydni slapped Willy's arm and said, "You never told me, who is it?"

Willy smiled. "That little bio-tech where we hand in the collections. The one with the blonde hair."

"You dog."

"But she doesn't want anyone to know, and like the others, I am certain I am just some passing fancy."

"You never know," Sydni said.

Shrugging his shoulders, Willy just continued to admire the landscape as he said, "You never know, but to tell you the truth Sydni, I've been down this avenue so many times, and it gravitates the same way each time. Another man, one more acceptable in society life, will come along, or our assignments will change." Willy paused long enough to take a deep breath. "I'm not saying that I'm not enjoying it one bit, she's a lot of fun."

Sydni reached over and smacked her brother's arm again. "You're just another pig."

"She's having as much fun as I, but you call me the pig."

"Live with it," she said. "Well, brother, what do you say we pack it in and head shipside?"

Willy closed his eyes as he sniffed the air. "Another moment, please, sis. I want to remember what pollution free air smells like, because once we've informed the ambassador and the captain, this planet will never be the same."

* * * *

Silent halls always pleased Willy, when he made his way through the Orion, and it didn't hurt that Conrad's quarters were only a deck away from his. After a quick check in either direction, Willy slipped his cloak off, revealing his crisp, white shirt, black vest, and black pants. He wore his shiny dress boots from his formal uniform for lack of any casual attire. He ran his hand over the scanner on the control panel to the right of the door. The door opened with the soft swishing of air, and music drifted into the hall.

Willy stepped inside and was quickly greeted by Conrad, who wore a dark blue suit and white shirt. Conrad bowed and said, "Thank you for coming tonight. As always in my home, make yourself comfortable. May I take your cloak?"

Bowing slightly in return, Willy handed over his cloak. "Thanks for having me, Doc."

The main room was large, befitting his rank, with windows along the far wall. Conrad had two extra long couches, one along the windows, while the other one faced the first, with a comfortable chair on each end. The coffee table in the middle was made from black wood and hand carved, from the last planet they had visited; it was a gift from Willy and Sydni. The wall to the right was half entertainment center and half bookcase. Conrad had a prize collection of antique books that he was extremely proud of. Around the corner to the left was the dining table, large enough for six people, which was usually stacked with specimens that Conrad was working with. Today the table was set for three with enough silverware and glasses for six people to dine. In the center was a crystal just over a foot tall out of which thin tendrils had grown and twisted among themselves, and as the music played, the crystal changed colors with the rhythm. Just past the table was the food preparation area, and Willy could see the cook had been by already, as several warming trays were covered with steam escaping out the sides. Both the door into the office and the door into the bedroom suite were closed.

"May I fix you something to drink?" Conrad asked

Willy nodded. "Whatever you're having is fine by me, Doc."

Conrad walked past Willy, after hanging his cloak on a hook to the right of the door. "We just made a new batch of SynthWine in the lab, which I have to say, actually tastes like some kind of wine."

"If that's what you happen to have open, then we shall drink SynthWine."

The green plastic bottle, with a cork-colored cap, was the telltale sign of SynthWine. As Conrad started pouring the deep burgundy liquid. It had the same alcohol content as real wine, but always seemed laced with a plastic aftertaste, the door chimed. Conrad, who was filling the second of three glasses, looked up and said, "Come in."

The door swished open, and Sydni stepped in. She was wearing a black jumpsuit, which seemed to be the current fashion craze on the ship, although Willy didn't understand how she could dress in a jumpsuit most of the day for work and then consider it to be perfect casual wear. Of course the bright blue sash tied at her waist was her way of specializing the outfit. So Willy pretended to understand fashion, but figured he never would.

Conrad carried over the three glasses and paused when he saw Sydni, who had joined Willy. "You look spectacular tonight, Sydni," he said with a hint of a smile on his face.

The smile that Conrad induced in Sydni was so infectious that Willy smiled as well. Handing each of them a glass, Conrad held his up and said, "I would like to make a toast to us. To friends."

Willy and Sydni clinked glasses with Conrad. As the other two sipped their wine, Willy held his glass underneath his nose as the two slits widened and he breathed deeply. Squinting, he glanced at Conrad, who was now paying close attention to him. Willy tipped up his glass and sipped.

Sydni said, "This is the best batch of SynthWine ever, Conrad."

Conrad nodded, but kept his eyes on Willy, who after swallowing his wine grinned enough to show the points of his teeth. "It's the best SynthWine you'll ever taste, sis," Willy said. "Only because it tastes more like barrel-aged Alpha One wine."

Conrad smiled and nodded. "I guess there is no fooling the master of the senses, because, my friend, you are correct."

"You secured a bottle of real wine?" Sydni asked.

Conrad winked at Sydni and said, "Being Chief Science Officer has its rewards, and keeping home in the ship provides me with extra money for, how shall we call it, extra provisions."

Sniffing again, Willy said, "I would say a vintage from their early days of wine making, somewhere about 2205."

"Very impressive, indeed. It is a 2203. Both very dry years in the wine valleys."

"It has been years since I have had real wine," Sydni said. She sipped it again. "Even then it was never as old as this."

"But please, come in and sit down," Conrad said, sweeping his arm in the direction of the table. The wine will be best with dinner, and we should eat while the food is fresh."

They moved over to the table, and Conrad pulled out a chair for Sydni, who smiled and sat down. Willy sat down, as Conrad placed a small plate in front of each place, and removing a lid, revealed a spinach salad. "I already placed a dash of dressing on and it is ready to eat."

"A garden-fresh salad, you are full of surprises this evening, Mr. Singh," Sydni said.

Conrad bowed his head too her. "For such distinguished guests, this is no problem. Enjoy."

The salad disappeared quickly, and Willy removed the small plates as Conrad passed out the dinner plates. Steam curled up off the plates as the lids were removed. Each plate had a small bird with stuffing, a potato, and a small pile of carrots. Both Sydni and Willy sniffed the steam, and their mouths watered immediately. Conrad sitting straight in his chair was very proud of his find. "Quadra Three Pheasants. The cook had them stashed for the ambassador, but he owed me one."

"I can't believe it," Sydni said, picking up her knife and fork.

"This brings back a lot of memories, Doc," Willy said after his first mouthful. "We would eat almost this identical meal for Thanksgiving Holiday."

Sydni nodded in agreement with her own mouth full. Conrad was more pleased by the look on Sydni's face than he was by the food itself. She winked at him, which fueled his smile.

It wasn't long into the meal that the door chimed. Willy and Sydni looked at Conrad, who shrugged. "I am not expecting any company at this hour. Probably someone from the lab who has a minute difficulty with a test result." He waved it off with his fork and continued, "They can leave a message and I can take care of it in the morning."

Again the chime filled the room. Conrad went back to eating, but Sydni watched Willy, whose head was cocked to one side as he listened and sniffed the air. After a few seconds, Sydni asked, "What is it, Will?"

Without moving his head, Willy shifted his eyes to look at his sister. "Angry voices."

Looking up, Conrad realized something was going on. "What do you hear?"

"Somebody's very upset outside your door."

There was an electrical crackle, and the door to Conrad's quarters burst open. Vladimir, the assistant to the ambassador, stepped in. After looking at the table, he looked back out the door and said, "They are here." Vladimir was a large man, both tall and broad. He also served as the bodyguard to the ambassador, and by most people aboard ship, he was considered dangerous. He had won the ships hand-to-hand combat tournament that Willy and Sydni helped Chief Su, the Dojo Master, referee. He took a step back and Ambassador Jasper Gallagher walked in dressed in a black suit with a black shirt. He walked swiftly to the table, for someone of his girth, and stopped, pointing a finger at Conrad. Before the ambassador could speak, Conrad was on his feet. "What right do you have to barge into my quarters uninvited! On whose authority can you break the security lock..."

Conrad was cut off by the commanding voice of Bucky Dollinger, the ship's captain. "Dr. Singh, please pardon the intrusion, but it was on my authority." Bucky's eyes were dark orbs that matched the midnight color of his skin. His gray hair was cut close, and he walked up to the table, standing straight and tall. His black uniform was covered with many decorations from his service to the UWC.

Willy and Sydni stood to attention and all three saluted the captain, who returned the salute and said, "As you were, scouts."

"Don't flatter yourself, Captain," Gallagher said. "This was by authority of the UWC itself."

The look of menace Bucky gave the Ambassador was slight and brief. Willy saw that his captain would have enjoyed stuffing the ambassador into an escape pod and sending him on his own journey, however, the captain had his orders. Willy smiled; he felt the same way about both the ambassador and his assistant, who now loomed behind him.

"And this intrusion is at the lack of your duty to the UWC, Dr. Singh." The ambassador slammed his fleshy fist onto the table with a dull thud, making Willy wonder if his head would sound the same as it hit the table.

The ambassador continued with his voice, squeaking in anger, "There has been a discovery that has gone unreported to the Council."

Conrad's voice grew angry. "There has been a discovery, and had you taken the time to read my contract, you will see that as CSO I determine when reports are complete and to be filed, especially when the information is of a sensitive nature." Gallagher opened his mouth to speak again, but this time, Conrad's level tone silenced him. "If you read the last section of my contract, you will see that not even the ambassador has the power to override my authority in the science section."

Conrad walked back over to his chair and seated himself. After taking a deep breath, he sipped his wine and glanced at Sydni and Willy. Sydni grinned and Willy nodded. Looking back up at the ambassador, Conrad said, "Now if you will leave my quarters, I do have esteemed guests who are in the middle of dinner."

Vladimir handed a computer clipboard to the ambassador, who began scanning what must have been Conrad's contract. His face turned another shade of red, nearing purple, and a little squeak passed through his tightly pressed lips. He threw the clipboard back at Vladimir and stormed past Bucky. Vladimir spun on his heels and followed the ambassador out of the room.

"I guess I owe you an apology, Dr. Singh. I should have read your contract before I let Ambassador Gallagher talk me into overriding the security system."

Conrad waved his hand in the air. "Don't worry about it, Bucky, I understand your precarious position when dealing with the likes of the ambassador. I know how persuasive he can be."

Bucky laughed. "Persuasive is a very diplomatic way to put it. But I am also intruding. Commander Colton, Commander Colton, I offer my apologies for this interruption."

"Won't you please sit and have a glass of wine with us, Captain?" Conrad asked.

Bucky took a deep breath. "Come on, Captain," Sydni said.

If it had been any other person sitting down to dinner with them, Willy would have been uncomfortable, but the captain had seen Willy often.

Conrad poured a glass of wine, and then he set down the glass in front of where the captain seated himself. "Sorry I don't have more food, Bucky."

"Don't worry about it, Conrad, I was at the end of my meal when the good ambassador caught up with me." Bucky slumped in his chair a little and raised his glass. "To your health."

"And yours," Conrad returned.

Willy, who along with Sydni had continued his meal, cleared his throat and asked, "Doc, who did you tell about our find?"

Music filled the silence that followed while Conrad furrowed his brow, then he stood up and looked around his room until he picked up his scanner from the entertainment center. He walked back over and said, "Here it is. I did not discuss the Coppertroid fuel we found with anyone, and the only place I marked it down was in my personal scanner."

Conrad looked at Willy and said, "Did you tell anyone?"

"Not me."

When Conrad looked at Sydni, she shook her head. Bucky sat up again, glanced at Conrad, and then regarded Willy. "Will, just what are you getting at?"

Pushing his plate away, Willy took a moment before he spoke. "It would seem to me that the CSO has been bugged. Maybe they have the whole ship wired so they know exactly what is going on at all times."

"That is outrageous." Conrad said. "Bucky, is there anything we can do about this?"

Bucky shrugged. "It will bear looking into, but I'm not certain. I will have to review my powers over the ambassador and his duties and rights aboard ship. I will also need rock solid proof of his misconduct." Bucky finished his wine and held up the empty glass. "Thanks for the wine." After setting down the empty glass, he stood up and straightened his uniform as he walked toward the door. Back over his shoulder, he said, "Get me proof and I will see what I can find out."

Bucky pressed the control panel, and the door slid open and closed behind him. "This is distressing news," Conrad said.

"Definitely," Sydni agreed.

Conrad poured more wine in each glass, waiting to see what Willy had to say. Willy shrugged and said, "It's obvious that Gallagher is up to something, all we have to do is prove it. We have to keep our eyes and ears open, poke our noses in a few places, and examine our contracts. Gallagher thinks we're stupid, let's hope he thinks that way until we have what we need to sink him."

CHAPTER 2

Wind whipped down off the mountains and out over the foothills, sending clouds by at a furious pace, forcing leaves to dance wildly and the grasses to sway out of control. The morning sun shone down in patches that moved rapidly with the clouds, and not much could be heard over the wind, grasses, and leaves. Several smells carried on the wind, varying from plants to animals, but what had Willy's attention was the very faint smell of burning wood. Lying in the grasses next to Willy was an old Jolabwe hunter, whose greenish-gray scales shimmered in the sunlight. The Jolabwe's name was Sasanal, and he had taught Willy much about living in the wild on his planet. He also taught Willy the language of the Hingandu people.

Sasanal tapped Willy's arm with his scaly hands that only had three fingers and a thumb. The Jolabwe's head was shaped much like that of a rattlesnake, and his flat ears were covered with a thick membrane that would retract, depending on what they were listening for. Two little antennae, which protruded just above the eyes, were what the Jolabwe used to smell. Looking into Sasanal's black eyes, which had no pupil, Willy waited for the old hunter to speak in the Jolabwe language. "You smell now, yes, Willy?"

Willy nodded. "Yes, Sasanal. I smell the fire of those that I seek. I appreciate your patience and time."

Sasanal said, "Your path could be dangerous, as the Hingandu do not trust strangers, but I dare not go as that might ensure your chance of an altercation. That tribe and I have had previous dealings."

"I will be fine." Willy sat up on his knees, resting back on his heels. He pulled out his scanner and scanned the hills. After putting it away, he said, "I am wasting daylight."

Sasanal sat up as well and said, "I have seen your instincts out in our world, and they will serve you well, just watch yourself with them."

"Thank you. I will report back to you when time permits." Standing up, Willy faced Sasanal and held his fist just in front of his mouth, which was a sign of respect in the Jolabwe community. Sasanal returned the sign and Willy left, jogging off into the hills.

Wind rushing in his face urged Willy to break into a full run across the gentle rolling hills, but he knew that running into the territory of a people that could possibly be unfriendly could be the biggest mistake, especially if it was to be taken as an aggression. Although the wood was different on every planet, and fires were different in color and smell, fire was still distinct, and Willy could tell that the fire he smelled was deep in the mountains. Willy crested a hill and halted with the knee-high grasses swishing at his legs. He could hear the faint sounds of someone singing. He crouched down, sniffed the air again, and listened.

Faintly on the air Willy could now smell the Hingandu who was singing, and if he wasn't mistaken, the Hingandu who was singing was a female. Sniffing the air again, Willy was certain it was a female. He adjusted his course a little to the north. The next rise brought him to a deep gully with a fast stream running off the mountains. Along the same side as Willy was a single, red-leaf tree. On the far side of the gully, was a rounded hill which stood a little taller than most of the others immediately around. Standing on top of that hill was the Hingandu standing with arms spread wide, face lifted to the sun, and her voice rising loud against the wind.

Her voice carried such emotion with it that Willy would have sworn she was mourning the loss of someone near to her. Stopping at the tree, Willy pulled out the scanner and began taping her as he zoomed in to see her better. The texture of the Hingandu skin reminded Willy of his own, except the light brown color was interspersed with much darker stripes, much like stripes on a tiger back on Earth. Willy noted two longer stripes running from her hairline down to the corner of her eyes, two shorter ones moving across her temples to the outside corners of her eyes, and two more following up the jaw line ending just under her bottom lip. Willy didn't want to miss the song, so he turned up the gain on the scanner. She was wearing a tan, sleeveless tunic made from some sort of cloth or animal hide cinched in at her waist by a dark brown belt. Jet-black hair spilled down over her shoulders nearly to her waist, and it struck Willy how much the Hingandu female was shaped like a human female. He took a reading of her.

Willy slowly read the findings on his scanner and not willing to believe what he saw, he took a second reading. He typed in several sentences before he transmitted the signal directly to Conrad's computer. He put his scanner away and crouched down against the base of the tree, wanting to meet the Hingandu, but not wanting to disrupt her song.

Nothing felt better than exploring new lands, untouched by the pollutants and waste that humans brought with them, but if something came in second to that, it would be coming to understand and know a new race of people. Once he learned their language and could communicate freely with them, he often lived among different races for long periods while stationed somewhere. Of course, his sister always claimed that he was just avoiding the ship, but he reasoned it out to his duty as a scout to know all he could. Willy smiled and continued to watch the Hingandu sing.

The song faded off with the wind, and the Hingandu lowered her arms and bowed her head. Willy was certain that she knew he was there; most races are aware of their immediate surroundings, and he had just walked up into her line of sight, nearly facing her. After only a few breaths, the Hingandu turned toward Willy and started walking down her hill in his direction. Willy was taken aback by her graceful movements and easy stride, and finding nothing to compare her to, he just thought how beautiful she was. She stopped across the gorge from him and stared into his eyes. Her lavender eyes were cat-like. Unblinking, she paused for a while. Then in a clear voice and in the Hingandu language, she said, "Welcome to my land, I've been expecting you."

Willy's heart skipped a beat. Her voice was clear and crisp, much easier to understand than the Jolabwe's. Finding his own voice, Willy said, "You were expecting me?"

She made a motion with her hand for Willy to join her. So Willy backed up a few steps, ran, and leaped into the air. Landing on the far side, he took two steps and stopped facing her. Standing a few feet from her, Willy smiled and said, "My name is Willy Colton."

"Willy, my name is Dekonal, and I would very much like to speak with you."

"I am here."

Dekonal scanned the sky and looked back at Willy. "I have had many disturbing visions in the last cycle of life, and my visions of you have perplexed me. My questions could take a long time, and cover very much."

"I have much time for you."

Dekonal stepped even closer to Willy, and he could see flecks of silver in her eyes. Sweeping her hand across the sky, she asked, "When must you return to the stars?"

Willy had to concentrate to hear her words, for her scent was overpowering to him as he stood next to her. Her scent was like perfume in its nature, but very commanding of his attention. Shaking his head, Willy said, "Whenever I please. I do not have to return anytime soon."

Turning toward the crest of the hill, Dekonal started walking. Willy matched her stride and watched her out of the corner of his eye. He only stood a couple inches taller than she did. He matched her pace easily, yet realized just how much power pent up inside her well-defined legs. At the crest of the hill, Dekonal stooped down, picked up a brown pack, and slung it across her shoulder.

Willy looked around from her vantage point and could see why she chose to sing there. The scenery both facing the plains and into the mountains was breathtaking. The wind shifted and Dekonal's scent washed over him again. He could tell she was standing so close to him that she had to nearly have been touching him. He turned and her face was only inches away; she was sniffing him. She didn't back off once he noticed her, she just kept on sniffing him, and deep down in her she made what sounded like a growl. Willy took that as a good thing, and having the opportunity to be so open about it, he sniffed her. So powerful was her scent that Willy had to close his eyes and clench his fist, while the only word that came to mind for him was intoxicating.

Growling again, Dekonal said, "You have a wonderful smell, Willy."

"Yours is unlike anything I have ever encountered," Willy replied, feeling very unprofessional.

Dekonal held her hand next to his face for a moment, as if she was gathering the courage to touch him, then she ran three fingers across his cheek to the bump of his nose. Then she ran her hand along his brow and into his hair just above his ear. She ran her fingers through the length of his hair and then rested it on his shoulder. "You must see this," she said, taking Willy's arm with her free hand.

Just before he touched her face, he stopped his hand and said, "Your skin is like mine," he said. "Your hair is similar to mine."

"You know this already?" she asked.

Willy touched her cheek, and traced the same pattern that she just had, ending with his hand resting on her shoulder. "I did not realize it until we were standing this close, but since I first saw you, I thought it might be true. This also means that I have many questions for you."

Looking around, Dekonal hesitated. "We are in a very well traveled area, by both Jolabwe and Hingandu, and I would like our conversation private so we would not be disturbed. My people are very suspicious of strangers and you would be very perplexing."

"Any place you would like would be fine with me."

Again she looked to the mountains before she said, "Follow me."

Willy was correct about her ability to run, when she said to follow her, she took off in the direction of the mountains at a furious pace, which surprised Willy. Soon after he was pacing her, then, before the bottom of the second hill, they were running stride for stride next to each other.

✶ ✶ ✶ ✶

Conrad stepped into his office and let the door shut behind him. He leaned back against the door and shook his head as he thought about his meeting with Bucky and Ambassador Gallagher. He would have loved to see the ambassador banished to the moon of water for an indefinite period. The intercom on the door into the laboratory buzzed and brought Conrad out of his daydream. "Enter," he said.

The door slid open and in stepped a petite black woman dressed in a white jumpsuit that the lab Techs wear. She was Conrad's first assistant, Andrea, who held the rank of Lieutenant Commander with the UWC Navy. She was looking down at a clipboard and she started speaking without even greeting him, "I've prepped a collection team for the extraction of the Coppertroid fuel and have them waiting for the go ahead from Commander Colton. I have assigned two Techs to your personal scanner and given you a replacement one, which is on your desk." She pointed with her thumb to Conrad's desk along the wall. "I have two more Techs and three hangar crew fitting two of the shuttles for use on the moon and fitting it with the correct equipment."

Andrea looked up and Conrad was shaking his head. "Such efficiency, Commander, but a simple good morning would have sufficed."

Smiling, Andrea shrugged. "I got to the coffee pot early and have been hyper all morning." Placing the electronic clipboard under her arm, Andrea said, "I really want to watch over the preparation of the shuttle, sir. I spent several years on a larger vessel in the waters of Quadra Three, and if you wouldn't mind, I want to spend a little time out there."

"Certainly. With you there, then I would certainly know the data coming back would be precise and thorough. Do we keep a deep sea probe aboard?"

"Yes, that is part of the preparation."

"Very well, Andrea. Just remind me before you go, so I'm not sitting here walking in circles looking for you."

Andrea cracked a smile. "You got it, boss, and while I'm down there, I'll send you memos on your computer so you don't forget."

Conrad laughed, and as Andrea turned to walk away, Conrad added, "Give me a buzz when the extraction team goes planetside, I'd like a look at the findings again."

"You got it, boss."

The door shut. Conrad walked over to his desk to check out any pending messages, or urgent forms waiting to be signed, or problems to be fixed, but when he logged on the computer, he found a message from Willy. Conrad knew Willy was going planet-side today, but he wondered how he could have found something so early. Breakfast call was barely even over, how could he have found something so soon? Conrad read the message aloud, "Doc, check out these readings. I am sending you only part of this information to get your attention. Tell me who I just scanned." Conrad studied the information and scratched his jaw before he laughed, then he stopped and sat up in his chair. "You are pulling my leg, right my friend?" Then using his computer, he paged Sydni on her scanner and turned back to the computer data.

Just as Conrad was about to check on Sydni's status to see if she had gone planetside, his hallway door buzzed. "Enter," Conrad said.

Sydni stepped in wearing her flight suit and carrying her flight bag. "I was already nearby, so I thought I would just stop in."

"It is much better to see you in person, especially for this." Motioning with one hand, he looked back to his computer screen. When she was standing behind him, he said, "What do you make of this?"

Sydni placed a hand on his back and leaned forward to read the screen. After a few moments, she stood up and said, "He sent you a scan of himself, he had to have."

"That's what I thought, but why?"

"Silly," Sydni said. "He's playing a joke on you. Besides, we haven't seen anything on the planet that could remotely produce such a reading."

"What about the Hingandu?" Conrad asked.

"We have had no contact at this point, but what would be the odds on that happening on a planet with the genetic structure of everything else we've seen."

"Well," Conrad said, rubbing his chin again. "The odds would be staggering. Downright astronomical."

Patting his shoulder, Sydni laughed a little. "He's just trying to brighten your day a little, after what happened last night. If you think about it, it not only is funny, it's right up his alley."

"Of course, you are correct, Sydni." Conrad stood up and cleared the message by touching his screen. "I apologize for dragging you away from your duties today."

Sydni waved her hand in the air as if to clear smoke and said, "Being called away from another boring satellite drop to come see you is not that bad, Conrad." Sydni kissed Conrad on the cheek and quickly moved for the door. "At least we know that Willy is all right. Let me know if you hear from him again."

"As soon as he sends another message, you'll be the first to know." Sydni left, and Conrad took a deep breath and sighed. Absent-mindedly he touched his cheek where Sydni had kissed him, and he smiled. Between Willy and Sydni, they were keeping his life interesting.

* * * *

Using up a greater part of the morning, they ran deep into the forest and into the mountains. Then they climbed up along a series of falls until they could see far out into the rolling hills and plains. When she stopped she observed Willy for a minute and was pleased that he was not worn out by their travel. "I am impressed by your ability to travel through the terrain as you did."

Willy smiled and said, "I grew up in a land similar to this. You have picked a very beautiful place to ask your questions."

"I find this place most peaceful, and very few of my tribe travel up here during this season. Food is plentiful here and we can build a fire to stay warm through the night as we talk." The outcropping that they had stopped on was more like a ridge that widened out farther to the north. The short grassy patch along the pool of water had a ring of rocks and a black patch where a fire had been. "Shall we take a walk and gather some wood and food?"

Willy motioned for her to lead the way as he said, "Certainly. I would like to see what you use for food."

As they walked along the ridge, Dekonal began pointing out the flora of the planet so he could learn the names. She picked up a few small twigs as they walked along, then stopped at a little tree that had fist-sized green fruit. She nodded when Willy reached up for one of the fruit, and Willy picked a few of them. Dekonal opened her pack and as Willy dropped them in, she said, "We call that Gombo. It is very nutritious and plentiful in the upper regions of the mountains. If one is lucky enough to find a tree that grows the Gombo in red, then it is truly a treat."

"I bet you know where there is one," Willy said.

Dekonal closed her bag and as they resumed their walk, she said, "Every year different trees grow differently depending on the sun, temperature and rain. Some years there are many, and some years there are none, but I have not found one at this time."

Further down the ridge they came to a row of bushes along the edge of the cliff. There were purple and red flowers covering them. Dekonal knelt down to smell them. Willy followed and took a long deep breath. The scent was spicy and tickled his nose, nearly making him sneeze. He drew his head back and looked at her, and he was uncertain, but she looked as if she was laughing at him. "You must be very careful of the Nalcota flowers, because in this present form they could either leave one unconscious or dead, depending on the amount consumed. The fruit that replaces it is as harmful while it is red, but once it turns white it is a spicy addition to other foods."

Willy decided not to scan anything that Dekonal showed him; he didn't want her to see the use of such tools until he knew the status and tools of the Hingandu people. He would just have to remember what she said, and scan it later for Conrad. Suddenly he realized that Dekonal was observing him, and he smiled saying, "I have much to learn from you."

"I have much to learn from you, Willy." She glanced to the sky again and in more of a tone that she was speaking to herself, she repeated, "I have much to learn from you, Willy." Then she was suddenly aware that Willy was watching her and she looked back to him. "Will you teach me, Willy? Will you teach me what I need to know to save my people?"

She stood up and started walking. Willy bent over and smelled the flowers again, wondering if he had heard her last sentence correctly. He straightened up and followed her. "Teach you what?" Willy asked.

Dekonal stopped and motioned toward the woods. "There should be plenty of wood we can use for a fire."

Willy knew not to push her. He knew that like most people and most species, Dekonal would reveal what she wanted soon enough. Willy was a scout and a hunter, and one thing he definitely had was the patience to wait for her to repeat the question.

The ridge widened and was enveloped by a thick forest. The ground was scattered with decaying leaves, branches and sticks from the trees. Underbrush was thick, but they could navigate through it. Willy's arms were full of wood, when he noticed that Dekonal was stuffing several roots in her pack. Then she began gathering wood as well, and soon her arms were full.

Without a word, they just headed back out to the ridge and started walking back to the pool. Several large birds in a V formation were hovering on a thermal about fifty yards out off the cliff-face just below them. The lead bird broke away and dove toward the base of the falls, and the other birds followed close behind.

Once back at the pool, Willy and Dekonal stacked the small pile of wood and seated themselves across from each other so they could each see out across the plain. They broke the branches and made a small pile in the circle of rocks without saying a word. Willy was beginning to wonder if Dekonal was going to want him to light the fire. From her pack, Dekonal pulled a long knife in an animal skin sheath decorated with red and copper-colored beads. When she slipped the sheath off, the copper-colored blade was brilliant in the sunlight. Willy couldn't take his eyes off the knife, and Dekonal held it out to him.

The knife was light in his hands, and the blade seemed to be made out of some opaque crystal, but as he tested it on the hair on the back of his hand, he realized the knife was razor sharp. The scout side of Willy wanted to scan the knife so he could get a look at it; in his whole time on the planet among the Jolabwe, he had never seen anything like that knife.

Dekonal pointed at the knife and she said, "Be careful of that weapon, it is dangerous." Willy quickly moved the knife away from his hand. "It is made from a crystal that will cut through or pierce anything, and if given the correct stimulus, it can burn or melt even rock."

She really had Willy's attention. He didn't understand what she meant by the word stimulus, but he had an idea. She said, "Rub the flat side of the blade against the wood." Moving her hands back and forth across each other, she continued, "The fire will start."

Willy did as she asked, and after only two strokes up and down one branch and the knife glowed and the stick burst into flames. Then he rubbed on other sticks deeper in the pile for the fire, and soon they had a nice fire burning. The blade was still glowing as Willy held it up to his hand, but he could barely feel any heat.

"How could you place this in a sheath or carry it in a pack if it would catch fire?" Willy asked.

"It is the friction. It takes the rubbing or a collision such as hitting rock." She again moved her hands across each other. "The blades make most effective weapons and tools."

"Where do you get the blades from?"

Dekonal seemed to take a minute to mull over this question before she answered him by pointing down into the ground. "Near our home."

Willy's heart was sinking faster and faster. He was certain that the blade was some form of crystallized Coppertroid fuel. He had never seen anything like the blade and this would be a major find for the UWC. They would want this and they would not be stopped in their efforts to retrieve their fuel. The mining would take place all to close to this race of people, who would have no idea, what was about to happen.

"What worries you, Willy?" Dekonal asked, leaning forward.

"Many things that we cannot control at this time. What is more important was that you needed to speak to me."

Dekonal paused and Willy handed her knife back. She sheathed it and set it back on her pack, then for several minutes she just stared into the fire. "I am a spiritual guide to my people, and when my father's time passes, I will become the Spirit Chief. I, like my father, and his father, and so on for generations, have had visions both waking and sleeping. However, increasingly I have the same vision of our way of life being disturbed forever and our people banished from the land which has been our home for generations gone by. I see strange birds falling from the sky, but within all of these visions, you are there, protecting our people." She twisted a piece of wood in the fire and green sparks scattered into the air. "I need to learn more about my visions. What you could tell me of these visions?"

"I will tell you what I can. It will take time. I am almost such a guide, as you, for my people. I must learn what I can of your people."

* * * *

Sydni dropped off her satellite and circled the moon twice, flying only meters above the water, kicking up a sea-spray behind her as she did. She circled twice and climbed as she watched massive shapes deep in the water, hoping that one would surface close enough that she could see it better. As she flew her thoughts drifted to Conrad. The more she thought about him, the more she liked the idea of being with him, but could she be happy with someone who was so opposed to surface life? She knew that someday soon Willy would find a home on a planet. She pulled back hard on her stick, and her ship cut straight up into some gathering thunderheads. She watched the water from the clouds streak her windshield and then evaporate at the higher elevations, when she started to see the stars. She flipped on her minimal shields and banked toward the planet.

She didn't know why she wanted to go to the planet, she just wasn't certain she was ready to return to the ship just yet. She clicked on her communications switch and glanced in the direction of the Orion. She could see the ship as it was just coming into view from around the planet. "Orion, this is Scout Leader Two. Do you copy?"

Her helmet filled with the voice of Sergeant Collins, "Go ahead, Scout Leader Two. What do you need, Sydni?"

"Asking permission to make a pass of the planet and catch up with you on my next pass."

"Standby," Collins said. Sydni could almost see him turning to the watch commander and passing on the request. Moments later, Collins said, "You have a green light, Sydni. Have a safe flight."

"Thank you, Sergeant, Scout Leader Two out."

She changed frequencies, looking for some good flying music. She found a new song on the ships rock station that broadcast constantly and she kicked in her thrusters. She didn't need to set coordinates to travel by; she had logged so many hours flying she knew the planet by its landmarks alone. She broke through the atmosphere to what looked like a picture-perfect day. After clicking on her cloaking device, she started humming to the tune on the radio and let her instincts guide her.

* * * *

Dekonal stopped in mid-sentence and looked to the sky, placing her hand above her eyes to shield them from the sun. "I would like you to explain that," she said pointing.

Willy didn't have to see what she was looking for, he heard it only moments after she had pointed. He knew right away that it was a ship from the Orion, and shortly after that, he knew it was a scout ship. He waited for her to look back to him and he said, "Do you understand where I come from, Dekonal?"

Nodding, Dekonal pointed to the sky and said, "From one of the stars in the night sky."

"How do you think I get from up there to here?" Willy asked, pointing from the sky to the ground.

Dekonal glanced up into the sky again and then looked back to Willy. Shrugging her shoulders, she said, "I really do not know."

"You know how the Jolabwe move across the plains in their carts, well, in a manner of speaking, we travel in something like their carts, but it can fly like a bird."

She looked up again, straining to hear the now faint sounds of the scout ship. "Do they travel so fast that I cannot even see them?"

"Yes they do travel very fast, but there is another reason that you cannot see them, but I have no words in your language for that."

Still looking away, Dekonal said, "I fear that there will be much that cannot pass between us for such a barrier, but we will just have to find a path around it."

Willy smiled. He liked her attitude and he was certain that with that attitude, they would find a way around any language impasse. "It would pass to say that they are hidden from view," Willy said.

Dekonal smiled as she looked back to Willy. "How many of your people come from the stars with you?"

"Have you seen a Jolabwe city?" Dekonal nodded. "Almost as many as that city." Willy paused and knew that what he was about to tell Dekonal could be construed as treason if someone were to twist the conversation, but he also knew that it was inevitable. "But I fear there are many more cities to come as the seasons pass."

"I have seen this and this is what makes me most fear for my people. But in all this I keep seeing you, their spirit chief, helping us. You must have great power with your people."

Willy contained a laugh, and Dekonal cocked her head a little at his reaction. "The many chiefs of my people are not very spiritual and my people do not always follow what would be the best path. My role within my people is to meet other people like yourself."

The fire shifted and again sparks flew up into the air. Dekonal added another stick to the flame. "This makes me afraid for us, Willy. It makes my heart sad, for I do not understand what my visions say." She shook her head and stared down into the fire. "I know I invited you to come sit with me to speak, but I must speak with my father."

"I understand," Willy said. "I would like to meet with you again soon."

Looking up at the sun and back, Dekonal said, "When the land has passed through the night, and once again, preparing to set again, can you meet me here?"

"Tomorrow evening," Willy muttered to himself. Then speaking in her language he said, "That is acceptable." Inside his pack, he pulled out his scanner. "With your permission, I would like to use this for a minute."

"What is its purpose?"

Willy glanced down at it and shrugged. "The best words I have in your language would be that it stores information." He paused. "It would store information about you and help me understand you."

Running her hand through her hair, Dekonal nodded and said, "You may."

The scanner needed only seconds before it had obtained all the information it could. Bowing low, Willy said, "Thank you. I look forward to our meeting tomorrow."

"As do I," Dekonal said, standing up in one swift motion. She stepped over next to Willy and sniffed. Then she smiled at him. "I just wanted to remember that smell until tomorrow."

Sniffing her again, Willy nodded, "I will not soon forget your scent, Dekonal."

Willy turned back along the ridge where they had collected the wood and walked along, scanning the Nalcota flowers. Once in the trees, he scanned the Gombo fruit. He was certain that Dekonal's eyes were still on him, so he turned and smiled at her. She smiled back and he disappeared into the thicker woods.

The meeting had been shorter than he had wanted, but his first visit had gone smoother than any other first contact; it hadn't hurt that Sansanal had taught him the Hingandu language. As Willy moved along the ridge, looking for a place to call his ship in for a pick-up, he wondered about her knowledge of his presence. He had seen a couple of other races that had tremendous mental powers, but none had ever exhibited such powers in person.

Willy searched below, along the cliff wall was a large rock outcropping. More than enough to bring in his ship, but he wasn't certain if it would hold its weight. He adjusted the scanner and scanned the outcropping.

When he was given the green light he jumped down the twelve feet. Then he adjusted his scanner again, which could be used for a remote to call his ship to his position. He calculated the time for his ship to arrive at five minutes, so he sat down with his back to the cliff, looked out across the valley below, and, for no reason, smiled.

* * * *

Conrad sat in his suite with a drink in one hand staring at his computer screen. The message Willy had sent still bothered him. Even though Sydni had dismissed it as a practical joke, something about the message nagged him. His door chimed and he said, "Please enter."

The door slid open and Willy walked in. He was dressed in his cloak, but underneath was his flight suit. Willy had come straight from his flight to Conrad's suite. As he pulled off his cloak, Conrad was studying him. Willy's smile was uncontained.

"What has you in such a mood today, Willy?"

Throwing himself down in a chair across from Conrad's desk, Willy shrugged and said, "You wouldn't believe the day I've had."

"So I would gather, but could I talk you into elaborating on that?"

"Doc, Sydni should really hear this, too. Have you spoken with her, recently?"

"Just after you had sent me the message she was here. I haven't seen her since." He looked down to his computer and back to Willy. "I can page her."

"Certainly. While we wait, I shall make a drink."

As Willy crossed the room to where Conrad kept is liquor supply, Conrad started typing into his computer, shaking his head. "Some bloody mood. I haven't seen you like this before."

Throwing a glance back over his shoulder, Willy said, "Just you wait, Doc. This one nearly knocked the flight suit off of me, it is going to blow a hole in your bulkhead." Willy raised his glass to Conrad, who raised his in return. As they both drank, the door chimed.

"Please enter," Conrad said.

Sydni entered the room with her usual flair and said, "You rang?"

"Your sibling has news for us, but was waiting for a full audience."

Sydni stopped next to Willy and stared into his eyes. "I haven't seen that kind of cheerful look in your eyes since the time we pulled that practical joke on the Ambassador to Centara Eight."

"You pulled a practical joke on the Ambassador of Centara Eight?" Conrad asked. "Which one?"

Willy, ignoring Conrad's question, reached out and hugged his sister. She was always elated when he expressed his feelings in front of others, since he rarely did. As they held each other tight, he whispered, "I have found that which I have been seeking all my life."

Pulling back, Sydni studied his eyes again, but now she was grinning from ear to ear. "Certainly not here?" she asked.

He nodded. Sweeping a hand toward Conrad, he said, "Please if you have a seat where you can see Doc's computer screen, you will understand very soon." Sydni pulled away and moved over to Conrad and sat on the desk facing the computer screen.

She nudged Conrad's thigh with the toe of her boot and said, "This is becoming habit-forming. You page. I come running."

Conrad broke into a wide grin as he said, "Some habits can be very good." Sydni winked at him. "But are you two going to tell me which Ambassador you pulled a prank on?"

Sydni looked at Willy, who had sat back down and was pulling his scanner from his pack. Willy shrugged. Sydni said, "Let's just say it was the one who made disparaging remarks about my brother, and a month later had to be escorted home by a squad of troopers and is now quietly retired."

"That scandal was your doing?"

"Doc, I didn't get him in trouble for anything he wasn't doing. I expedited the process." Willy smiled, showing his fangs. "He made the wrong two enemies."

Sydni laughed her infectious laugh. "Enough of the old days, let us see what has you grinning."

Willy was typing with one hand and holding his drink with the other hand. "My main objective was to have first contact with the Hingandu people today. I found one, and get this, she walked up to me and said she was expecting me."

Sydni squinted her eyes to study her brother, and Conrad asked, "You mean to tell me they have psychic powers?"

Willy shrugged and said, "Precognitive, possibly. She called them visions. Even though we did not have the words to discuss everything we wanted, she knew much." Willy typed more on his scanner. "This is the visual I have."

The screen showed Dekonal singing her song, then the last little bit when he scanned her before he left. "Remarkable creature," Conrad said.

When the screen held the last scan of her, Sydni glanced back and forth to her brother. "Remarkable indeed."

"Here is a replay of her with sound."

Conrad scratched his chin. "A very clear voice. Much in contrast with the Jolabwe recordings I have heard."

"You have taught me much of the language, Willy, and I could understand her perfectly."

They both looked at Willy, "Now hold on tight, because this one is going to throw you for a loop. I am sending you her complete scan, and Doc, I am not playing a joke here."

Sydni reacted first as she turned to Willy. She had studied the genetic differences between the two of them since the day she knew what the word meant. "Willy, she has the same genetic structure that you do."

"It says it right here," Conrad said. "These scans don't lie, but how could she have such a make-up? That would mean that she is human as well." Conrad went into his own thoughts as he stared at the readings on his screen. Then, in a voice barely more than a whisper, he said, "That would mean that the humans were introduced to the same genetic mutation and placed on this planet. I would need tissue samples and blood samples, not to mention the necessity of a team of anthropologists to dig through their histories and myths and legends." Conrad typed a few more keys on his keyboard, and squinted at the screen. "Generations upon generations." Sydni put a hand on Conrad's shoulder and he looked up at her as if it was the first time he realized that she was in the room. He smiled and looked at Willy. "According to my calculations, albeit rough, these people have been on this planet for at least 500 years before we had the ability to travel from one solar system to the next."

"Okay, Doc, then we have to ask who brought them here, and does this planet have the potential to mutate humans like Quadra Three?"

Sydni shook her head and said, "In all our travels, we have only encountered a few races capable of space travel, none of which has ever ventured as far as Earth."

Shaking his head, Conrad said, "I am afraid that your discovery has given us more questions than answers." He raised his palms to the sky and shrugged his shoulders. "I need more. Much more information is needed before we can obtain clues to this mystery. When do you again speak with this wonderful creature?"

"Tomorrow afternoon."

"I think I will delay taking our findings to the ambassador until we know more."

"Sounds like a good idea," Sydni said.

Willy nodded. "I do not trust that Gallagher. Ever since we arrived here, he has been very secretive, and that whole outburst over the discovery of the fuel…."

Lowering his voice, Conrad said, "I have one of the Techs checking out my scanner for anything unusual. I just don't understand how he knew about the fuel. Only the three of us had that information."

"Good point," Sydni added. "But what could he be up to? The finding of the fuel itself has happened on many planets between here and Earth."

Willy held up his index finger and shook his head a little. "But none this far out in the quadrant."

"To what end, my brother?"

Conrad typed on his computer and pulled up a map of the quadrant. He shook his head and typed in again. "That is peculiar. There are no significant reports from beyond this system, and I know there have been probes sent out in that direction."

"I would bet the ambassador has that information available on his computer."

"Willy, I have my misgivings about the trustworthiness of Jasper Gallagher, but certainly he would not have such important information withheld from the Chief Science Officer."

Sydni laughed and Willy said, "Doc, you and I grew up in totally different worlds, and I always hope that you retain your optimistic view of the world, but I have no such belief. Gallagher has only his own welfare and that of the UWC on his mind. He will claw over anyone or anything he can to advance his pitiful career."

Conrad looked back to his computer and the starscreen with only a few labeled stars. He slowly shook his head a little and mumbled half to himself, "This whole operation is beginning to smell."

Sydni put a hand on his shoulder and said, "Don't you worry, Conrad, Willy and I are like air fresheners. We'll find out what is going on."

A smile shone through on Conrad. "What can I do to help you?"

Willy said, "Well, I will have to meet with Dekonal tomorrow, but I will start an investigation the day after that. From there, we'll just have to see."

CHAPTER 3

The observation deck was empty when Willy entered and opened the dome. He took off his cloak and walked to the center of the room and looked up. The stars were dimmed against the reflection from the room. "Turn off lights," Willy said softly, and the lights faded to blackness, lighting up the dome with the stars. Willy sat cross-legged under the dome and breathed deeply. He imagined himself in the mountains behind his childhood home, where he had spent many nights. The Nightloon called out its sad song, as the Black and Red Gibbons chatted incessantly as they foraged through the night, while the Quadra Three version of crickets droned on. Distantly through the night a pack of coyotes would howl.

These sounds were not being played back on the Orion's computerized sound system, the night sounds of Quadra Three were ingrained in Willy. Although he had no love for the people on the planet, before he left the fleet altogether, he hoped to visit the mountain behind his parents house and listen to the wildlife create its song.

Willy's mind had been racing ever since he saw Dekonal singing. Through the night he had barely slept, and what few hours he had slept were filled with dreams of her. He knew she had triggered something deep within him that he needed to control before he lost himself with her in the hills of the planet. After all, he had a duty to his ship to perform. So only hours into his sleep period, Willy had risen, swam in one of the ships pools, and dove from the platform several time1

s. Then, after cleaning up, he came to the observation deck to meditate.

Usually he went deep within himself and remembered the most comforting sounds he ever knew, nighttime on Quadra Three. As he breathed deeply, he scanned the sky and longed for the pattern of stars he grew up knowing. In just more than a whisper, he said, "Bring up star map of Quadra Three, Saratoga Colony, summer solstice." The stars above shimmered and shifted until they took that familiar pattern. As much as his animal instincts urged him to run and find Dekonal, he knew there were many things he had to focus on aboard ship; questions needed to be answered, and mysteries needed to be solved. Finally a peace came over him with his long deep breaths as he stared upward. He would be able to tackle the many tasks set forth with a clear mind.

Conrad, unable to sleep with the significant discoveries of the past two days, poured over his computer until his eyes were bloodshot and a dull ache crept up his neck and into his head. After trying to sleep for an hour, he changed and ran laps around the Command Officer's Gym, then continued on the climber for twenty minutes. Fatigued, but feeling better than he had all night, Conrad sat himself in a small whirlpool in the far corner of the jacuzzi room.

Relaxing as the jets of warm water worked over his body, he knew he had to pull himself away from the speculation of the Forest Dwellers' origin and the quite possible reality that all his work was being spied upon by Gallagher for the UWC. So Conrad let his thoughts drift like the rising steam to Sydni. Taking a deep breath, Conrad sighed. She understood him, and he really liked that. Also, her brother was possibly his best friend. He wondered at the possibility of a relationship forming when he had a professional relationship that would not be terminated for some time.

He scooped a handful of water up across his face and another over his hair. Their contracts both stated that relationships between officers were permitted, but some would say that indirectly she was partially under his command. He knew that under contract though, they only had to report to the Captain and under certain circumstances to Gallagher.

Conrad's laugh filled the empty room. "I have reduced such a grand thing as love to a study of bloody contracts. Oh, my grandfather would be so disappointed."

Forcing himself up, he continued to laugh to himself as he picked up his towel and walked for the showers, drying himself off. As he was drying off his hair and had the towel draped over his head, the sliding door to the showers opened, and Vladimir burst through, knocking Conrad aside.

Vladimir's unmistakable baritone resounded in the hall, "Out of my way."

Conrad, knowing full well who had just pushed past him, ripped down his towel and straightened himself as an officer of the UWC Navy and let his own voice fill the room. "I beg your pardon, Major!"

Vladimir stopped in mid-stride and slowly raised himself to his full height. While the assistant to the Ambassador was usually of a high rank, the Chief Science Officer was part of the Senior Command of a ship. Conrad had worked many years to obtain his rank of Lieutenant Admiral and was not about to let Gallagher's assistant push him around. Trying not to feel foolish standing up to someone twice his size in dripping swim trunks, he decided to push himself. "I don't believe you realize who you are addressing, Major."

Vladimir spun around, faced forward and nearly growled as he stared at Conrad. Conrad squinted his eyes and stepped forward. Thinking better of a confrontation with a senior officer, Vladimir snapped to attention and stared straight down the hall. "I beg your pardon, Doctor Singh. I forget both myself and my rank."

Conrad wanted to laugh. He knew it was eating Vladimir up to apologize and stand at attention. He also knew he never wanted to meet Vladimir in a dark, unmonitored hall, so he thought better of holding him there too long. With the wave of a hand, Conrad said, "Dismissed."

With one quick movement, Vladimir was turned away and walking down the hall. Conrad watched him until he was gone before he started on his way again, making a mental note to talk to the captain about Vladimir.

* * * *

Willy found what he was looking for. He lay stretched out on the floor of the observation deck staring up at the configuration of stars, as they would look on Quadra Three. The level of meditation he achieved left him feeling weightless, floating just above the floor.

Suddenly the stars wavered as the computer voice broke the still room. "Security override of locked door initiated."

The sound of the opening door was distinct, and moments later, the lights flashed on at full strength. The footsteps were fast, hard, and familiar. Willy had met everyone aboard ship who was big enough to make those footfalls and only one walked with such intensity. Before the voice, thick with his eastern European accent from earth, cut the air, Willy knew it was Vladimir. "Stand at attention."

Willy hadn't realized it was going to be such an amusing day. "I gave you an order, Colton. Get up."

Rolling back on his shoulders and bringing up his legs, Willy paused before he snapped out his legs, flipped up, and stood facing Vladimir. Willy smiled before he said, "Insubordination is an ugly word, Major, and I don't think that ignorance is a defense. But since you cannot spell it out for yourself, I will tell you, major. I out-rank you. The next time you address me, it will be as Commander Colton."

Vladimir snapped back out of Willy's face. "Commander? You're a scout, how do you rank as a Commander? I am the Liaison to and Chief of Ambassador Security, which must out-rank you."

Both Willy and Sydni had graduated at the top of their class in the academy, and they both logged more hours planetside than any of the squads in which they had been assigned. Their time coupled with their performance in the skirmish and the war, made them early candidates for promotion twice in their career, not to mention they had served under and impressed several high-ranking officers who now made such decisions in the UWC fleet. Willy shook his head and said, "No."

"How can a stinking scout, who isn't even human, hold a higher rank than me?"

Willy's smile disappeared. "You forget yourself, Major, but I grow weary of your comments. One more outburst and I will have you charged."

Vladimir, unbelieving that he let his thoughts slip, looked at Willy as if for the first time. "You have something else to say to me?" Willy questioned.

Snapping to attention, Vladimir said, "Sorry for the intrusion, Commander." Vladimir couldn't believe it was his second dressing down by a superior officer since he woke up this morning.

"Did you have something constructive to bring to my attention, Major, or did you just want to brighten my morning?"

"I was looking for someone other than Su to spar with, and he told me you were the best hand to hand combatant aboard ship."

"Chief Su is the Master of the Dojo aboard this ship and I would have to say he is the best."

"I need a new sparring partner. He says you have studied under some of the best masters in the fleet."

Shrugging, Willy said, "I do not spar with anyone else aboard ship, Major. Good day."

Willy walked past Vladimir, but Vladimir grabbed Willy's forearm and said, "Why will you not spar with me?"

"I need to spar with someone with the control of a master," Willy said.

"I hold the master level of martial arts."

"No." Willy said shaking his head. "You are excellent, but you do not have the control of a master and you do not hold the belt of a master: self-control, inner peace, level-headedness, and emotional control. I have seen you fight, I have seen you interact with people, and no, I will not spar with you." Willy moved toward the door and Vladimir let go of his arm.

At the door, Willy picked up his cloak and slipped it on before he opened the door to the hallway. "Computer, end star simulation."

Standing in the center of the room, Vladimir watched until after Willy had left. His face grew red, and his clenched fists shook uncontrollably. He looked for something to strike out at, but there was nothing in the room. He left with rage still in his heart and a vein popping out on the left side of his neck.

* * * *

Sydni slept deeply, dreaming of happy times with her brother and Conrad. When she woke in the morning, she could not remember the details of her dream, only that they had all been happy. Even though she had seen her brother content, she never truly believed he was happy, and so it happened that she did not believe she had truly been happy. She stretched out and ran through a quick series of aerobics to the sound of the latest band from Quadra Three.

She checked her flight schedule and found that her drop of another satellite had been scrubbed, thus giving her a free day in which she could amuse herself on board the ship, or she could go planetside and scout around where Willy would be, in case he needed back-up. She typed in a message to Willy so he would see her before he went to the planet and decided she would have time for a lesson with Master Su.

Sydni ran through the halls of the Orion and scurried up several decks in the access tubes to limber herself up. When she reached the Dojo, she pressed the access button. After no one answered, she repeated her action.

It was possible that he was introducing someone to the fine art of meditation as he had her, but usually the bell would at least bring an answer. She tried the access button one last time before she tried the entrance button. The door slid away. Entering any non-public door without verbal permission was frowned upon, even in the case of the Dojo, but she was worried.

Immediately she could tell there was a different odor in the room over the usual smell of incense burning. She bowed toward the far back wall where she could see the Japanese writing faintly, and then she slipped off her shoes. "Master Su," she called out.

As she walked forward, she found the dressing room empty and Master Su's office as well. When she approached the door to the training room, the smell was stronger, and suddenly she recognized the mixture of sweat and blood. Once she realized what the smell was, she ran into the training room.

"Chief," she yelled. He lay crumpled up against the wall to the right in a growing pool of his own blood that seemed vivid against the white room. He moaned and tried to move, never really fixing his eyes on her. She had barely reached him when she said, "Computer, alert sick bay and security to a medical emergency, priority one."

Reaching out to Su in a natural reaction to comfort him, she hesitated and only touched his bloody cheek. "Can you speak, Chief? Can you tell me who did this to you?"

Su could hear her voice like she was talking to him underwater, but as much as he tried; he couldn't see anyone or anything. To him, he clearly replied, "It was that bastard, Vladimir."

All Sydni heard was another series of moans. "Hang in there, Chief. The emergency team will be here soon." Annoyed that no one had responded to her call for help yet, she spoke into the air, "Computer, ETA on emergency team?"

After a short pause, the dry voice of the computer said, "Estimated arrival two minutes."

"Computer, call all scouts who are shipside and bring them to the Dojo, priority two."

What was only minutes seemed like half an hour to Sydni, who felt helpless to assist her colleague. The door opened and in rushed four workers in gray jumpsuits carrying an anti-gravity sled filled with medical equipment. Sydni backed up as they approached and the Lieutenant spoke to her without looking up from his patient. "What happened here?"

"I don't know. I came in for a lesson and found him here."

A sergeant quipped, "Looks like someone gave him a lesson."

"This is no time for jokes!" Sydni yelled, trying to keep her emotions in check.

They fell silent as they worked on him, the sergeant hoping not to lose another stripe for his jokes. Sydni had advanced survival training, but her knowledge of field first aid failed to let her understand all they did to Su. Once he was immobilized and on the sled, a security detail arrived wearing their deep blue jackets and pants with a maroon stripe down the outside seam. "What is the emergency, Commander?"

Sydni recognized the major from the mess hall or from a party or from some ship function, but if his name hadn't been written on his chest, it would have eluded her. "I came in for a lesson and found Chief Su injured and bleeding."

Glancing at the emergency team, the major asked, "How's it look, Chuck?"

Already starting to pull him away on the sled as one person tended to him, the lieutenant looked up and said, "Not very good, Bob. I'll call you when I know more."

Nodding, Bob looked back at Sydni and said, "Was anyone else here when you arrived?"

"No."

"Did you see anyone in the hall as you approached?"

"No."

"Do you know of any enemies he might have?"

"No."

The door opened again and three of the scouts rushed in. The two other security officers turned to block their way. "Sorry, but you can't come in any further." Sydni caught the eye of Tanya and gave her the hand signal to regroup and wait further orders.

Tanya raised her arms up, palms forward and said, "Easy, man. We'll go, no problem."

The two security officers stood with their arms crossed all puffed up as if they had just repelled some onslaught. Looking from the door to Sydni, Bob said, "This doesn't give us much to go on, but we will start a full investigation, including any tapes of conversation, forensics, and scheduled appointments. I will ask you to leave since we will have to seal the room."

"Let me know what you come up with, Major."

"Please, call me Bob."

"Okay, Bob. Just keep me informed."

"Sure thing."

Sydni walked past them and headed for the door. She wondered who could defeat Chief Su, or how many people it would take. As far as she could remember, there was never a case of such violence among the crewmembers. She knew that Chief Su was part of the UWC Marine Corps like the security detail was, but those definitions usually didn't call for problems while aboard ship and out for duty in deep space.

Sydni had called the scouts together, because Willy, who was officially in charge of them, insisted that they take lessons three days a week. They all liked Su and considered him a friend. Outside, Tanya, Gordo, and Barkley waited for her. Lieutenant Tanya Williston looked up at Sydni and waited for her to speak. Master Sergeant Gordo Diego paced back and forth clenching his fists, while Master Sergeant Barkley Billings leaned up against a wall with his arms crossed and his squinted eyes watching Sydni.

"Did you see him?" Sydni asked.

"He looked bad," Gordo said. "I was a medic for five years while I waited for scout school, it looked bad."

"What do we know?" Tanya asked.

"Nothing," Sydni said. "Not a damn thing. Somebody hurt him bad, and I want to know who."

"Isn't security taking care of it?" Barkley asked. "The marines always come in and clean up this kind of thing."

"They are proceeding in their conventional ways, but I want you guys to keep your eyes and ears open and find out what you can."

"You got it," Tanya said.

"No problemo," Diego said, accenting his Spanish.

Barkley stood up straight and nodded. "We'll find whoever did this, Sydni."

"Good," Sydni said. "Carry on."

The three scouts stood at attention and saluted Sydni, who returned the salute before they walked away, talking in hushed voices.

Sydni just looked at Su's door for a moment, wondering who could possibly want to hurt him. Down the hall from the opposite direction that the other scouts went, there was movement. Willy was running down the hall. She could just make out the faint outlines of Willy's face, hidden in the shadows of his hood.

"Are you okay?" Willy asked. "What happened?"

"My flight was canceled, so I came for a workout and found Chief Su badly beaten. He doesn't look good."

"Where is he?"

"They've already taken him to sick bay."

Willy cursed under his breath. It didn't take him any time to figure out who had beaten Su. "I should have seen this coming. I should have warned him that it could have happened."

Laying a hand on Willy's forearm, Sydni said, "You mean you knew about this? Who did it?"

Willy pulled back his hood a little so she could see his face. "Vladimir did it! As I live and breathe."

As he sniffed the air of the corridor, Sydni asked, "What are you talking about? How would you know?"

"He came to me today, saying he wanted to spar. Master Su told him that I was the best on the ship. I told him that I would not spar with someone without control. I left him fuming." Willy shook his head. "How could I not have warned Su?"

"You have a mission on your mind. A very important mission I might remind you. There was no way that you could have foreseen such a brutal act."

Willy spun around and opened the door to the Dojo. As he walked across the foyer with Sydni right behind him, one of the security guards stepped out of the office to block his way. "This area is off limits, Sir."

"I want to speak with the officer in charge."

"He is busy at this moment, Sir."

"Look, Corporal, I have knowledge that may help this case."

"If you could just wait..."

Bob came around the corner and said, "It's okay, Corporal, I can speak with Commander Colton now."

Bob saluted Willy and his hand was covered with a surgical glove. Willy returned the salute and Bob said, "Please excuse the gloves, Sir. I am collecting evidence."

"Understood, Major."

The security guard walked back into the office of the dojo. "Now, you were saying."

"I will get straight to the point. I am very close with Chief Su, and I know the people on the ship that have obtained Master level. There are only a handful, and only one of them has a problem with Su."

"Who?"

"Do you know the Assistant to the Ambassador?"

"Unfortunately. Vladimir has been a constant problem since he boarded back at Galvantina Asteroid belt."

"He is very violent and early this morning was looking to pick a fight with me."

Bob smiled. "I hope you're correct, Commander. There is nothing that would make this deployment more enjoyable than expected. Do you have any evidence?"

"Nothing concrete, yet."

"Well, I will keep both you and Commander Colton appraised of the investigation."

Willy stepped in closer and lowered his voice. "If I can help in any way, or if you need assistance, my staff is ready to help."

"Appreciated, Commander."

Willy looked at his sister and asked her, "Anything else?" When she shook her head, he turned back to Bob and said, "We will let you get back to your task, Major."

Once back out in the hallway, Sydni said, "I have already sent out Tanya, Gordo, and Barkley to start an investigation. I guess we should call them back and redirect them."

"Maybe we shouldn't," Willy said. "Let's see what they come up with."

"Okay."

Checking his watch, Willy said, "I'll have just enough time to check in sick bay before I have to finish packing and complete my pre-flight check.

* * * *

The office door was already open, and Conrad paused for a moment. He peeked in. Andrea was sitting at his desk writing on an electronic clipboard. She looked up as Conrad stepped inside. "Good morning, Sir," Andrea said.

"Good morning, Commander. You are working early today."

Glancing down at the clipboard one more time and writing, she said, "The work on the water vessel is going better than planned. Scans have revealed several large aquatic creatures that we do not want attacking the vessel, and it looks like several crewmembers want to take some leave time down there." She slid the clipboard back and set down the light pen. "Since I will be leaving, here are the reports due in, the people on assignment, current tests running, and a reminder that my paging code will be delayed when you inevitably need to get in touch with me."

Conrad smiled as he walked over to the coffee dispenser and poured himself a cup. "Save a place for me down there, I may just pop down for a visit."

"That would be great, sir."

"We'll have to see what my schedule will permit, but maybe."

"When is scheduled deployment?"

"Five hours from now."

Holding up his coffee mug, Conrad said, "Andrea, go, relax and make certain you are ready for your mission. I'll be fine. The department will get by until you return."

He could almost see her relax as she took a deep breath. "Thank you," she said.

Conrad would miss her greatly during her stay on the moon, but it wouldn't be the first time he had to do the work of Assistant to the Science Officer. She seemed to be in great spirits as she said her good-byes and left.

Sipping his coffee, Conrad sat down at his desk and looked over Andrea's list on the clipboard. He shook his head. He may have attained his position off a lot of hard work, and he may have made a decent administrator, but he missed the research end of the job. He missed pouring over analyses, maps, scans, and reports to try and figure out what was what on a planet.

The landing zone that Willy wanted to use was in the middle of a fast moving electrical storm. He made a wide circle high in the atmosphere as he waited. He had been over the planet many times as he scouted, but today, high in the mountains above the tree line, yet below the snow-capped peak, he spotted a mile long stretch that glittered in the sun. Lowering his altitude, he inverted his ship for a better view. After watching the glitter for a little while, he scanned it and checked the readout. Typical rocks, grasses, and scrub-brush reading, but there was a substance that did not register as a known element.

Straightening out his ship, he typed in a note of the location and what he had seen into his personal ship's log so he could access it some time when he could land and take a sample for Conrad. When he passed his landing zone again, the furious part of the storm had moved on, so he landed. He looked around and waited, as rain pelted his canopy.

Willy liked the rain, and being wet was never a problem with him. So he took off his helmet and popped the canopy. After hopping down from his ship, he hit the remote button and locked up his ship. Then from his outside compartment, he pulled his pack and his rifle. Once these were slung on his back, he hit another button and his ship shimmered before it disappeared.

Then he started off in the direction in which he was to meet Dekonal. He was almost in the woods when he heard a flock of birds take flight out of a stand of trees not far from him. He crouched down and unslung his rifle in one motion. Once the birds had receded behind him, Willy listened intently before he moved on. When the trees hid him from view, he turned and circled back through the woods toward where the birds had flown. He found two imprints in the wet grass where someone had been standing for some time. Whoever it was had probably seen him land and exit his ship. The rain was quickly washing away any scent that might have been left behind. Unable to see which way the person had gone, Willy decided to head toward Dekonal without waiting.

Even through the thick underbrush, Willy made his way silently for a long while, listening for any sounds of someone following him. After covering several hundred yards, he crouched down, concealed in a thick clump of brush. He flicked the safety off his rifle and was prepared to strike.

The steady rain beat out its cadence, and nearby a bird sang a soft, steady tune. Willy listened intently through the rain and the bird. Then, as silently as he had gone, a Hingandu male moved along the path almost directly where Willy had walked. His skin was lighter than Dekonal's and his stripes were more pronounced. His hair was long and matted down with the rain, and he was dressed in shirt and pants that blended in with the vegetation. He was carrying a crossbow and a pack on his back.

Willy realized that the Hingandu had lost his trail when he stood up straight and began looking around in a circle and sniffing. The Hingandu stopped when the forest nearby erupted in a fluttering of wings and high-pitched growling. Raising his crossbow, he moved off in the direction of the commotion. Willy would have sighed in relief, but he didn't want the Hingandu to hear him, so he dropped to the forest floor and crawled along, catching glimpses of the Hingandu's feet. Willy worked his way around the Hingandu, in an attempt to stay downwind.

Then after twenty minutes, Willy could see a feline bigger than a bobcat on Earth, tearing apart a large bird. The Hingandu was working his way in close. Willy had caught a glimpse of the feline before, but never this close. Ahead the forest gave way to open rolling with spotted forest and scrub brush.

The feline stopped eating and shot a glance back toward the Hingandu, who froze in half step. Willy anticipated that the feline would take off into the open and that the Hingandu would follow, so he kept up a quiet pace toward the edge of the trees. At the same time the feline bolted, the Hingandu did. With all the noise, Willy made it to the edge of the forest quickly.

The feline was at a dead run. Even carrying the large bird, flopping in its mouth, it was making good time. Just when Willy thought it was safely out of the range of the Hingandu, the soft twang of the crossbow's string startled Willy. He saw the bolt fly straight across the plain, however, where he had expected it to fall short into the ground, it was flying straight, leaving a faint orange trail. The feline stopped and turned back to look at the tree line, and the arrow caught it behind the shoulder, sending it tumbling over.

A million questions flooded Willy's mind. He had a whole new category of questions for Dekonal, but he didn't want to frighten her with military-sounding questions. The Hingandu waited for a minute. He was so close that Willy could hear him sniffing. Then the Hingandu walked into the plain before he broke into a jog.

Knowing that the Hingandu was otherwise involved now, Willy stood up and knew he could head toward his appointment with Dekonal.

* * * *

The rest of the jog to where Dekonal waited for him was uneventful, and he could smell the fire long before he reached the waterfall. Dekonal was sitting cross-legged with her hands resting on her thighs. Willy observed her for a moment, before walking up and sitting next to her so he could look out over the vast horizon. Taking his rifle off his back, he set it down next to him before he closed his eyes, and breathed deeply.

"You seem troubled, Willy," she said in a voice barely louder than the waterfall. "Are you concerned about something?"

"Many things, however, the only one that I think you should know is that I believe I was discovered by one of your people today." Willy heard what he thought was a laugh, and he glanced at her.

Dekonal had laughed. She had told her father and brothers that she had met the outsider of her dreams and that she would be meeting him again. Her oldest brother did not want her to go alone to meet the outsider, but then again he was always looking out for her even when it was unwanted. "It was probably my brother. He wanted to know where I was meeting you today, but I would not tell him."

"Why not?"

"He would have many questions for you, as he is very suspicious, but I want to speak with you without his interruptions. He will meet you soon enough." Dekonal opened her eyes and placed several large sticks on the fire before she looked at Willy. She had to control the deep feeling that she had formed for him since she had seen him in her visions. He looked into her eyes. "But tell me what else you are concerned about."

Willy wasn't certain he wanted to get into the problems going on aboard the Orion. He felt as though he could tell her anything and she would understand; deep down he trusted her, but something in him resisted. To keep trust though, he knew he must give her something, just not all. "My friend, from where I live, was badly injured today. I have no proof, but I believe I know who hurt him."

"I am sorry about your friend. I hope you can prove it."

"Thank you."

"I thought I would have many questions for you, but I can clearly see that we need to form a trust between us before we can ask many of the more difficult questions."

Willy nodded. He wanted to trust her, but he wasn't so certain that it was more because of his knowledge that she was the same as he was, because her scent was attracting him so much, or because he was reading her intentions as truly peaceful. He also wanted to know more about her visions and what she saw of the future. He had heard of such abilities in people, but he was a skeptic. "How do you propose we form such a trust?" he asked.

"I spoke with my father on the very same subject, and he spoke in turn to the council of elders. I am going to ask you to go with me to my home. There you can see how we live and we can come to know you better. The constant use of our language will increase your knowledge of it, and maybe we can come to know one another better."

Deep inside Willy felt a twinge of guilt. He felt as though he should go back to the ship to pursue Vladimir in the beating of Chief Su, but he knew he had to go with Dekonal. Sydni and the others could handle what investigation he could, without stepping on ship security's toes. He would send a message to Sydni and Conrad that he would be staying indefinitely on the planet. This would be the ship's first priority, since the Coppertroid fuel was located on what would be disputed as Hingandu land. It wasn't all bad; he would have time to get to know Dekonal. "I accept," he said, looking into her eyes. "I just have to do something first, but it will only take a moment."

"Whenever you are ready." She turned and closed her eyes again.

Willy slipped his pack off and placed it in his lap. He pulled out his scanner and turned it on. He typed in a quick message to Sydni and warned her that she could become a target if his suspicions were correct. He told her not to worry about him; that he was staying planetside for a while to study the Hingandu. Then he sent Conrad the same basic message.

Out of the corner of her barely open eyes, Dekonal watched him work on his recording box. The urge to know what he knew overcame her. She knew that such things, as his recording box, were what the old ones had used. She just wished she could see the day foretold in her visions. As Willy put his box away in his pack, she softly said, "Willy, teach me your language."

Sydni was sipping a cup of coffee in the aft bar called *Six O'Clock High*. She had her legs drawn up underneath her in a booth, looking out a small portal. She could just barely see the planet below. Willy's message had concerned her; she had never considered Vladimir as a threat, but it made sense as Willy had put it. The thought of the beating that Chief Su had taken gave her a chill, and that was why she had gone for coffee. Not to mention that *Six O'Clock High* was mostly the pilot's place to hang out. With all of the scouts having to be pilots, they were accepted as well. Vladimir usually stayed in the mess hall and the forward officer's rec hall, so she figured she could avoid contact. Feeling how she did, she would just as soon not see Vladimir and start an incident. She forced a smile and whispered, "Incidents are Willy's strong point."

She wondered how the investigation was going. However, the more she mulled it over, the more it seemed to give her a headache. As she pushed that from her mind, she thought about her brother. For the first time since they were children, she worried about him. She worried that since this race of people was more like him than she was that he would actually do what he had threatened to do for so long and disappear into the mountains forever. "Go deep," she whispered to herself. She then chuckled to herself as she thought that their connection was as deep as his call to the wild, and that he would never totally leave her behind. Besides she could find him in any forest, she had been training almost as long as he.

The waiter brought her out of her concentration by asking, "More coffee, Sydni?"

She stared at him but only nodded, holding out her cup. "Thanks," she said as she tried to refocus her thoughts on the present.

Her cup grew warm again and she looked back out the window. A shadow passed over her table, and she caught the reflection of someone in the portal. She tensed to defend herself, but Conrad's smooth voice made her relax. "May I join you?"

Instantly Sydni was alert. "Yes you may," she said, sweeping her hand across the table. With Conrad present, her chill was wearing off fast.

"Any word?" he asked.

Shaking her head, she said, "No, I am still waiting to hear. When I tried to call an hour ago, Bob was in with his superior officers, so I left a message. What have you been doing?" she asked, patting his hands that were clasped together on the table.

"Some admin work that Andrea usually takes care of. I don't know what I would do without her full-time." He unclasped his hands and took hers in it. "This may seem like a very awkward time to do this, but maybe it will help take your mind off everything that has gone on today." Sydni cocked her head a little and squinted as she stared into Conrad's eyes. "Will you go out with me? Dinner and maybe a walk through the gardens."

Sydni smiled. She set down her cup and used both hands to hold Conrad's. She searched for something to say, but wasn't certain what the appropriate words would be, so she just said, "Yes."

Conrad relaxed, and Sydni realized just how tense he had been when his shoulders slumped a little and his knotted brow relaxed. "Good, because

I made reservations at the *Orion's Belt* for a seven o'clock dinner, and I have reserved the gardens from nine to ten for a private stroll."

"You have it all planned out, don't you?" she asked.

Conrad grinned and motioned for the waiter. Sydni glanced at the waiter, he was walking up with a cup of coffee and a dozen red Quadra-Three Miniature Lilies. She let out a gasp of air and looked back and forth, from Conrad to the flowers.

"You had said these are your favorite, right?" Conrad asked. The waiter left without a word and Sydni held the flowers under her nose and inhaled deeply.

"You are a dear," she said. "How did you ever remember such a detail? These are my absolute favorite." After another deep breath, she said, "They remind me of my favorite summer nights sitting deep in the woods with Willy when I would find a grove of these and we would lie down and stare up through the trees at the stars." Reaching up she touched his face and said, "Thank you. They must have cost a fortune."

After sipping his coffee, Conrad said, "Not to worry. You just enjoy them."

* * * *

The arboretum canopy, which was lit like the sun and was warm to walk under, was now clear and showing the stars. Conrad and Sydni walked hand in hand winding along the paths. Sydni knew the paths well because Willy could often be found here during their space travel, since this was as close to a planet as could be found.

Over dinner they talked about the planet and the moon. For a while they even speculated about Willy's find on the planet, but decided that maybe his little stay would help solve that mystery.

Alpha One violet vines grew like a wall between two trees, and Conrad stopped to smell one. Their conversation had lapsed, and Conrad knew how he wanted to fill the empty space. He turned to face her and pulled her closer. Looking up into his eyes, she wondered what had taken him so long. He slipped his arm around her waist and dipped his head toward hers, pausing to see if she would withdraw. Sydni met him halfway and they kissed. He drew her body up against his and placed his free hand on her side. She ran her fingers through the back of his hair and embraced his neck.

They kissed for several minutes before they parted, and when they did, he didn't let her go far. "I was wondering when you would get around to that," Sydni said.

"I did not want to rush it," he replied. She ran her fingers through his hair and straightened out where she had messed it up. He said, "It was worth the wait."

"Was it?" she asked with what Conrad would have described as a devilish grin.

"Definitely." They kissed again.

Sydni pulled away and put a finger to her lips to hush Conrad. She motioned for him to walk through the vines and hide on the far side. She sniffed the air, artificially blowing like a summer breeze. Whoever it was wasn't being too careful, because they were walking with the wind and smelled of synth-alcohol.

Glancing around, she saw that Conrad had managed to clear a hole in the vines and his leg was disappearing within. She backed up to the hole and slid in, grabbing a couple of flowers that had fallen while they went through. She crouched down and looked out where they had come in as Conrad was peeking through a spot higher up.

She heard the shuffling footsteps before she saw the slightly swaying body of Bob walk down the path. "Bob," she said very loud in the silence. Bob jerked his head up and took a staggering step back. "What are you doing here, Major?" she asked.

"Looking for you, Commander."

"What is it?"

Conrad pushed his way back through the vines and said, "Have you heard anything, Major?"

Bob nodded and paused. "I am sorry, but I had such a bad day, I went and had a drink before I came to find you." He paused and swayed.

"Maybe a whole bottle or so?" Conrad asked.

Managing a grin, Bob's smile broadened. "Or so, sir."

"What news?" Sydni asked.

"I was getting too close to something. As your brother said, I checked into Vladimir's possible involvement. I must have come too close to home. My C.O. called me in and removed me from the case, stating that the Ambassador's personal security team would lead the investigation."

Sydni felt her heart sink. "Not only was Willy right, they are taking great pains to cover it up."

"All the tapes for the dojo were confiscated just before I could get there, and someone tampered with the security and locator programs."

"Damn!" Sydni said. "Damn that miserable, low-life, Gallagher. We have to find proof that he is up to something or at least covering up something."

"Well, if I can help, I would like to see Vladimir in my brig."

Sydni patted Bob's shoulder and said, "Thanks, Bob. If we need your help, we'll come get you first."

Turning to Conrad, Sydni said, "We should go take care of some things before Vladimir tries to pin this on Willy or me or you."

"Agreed. Indeed, there are several things we could use to prove otherwise if we get to them before he does."

Sydni took Conrad's hand and they ran off down the path, leaving Bob wondering how they had just disappeared.

Chapter 4

Darkness came over the mountains quickly, but Dekonal did not rush her walk through the woods back to her village. Willy had his pack and rifle slung over his back and walked alongside her where the path permitted. "Outside my village, we will meet my father and the three elders who sit on the war council so they can approve your stay. Then you will come to my family's home for a meal and you will meet my brothers who will be waiting because they are anxious to see you."

"What about my weapon?"

"Weapon?"

Reaching up, Willy tapped the barrel of his rifle. "This is a weapon for the hunt and protection."

She dropped back behind him and he stopped. She touched it and looked at it for a moment before she resumed walking. "I had not thought about that, but the elders probably will." She looked sideways at Willy and asked, "What if they ask to take it until you are ready to depart?"

"I would have no problem with that."

Dekonal was pleased with the answer. Many of the men of her tribe would be very suspicious of Willy in the first place, but if they were in his place they probably wouldn't give up their weapons. She knew he would not cause any problems.

The path turned and followed a stream down into a deep, narrow valley that seemed to head for the heart of the mountains. Every now and then, with the shifting of the wind, Willy could smell fires and the unmistakable smell of roasting meat. Soon the mountain loomed over them, and the valley grew very narrow. The woods grew more sparse with a thick carpeting of fern-like growth and sparse shrubs. The moon was bright enough for Willy to be able to see really well.

Three people shadowed the couple for at least a mile before Willy said, "You do know we are being watched, right?"

She nodded and smiled. "I am certain they are cursing their luck that it is not daytime so they can get a better view of you from a distance." She stopped and turned around. "You can come out. He knows you have been following us."

Three shadows slowly solidified from behind the trees and took the form of three Hingandu. One stood taller than Willy, his hair was just beginning to show signs of graying at the temples. The two others were about a head shorter than the first, and their hair was stark white in the moonlight. When they were close to Willy, the tallest pulled a round tube out of his belt that he pulled apart, showing a glass center as long as each end. With a little twist, the center glowed bright, like a piece of the sun. A lantern.

Motioning toward the one with the lantern, Dekonal said, "My Father, Chakdon." Willy bowed a little in his direction. Then motioning to each of the two older men, she said, "This is Klisk, and this is Watkil."

Willy bowed in their direction and they returned the motion. He looked at Dekonal and said, "And the fourth."

A quick jab of a stick in the back made Willy realize that someone had walked up behind him. A deep and gravelly voice from behind him said, "I would be the fourth." Willy turned and looked down at a Hingandu who was hunched over holding onto a gnarled walking stick. His skin was lighter than the others, which made his stripes stand out more. "Tell me your name," the Hingandu demanded as he swiped some of his long gray hair out of his face with a shaky hand.

"William Colton, but most just call me Willy."

"Willy," the old Hingandu said as if he were trying out the name for himself. Using his walking stick for support, the Hingandu stood a little taller and very loudly said, "I am Douka and most just call me old." Willy, uncertain if it was meant as a joke, laughed anyway. Douka smiled and motioned like an impatient father to Chakdon as he said, "Give me that light."

Chakdon handed the light to Douka, who held it up near Willy's face. "Look at me, Willy. Look into my eyes and let me see you." Willy stared into Douka's eyes. "What are your intentions?" Douka asked.

Willy wondered exactly what he meant by intentions, but he gave the standard answer for his scouts to give. "It is my duty to understand you, to get to know you, and to make peace with you so my chiefs will be able to speak with you."

Douka bobbed his head and snorted before he said, "Very political. Do you understand that word in our language, political?"

Willy shook his head and said, "No, I do not understand, political."

Douka looked at Dekonal and then back to Willy, then he said, "Something your council leaders would expect you to say."

"I understand," Willy said with a nod.

"You, I believe, have reason, from what Dekonal and Chakdon have told me, to be here."

All the training at the academy and at scout training nagged at him not to give any other answer than the usual, but deep down, he had an answer to that question and he wanted them to know it. He glanced at Dekonal and back to Douka. "I do have my own reasons. I have traveled to many places, and almost always I have been out of place because I am different. You and your people are like me. I am like you, and I want to know why I am like you. Why, so far from where I live, are we the same?"

Douka stopped bobbing his head and smiled. "A truthful answer, Willy. I see no reason we should not search with you to find out these answers for ourselves. What say you, Klisk?"

Klisk walked over next to Douka and said, "I am in agreement. What say you, Watkil?"

Watkil said, "What weapons do you bring with you, Willy?"

Tapping the barrel of his rifle again, Willy said, "This and a knife."

"Should we allow him to carry a weapon among us?" Watkil asked, looking at Douka.

"What does Chakdon say?" Douka asked.

Chakdon had been staring at Willy the whole time, studying his answers and his body language. "I do not sense that we need to fear his weapon."

Willy unslung his rifle and held it in his open palms toward Douka and Klisk. "I freely give it into your possession while I am in your village. I have no need for it while I am here."

Watkil and Klisk looked at Douka, who seemed to shrug. Klisk reached out and took the rifle. "Thank you, Willy."

Douka and Klisk turned and started walking down the path, and Watkil said, "You are welcome to stay in our village." He then turned and caught up with the other two elders.

Chakdon turned to Dekonal and said, "Willy, welcome into our village. Dekonal, you have done well, my child. We will see you for dinner, right?"

"We will be there in time, father."

Chakdon then turned and trotted off toward the others. Douka moved fast despite his bent figure and reliance on the stick. Dekonal placed a hand on Willy's arm, saying, "You were wonderful, Willy. Now, let's go into my village so you can meet many others who are like you."

* * * *

Sydni and Conrad sat on the couch of Conrad's room with her scanner in front of them. "Okay," she said, "We have copied the access codes to all the places we were at today and all those Willy was at today so that if Vladimir tries to augment those to say that one or all of us attacked Chief Su, then we will have the conflicting evidence."

"One slick lady," Conrad said, sitting back.

"Well, Willy and I both cross-trained for intelligence in case scouting didn't work out, besides, this isn't bad stuff to know. If you are careful, a lot of this stuff could be bypassed when you are aboard ship and trying to move undetected."

"Anything else we need to cover?"

"That's it for now. Tomorrow we can go to Bucky and find out why the Ambassador is covering this investigation. Also, if we can gain access to the computer and communications core, there is a backup security system in there that Bob doesn't even know exists."

"Why can't we go take care of it?"

"Because Willy is much more knowledgeable about this ship and when it comes to electrical and communication boards, he is as good as a tech."

Conrad stretched his arms out along the back of the sofa and said, "Is there anything he isn't good at?"

"He certainly is thorough, but I would say his social and communications skills among others could use a little boost." Sydni sat back and leaned against Conrad. "Of course that is not quite fair. Most people don't give him the chance to be very social."

"It is difficult to believe, since he is one of the nicest people I have ever met. A few people give him a chance." Conrad paused, and then said, "What about the scouts under his command, how do they treat him?"

Sydni twisted around so she could see Conrad's face. She wanted to stop talking and get back to what they had started in the arboretum. Instead she said, "They treat him with the utmost respect. They trained with us for three months on the moon of Alpha One before we embarked. He will eat with them and sometimes, very rarely, he will have a drink with them, but not very often."

Conrad nodded. "And he has you to look out for him."

She placed a hand on his chest and raised herself up. "And what about you?"

"Me?"

"Yes you. You have taken up the cause of Willy Colton as well and you have become good friends with him." She brought her knees up on the couch and leaned in. "That means a lot to me." She kissed him. They embraced and he pulled her off her knees so her weight was on him.

"That means a lot to you?"

"Kind of," she said as she moved in to kiss him again. "But we can talk about my brother tomorrow." She kissed him again before she added, "Over breakfast."

Conrad laughed. "Computer, dim lights eighty-five percent and lock the doors."

The valley opened up on either side, paralleling a high cliff face, rising above the trees. Willy couldn't be certain, but he thought he saw dark spots up on the cliff face, which would mean there were caves up there. Smoke curled up along the cliff face like wisps of ghosts in the moonlight. The tree line turned into cleared fields with a waist-high crop growing in neat rows, and there was the village beyond. The buildings were one and two story structures that extended back into the cliff face, they reminded Willy of some tribal buildings back on Earth where some natives had lived, but at the moment the names of the tribes and the continent they lived on escaped him. He couldn't wait to get a scan and see this very sight in the morning, but he knew that he had to wait until later, after he met those that Dekonal wanted him to meet. He figured he would have more than enough time to explore the massive village, although his initial judgment told him that thousands of people had to live in this village.

He knew that his English version of the word village was maybe the wrong description of the Hingandu's home. Willy had stopped in his tracks and looked again toward the mountain peaks. Then he looked back the way they had come. He wondered where they were that he had missed their village in both sight and on the scanners. Dekonal placed a hand on Willy's arm again and asked, "What is it?"

"Nothing," he said, almost to himself. Remembering where he was, he turned to Dekonal and said, "Really, I was surprised to see how big this place was. I expected something smaller."

Willy wasn't certain whether her smile was from amusement or from enjoyment at his wonder, but she pulled on his arm a little and said, "Come, let us not be late for dinner. Tomorrow I will give you a tour of the whole village and you can ask any questions you may have."

Again they followed the path that now was worn between two fields and heading for the heart of the village. A small group of children was playing along a thigh-high wall that marked the edge of the village. As Dekonal and Willy passed through the wooden gate, the group of children came close. Then laughing, the children scattered. Willy wasn't certain, but he realized he was smiling at their mirth. He never remembered laughing like that, with a group of other children.

Then the walls of the buildings crowded close, and people passed by, looking as closely as they could at Willy in the moonlight. He wondered if his lack of stripes showed up very well in the dark. People talked from windows with other people in doorways or windows and lamplight spilled into the street. As with any new place, the smells were unique and some seemed familiar, but with such an overpowering amount, he couldn't decipher any of them.

Some people greeted Dekonal as she passed, but many just kept to their own business. After several turns, they came to an open plaza with tile-like flooring set in a pattern Willy couldn't quite make out and several short trees in the middle with benches and tables between them. The tables and benches were all taken, and many people sat around the base of the trees and talked with others. Two groups of children played, running back and forth and all around the plaza; in his walk across the plaza, he deduced that their game was an elaborate type of team tag.

No vehicles, power lines, wells, or even trash were some of the mental notes that Willy made as they walked. On the far side of the plaza, they followed another large street until it ended in a very small plaza. There were two doors on each side of the plaza, and Dekonal pushed through the first door on the right. In the center of the courtyard, which was set with stone, was a fire, over which roasted an animal on a spit. As they neared the fire, Dekonal's brother, Doqui stepped away from the spit and ran over to them. "Dekonal, I am glad you are here, it is nearing time to take the Saka off the fire."

"Doqui, this is our guest, Willy, who will be joining us for a few days."

Doqui bowed a little and said, "Welcome to our home, Willy."

Willy bowed in return. "Thank you."

Dekonal looked past Doqui and asked, "How long has he been sitting there like that?"

Glancing back over his shoulder, Doqui snorted and asked, "Quistqui? Ever since he came home. I don't think he even said a word to anyone." Doqui looked at Willy again, squinted, leaned in a little, and whispered, "I tried speaking to him, but he says nothing."

Placing a hand on Doqui's shoulder, Dekonal said, "Please don't be so shocked at our visitor and tend to the Saka."

"Sorry," he said, looking down. He turned and went back to the fire.

Over the years and the many new worlds Willy had visited, he had been looked at, poked, touched and even pushed around, and he knew that Doqui's reaction was just ordinary for any species. "I apologize for his manner," Dekonal said.

Shaking his head, Willy said, "It is normal to want to examine one that is new, and I am quite used to it."

"Come," she said, moving toward the fire. "Let us introduce you to everyone before we must sit down and eat, and maybe they will stop gawking at you."

Willy hadn't understood the word, gawking, in the Hingandu language. "Please explain 'gawking'."

She thought about it and said, "Looking at you as if you were a creature that was very different," she paused, "with a fixed look." Straightening herself she looked at Willy and widened her eyes, parted her lips and tilted her head a little.

Trying not to laugh, Willy nodded. "I understand."

They stopped at the fire and Willy sniffed the meat, which made his mouth water. Then he crouched at the fire and extended his hands, palms to the warmth. He stretched his back and flexed out his claws. Dekonal had crouched next to Quistqui and was whispering. Quistqui, whose eyes had seemed to stare off into the far distance, suddenly jolted, as if someone had thrown a cold bucket of water on him. He popped to his feet and looked around. Dekonal stood up and was smiling.

Willy figured that Quistqui was looking for him, since Quistqui was the Hingandu that had been following him earlier in the day. Willy stood up, uncertain how Quistqui would take seeing him. In other cultures the male species would push around or even fight to prove their worthiness, but Sansanal had been unable to inform Willy about that aspect of Hingandu life.

The fire was between them and they stared across at each other for several minutes before Quistqui started to walk toward Willy without taking his eyes off of him. Quistqui moved to within an arm's length and sniffed. Willy sniffed as well and suppressed a smile. From one hunter to another, he had won, he had given the other the slip. Dekonal walked up and stood next to both of them and said, "Willy, this is my brother, Quistqui."

"We have met," Willy said. "Sort of."

"Yes," Quistqui said. "In the lower forest this afternoon." Quistqui knew that if he did not show friendship to the stranger, that both his father and his sister would be angry with him. Besides, the stranger had given him the slip. At least he was worthy of respect. Quistqui had many questions that he wanted answered. Friendship often answered questions better than rivalry, so he must befriend this stranger, Willy. After another moment, Quistqui smiled and bowed a little. "Welcome to our home, Willy. It will be an honor to have you sit at our table."

"Thank you, Quistqui." Willy said, bowing.

Dekonal was relieved; she knew that sometimes her brother could be headstrong and suspicious. His response was a welcome relief.

Pointing toward the roasting animal on the spit, Willy asked, "Is this what you keep referring to as a Saka?"

"Yes," Quistqui said. "A herd animal that sticks to the lower mountains and flatlands." Nodding toward Doqui, he continued, "My young brother brought it home for dinner just for this occasion."

Stepping back, Dekonal raised her hand. "That is all for now. You three can discuss hunting after introductions have been made and we have eaten dinner."

"As you wish," Quistqui said, bowing very low to his sister.

"Stop that," she said, smacking him on the shoulder. Then, to Willy, she said, "Come on, we must go before he starts giving you bad habits."

As Dekonal led Willy away, Doqui looked at his brother and asked, "After brooding all evening, why were you so nice to him now?"

"Doqui, you have much to learn, and the first thing is that our sister and father are seldom wrong when it comes to the good of our people. Father is probably right when he told me to watch the stranger, because he may be able to teach us some things to help us in the future." Then, still staring at Willy as he went inside the house, Quistqui lowered his voice and said, "He slipped away from me today, and that alone is cause to respect him."

The ambassador's desk took up a major portion of a wall in his office, and Jasper Gallagher looked small in his high-back chair. Vladimir stood in front of the desk with his head bowed and hands folded behind his back. Jasper slammed his fist onto the top of the desk, yelling, "I can't believe you did that! What kind of idiot are you?" Jasper threw his arms up in the air and his chair rocked back. "Then you start a cover-up without going through my channels. What the hell kind of power do you think you have on this ship?"

Vladimir took the question as an opportunity to give his side of the facts. "I thought that I could..."

"You thought! Stop thinking and do as I tell you." Jasper was red, turning almost purple as he sputtered when he spoke. "You don't have any power that I don't give you. There is an ultimate plan at work here, Vladimir, and I will not allow you to screw it up."

Vladimir looked up at Jasper, and now Vladimir was turning red. He didn't like being dressed down by any commander, not to mention an overweight, lazy ambassador.

Jasper recognized that look and was not intimidated by Vladimir's size, because he knew the power that backed him. Standing up, Jasper lowered his voice and pointed at Vladimir. "Do not get any smart ideas, Major. You could break me in half or pound me like Chief Su, but you could also disappear out an air lock, or be reassigned to the Coppertroid mines in the Alpha-Earth Asteroid belt with the rank of prisoner." Jasper took a deep breath and straightened himself out. Walking around his desk, he stood directly in front of Vladimir. "I have read your dossier, Vladimir. You should be dead. If I had been Admiral Costigliano, after you sent those four Cooperstown boys to the hospital I would have participated in the local mob that showed up to rip you apart. The UWC has taken pity on you. There is a time that someone as ruthless as you is needed, but they did not send me here out of pity. If you hinder my job, you will be dealt with."

Vladimir swallowed hard, because Jasper had pushed all the right buttons. Vladimir knew that even the actions he had already taken might bring down the UWC on him. He had erased the evidence of his brutal attack, but somehow, the UWC always seemed to know the truth. "It will not happen again." He said, looking down again.

"How come I don't believe you? You are confined to your quarters tonight, and this will go into your UWC file, but I expect no action to come of it for now." Turning away, he motioned back over his shoulder for Vladimir to leave. "Dismissed."

Vladimir left and Jasper walked over to a bar and poured himself a drink of Synth-Ale. After a sip, he returned to his desk and pushed a button on the under side of his desktop. The top slid apart and a computer console and keyboard came up. Jasper drank again before he pushed several keys with his free hand and said, "Alpha-alpha, coded and scrambled channel."

The computer voice said, "Coded and scrambled channel alpha-alpha opened. Recipient?"

"UWC Command Office, Chancellor Chambers."

The computer said, "Aligning main communications dish, please wait."

Jasper punched a few more keys and watched as the brutal beating of Chief Su replayed on his screen. Su had put up a struggle, but in the end, Vladimir's onslaught had been too much. Shaking his head, he said, "What the hell were you thinking about, Vladimir? Don't make me take you out of the program."

The view screen cut in half and a man's face appeared. It was Chancellor Chambers. His gray hair was neat and to Jasper, Chambers' smile always seemed fake. "Jasper, sport, how is life on the outer edge of civilization?"

"Interesting as usual, Chancellor. I have news for you. Your initial thoughts on the possibility of the existence of Coppertroid fuel is correct. It has been confirmed. Specimens have been delayed. The readily available sites are under control of a population we are just now contacting."

Chambers looked away from the screen for a moment and then, as if it were even possible, his smile widened. "Jasper that is excellent news. Oh, very excellent. I want a sample soon. Make it happen. What of your other search?"

Jasper shook his head and said, "I have seen no evidence of any life-forms with any more intelligence than those on industrial Earth."

Chambers bit his lower lip. "Look, sport, I need you to investigate further."

The same conversation had taken place over and over, but it was only frustrating to Jasper. Chambers would not tell him what to look for, but insisted there was a technologically advanced intelligence in the vicinity. As part of the Orion's orders, several science shuttles were dispatched for week-long surveys of the solar system and nearby asteroid belt. "I understand, Chancellor. We are taking all the surveys and scans as you suggested, but maybe you could tell me what I am looking for in more detail."

"Okay, Jasper, what I am about to do is going against the Council's wishes, but I am going to show you some digital feed from one of our first satellites to reach this system. This goes no further than you and me."

"Yes, Sir," Jasper said. He fidgeted in his chair and gulped down part of his drink. Then, as Chambers' image moved away from the screen, Jasper enlarged the feed from the Chancellor and began recording the message.

Chambers reappeared, "Here it is, Jasper, pay attention."

The image shifted and a star field appeared. "This is the solar system where you are now," Chambers said. Then the planet they were currently orbiting appeared. "That is where you are now. Watch." There was a burst of golden light near the planet and then the light grew brighter. Suddenly the light turned at a ninety-degree angle and went out of sight, leaving a fading after-trail. "All our experts say that this is a ship that was either orbiting the planet or leaving the surface. Someone has to know about this."

"Wow," Jasper whispered. "That's incredible." The recording played again and Jasper stared mesmerized.

"Exactly. Now do you understand why I am so interested? The whole project could be jeopardized if we don't find out who this is."

"I understand, Chancellor."

Chambers' face filled the screen again and he lowered his voice. "Do you, Jasper? Don't forget the history lesson I gave you before you left. If we have another incident like the Doreea Star War, I will hold you personally responsible. We need that sample, but we cannot afford to instigate a war, at least not between us and the locals." Chambers paused and snapped his fingers up in the screen so Jasper could see it. "You were a junior assistant to the ambassador back on Earth at the time, right? You remember, don't you?"

Jasper swallowed hard. "I remember, Chancellor. Vividly."

"Good. I just wanted to make certain that we both had the same vision of how events could unfold."

"Anything else, Sir?" Jasper asked.

"No. Was that your whole report?"

Jasper remembered Vladimir's indiscretion and informed Chambers of the events. Chambers rested his forehead in one of his hands as he mumbled something. "Give him this message from me. Tell him, that if he screws up again, I will have him taken care of. You do realize that I have staff aboard the Orion to deal with any problems that may creep up?"

Nodding, Jasper said, "I know, Sir."

"Can you cover up his indiscretion?"

"It was handled, but not very cleanly."

"Don't let him start accusing others aboard, Jasper, I don't want any more feathers ruffled than possible. We don't need someone to come up with evidence and fry him right now."

"Understood."

"Chambers out."

The screen went blank and Chambers' image was gone. Jasper raised his glass and drained it in two gulps. After setting down his glass, he replayed the recording from Chambers. Goose bumps covered his arms and the hair on the back of his neck bristled. Suddenly, his droll Ambassador, exile-like job on the Orion had taken a whole new meaning. Chambers had thought enough of him to give him such an important assignment.

He hit another key, and his screen went blank. He was paging his secretary. A sleepy voice answered, "Hello?"

"Tristina, this is Ambassador Gallagher. I have a job for you tomorrow."

"Yes, Sir. No problem, what is it?"

"Call in the Scout officers, I need to have a conference with them."

There was a pause and the sound of a yawn. "It will be done."

Jasper, already replaying the recording again faintly said, "Dismissed."

He sat watching the recording over and over, stopping only to pour another drink at the bar. In the flash of a few seconds, he was more important to the UWC than he had ever thought he could be.

*   *   *   *

Dinner in the house of Dekonal's parents was simple; they had the Saka and a salad of nearby flora, and a crushed root that had the texture of mashed potatoes and a distinctively sweet flavor. They drank water, and milk from what Willy deduced was a herd animal they kept locally called a Warniger. Dinner was eaten at a long table, but only set for seven people, and Willy had been introduced to everyone, including Madak, Dekonal's mother and Nurian, Quistqui's girlfriend.

Never had one of his first contacts gone so smoothly, but then again, he had never had an encounter quite like this one. These people had given him full access to their home. There was much he wanted to learn from them, and to figure out how humans ended up on this part of the galaxy, he would have to dig into their past, which was a first for him. Then he wanted to know how they were cooking without a fire and how the lights functioned. Usually his scouting missions were clear-cut and direct; he had to gain the confidence of the local population, learn to communicate with them, and look out for any sign of aggression.

Conversation at dinner had been very general, usually pertaining to the crops or the herds of flying creatures that were called Brotus. Willy asked a few generic questions, but didn't want to sound overly inquisitive about anything, especially about something that gave them a decisive aerial advantage over the Jolabwe. Dekonal stood up and motioned for Willy to follow her. Once he was through the doorway, everyone sitting at the table began talking in hushed tones, so he could not understand what they were saying.

He glanced back over his shoulder, and Dekonal said, "They are talking about you."

Willy, trying to contain his amusement, asked, "Is that good or bad?"

Dekonal, looking back past Willy laughed and then looked back at him. "By our people's standard, you are a very handsome man, even though you lack stripes."

Willy stopped. "I understood your use of your standards and handsome, but what was the last thing you said?"

Facing him, she said, "Stripes are these." She traced the lines on her face. "You do not have them."

Willy nodded and said, "Now I understand. Thank you."

"As much as one of my people can have very distinctive stripes, your lack of stripes is also very distinctive." She reached up and touched his cheek and then his forehead. Her eyes seemed to look past Willy, as she remembered some of her visions of the future, and her voice said, "I have seen what is to be, and I am very happy that you have chosen to come here."

Her touch sent a chill down the back of his spine and his arms prickled with goose bumps. He wanted to know what these glimpses of the future were. What did she see? What could she know, or what did she know? "We need to talk, Dekonal. I cannot wait any longer to ask some questions of you."

"I know," she said, still tracing imaginary lines on his face. "Come, I will take you to one of my favorite places, and we can talk privately as long as you want."

* * * *

Using a lantern as her father had, Dekonal led Willy to the back of the village, up under the cliff and into a series of caves. They climbed ladders, twisted and turned up corkscrew passages, and eventually ended up at the mouth of a cave overlooking the village. The mouth of the cave was wide, about thirty feet across. It was equipped with several chairs made of wood and tied together with rope, and the seats were tightly woven material. The three-quarter moon lit up the village below and the forest and valley up into the mountains. Dekonal motioned for him to sit down as she hung the lantern from a peg on the wall.

Willy opened his mouth to speak, but Dekonal held up a hand to hush him. She sat down in a chair facing him and before she spoke. "Willy, I am allowed to tell you as much about our people as I feel comfortable. The Council is very confident in my father's ability to guide them and he is very confident in my ability to guide as well. The war council asked to see you first, as much a formality as for security reasons, and that was my final approval." She shifted in her chair. "I trust you for many reasons, Willy Colton, but most of all, I believe that you will not allow us to come to harm, nor will you tell our secrets to those who would try to exploit us or destroy us."

Willy took a deep breath and paused. "How do you know you can trust me that much?"

"My visions have told me as much."

"May I ask what your visions are? How do you see me or the future?"

"Do you see visions while you sleep, Willy?"

Willy understood that she meant dreams. "Yes."

"My people call these dreams," Dekonal said. Willy nodded, taking note of the new word. "People only have these dreams when they sleep. But I can see them when I am awake, in the daytime as well as the night. My father has the same ability that I do and therefore we are the guides to our council so that they may take the correct path in life for the future of the people. Do you understand what I am talking about?"

"Yes, I do understand. What do you see of my future?"

She hesitated and looked out at the village below. "I could tell you, but I do not want to cloud your vision by my words. My visions could give me great power over people to serve my purposes, if I chose to use them in that manner."

"So you won't tell me anything that you see?"

She looked back at him and said, "If I must, I will tell you some, but not all. I see a great war looming in our future, with the Jolabwe and another people I do not know. I see some of the race I do not know helping us as I see you helping us. I see people close to me dying in this war. I also see great things happening for both you and me in this same future."

"Great things?" Willy asked. "What great things for you and what great things for me?"

Dekonal only smiled, shaking her head. "I could sway your actions by telling you, and especially in your case I cannot and do not want that to happen." Dekonal wanted to tell Willy what a great future she saw for them together, but she knew she must not sway him in such a manner. She knew that he had to fall in love with her and let her know it in order for their relationship to be true.

"Why is there war?"

"Remember the knife I showed you? For the liquid that formed that crystal."

"Do you see the outcome of the war?"

"I do not see the outcome, but I know how it must turn out. My people cannot lose that battle."

Willy's heart sank. He didn't think that her crystal weapons could hold up against the bombs and attack ships a star cruiser could unleash on a planet. He would have to deal with that issue later. Also, if she saw him helping them fight the Jolabwe and another race, then the other race was probably humans and that would put him in a very awkward position. That thought alone did not sit well with him.

He didn't want to pause too long, so he said, "You know how we are so similar. Our skin, hair, eyes, and hands are much the same, but we have come from different homes. Do you keep a record of your past?"

"Yes, we have a past and we have kept records over the generations." She paused and thought over how she could tell him what he wanted. "The past becomes more and more faint the longer it is gone."

Willy thought about her sentence, and he was certain what she meant. The farther back you go, the less clear history was. Information was less accurate, and less information was recorded. "I want to know more about your past from when it is the faintest."

She smiled with the realization of what he was looking for. "You want to know about the old ones."

"Yes, that is what I am looking for. To see if you and I come from the same place."

"How can that be?" Dekonal asked, chuckling. "You come from the stars in cities that fly, when my people have always been here."

"You know my box that records you," he paused until she nodded. "That tells me that you and I are exactly the same. From my home to here, up in the stars, we have never found another people that are exactly the same."

Dekonal looked perplexed and turned to stare out of the cave again. Willy wasn't certain if his words conveyed the meaning that he wanted her to understand, so he thought he would give her a minute before pushing further. She said, "We have seen another race, a long, long time ago our stories tell us, but they are the only other ones."

Willy looked up into the sky and it didn't take him long to spot the Orion as it sped across the night sky making its orbit. Then he spotted a satellite, moving much more slowly. He noticed that she had shifted and was looking at him now, so he faced her again.

"You mean to tell me," she said before she paused. Then after clearing her throat, she continued, "That there are many more who travel through the stars?"

Searching for a way to explain the planets in a solar system he pointed to the stars and said, "Each point of light is like your sun, but it is so far away, that they appear as stars. Like your mountains and the lowlands around the Jolabwe cities and the great waters, there are other such places near those points of light. Other people live there as you live here. Very few have cities that travel to other places. I have traveled over many lands and eaten dinner at many tables, but the people have been very, very different."

He paused again, listening to a faint, wolf-like call. "Never, in your travel from light to light, have you met anyone like us?" she asked.

"Your ancient peoples and my ancient peoples all have come from the same place. My people have a way of knowing such things that I cannot even begin to explain, especially since the words to explain it would have no meaning to you."

"I think I understand. But why do you travel with others that are not like you?"

Laughing, Willy said, "They are like me and they are like you. They look different, but they have the same ancient peoples that we have."

"How?" she asked.

"You know there are things that we cannot explain to each other, but it is simply a matter of language." Willy paused and tried to not let his inability to describe DNA and mutation frustrated him. So he thought of only one example. "Those people you see, in your visions, well my sister looks like that. We were born at the very same time."

She said a word that Willy took for twins and nodded. Then holding up two fingers, she said, "Two births from the same mother at the same time."

Willy smiled and nodded. "Twins, yes. My sister and I are twins, yet she looks like the others and I am like you."

Dekonal's head jerked back and she made a sound much like a gasp. Willy gestured toward the stars and said, "Somewhere in time, somewhere out there, our peoples have met before." Willy could sense her shaking minutely.

Dekonal's skin prickled with bumps, and she wondered if she had spoken of war with one she would have to fight. Could her visions have been wrong and he was fighting for the other side against them? As she let her thoughts run, Willy reached over and touched her forearm.

"Dekonal, you have nothing to fear from me, and any secrets you confide in me I will not betray you to those that would hurt you and your people."

She looked into his eyes in the faint light, but she already had the answer to her question and she wondered why she had doubted herself. He was the one, and she could trust him. She also knew that it made her fall even more in love with him than she was already. The touch of his hand on her arm sent chills through her body. She wanted to kiss him, but she did not want to rush that which she saw as the inevitable.

At that same moment Willy was looking in her eyes. Part of him wanted the same thing, but he knew that if he gave into her deep brown eyes and kissed her now, any other work would take second place to her. She put her hand on his and squeezed. They both knew that there would be a time that was right.

Keeping his hand in hers, she asked, "So why is it important to know about the old ones?"

"It is important to see where our people were separated and maybe we can avert a war among our people and save your village."

"I can take you to the hut that holds our past in the morning."

"That will be the best place to start. In the morning."

Chapter 5

The two portals in Conrad's room could easily be seen from the bed. Sydni lay nestled next to Conrad with the covers pulled up to her neck. She had been awake for a long time listening to his deep breaths that denoted sound sleep. That night had left her the happiest she had been in a long time, and she could not remember the last time anyone had treated her with such tenderness and caring. She wanted to stay in bed with him for a long time, denying the morning hours and the inevitable work ahead.

The planet came into view, brightening the room although where they were looking was half covered with the night. She knew that somewhere planetside was her brother. She wondered where he was and if he was finding the answers he had hoped. Calculating ship hours versus the sunrise and sunset on the planet, she figured it to be the early hours of the morning where Willy had planned on landing.

Then the quiet morning was ripped apart by the blaring sound of Sydni's scanner. She jumped out of bed, wondering who would be paging her at this hour. She picked up her scanner from her pile of clothing and stopped the beeping. Under her breath she cursed as she read the message to report to Gallagher's office immediately. Shaking her head, she set her scanner down and ran her fingers through her hair. As she turned back to the bed, she noticed that Conrad was awake and had raised himself up on one hand to watch her.

He was watching her naked body in the light filtering in from the planet. When she realized she was being watched, she smiled and walked back over to him.

"Sorry to wake you," she said, leaning over and kissing him. "Duty calls."

"So early?" he asked, yawning.

"I'm not certain what's up. It's that bastard, Gallagher, calling in all the scouts."

Conrad sat up, and Sydni sat on the bed next to him. "Be careful around him, Sydni. There is something going on, and also the whole thing with Vladimir."

Running her hand along Conrad's shoulder and arm, she said, "I will be careful, don't worry."

Leaning toward her, he wrapped one arm around her waist and pulled her closer. He kissed her. "Last night was wonderful, Miss Colton."

"I agree," she said, winking at him. "Would you care for an encore presentation tonight?"

"I would be most delighted."

"Great." Sydni stood up and reached for her clothes. "Now you get some more sleep and I will check in with you later today."

Conrad leaned back, but continued to watch Sydni dress. Once she was fully clothed, she glanced at him one more time and waved as she left. It did not take long for Conrad to fall back to sleep once she was gone.

* * * *

Once Sydni left Conrad's room, she jogged back to her room, where she quickly showered and threw on a flight suit before heading to Gallagher's office. On her way, she sent out a message for the other scouts to meet her at the dojo before going to Gallagher's office.

She found Tanya, Gordo, and Barkley sitting in the hall, passing a thermal bottle around. She could smell the coffee in the hall and she smiled. Once she stopped, Barkley held up the bottle and said, "You want a shot of café, Commander?"

"Certainly," she said, taking the bottle and opening the top. Steam curled up from the opening and she sniffed it before she sipped it. "Well, I know Gordo didn't make it, so who do I thank?"

Tanya raised her hand and said, "I was on third shift just coming in from retrieving a malfunctioning satellite when the page went off, so I thought you guys might need a fix."

Sydni took another sip and passed it on to Gordo. "Thanks."

Barkley, whose barely open, red eyes betrayed his long night of having fun, cleared his throat and asked, "Did you find out anything?"

Sydni shook her head. "I found out that the investigation has been taken over by the ambassador's office."

Gordo sat up straight and passed the bottle to Tanya. "That son-of-a-bitch Vladimir is now in charge!" Gordo nearly shouted. Easing back against the wall, he continued in a lower tone of voice, "Wouldn't surprise me any if he's the guilty one."

Tanya yawned as she said, "He is one of the few with both the temper and the ability."

Sydni nodded. "Willy thinks so as well. So watch your backs around Vladimir."

"Where is Commander Colton?" Tanya asked. "Gallagher is probably stewing already, and Willy is the first one usually here."

"He won't be showing, by my figuring." Sydni said. "He was going to go down to stay planetside last night, so I don't think he'll be back."

Tanya groaned and pushed her self to her feet. "Let's go see this smelly slob so I can hit the rack."

"Me, too," Barkley added.

Gordo laughed as he reached across the corridor and grabbed Barkley's hand, pulling each other up as they stood. "Here I was thinking about hitting the galley for a giant sized breakfast followed by a sprint to the top of the tail and back."

"You're a sick man, Gordo." Tanya said, not even looking back.

"I agree, Tanya," Sydni said. "And I just woke up."

"I just wish that all three of you would shut up so I can get some shut-eye while we walk."

"Sorry, Barkley," Sydni said. "We are late. We need to go double time." Sydni smiled. Without any complaint or groans, they all broke into a jog in unison. They all had worked long, hard hours together, which had earned both Willy and Sydni their respect. She knew that they would push themselves as long and hard as they were asked.

They arrived at Gallagher's office, and his secretary was sitting at her desk, one hand holding up her head, the other wrapped around a cup of tea. She looked up as they came into the door. She did not sound amused when she said, "He's been expecting you. Through the double doors."

They all fell in behind Sydni and as she approached the double doors, they slid open. Gallagher was drumming his fingers on his desktop and he was staring into his monitor.

"You're late, Commander." Gallagher looked up and squinted. "Where is Commander William Colton?"

"He is on the surface, Ambassador."

"Why hasn't he returned?"

"Sir, he is investigating the Hingandu people, and he is probably going to be gone for several days."

Gallagher stopped drumming his fingers and he touched his screen to turn off the video of the planet that he had received the night before. He brought up the scout contract and reread something he had highlighted. Looking back at Sydni he said, "Unfortunate. Then since you both have equal command, I will direct you. I want two long-range scouting missions." He brought up a holo image of the solar system and the Orion over his desk. There were two sets of coordinates and highlighted flight plans. "I want Lieutenant Williston and Sergeant Diego to go into the long range missions, and I want you to go into the city of the Jolabwe and use some of your contacts. I am looking for information about myths and legends. Then I want Sergeant Barkley to pursue detailed scans of planets two, four, and five. I want all this to take place immediately."

"Sir, I am going to have to change your arrangements, though..."

Gallagher slammed his pudgy fist onto his desktop and cut off Sydni. "Why? I have studied the contract and each of your files and I have decided which of you would best serve my purposes."

"However, if you read the scouting contract, both Willy and I have the right to assign our scouts as we see fit, even in a crisis. By flight standards I cannot send Lieutenant Williston back out on a long-range mission. Now, I do not care to argue the fine points of the contract with you, and your orders will be completed as soon as possible."

Sydni held up her scanner and copied the holo with the coordinates. She glanced up at Gallagher who was staring at her with his mouth wide open. She shut down her scanner and stood at attention, before saying, "Anything else, Sir?"

Gallagher sat up straight and waved them off. "No, but I want reports as soon as we have any information."

"Sir, what exactly are we scanning for? What kind of myths and legends are we interested in?"

"Never mind. You just carry out the orders and report, and I will decide what information is good. You are dismissed. Leave."

Sydni turned and walked out his door. The others followed her as she passed them. The secretary was asleep at her desk in the same position as when they came past her before.

As she walked, Sydni tried not to let her face flush, but it was too late; Gallagher had made her really angry with his demands. When the door to Gallagher's outer office closed, Diego said, "Wow, Sydni. That was incredible."

Tanya patted her on the back and said, "Go, Commander."

Sydni stopped and faced the others. "That pig has some nerve. Trying to order us around like that. I was not going to be bullied, and I am not sending someone coming off third shift into a long range flight when I am just waking up."

"I appreciate it," Tanya said, "but I'll go if you want me to."

"Let's not talk about it here, one of his flunkies may walk by. Come on."

* * * *

Willy sat in the cave where Dekonal had taken him early in the evening. She had sat with him in silence for a couple of hours watching the night with him. A place to sleep had been offered back at her parents' house, but Willy was so enchanted with the view from mouth of the cave that he had asked to stay where he was. For a few hours, sitting with Dekonal, her hand on his arm, watching the stars, and for the few hours of peaceful sleep, he had forgotten the Orion, Chief Su, Vladimir, and Gallagher. He had felt comfortable. When the scanner woke him, it all came rushing back. When he had seen it was a general call for scouts to go to Gallagher's office, he didn't respond. Sydni would take care of it. He tried to scan the city then, to have a birds-eye view, but his scanner didn't register anything. The scanner was working, because he had just received a page. Very curious.

The sky was turning gray, chasing away the stars, and the singing of birds lifted up from below on a small breeze. He stretched out on his back to watch the stars fade fast between the intermittent clouds. There was a flapping sound from above him, and one of the flying feline creatures with a rider swooped past. Willy craned his neck to watch them for a while as they rode down the valley before they disappeared into the morning shadows. He imagined the wind in his face and the sudden drop as the creature first dove off the cliff. Dekonal would wrap her arms around him and hold tight as they cruised up through the valley. The thought of that ride suddenly jolted him. Never before since he could remember, had he actually fantasized about a woman. It had always been the hunt, or the mission, or even of people not being afraid of him; at one time he had daydreamed that his own parents would feel that way about him, but never had he considered himself a romantic or entertained romantic ideals. Sydni would get a good laugh at this, if he decided to tell her.

The soft scrape of a foot on the stone stairs was loud in the cave. Willy rolled onto his side, resting on one elbow, and zipped up his flight suit. Dekonal emerged from the last turn in the corridor. She was wearing a dress that wrapped around her starting at the neck and winding its way around her, and then hung from her hips like a skirt. The outfit was a deep reddish-purple with thin gold and silver lines that followed the movement of the dress. The dress allowed both her shoulders and midriff to show, and it didn't take long for Willy to realize that he was staring. "Good morning, Willy. Did you sleep well?"

"Yes," he said, sitting up and stuffing his scanner back into his pack. Then he stood up and hoisted his pack onto his back. "Did you sleep well?"

She wanted to blurt out that she had not slept well, knowing that he was this close, yet so unobtainable. The time would come; their time would come and then all of this waiting would no longer be relevant, so she just smiled and said, "I slept very well. This morning I have arranged for us to use the hut of the past without any interference from the council or other curious people. I have started preparing the morning meal and thought you might like something to eat."

"I am hungry."

"Good, follow me," she said. As she turned and started back down the corridor, she continued, "I have asked my brother to let you use his sleeping quarters if you wish to..." She paused and waved her hand back and forth as she looked for the right word that he would understand. "Clean yourself."

Nodding, Willy said, "I would like that very much." As Dekonal continued to walk, Willy stared at her hair, pulled back and tied with a long piece of cloth that was an exact match for her dress, and then his eyes lingered on her bare shoulders and arms. The stripes on her body were very curious to him, and he knew it was just a pigment mutation and it almost made him wish he was striped as well.

"Your dress is very beautiful."

Dekonal glanced at Willy over her shoulder and he thought he could see her blushing. "Thank you. My mother and Grandmother made the material, and the three of us made the whole dress. I prefer to wear something like this for official meetings and entering the hut of the past."

"Will I be okay wearing this?" he asked, pinching the material of his flight suit.

Dekonal nodded, "Yes. Most people do not change their clothes for the occasion, however, with my position in the tribe, I do not want to give anyone a chance to say I should have done otherwise."

Willy smiled and reminded himself that they were human too and probably had the same tendencies as any group of people on the Orion. She led him through the city and back to her family's home. Madak and Chakdon were at the table eating and speaking in hushed tones when they walked in. When Madak saw Dekonal and Willy, she stopped speaking and stood up. "Please, sit down and I will bring you something to eat."

"I do not want to be any trouble, Madak."

She held up her hand and then motioned for Willy and Dekonal to sit down. "I am finished with my meal, so it is no trouble." Her movements reminded Willy of the way his own mother would have hushed him as a small boy. He tried to remember his mother, but she was not very vivid in his memory. His mother had been protective at one time, when he was very little, but once he was older, and not tormented by the children of his community, she withdrew from him and became distant. She seemed to focus on Sydni more, fussing over her dates and dances.

Willy snapped himself out of his memories, realizing that Dekonal had already seated herself and was looking up at him. As Madak picked up a plate from her place and a bowl from Chakdon's place, Willy said, "Thank you," and sat down.

"You are going into the Hut of the Past?" Chakdon asked.

"Yes, Willy has some questions concerning the old ones, so we are going to see what we can find out."

"Why the Old Ones?" Chakdon asked, looking at Willy.

"Because I feel that my," he paused and looked at Dekonal to make certain that his words were understandable, "ancient peoples and your ancient peoples are the same." Willy looked back to Chakdon in time to see his look of surprise fading back into his passive look. "Since we are the same, I want to know how that can be since we are so far from my home."

Chakdon nodded. His daughter had explained most of this to him when she came down from speaking with Willy, but actually hearing it from Willy had surprised him. He had helped her arrange to have the Hut of the Past to themselves. Many in the community were very curious about the stranger who bore no stripes on his body, and many would try to speak with him. The elders listened intently to any request by Chakdon or his daughter, as their guidance had proven beneficial to the tribe. His own visions had not provided much to him on the subject of the stranger. His recent visions had him concerned about the Jolabwe. He had sent many of the tribe's best warriors and hunters out on many missions to see what the Jolabwe were doing, but so far nothing could be ascertained.

Madak returned with two bowls of steaming food. It looked like she had fried the Saka and the potato like substance together in a sort of hash fashion. She gave them each a utensil that resembled a spoon with two points on the end. Steam curled around Willy's face as he sniffed it. There was a new spice or something added to this dish. He had no comparison for the smell, but it made his mouth water.

Madak sat back down next to Chakdon and placed her hand on one of his. He looked at her and smiled. Willy glanced at Dekonal who was already eating, and looking back at Madak said, "Thank you."

After he was done eating, Dekonal showed him to Quistqui's room and showed him the equivalent of the bathroom. The shower was simple, with one control for the water and marking for hot and cold. While trying to explain the use of the toilet, which to Willy's surprise looked much like a toilet from home, Dekonal blushed. Willy assured her that he understood its use before she pulled a very thin, but oversized, towel out of a cupboard.

"When you are finished, I will be in the cooking area."

Willy thanked her before she shut the door and left. He shook his head then and said, "Hot and cold running water, indoor plumbing, and indoor cooking without a fire. This is not as primitive a culture as I was led to believe."

Madak was cleaning up the bowls and plates from the meal while Chakdon leaned against a counter. When Dekonal walked in, they were laughing. Chakdon noticed Dekonal first and he also noticed the pensive look on her face. "What troubles you, Dekonal?" he asked.

"I must speak with you concerning my visions. I am troubled by something."

"Do you want me to leave?" Madak asked, having grown used to the bond they shared.

"No, but I must ask you not to be shocked by anything I may say."

"I give you my word."

"Father, did any of your visions ever prove to be false?"

Chakdon shook his head and his brow furrowed. "I can say that some of them have misled me or that I misread them, but never have I had one that has been false."

"Did you know that it was Mother you would mate with?"

Chakdon laughed, and the laughter was so contagious that quickly both Madak and Dekonal were laughing with him. He caught his breath and said, "You know, I knew it was your mother that I would mate with when I met her."

Madak moved over next to Chakdon, where he hugged her. "So he says," Madak said. "It seemed like I had to drag him to the mating ceremony." They both laughed even more and Madak poked Chakdon in the ribs with her elbow.

Suddenly, Chakdon stopped laughing and looked at Dekonal. "And you ask because you have seen?"

Dekonal nodded and said, "I believe I have seen, but it is that same vision that perplexes me."

Madak became silent and stood still. Chakdon wanted to ask, but he knew his daughter would tell him in her own way.

"I have seen much concerning the stranger lately and of the impending war, but I have seen something else. I have seen your grandchildren, and I have seen my mate, and I have seen happy times ahead and sad times ahead."

"Grandchildren?" Madak asked.

"Yes, Mother," Dekonal said with a smile. "Your grandchildren. My children. I also see their father to be the very same stranger from the sky."

Madak gasped, and Chakdon shook her shoulder a little, annoyed that she showed such an emotion at something that would be. He knew his daughter's intuition where her visions were concerned, and if she thought that Willy was to be her mate, then he more than likely would be. "I know you well, and I know you are probably correct. I must caution you about the urge to tell him that is what you see."

"I have not spoken of this to him."

"It would be best if you let him come to you." He held up his hand and said, "Wait, let us go sit down."

Chakdon and Dekonal moved toward the doorway to the dining area, while Madak returned to the sink. "You may come, as well," Dekonal said.

"I do not need to know too much of the future. I would rather have it happen and be surprised."

Dekonal sat across from Chakdon, and he held up his hands as if they would help to explain his thoughts. "I do not have to give you the same speech I have given you so many times, for you know how things will turn out. However, where love is concerned you must be extra careful. If you care for him, you must not push him away either. But most of all Dekonal you must follow your heart when it comes to love."

"I understand."

"Do you care about him?"

She nodded. "Father, from the first time I saw him in my visions, I was interested. From the first time I looked into his eyes and smelled him, I loved him."

"You must trust your feelings." He paused and smiled. "As much as it frightens me to say so, if he is the one you have seen, then you must trust your feelings."

"Thank you," Dekonal said, standing up. "I am going to help Mother with the dishes."

Chakdon nodded and smiled, knowing she really meant she was going to talk to her mother about what had been said. He knew it would be a good time for him to take a walk.

Sydni jogged back through the corridors, hoping to catch Conrad still in bed. She knew that going on a long-range patrol would send her on a loop past the solar system and take about four days. She sighed to herself. The first man she found on the Orion worth spending any nights with, and now she'd have to leave for days alone in the cockpit of her ship. Diego had given her more time by promising to start the preparations for her ship so she could get her affairs in order, she had never exactly told them what affairs needed attention. They had never questioned her before, she knew they wouldn't start then. She smiled as she touched the keypad to open the door.

The night before, she had watched as Conrad typed in the access code, and her memory had not failed her. With the slight rush of air, the door slid open. Not turning on any lights, she navigated through his living space to his bedroom. Peeking in around the doorjamb, she saw Conrad sprawled out on the bed, his naked body half covered by the sheets. She paused at the bedside and nudged the mattress with her knee.

Conrad stirred and mumbled something unintelligible before he settled back into his original position. She nudged the bed harder and cleared her throat. This time Conrad opened his eyes and said, "I'm up. I'm up." When he saw Sydni through his sleepy haze, he said, "Either I overslept most of the day, or your meeting went quick."

She just grinned at him and started unzipping her flight suit very slowly. "Conrad, Darling, I have good news and really bad news."

Through a yawn, Conrad said, "I can play this game. What's up?"

"I have to run a long range scouting mission."

"The standard four days?" he questioned, trying to straighten his hair.

"Four days."

"What is the good news?"

When she finished unzipping her flightsuit, she slid it off one shoulder and said, "I have at least half an hour to report to the flight deck."

For the second day in a row, Vladimir found himself standing in front of Ambassador Gallagher's desk with his hands clasped behind his back. Jasper paced back and forth for a few moments before he started to speak.

"Vladimir, I don't know why you are not now in the brig, just plain gone, or vanished, as happens to so many when they keep crossing the UWC, but Chancellor Chambers seems to have you in mind for something."

Vladimir swallowed hard at the sound of the name. In the intelligence community he was known to be the strong arm of the Security Council who made problems vanish without a trace. He had saved him from the mines the last time he was in trouble.

"I have a message from the Chancellor," Gallagher continued. "He told me to tell you that he had people in place that would remove you if you continued to be a problem." Stopping in front of Vladimir, Gallagher faced him. "Do you understand?"

"Yes, Sir," Vladimir said.

"Good, then on to new business. Stall in your investigation."

"Sir, if I may. I was going to give information and lead the investigation toward those nosy scouts, especially Willy Colton."

"No! You absolutely may not! We need those scouts right now for other things and I will not have you subverting them. Understood."

"Yes, Sir."

"Good. Then as I said, stall your investigation, interview people, make it look official. There is more at stake in this than you, your career, your life, or me, and if I have to report back to Chancellor Chambers with any problems, I will have already set in motion steps to solve my biggest problem. Now, get out of my face and out of my office."

Vladimir was at the door when the intercom buzzed. Gallagher's secretary said, "Ambassador, I have Captain Dollinger here, wishing to see you."

"Send him in when Vladimir leaves."

Vladimir had stopped at the door and was looking at Gallagher who was holding his head and slowly shaking it. Then, in a voice that put fear into Vladimir for the first time from the Ambassador, Gallagher said, "You better give the performance of your lifetime, Vladimir, because your life depends on it."

Vladimir opened the door and saluted to Captain Dollinger who was standing and facing the door. Bucky saluted back, although he did not trust Vladimir, who was just a lackey of the ambassador. Once Vladimir passed him, the secretary said, "Captain, you may go in now."

Bucky stepped through the double doors. He knew that Ambassador Gallagher would start with his best diplomatic voice, but when he heard that voice he grew furious. "Captain, please come in and sit down. I am very sorry to hear about Chief..."

"Cut the bullshit, Gallagher. I am tired of your diplomatic corps attitude. This is my ship, and when one of my people is attacked, I want to conduct the investigation. I have no need for your security to take over."

"It is within my right, Captain. I want this trip to go smoothly, and if someone is attacked so brutally, I want to know by whom. This trip is important to the UWC and I will not have it spoiled."

Under his breath, Bucky said, "Or you want to cover something up."

"Excuse me, Captain, what was that?"

"I am going to be sending this report to my superiors, Ambassador. This may be within your scope, but it is highly irregular and to me inappropriate. Before I report, I wanted you to have a chance to change the investigation back over to the Marines."

"I will not give up the investigation, and Bucky, let me tell you as a friend, do not make waves."

"Is that a threat, Ambassador?"

"I would not call it a threat; I would call it a reminder."

Bucky had had enough. He was recording this message for future difficulties with the ambassador, but he was beginning to believe that both Commanders Colton and Vice Admiral Singh were correct in their suspicions of the Ambassador. "A reminder. What a gesture, Ambassador, but remember, you are not my friend, and if I find that you are hindering the investigation, I will see that the proper authorities are notified."

Bucky stood up and walked to the door as Gallagher called from behind, "Have a good day, Captain."

The computer screen was scrolling through the new electronic messages, but Conrad only saw Sydni's eyes as he stared far past the screen. He had fallen for her fast, but he had doubted that she would fall for someone who lacked her adventurous spirit, which was one of the things that he liked about her. He vowed to himself that he would be more willing to go with her on some of her outings on the surface. The electronic messages were piling up in Conrad's computer, and he was sitting at his desk, trying to take care of all the things that Andrea usually did but could not do while she was assigned to the water vessel on the moon. He had a message from her that the vessel was operational and running smoothly. They were placing scanning buoys around the moon to begin its mapping and investigate the moon's animal life forms. He was glad she was having a good time. A new message stood out, for it was a reply to his inquiry of the test of his scanner. The techs had finished their investigation and wanted him to go to the lab for their report.

It was unlike any of his techs not to send a message. Only when something was really important would they call him in.

So he shut down his computer and decided to go have a look. The lab was just down the hall from the administrative offices. He entered the anterior room and spoke with the clerk at the intake desk. "Anna, I have to see Techs Johnson and Silva."

"They are in the vault, Sir."

"The vault? What are they doing in the vault?"

Anna shrugged and said, "They told me to have you go in alone."

Conrad nodded. "Okay, buzz me in please." The first door was marked with a red sign that read: Authorized Personnel Only. At the second set of doors he had to have his retina scanned and his hand scanned before the doors would open. A couple of techs saluted him as they worked over samples of rock from the planet. He walked around the rows of tables with various scanners, microscopes and electroscopes to a hallway in the back where there were several more testing rooms. In the very back there was what they called the vault. This was an explosion-proof, soundproof, microwave-proof room. Nothing could penetrate the field that was activated around the room. Conrad punched in a security code on a screen and the computer said, "Voice print mode, please state your name."

"Dr. Conrad Singh."

"Voice confirmed."

There was a series of clicking sounds and the vault door opened. There was a separate computer system and a copy of every scanning device available in this room. Two techs sat at a small table with his scanner lying there in several pieces.

The two techs stood to attention and saluted Conrad. "As you were. In here gentlemen, I am just Dr. Singh, so please don't salute me."

"No problem, Dr. Singh," Silva said.

"What do you have for me?"

Silva and Johnson looked at each other and Johnson said, "You discovered it, you can tell him."

Clearing her throat, Silva said, "Sir, someone has tapped your scanner, with a very sophisticated device that is usually used by the spooks. Whoever planted this knew exactly what to do, and you never would have found it unless we tore it apart like this."

"Can you scan for any sign of who planted it?"

"We tried everything we could, but they left no sign," Johnson said. "That is why we moved it into the vault. We did not want whoever planted this to know that we found it."

"Any theories as to where it sends information?"

Again Silva and Johnson looked at each other. "No," Johnson said. "It would take finding the receiver and tracing it. That would be up to engineering, though."

"Now that you know what you are looking for, could you check the other scanners with minimal effort?" They both nodded. "Okay, I want every scanner checked, and I want a clean one issued to everyone. Remove them if there are more, on my orders. I want this one back together." Both techs smiled. They liked Conrad because on several occasions, he had stood up for their department and allocated funds and demanded a great contract. They were both eager to work on something out of their mundane tasks. "Speak of this to no one, or over electronics. Inform all those with scanners personally."

"You've got it, Doctor," Silva said.

Johnson added, "We'll have another scanner to you in a couple of hours."

"Thanks," Conrad said. "And thank you two for your great work. I guess I need not mention that this is highly classified until we find out who is behind all this."

The star field ahead was spectacular, including a nearby comet of which she would have a spectacular view. Sydni glanced back over her shoulder and could just see the fading planet, and circling that planet would be the Orion and Conrad. She needed to keep him out of her mind, or the four-day flight would drive her nuts. She had packed a book and four movies, the most recent releases before they left Quadra Three. Of course she had seen all of them during their flight to the planet, but she would watch them again. Gordo had packed her snacks with her food supplements, so that would mean there would be plenty of junk to tide her over. She adjusted her seat back and stretched.

The scout ships were the latest design. Finally, someone had made a scout ship that not only could carry a payload, but a two-seater, with a primary seat that leaned back into a full bed so their downtime was actually downtime. Her first long-range patrol had left her with a severely cramped neck and legs. Exercise was impossible in the cockpit, but being able to stretch out allowed her to meditate better.

For the second time since departing the Orion, she checked her payload. Everything was fine. Then she ran through the full array of scanners, even though the alarms were all set to record if anything was picked up. Something about checking them visually reassured her. That way there would be no surprises. She slipped in a disk and started listening to a band that formed on the Orion and had a pretty decent sound. With her scanner hooked into its docking station in the control panel, she could convert her ship's computer to send out a message to Willy.' Now if he went to find her, he would know where she was.

Her message relayed what Gallagher had set up for their missions and about his attitude and vagueness to what they were looking for. She also transmitted her long-range route. She liked having Willy as a back up, just in case.

She leaned her seat back a little and stared at the comet as she tried not to think about Conrad.

✶ ✶ ✶ ✶

The scanner did not respond for the third time as he tried to scan the structure where he had taken a shower. When he completed the system diagnostic check, it read that everything was fine. Willy was even more confused when he received a message from Sydni. So he finished up; he did not want to keep Dekonal waiting.

The Hut of the Past looked very plain from the outside, but inside was a series of rooms with tables and shelves lined with books, scrolls, etchings, carvings, paintings, sculptures and intricately designed and jeweled weapons and goblets. Dekonal walked him through several rooms until Willy stood in awe, looking from sketch to painting to sculpture. He had figured the Hingandu people were simple hunter-gatherers, but this along with the shower and lanterns and what weapons he had seen, raised their culture into a much more enlightened and skilled age. No such artifacts or paintings adorned the walls of Dekonal's home, though.

Without looking at Willy, Dekonal stood in front of a sketch of a Hingandu at some sort of celebration. The Hingandu was adorned with necklaces and a headdress of sorts. "There was a time, where my people longed to have their house full of such things and hoard wealth among their own family, but over many years there has been," she paused and placed a hand over her chest, "how would you say it; shift to a spiritual nature." Understanding, Willy nodded. "Some such items are made and given for gifts at times of ceremonies or anniversaries. Many people have paintings and art in their homes, but my father says that it is distracting to his visions." She glanced around and lowered her voice, "But I know my father is fashioning a ceremonial ax for my brother's mating ceremony." She smiled. "I think in his older age, as I take over his position in the tribe, he will adorn his walls with gifts he has received over his many years of service."

Dekonal had not smiled very much since he met her, and he never really looked at his own smile in the mirror. Her smile was infectious to him and soon he was smiling as well. "This may be inappropriate at this time, Dekonal, but I just noticed what a pretty smile you have."

Her smile broadened even more and she even blushed a little. With a barely noticeable nod, she said, "Thank you." She pointed toward the back room and continued, "That is where you said you wanted to start. With the faintest memories."

So the day passed with Willy and Dekonal sitting at a table working their way through stacks of books and drawings. Dekonal had to read aloud to Willy, as he could not read their written language, although the letters reminded him of Old Russian from Earth. He tried scanning several more times, but still his scanner would not work, so he taped long sections of what Dekonal said so that he could later transcribe it into English.

Neither had realized exactly how much time had passed until there was a faint knock on the hut's door in the front. Before either of them could stand, they faintly heard Douka calling their names.

"Back here, Douka," Dekonal yelled.

Immediately Willy could hear the thump of Douka's staff and then the shuffle of his feet. He rounded the last corner before them and then smiled. "You two I saw walk in here when the day was young, and now, when the day is old, I find you here still seeking something in the Hut of the Past. I have already eaten my evening meal and cooking fires are still burning. Go enjoy a meal. The past will still be here tomorrow."

Without giving them time to respond, Douka turned and started walking back out of the hut. Before he turned the corner again, he looked back. He was grinning like he had just told himself a great joke. "It is great to see you two so happy together." Laughing Douka left, and they could hear his laughter until the door shut.

Willy looked at Dekonal, who was staring where Douka had been with her mouth open and eyes fixed. "What did he mean by that?" Willy asked.

Again she flushed before she straightened herself out and looked at him. "I am not certain, but he is right about the evening meal. We should have something to eat."

Willy shut down his scanner and Dekonal closed the book she had been reading from. "Was any of this helpful?"

"Yes, I am learning much."

At the front door, she said, "Do you mind eating with my family again, or would you prefer to eat elsewhere?"

"Where else is there to eat?"

She said a word, but Willy didn't understand. So she thought about it then said, "It is a place where people gather and eat and drink. There is different kinds of food." Willy was nodding so Dekonal stopped. Restaurants. Very interesting. "I will go wherever you want. However, I would like to go for a run at some point."

"A run?" she asked, pantomiming running.

"Yes. After sitting so long, I feel better if I run. I run to keep in shape. Do you understand?"

"Like the day I met you we ran to get up the mountain?"

"Yes, except we end up in the same place we started."

As Dekonal closed up the door to the hut, she asked, "Would it be wiser to go before we eat or after?"

"Let's go before so we are not weighted down with food."

They started the short walk back to Dekonal's home, and in the air was the scent of many different foods being cooked. The sky was dimming and a couple of stars shone brightly in the sky. "Douka was right, though," Willy said.

"About what?" Dekonal asked, looking up at the sky with Willy.

"I am happy when I am with you."

Dekonal smiled. Willy saw it out of the corner of his eye. He was smiling as well, but Dekonal didn't need to look at him to see it. She just knew.

CHAPTER 6

The first day in the hut set a pattern for several more days. They spent most of the day reading and searching through old text, and then in the late afternoon they would go for a run before dinner. In the evening they would visit with different people in the tribe, but Willy was concerned, because her father and brothers still did not say much to him. Every morning, Willy then transcribed Dekonal's reading into English. He had some ideas he was turning into theories that he was excited to discuss with Sydni and Conrad. He was keeping track of Sydni's time-line, and if everything was going according to schedule, she would be returning in the evening. He did not receive any further messages from her, but one message from Conrad was perplexing in its vagueness. It only read: *I need to speak with you immediately upon your return.* Conrad's messages were usually concise and well spoken. However, another day in the hut and he figured he would have what he needed about their past for now.

The Hingandu were very secretive about certain aspects of their lives. There was power in the village, possibly some sort of electrical power. He had no idea of the source, but there were powered lights and cooking areas. He hinted around the subject with Dekonal, but she always sidetracked him and changed the subject. Over time, he knew he would figure it out; he wished his scanner would work. If pushed to theorize what the source of power was, he would have said Coppertroid. At one point, he almost was ready to return to the ship to retrieve another scanner, but the rapport he was building was much more important at the time.

Once again they were sitting at the same table as they had the first day, poring through text, and Dekonal was showing Willy a word. She had inadvertently begun teaching him her written language, and Willy was so adept at reading that he was picking it up rapidly. Willy looked away from the book and cocked his head to listen. Dekonal's voice faded away as she realized that he was no longer listening. Turning off his scanner's voice recording, he looked at her, but kept his head cocked. "What do you hear?" she whispered.

"I don't know," he whispered back.

They both pushed their chairs back and headed for the front door. Dekonal began to smile, for she only heard one thing. She was not certain if he was hearing something else. Willy opened the door of the hut, and the noise burst into the room as if a band had begun to play. It was laughter. The unchecked laughter of children playing was louder than almost every other noise nearby. Willy watched in awe as they played a game with a ball the size of a softball and each had a stick with the end scooped out like a giant spoon. Willy was less interested in the game than he was in the children. He had only seen a couple of children from a distance, and he figured that most people were keeping their children far away from the stranger. But there they were, nearly two dozen children of varying sizes and color, each with the distinct facial features that he had, and each with varying stripes.

Willy's heart swelled. As often as he had played sports in school and laughed with Sydni, never had he been involved in something like what he saw before him. He would have fit in here. They watched until the game took them out of view, but the laughter lingered for quite some time. As he leaned against the doorjamb, the next thought to cross Willy's mind was that his children would be accepted here. His children would not be secluded from the rest of the world by fear and hate, they would be accepted. It was at that time and on that spot that Willy knew that he had found his home. Damn the UWC and Gallagher and especially Quadra Three, he would live here if the Hingandu would let him. He would find a way to convince whoever needed convincing that a spaceport and Coppertroid mine would be disastrous here and that another site somewhere far away would be more appropriate. He would stay on long enough to find out what had been going on aboard the Orion, fix it, and put his affairs in order...he stopped his train of thought with one word, Sydni. He would have to talk to her first. They would have to make some sort of plan for the future. As much as he wanted to stay here, he could not abandon her either.

Suddenly something touched his face. Looking over, he realized that Dekonal held her hand against his cheek. "You are sad?" she asked, wiping away a tear.

Realizing that tears had brimmed over his eyes, Willy shook his head. "Not sad. I am happy."

Holding her hand up so Willy could see, she said a word. He knew she meant the same thing as a tear. Then she said, "I understand tears of happiness, but I do not understand why you have them now. Are there no children where you come from?"

Sliding down the doorjamb, Willy sat. As he looked up at Dekonal she mimicked his movements and sat down. Their legs touched, and Dekonal gathered up her skirt showing her legs, but making certain nothing else was revealed. Willy heard a new outburst of children and he smiled. "Remember when I told you that my people look different than me?" She nodded. "Okay, well, I was the only one that was different. Never in my life did I laugh and play with the other children like that. If I have children on my home planet, the same would happen to them. Because I look different, I am feared among my people. Even my parents were sort of scared of me." Willy watched as the gaggle of children ran past a cross street. "Only one woman has ever truly cared for me, but we were young and her father thought me a monster and so quickly we were separated."

Dekonal reached out and paused. Her hand hovered near Willy's face, but she was afraid to comfort him. There eyes locked for a moment, then Willy continued, "It took those children to make me realize that here I could be happy. In your world I could have a home and children that would be accepted."

"You want to stay?" she asked, and he noted the tone of excitement in her voice.

"Yes. I have many things I need to do before I could stay here, but I want to live here, or near here."

Willy thought he had read her voice correctly, but when she smiled at his revelation, he knew she cared for him. She started to withdraw her hand. Willy stopped her and took her hand. He drew her closer until their thighs were touching. She leaned in at the same time.

"Dekonal, I do not know your custom here, but where I am from, when a man cares for a woman, we express it with what we call a kiss."

"A kiss?" she repeated hesitantly in English.

"Yes." He leaned forward until their noses nearly touched. Her scent filled his nostrils and tilting his head, he pressed his lips to hers. She responded immediately. The breeze stopped blowing, the sun stopped shining, and the world stopped spinning. All that Willy and Dekonal were aware of was the fast beating of their hearts and the warm, moist kiss. After a few minutes the world came rushing back. The children's laughter had turned to giggling. When they turned to look, the children had paused their game and were watching them kiss. Once the children realized the grown ups were watching them, they ran off, laughing louder than ever.

Willy and Dekonal stared into each other's eyes and held opposite hands. Dekonal asked, "Why don't we stop the investigation for the day and run early so we can spend the rest of the day together, outside the Hut of the Past?"

Willy gathered his legs underneath himself and stood up, pulling Dekonal up also. As they stood nose-to-nose again, the urge to kiss was irresistible. This time Dekonal wrapped her arms around his neck and he placed his hands on her hips. He guided her back a step into the hut and used his foot to close the door. When they parted again, Dekonal breathed deeply and breathed out in a sigh. Softly under her breath she said an exclamation that Willy did not recognize, but he felt the same way and did not need a translation.

He touched her cheek and traced a line down her jaw line to her neck. Half of Willy just wanted to clear a desk and continue but until he knew the exact customs of these people, he thought he'd better stop. He leaned his forehead against hers. "It would be better if we stopped here, and go for our run, right?"

Dekonal smiled. "It is a good place to start, with a kiss." She used the English word for kiss and then repeated a word in her language. Willy repeated it and then kissed her lips again.

"A kiss is a wonderful place to start."

He watched her place the books back in their places as he replaced his scanner in his pack. "Your clothes should be clean now. Mother usually has her clothes washed and dried by this time. Then after we run, you can speak with some of the men about hunting."

"I am so glad you came to stay with us."

"I am too. I have not spoken of returning to my home, but I must go tonight. My sister and a friend will be there and I need to speak with them."

Dekonal's face showed her disappointment, but quickly she controlled that emotion. She knew he would have to return to his home, maybe several times. Selfishness was something she could not allow right now; had he offered to take her away, she probably would follow him, but she could not go immediately. "I understand. Really, I do. When must you leave?"

"After the evening meal."

"Shall we go? I do not wish to waste any of our time here."

* * * *

Sydni's flight had gone as planned. She dropped a long-range probe that was speeding away from her, relaying information as programmed. The static sensor beacon she dropped was also functioning well. The comet was spectacular, and she had taken several digital images and scanned it. She watched her movies and one she watched three times. She had finished one book and was starting another.

Diego was showing up on her short-range scan, and he would come into view momentarily. She knew Diego well enough to realize that he would come swooping in cloaked and fire a couple of shots across her bow to try and startle her, so this time she was ready. She switched to her battle computer and waited. He tried to hide behind one of the outer planets of the system to shield himself, but she had caught a glimpse of him just before he disappeared.

She quickly calculated how long before he would shoot if he arced around the planet with his boosters at full throttle. It would not take long for his ship to be on top of hers. Little did the scouts know that Willy and Sydni had placed a beacon on each ship, so they would know where the ships were; Sydni's battle computer screamed at her when Diego rounded the planet aimed at her with his weapons armed. Not only was she ready, she had practiced the maneuver. She kicked in her boosters and was thrown back against her seat. With ease, she corkscrewed around him and pulled up behind him, inverted from his flight path. She fired three quick bursts that passed just over Diego's cockpit and she yelled to herself, "Ye-haaa! Diego, you are dead."

"Diós mio, Commander!" Diego exclaimed. "How'd you do that?"

Sydni decided to partly lie and said, "I caught sight of you before you ducked behind the planet and then I just calculated your time and guessed at your arc. Then behind you I had my sensor array set up for Coppertroid particles." It wasn't a total lie, she could have done it that way, but this had just made it easier.

Diego's ship wavered and then was fully visible. Sydni corkscrewed again and ended up flying even with Diego. "I just have to be the best to keep up with you," she said as she looked over. She could see Diego in his cockpit look at her and wave. She waved back. "How was your trip, Gordo?"

"Uneventful. You?"

"Same. I could see the comet really well."

Suddenly, they were cut off by a message from the Orion. "Scout Two, Scout Two, this is the Orion. We read that weapons were discharged, do you need assistance?"

Sydni and Diego looked at each other. After she switched channels to respond, Sydni said, "No, we were just performing a weapons check."

"Affirmative. Welcome home, Commander Colton."

"Thanks, Sergeant Rodolfo. Sergeant Gordo and I will be on final approach in another twenty minutes. Scout Two out."

"Orion out."

Once she was back on the channel with Diego, she said, "You must have shot like that a dozen times coming back from long range patrols, I wonder what has them so edgy?"

"Probably Ambassador Gallagher. Look how edgy he was when we were in his office. Also, when you asked him what he was looking for, he went haywire. He probably has the deck crew on pins and needles."

"No doubt," she replied. "I just wish I knew what it was he was looking for. What had him wound up so tight?"

"All I know is that I am ready for a hot shower, hot food, and I have this incredible date lined up after I take care of the first two."

"Who is your date?" Sydni asked, thinking she couldn't wait to see Conrad.

"Bed. I want to stretch out and sleep."

"Well, add one other item to your equation."

"What, Commander?"

"We need to report in with Gallagher. Nothing to report does not take long to say, so it won't add much time to your duties." She could hear Diego sigh. She didn't like it any more than he did, but with Gallagher being so edgy, she had no other choice but to make certain every "I" was dotted and every "T" was crossed.

The Orion grew quickly in front of them. It was now in even higher orbit, circling well outside the moon. There was a flash near the launching bays, and Sydni recognized it as ships leaving the Orion. Quickly the squadron of 8 fighters was within visual range. Sydni recognized the insignia; it was the 21st flight squadron also known as the Black Jack Brigade. Over the intercom, she heard their leader, Jackson Jeffries say, "Welcome home, Commander Colton. How was your flight?"

"Uneventful, Commander Jeffries," she replied. "Where are you headed?"

She caught a glance of Commander Jeffries hands being thrown up in the air in a gesture of uncertainty. "Sydni, we have been scheduled for routine patrols of the system. Two squads per shift, around the clock."

"On whose orders, Jack?" she asked.

"The ambassador himself."

She shook her head and glanced back over her shoulder at the eight engines burning. "Well, take it easy out there."

"Sure thing, scout. Later."

One by one they hit their boosters and were gone. "Later," she said, knowing they would still hear her. The *Lucky 21* was a fun squad to drink with, and Sydni and Willy had played war games against them to help sharpen the flying skills of the scouts. At last count, the score was even. She hoped that Willy would be home tonight. She felt like they needed to talk, but she was uncertain as to exactly why.

* * * *

Willy and Dekonal ran back down the valley toward the village side by side, sometimes splitting apart to dodge trees or rocks. They even startled a Hingandu returning home with his prey, a small Saka, thrown across his shoulders, but before he had a chance to even say hello to them, they had passed. As they neared the village, Willy saw Douka sitting on a large rock staring away from them. Willy slowly came to a halt, and Dekonal turned and jogged back to him asking, "Is something wrong?"

"No," Willy said, smiling. "However, I see Douka and would speak with him before I leave your village."

She looked around and spotted Douka. "The evening meal is yet to begin preparation. I will go and help prepare. You speak with Douka." After looking around, Willy stepped up close to her, dipped his head down, and paused. They kissed. "I will see you at the evening meal."

Dekonal turned and continued on down the path. Willy watched her until she was out of sight, then he walked toward Douka; he moved into the breeze to allow his scent to announce him. Douka's head bobbed and he said, "Why do you seek my counsel, Willy of the stars?"

"There are customs that I would ask you about."

Douka leaned harder on his cane and stood up before he faced Willy. "Would the customs concern female Hingandu?"

Douka was usually straight to the point, and Willy liked that. No wasted time. "Yes."

"So my hunch is correct. You and Dekonal are..." he made a gesture as if he were looking for the right word, "In love?"

Willy nodded. "But I do not know of your customs."

"What is proper, what is not depends on the person," Douka said. I am certain that if you ask me, Quistqui, and another young male Hingandu what is proper between Dekonal and you, you will certainly have three different answers." A laugh was simultaneous between Willy and Douka. "Yes. In general, what is in your heart is proper." He tapped Willy's chest. "Kissing is proper in public. The interlocking of arms and hands is also considered proper." He leaned in and nudged Willy with his bony elbow and snickered.

"And they generally like the showing of emotion, interlocking of hands and holding one another."

Willy couldn't resist a grin; for the first time in his life, another man was treating him like a guy. One thing no other man ever discussed with Willy had been women. "Thank you, Douka. I just did not want to make any mistakes that would endanger my ability to see Dekonal."

"Come. Walk with me to the village." Douka started walking, faster than it looked like he could walk, keeping a thumping pace with his staff. "Does this mean that you will be staying with us?"

"I would like to, if I would be welcome."

Douka pulled at his chin and looked at Willy with a sideways glance. "There would be those who would take longer to accept you, but of all the families you could want to become a part of, Chakdon's would cause the least apprehension, since he is the tribal advisor." Douka chuckled and continued, "But the most suspicious person would be her own brother, Quistqui."

"Are you implying that he would be a challenge?"

Douka stopped. "No, I am not implying it. I know it. He will challenge you. It is unfortunate, but if he does not trust you, he will test you. My only advice would be to both lose and win gracefully."

They resumed walking and Willy wondered how Quistqui would test him. He thought of his first kiss, sitting in the doorway to the hut of the past, and he knew that no matter what Quistqui could dream up to test him, for Dekonal he would do whatever it took.

Douka tapped Willy on the shoulder with his staff and said, "Do not let this weigh heavy on your heart. Your heart is free. Focus on Dekonal, for her spirit will see you through anything."

"So you would have no problem with me joining your tribe?"

"In your heart, have you not joined already?"

Douka's words stayed with Willy, long after Douka left him at Chakdon's home. He again cleaned up in Quistqui's room and changed into his flight suit that Madak had cleaned that morning. He wondered where Quistqui was, and what would happen at dinner. Neither he nor Dekonal had discussed telling her family, but how could they not know just by the look in their daughter's eyes? Was he nervous? He laughed.

Before he went down for dinner, he checked his scanner for messages. He had one from Sydni that said: I am home.

He typed in a reply that said: Behind you a couple of hours. I need to speak with you upon arrival, please be available.

Once he sent it, he packed up his bag and headed down to the family meal. Dekonal met him at the base of the steps. Immediately she smothered him with a kiss. He did what came naturally. He wrapped his arms around her and pulled her closer. She pulled her head back and said, "Please do not be mad, but I have informed my family just how much you mean to me."

"Why would I be mad?" he whispered into her ear.

"Well, maybe it was something we should have been together to say, but I thought under the circumstances..."

He stroked the side of her face and looked into her eyes. "I have no problem with you telling your family. I wish you could be there when I tell my sister tonight, but I cannot take you. Now, let's go eat. I have a long way to go tonight."

Dekonal turned to walk back toward the dining room, but he touched her arm. She stopped long enough for him to take her hand and interlock his fingers through hers. They made their appearance into the room as Quistqui was speaking loudly. "You must speak with her, father. How can she love an outsider? Tell her this is not right."

They stopped in the doorway as Chakdon answered, "You know full well that Dekonal and I know more of the future. If that is who she has seen as her mate, you have no right to question it."

Doqui cleared his throat and then picked up his cup to take a drink, trying not to stare at anyone involved.

Quistqui stood up when he saw Dekonal and Willy standing in the doorway. Willy resisted the urge to be defensive and speak up. He figured it was not his place to say anything, yet.

Chakdon turned and saw what had startled his son. He knew they had heard more than enough. All he wanted was to have a peaceful dinner, and in this growing atmosphere, that was beyond impossible. The couple stood just inside the door holding hands. He could see the happiness in their eyes. Quistqui and his mate-to-be, Nurian, were happy, but neither held the look in their eyes that Dekonal and Willy had. Willy: he would have to get used to that name for his daughter's sake. Chakdon took a long hard look at the stranger. He was big and healthy, and from the way he had seen Willy run, he knew he had endurance and strength. His daughter had made a wonderful choice, yet his son, who had no real idea of his sister's potential for anger, was jealous.

"Quistqui," Dekonal said in a very calm but icy voice. "What right do you have to question who I chose to love? If you had a problem with me or my choices, why do you not ask me?" Quistqui started to speak, but she wouldn't let him have a word. "I will not take lightly any attempt of yours to come between Willy and me." She still had Willy's hand, and was shaking her finger at Quistqui with her claw extended.

"I hear you and father speak of the future of our tribe. I am concerned with any up-coming war, but you bring a stranger in among us, let him into our home, and then tell us that you are in love with him." He moved forward and now was standing just in front of them. "I don't have visions to tell me anything. I must trust myself, and I don't trust him." Quistqui now had his finger pointed at Willy and was only inches from his nose.

Remaining relaxed, Willy was ready to react if Quistqui attacked him. "Why?" Dekonal asked. "What do you have against him?"

"He is unproven."

"Unproven," Dekonal said, throwing her arms up in the air. "Please don't throw your ancient male rituals around." Then she used a word for it that Willy believed would equal *machismo* in English.

Suddenly Madak came in the room, her voice raised above the others. "This will not take place in my home. I will not abide any fighting around my table. If you cannot have a peaceful meal, leave my house." Everyone grew quiet, with Quistqui staring down Willy, who gave no sign of backing off. Willy then realized where Dekonal got her icy tone. Madak, in much the same tone, said, "Quistqui, if you do not back off, you are not welcome here."

Quistqui glanced at his mother before he stepped back, then, Quistqui turned and ran, dodging his father's hand that tried to stop him. "Quist," Chakdon yelled after him, but Quistqui was already gone.

Dekonal turned to face Willy and she sighed. "I am sorry, Willy. I did not know he would react that way."

Everyone in the room looked at Willy. He took her hands in his and he cleared his throat. "I actually understand somewhat how he feels. I too have a beautiful sister that I worry about. He is protective of his family and his tribe. I cannot blame him. However, maybe it would be best if I left now and give your family some time."

Willy could see that Dekonal wanted to say no to his request, but she thought about it. She squeezed his hands and nodded. "Do you know when you can return?"

"Maybe tomorrow, but no later than the next day."

"Okay. I will miss you."

"I am so sorry," Chakdon said. "You are always welcome in my home."

Willy nodded to Chakdon. "Thank you." Then, turning to Madak, he said, "Madak, your hospitality has been great, and your food plentiful. Thank you."

Madak forced a smile. Doqui just sat there with a blank look on his face, still holding his drink up to his lips. Dekonal escorted Willy to the front door and they stepped out into the cool night. Light spilled out the door from inside and there they embraced. Their embrace quickly turned into a long kiss.

"I will really miss you," he whispered into her ear.

"Hurry back to me," she whispered back.

Willy turned to leave, but Quistqui stood several yards away. "To leave our village and return, you have to go through me."

"Quistqui, how dare you…." Dekonal started, but Willy held up a hand to quiet her. She took his cue and hushed herself.

"I will not fight you," Willy said, stepping forward.

"You are a coward?" Quistqui said, but Willy did not understand the word coward.

Behind him, Dekonal said, "It means afraid."

"No. I am not afraid. I just do not believe in fighting."

Quistqui said, "I am going to fight you."

Willy had no idea if they had any type of formal fighting style, so he just poised himself, ready to react. Quistqui struck with the speed of lightning, but Willy's reflexes blocked the punch, and his second motion used Quistqui's momentum to send him flying. Quistqui rolled in the dirt and stood up charging. Willy could see Quistqui's mouth move, but he did not hear what he said. He just ducked and came up under Quistqui, sending him rolling in the dirt again.

This time Willy followed. As Quistqui came to a halt, Willy was on top of him, dragging him up by the arm and shoulder. He had underestimated Quistqui's reaction time, and received two elbows in the face before he flipped Quistqui hard. Willy jumped back and waited while Quistqui stood up. This time Quistqui walked up to battle in closer. As he reached out to jab at Willy, Willy spun and swept Quistqui's legs out from under him.

Quistqui jumped up to his feet, too late to see the roundhouse kick coming. Down he went again. Suddenly sound came rushing back to Willy, and he heard several people shouting from behind him. It was Dekonal and her family, mostly yelling at Quistqui to stop.

Dekonal was saying something else, and Willy realized he had looked away from Quistqui too long. The sharp pain hit him in the ribs, then his face. He rolled with the punch and tumbled twice. This time he came at the rushing Quistqui with the intention of stopping him. He landed three punches in the face, one to the chest, and a kick to Quistqui's abdomen before Quistqui went down.

Blood trickled down from Quistqui's nose, cutting a path in the dust on his face. Quistqui stood up and faced Willy. Quistqui's face was bloody and dusty, but now his posture was relaxed as he wiped blood away. In the dim light from the doorway, Willy could see that Quistqui was smiling. He bowed to Willy before he turned and walked down the street. Dekonal rushed up to Willy gently placing a hand on his shoulder. "Are you injured?"

"Nothing too damaging. He was not trying to injure me."

"It did not look that way to me," Dekonal said, using her thumb to wipe some of the blood from Willy's nose.

Willy picked up his pack, pulled out a bandanna from a side pocket, and wiped his face. Then he pressed it against his nostril and tilted his head back to stop the bleeding. "Your brother could have been more violent, especially when I turned my back."

"I will speak with him before you come back," she said as she took Willy's hand away and held the bandanna for him. Willy could taste the blood in the back of his mouth.

"Please do not. I have gained some respect in his eyes tonight. Let me work it out with him." He tilted his head a little to one side so he could see her face. Her lips pressed tightly together and she squinted as she looked up at him. "I will be able to come to terms with him, even if it has to be on his terms."

"Why do men have to partake in such foolishness?" she asked. He wiped his hand on his flightsuit and then found her hair. After stroking her hair, he cupped the side of her face in his hand and she leaned into it.

"It is foolish to you and me, but it is not to Quistqui. As I said, I will deal with him when I return."

"But why such violence?"

Willy shook his head and looked down at her. "That was not violent. Had we really been fighting, I could have crippled or killed him on his first pass, and he could have me when I turned to look at you." Taking the bandanna away, he said, "Do not worry. I am worthy of your love, and I will prove it to Quistqui."

She tiptoed and kissed him on the cheek. "Go with the speed of the wind, and return to me safely."

After kissing her forehead, he waved to her family, who was still standing in the doorway. He turned and saw Douka standing in the street, carrying both his staff and Willy's rifle.

Willy jogged over to Douka and accepted his rifle. Douka did not say a word, but he stood there with his head bobbing in what looked like approval to Willy. Once he had slung the rifle across his back and glanced again at Dekonal, he jogged out of the village.

"Computer," Conrad said. "Check status of Commander William Colton."

The computer voice came back and said, "Landing in Hangar Three."

"I told you," Sydni said, clinking her glass against Conrad's glass. "He said he needed to speak with me." She stretched her neck and kissed Conrad on the corner of the mouth. "Then once we have caught up, you and I can spend a leisurely night and morning alone."

"Did I tell you I missed you while you were gone?"

Sydni nodded. "Yes, and since you were a good boy while I was gone, we can take this time to get reacquainted." Sydni took his glass and set them on the coffee table. Then she turned on him and began kissing him with breathtaking passion. Conrad rolled her down on the sofa and stretched out with her, without ever removing his lips from hers. Neither of them was aware just how long they had been kissing until the door chimed.

It took them a minute to stop and sit up before Sydni said, "May I help you?"

"Sydni, it's me, Willy, may I come in?"

"Of course," she said, "Open door."

No sooner had the door opened when Sydni recognized the dark stains on his flight suit and the swollen nose. She jumped up, asking, "What happened? Are you okay?"

Willy put up his hands in a gesture to stop her, but she had to inspect him anyway. "It is all part of the story I need to tell you."

Sydni swatted Willy's hands away and examined his face and nose. "Does it hurt? Are you injured?"

Willy dropped his hands and sighed. "Nothing substantial, sis." Then he gave her a grin so wide that Sydni stepped back almost shocked. "It was worth it."

"What was worth it?"

"You are impatient. If you give me a drink and sit down, I will explain my days planetside." Sydni handed Willy her nearly full glass of SynthWine and sat back down, nestling in next to Conrad.

Sitting in a chair opposite them, Willy sipped his wine and looked up. He realized that Conrad's arm was around Sydni. Willy pointed back and forth between the two of them and said, "You two are ... together?"

Conrad had not thought about how Willy would react, and for a split second his heart skipped a beat. Sydni and he smiled simultaneously and Sydni said, "Yes we are!"

Willy was staring at Conrad, who continued to grin. "Congratulations," Willy said holding up his glass. "You two make a great couple."

Conrad's sigh of relief was not audible, but Willy could see the relief on his face. "I am very pleased you think so, Willy. It means a lot to me."

Slapping Conrad's thigh, Sydni said, "We can talk about us later. What is going on?"

Willy took a big gulp of the SynthWine and a cut inside his mouth stung. "I have been staying in the Hingandu village for the past four nights. I have learned much about their past, and I have heard many of their tales and myths. I have eaten among them and lived like them. All that aside, I have come to another conclusion." Willy paused for more wine, and he could see the impatience of his sister showing in the twitching of her leg. Willy smiled, showing all of his sharp teeth. "I have fallen in love."

That statement coming from her brother left Sydni speechless and staring at him. He used the word *love*. Willy was in love. "With who?" Sydni asked.

"Dekonal is her name. She is the very same woman that I met and recorded that day."

"You're in love," Sydni said aloud, barely believing herself.

Sydni stood up, and Willy did the same. "And she is in love with me."

She rushed forward and threw her arms around her brother. "Oh, my God, Willy."

"Sydni, you won't believe it. It is a village full of people like me. Men, women and children. Today a group of children choked a street laughing and playing, and it was then that I knew. I have found a place where I can be happy and raise a family and be accepted."

"And why do you have a bloody nose?"

"For lack of a better term, I will call it a male ritual. I was not proven."

"Not proven?" Conrad asked.

"Yes. It was a brother protecting a sister when he thought I was the wrong choice. He wouldn't let me leave the village without a fight."

"And that is acceptance?" Sydni asked.

Willy laughed and Sydni finally let go of him. "I proved to him that I could fight. When I return, he may try and test me more, but it is something he and I will work out with time."

Sydni felt tears well up in her eyes and a lump in her throat; if she had always prayed for happiness for her brother, then why was she about to cry at his good fortune? Willy was on top of it though; he instantly moved into his big brother tone. "Hey, I am not leaving today. We have some things to figure out and I could not just resign my commission so quickly. I promise I will not just pick up and disappear on you."

"We aren't both just about to be happy all at the same time, are we?" Sydni asked.

"Too late," Willy said. "It already happened. So what is on our agenda for tomorrow, or the next few days?"

"Gallagher has everyone jumping through hoops on the bridge. He has patrols flying around the clock. I sent you a message about what he ordered us to do. Something big is going on, but he will not say what it is."

"I need to see your scanner as well," Conrad said. "Two of my techs have found a bug in mine, and I am trying to trace down where the information is sent."

"Doc, it has to be Gallagher. He is the one who barged in to your quarters demanding to know why he wasn't notified about the Coppertroid fuel."

"To be on the safe side, I have Chief Watkinson checking into it."

"How about Chief Su?"

Sydni shrugged her shoulders and said, "Still critical and still unconscious."

"I have to transcribe my notes, but not until my scanner is checked," Willy said staring off into space. Once they are transcribed, I will discuss them with you two, but I want to go back to the planet as soon as time permits."

* * * *

The cold water ran in the sink and mixed with blood as it swirled down the drain. Quistqui heard the heavy footsteps enter his room, and he knew it was not Dekonal as he was expecting. After rinsing out his mouth, Quistqui spat the bloody water into the sink. "Can I help you?"

"I hope so," Chakdon said, his voice rising above the running water. Quistqui looked up sharply; water ran in streaks down his chest. "Maybe you can tell me just what my oldest son had on his mind when he attacked a guest outside my home?"

"You know all to well what I was doing, father."

"Do you not trust your sister's or my abilities to foresee the future?"

Quistqui lowered his own voice and said, "I would follow either of you to the end of the world if you asked me to, but that does not mean I have to trust an unproven stranger."

"Unproven," Chakdon said in almost a snort. "That is old and...."

Quistqui cut him off with a laugh. "You yourself accused your sister's husband, my uncle, of being unproven and fought him." Chakdon had not been ready for that. He had never told that story to his family. Chakdon slowly shook his head and sighed. "Are you saying that is a lie?" demanded Quistqui.

Before he had to answer, Dekonal came in and saved him. "Father, please do not take up against Quist. I wish to speak with him and will settle things between us." She rested a hand on Chakdon's shoulder and softly urged, "Please."

Letting his head sag a little and shaking it, he said, "As you wish, Dekonal." Then pointing a finger at Quistqui, he warned, "Do not instigate a fight in my household again. That I will not tolerate."

Quistqui bowed his head and looked at the floor. "For that I apologize and for disrupting your dinner."

Before he left, Chakdon reached out and put his hand on his son's bowed head and tousled his hair a little. Once Chakdon was gone, Quistqui avoided his sister's eyes and turned back to the sink, blood had started again from the corner of his mouth and nose. "Do not come in here expecting apologies from me," he said gruffly.

As he splashed water on his face again, Dekonal said, "I do not require an apology." When her brother looked up, she stepped up closer and examined his cuts. "I came to see if my brother was injured."

Tilting his head and squinting, Quistqui looked at his sister, trying to imagine what she was up to. "Not seriously. Although Willy had a couple chances to cause me some serious harm, but held himself back." Dekonal laughed. "What?" he asked.

"Willy said the same of you before he left."

Quistqui started to smile but suppressed it. Dekonal snatched a rag already spotted with blood off the sink and held his chin with her other hand. As she blotted blood off his face, she said, "I think I understand just what you are doing, Quist. All I wanted to tell you was that Willy is no infatuation. There is something about him that I am drawn to. I truly love him." She turned his head and tiptoed to kiss his cheek. "I love you, too, big brother." Jamming the rag into his hands, Dekonal turned and left, patting Doqui on the shoulder as he walked in the door.

Doqui looked back out the door and watched Dekonal leave, then he looked at Quistqui and said, "She looked calm for just yelling at you."

"She didn't scold me, and she stopped father from trying."

"Why?"

"Little Brother, with Dekonal, you can never tell. Just roll with it."

"Why do you not like Willy? You told me yourself that we should respect him."

Picking up a towel and wiping off his chest, he said, "To prove him. Test him. See if he can protect her and provide for her."

Doqui was so intent on what his brother was telling him that he did not notice as Quistqui was rolling the towel from both ends. Then with a quick snap of the towel and a sharp crack, Quistqui had left a welt on Doqui's thigh.

"Ow..." Doqui howled as he jumped on one leg, clutching where he was stung.

Quistqui pushed Doqui over on his sleeping mat and laughed. "Maybe I should be working with you instead of Willy, though."

* * * *

Willy lived in the officer quarters, only around the corner from Sydni's, and he had the standard commander's suite. It consisted of a living room, bathroom and sleep room. Willy was standing at the vidphone, which was between the hallway door and the desk with his computer. Just past the computer was his food prep counter. His wet hair was smoothed back and hung loosely about his shoulders. He had changed into a black tee shirt engraved with the 121st scout squadron insignia embroidered over the left breast. He also wore a pair of forest green sweats. The vidphone was punching in the number he had requested.

His living room consisted of a couch facing the wall that had a sound system and video screen and two rows of bookshelves. The wall opposite the hallway door held his arsenal of weapons he had collected. There was an antique flintlock and percussion black powder rifles from earth's twenty-first century, an even more ancient Sharps 45-70 government from the late twentieth century. He had several pistols from old revolvers, to early pulse pistols and his current UWC issue. Then he also had several centerfire and pulse rifles. His favorites were the centerfire rifles that were the favorite with hunters throughout the UWC.

Below the arsenal was a long bench and cabinets. Willy usually made all his own ammunition for the centerfire weapons. There were three pictures in frames on the cabinet, one of Sydni and himself at graduation, another of them at the conclusion of the Doreea Star War where they were promoted to Lt. Commander, and one of Willy and Jean-Pierre dressed in their full camouflage outfits during a hunting expedition.

On the third ring of the vidphone, a clump of Willy's hair fell across his brow and he pushed it back with a swipe of his hands. A sleep-filled voice answered, "Ambassador Gallagher here." Then the ambassador appeared with his mussed up hair and puffy eyes.

"Ambassador, Commander Colton reporting in."

Gallagher rubbed his eyes and said, "It's late, Commander."

"Sorry, Sir, but I just got in."

"Very well." He yawned. "What is your report?"

Willy knew he needed to stall, even if it included lying to Gallagher. "The Hingandu are a bit more complex than I was led to believe."

"Your initial report called them a forest-dwelling, village people."

"That was what I was led to believe by the Jolabwe. They have running water and some sort of power source, but I have not been able to find out what it is yet."

Gallagher nodded. "I want you to return there and continue your investigation."

Willy knew how to play the ambassador, "But I have..."

"I don't care, Commander. This takes priority. Reassign your other duties and I will even remove the scouts from long-range missions until you have concluded your business planetside."

"Yes, Sir."

"Be very thorough. Gallagher out."

The screen went blank and Willy turned off his vidphone. That was the first nice thing Gallagher had done for him. Of course Gallagher had no idea he was ordering Willy to do exactly what Willy wanted. Willy stretched and yawned. He felt a dribble of warmth just under his nose. He touched the wetness and knew it was blood before he looked at his finger. Smiling, he went into the bathroom and pulled off some toilet paper and leaned against the sink with his head tilted back. Quistqui had some very good shots and he moved faster than Willy had anticipated. While he waited for the blood to stop, he wondered what else Quistqui would throw at him, and deep down, he was thrilled at the challenge. There was one way to gain Dekonal's brother's respect and that was to meet his challenges.

After the blood stopped again, Willy went into his bedroom, which was quite sparse for a commander. The walls were bare, and there was one small portal looking out to the stars. There were two dressers and a closet. The tops of the dressers were covered with animal pelts, as was the thin mattress that was on the floor in the far corner.

Willy wanted to be fresh for tomorrow. There were many things he wanted to get done before he went planetside again to see Dekonal. So, sitting on his mattress with his legs crossed and the backs of his hands resting on his knees, he breathed deeply and closed his eyes. For a brief moment he wondered how Chief Su was, and how Vladimir slept at night, but that, he figured, would have to wait until tomorrow.

CHAPTER 7

Chief Su lay on a bed in the sick bay with tubes sticking out of his arms and mouth, connecting to the wall. The readout of the scanner showed steady heartbeat and breaths. The nurse came in and paused. "A friend of yours?"

Turning to face her, Willy said, "Yes, what is his status?" The nurse, a petite woman dressed in gray scrubs and a white coat, seemed not to hear Willy's question, she just stared at him. Willy knew it was the first time she had seen him, so he smiled and said, "Nurse, his status?"

She blinked and then said, "My apologies, Sir." She walked over next to the bed and punched a code into the computer. His medical record flashed and she paused it. "Severe trauma to the head, chest and abdomen. Ruptured spleen and an injured kidney were both removed. Unable to ascertain if there was any brain damage, although the doctor on call at the time thinks he was found early enough. We will not know for certain until he wakes from the coma. There was so much trauma to the head that we have had to relieve the pressure two times and he was under the laser for five hours to fix his internal injuries."

She looked up to see Willy shaking his head. "I promise, Chief," he said. "I will take vengeance for you. You rest and concentrate all your power to healing, and I will bring your assailant to justice."

"You think one person did this to him?" the nurse asked. You know this is Chief Su, the master of the dojo. No one person aboard the Orion could have done this to him."

Willy looked at her. "There are four qualified masters aboard ship. Any one of them could have at least given him a run for his money." Turning back to Su, Willy continued, "Keep the faith, Chief. I ran your class through this morning and Tanya is taking today's noon class. The scouts will cover when they can, and I have spoken to several other of the black belts who are willing to help. We'll take care of shop, you rest." Turning to the nurse, who was staring at him again, he said, "Thank you for the information."

Willy was almost out of the room when she said, "No problem, Sir."

* * * *

"No, Doctor Singh, there was nothing in this one or any of the others." One of the techs said, handing back Willy's scanner. "Since it was only yours that had the sensor, we took the liberty to check your office computer, but there was nothing there."

"Thank you, and as before, I would prefer if this stayed confidential. Any ideas on why mine was the only one to be tapped?"

One tech shrugged, but the other said, "Opportunity. It would be my guess that for someone to get their hands on anything of Commander Colton's, they would really have to be on top of their game, but your scanner would be easy access."

"I hadn't thought of that. Good day."

Conrad left the two techs in the vault and made his way out to the hall. He wished Andrea would return and resume her administrative duties, but he didn't have the heart to bring her back yet. She was enjoying herself too much. As he walked to his office, he thought of something. Sydni had thought the water moon was beautiful. Now that they had a research ship down there, maybe he could arrange for a picnic dinner aboard. He knew it would be unnerving to him, but it would be worth it for Sydni.

At his desk, he set up a direct link through his computer to the research vessel afloat on the moon. It took several minutes before anyone answered the call, and then it was a tech who wasn't even wearing a shirt. "Admiral, nice to hear from you."

Conrad smiled. "Thank you, may I please speak with the Major?"

"Hold on," he said moving away from the screen.

He drummed his fingers while he waited, then finally Andrea appeared wearing an open white blouse that looked wet and her hair glistened with water. "Sorry to keep you waiting Admiral. Do you need me to return?"

"No. Nothing like that," Conrad said holding up his hands. "I was actually thinking of bringing a guest down for a visit. Maybe an afternoon in the sun, and an evening meal on the top deck."

"A social visit?" She asked with her bright smile even broader than before.

"Nothing official about the visit. In fact, you do not even need to warn the others of my arrival and that way they won't have time to get nervous." He paused. "How about if I bring the rations for a cookout? You do have some sort of grill or cooking station set up."

"I see you have been in similar situations, Sir."

Conrad had been aboard research facilities that were land or water based. He had drawn up the original plans to turn shuttles into a floating research facility. He had not been happy about the wide-open ocean, but it was his job, and he had participated in many parties aboard such places. Usually the CSO would not be instigating such a party, but he wanted his subordinates to enjoy the experience. Maybe it would help them grow to be good leaders when it was their turn. "Affirmative. Let's see, I will aim for four hours before the sun sets on your facility for some time in the sun."

"Aye, aye. Looking forward to your visit, sir."

Conrad shut down the link and then sent a message to Sydni, so she would free up her time. He did not tell her what he was doing, just that he needed all evening. It wouldn't quite be what she expected, but he wanted to keep her on her toes.

* * * *

After seeing Su, Willy spent most of his afternoon transcribing notes from his scanner to his computer. He would then download them to Conrad's computer and scanner for further examination. He was about halfway done with the task when the alarm on his computer chimed. There was to be a Scout meeting before lunch to check on the progress of their investigation. As he shut down the scanner and computer, his door beeped. "Enter," he said as he turned to greet his guest.

It was Tanya and Gordo. "Hola, Willy," Gordo said as the door shut. "How was your visit to the Hingandu?"

"Very informative. One of the reasons we are having this meeting is that I will be returning there for an extended period of time. How was your four-day run?"

"Monotonous and uneventful."

The door beeped again and Sydni entered with Barkley. "I found this one straggling along in the halls and took pity on him," Sydni said, pointing her thumb at Barkley behind her.

"Come on in. Everyone and have a seat somewhere." Sydni and Willy tried not to show their sibling affection around the scouts, but Sydni was very happy and she knew Willy was too. She kissed his cheek as she passed and said, "Hello."

"Hey," he said as he returned her kiss.

"Anyone want a drink or something to eat, feel free to raid my kitchen," Willy said. Barkley lay down along the wall with the video screen, and Tanya flopped down on one end of the couch.

Gordo veered into the kitchen and opened the refrigeration unit. Sydni said, "Gord, will you bring me one of those juices?" He nodded as he looked through the contents, knowing she would prefer apple or orange. Sydni sat on the other end of the couch from Tanya and Willy sat on the cabinet along his arsenal.

"Well, we really don't have much of an agenda, but we just wanted to check in." Willy said.

Sydni took a juice container from Diego and said, "Thanks. Does anyone have any information on Chief Su?"

Diego sat on the floor with his back against the middle of the couch. "Not me, my long range gave me little time."

Tanya shook her head. Barkley raised his hand and said, "I don't have any real information, but Vladimir is asking a lot of questions. However, they are all general and unfocused. I'd say he is doing it just to make people think he is trying."

"Agreed," Willy said. "I saw Chief this morning. He is not good and his status is still not stable. Tell the classes we teach to go visit him. He is in a coma, but probably knows we are there. And I would like to thank you for volunteering to take some of Chief's classes. I still want you to remember that if Vladimir comes into class, notify us immediately. Drop what you are doing and respond to that call. I do not want a repeat of what happened to Chief."

"Can't we just remove him the same way?" Barkley asked.

Tanya laughed and said, "Yeah, right, the great Scout Uprising aboard the UWC Orion."

"No, really," Diego said. "Deal a little to him that he dealt out."

"I want to take him down, too," Willy said, "but I want it to be officially. There are some other weird things going on with the Ambassador, and I want to find out what it is before we act."

"I agree," Sydni said. "We need to know what is going on; something is very suspicious."

Gordo swallowed some of his drink and said, "I heard from some guys coming in this morning that there are round-the-clock-patrols going on. Is that true?"

"True," Sydni said. "Undetermined why, though."

They all turned to Willy. Usually he had an inside track as to what was going on aboard the ship, but all he could do was shrug and smile. "Really, I don't know. It has something to do with the ambassador. I have been ordered back to the Hingandu to learn what I can about them. Gallagher has seen something that has piqued his interest."

That sparked a memory in Willy's head that he had forgotten. He remembered seeing the glitter of debris on the ground while he was flying. "I have seen something that looked like debris from a downed craft, but I couldn't get a good reading." He thought about it for a moment and said, "Whoever goes, take precautions. If it is an old wreck site, there could be hazardous residue."

"A crash site?" Tanya asked. "Any speculations?"

"None. I know this is generally Dr. Singh's area. Land first and then call in a team. I want first info on this. Relay anything to both Sydni and my scanners."

"I'd go," Barkley said, "but Gallagher's stuff I am doing has me pretty backed up."

"I can do it," Tanya said.

"I'll tag-team if it's okay," Gordo said.

Tanya patted his head and said, "Well, at least I don't have to worry about taking lunch with me."

"No, I'll have it covered."

"Great," Willy said, cutting in. "I will relay the coordinates to your ship, Tanya. Then, when you are checking, fly a random pattern and then tell the bridge you want to land. Take your time and be thorough before you call in a team. I want details."

"Affirmative," Tanya said.

Willy added, "If you need me, or Vladimir starts causing trouble, do not hesitate to call me. I may want to take care of Vladimir officially, but I will not endanger any of you in the meantime."

Barkley raised himself up on his elbow and looked at Willy. "No offense, Willy, but could you take him out?"

Willy grinned and it was a grin that always worried Barkley, showing Willy's sharp white teeth. "I would personally like to find out, but professionally, I really hope I do not have to." Then, with an involuntary flex of his claws, he said, "With all of you as backup, how could I go wrong."

Barkley lay back down and said, "Fair enough."

"As usual, when I am gone this time, feel free to come in and use my quarters. Gordo, just replace any food and Barkley," Barkley looked up again, "Stay out of my good liquor."

"Yes, Sir. Sorry, Sir."

"Sydni, anything to add?"

She sat up and said, "Just to keep the rumor mill at a dull gossip, I have news for you." That got all their attention quick. "I have been seeing Dr. Singh."

Gordo laughed and said, "On a professional basis?"

Tanya reached over and smacked him hard enough to bob his head forward. "No," Sydni said, "on a social basis."

"I hope you're happy," Tanya said.

"Me too," Barkley said.

Gordo laughed again and said, "He's no scout, but he is a Lt. Admiral." He ducked his head before Tanya swung at him again. He rolled away from the couch and stood up. Looking at Willy, Gordo shrugged and said, "What did I do?"

Willy laughed. "Gordo, you are dismissed, before you get into any more trouble. Everyone is dismissed. So everyone keep your eyes open, I want to know what is going on around here."

Sydni and Willy were walking down the corridor to Conrad's office for lunch. Sydni was watching her brother walk down the corridor without his cloak. Willy seemed not to notice that everyone was watching him. When they were side by side, she asked, "Are you going to tell them about her?"

"Dekonal?"

"Yes."

"I'll have to. They are a very good team, the best I have ever worked with. When the time is right, I will tell them."

"Have you made any conclusions about the nature of the humans on this planet?"

"A couple. I believe they were transplanted, but I will forward my info to both you and Doc so you guys can read up on it and decide for yourself."

"That debris, could it be a crashed ship? Humans crash-land and are stranded?"

Willy shook his head. "Doc said the mutation they had was generations and generations long. It would have to have been an ancient ship. I also gather that there are a couple of other villages of Hingandu north of there, so how could one ship have had enough to multiply that much. Could they?"

Sydni shrugged her shoulders. "Besides, I think we would have learned about a lost ship in History. Look how much Earth historians still debate the lost colonies, lost planes, and things like the lost city of Atlantis."

"It may never be solvable, but I think once we have more evidence, we will be able to come to a conclusion."

They stopped at Conrad's office and pushed the button. The door slid open and from behind his desk, Conrad said, "Come on in. I will be done in a moment."

Willy sat facing Conrad, while Sydni sat on the corner of the desk. Once he was finished, he looked up at Sydni and reached out for her hand. Then looking at Willy, he said, "I take it you got your scanner back."

"You can trust the tech you sent with it?"

"Yes. Not only as a colleague, but we have been close friends for ten years or more."

Willy nodded. "I am about halfway through my notes, but I did find something peculiar when I was planetside. My scanner would not work in the village, but when I leave the village, it works fine. Also, from the air I cannot detect the village or even see it visually for that matter."

"A dampening mechanism?" Sydni asked.

"Nothing I saw would suggest it."

"Maybe some sort of solar effect or polar effect, but that would not explain the visual. I would like to have more information on this when you are able to find out, or at least scan the area and maybe we can pull something off of that."

"What kind of scans?"

"Try the whole range and maybe we can come up with what it is."

In the pause, Sydni said, "My schedule is clear today and tomorrow. My days off. What's up?"

"Surprises."

Sydni's face lit up with excitement and she repeated, "Surprises! Like what?"

Conrad stood up and grinned. Grinned like a mischievous little boy. He kissed Sydni and said, "You will have to wait. Now we should have lunch. I had planned to have it here, but I did not have time to make the arrangements. Do you mind going to the Officers' Galley?"

They both looked at Willy, who stood up and said, "Not anymore. Let's go."

Willy had never gone to the Officers' Galley at the noon meal. The line extended down the hall. Conrad looked around in amazement before he turned to Willy and said, "I cannot believe it."

"What?"

"I see now how naive I must have seemed when we talked about people's reaction to you."

While Willy laughed, Sydni swung Conrad's arm back and forth, giggling. "Oh, Conrad," she finally said. "That is why I love you. You keep your ideals and I will be the cynic."

Willy said, "Doc, you would think people would get used to me, but I have found out that they never do. Growing up, in school, and in the academy, it was always the same. But it is nice that you now understand what I was talking about."

They went through the line and met again by the drink dispenser. "Looks like getting a table could be a bit difficult," Conrad said.

Willy's laughter came from deep within and he said, "Doc, I used to have this down to a science. Syd, if you'd please get me a drink, I will provide a table." Willy looked around. He was certain that half of the private conversations going on were about him, which would work to his advantage. Moving slowly but holding himself up straight and tall, he cruised through the tables looking for a group of young officers. They stopped speaking as he neared, and they had one extra seat. Willy stopped next to the chair. Using his deepest, most gravely voice, he asked, "Is this seat taken?"

They looked at each other and then a lieutenant almost stuttered, "No, Sir."

He sat down and looked at his food, growling deeply. He had all their attention, which was what he wanted. It only took a minute before they cleared the table around him, leaving more than enough room for Sydni and Conrad.

"How did you do that?" Conrad asked.

"He psyched them out. Young officers can be intimidated by a higher-ranking officer, and Willy adds a touch more to that."

"Kind of a mean thing to do," Willy said. "But here we are with all kinds of space."

They ate, trying to keep their discussion about anything but the planet, Chief Su, and Vladimir. It was difficult, because they each wanted to discuss what was going on. Willy was afraid someone might be trying to hear what they were talking about, and they could not afford a leak at this time. Sydni whispered, "I want to know more about her."

"If you have a few minutes after lunch, I will try and discuss it with you..." Willy was interrupted by his scanner going off. He glanced down at it because Tanya had paged him with the code that meant Vladimir just walked in on her session.

Willy stood up and looked at Sydni, who asked, "Who is it?"

"Tanya," Willy said. Then he turned and started running through the galley.

"Damn," Sydni said, pushing her tray back and standing up.

"What is it?" Conrad asked.

As she started running, she shouted back over her shoulder, saying, "I will explain later. I have to run."

Conrad watched as Willy dodged one last person and ran out into the hall. Sydni was not far behind him. Conrad knew that Tanya was one of the scouts, but he wondered why they would have to run if she paged. Looking down at what Willy always referred to as a synth-meal, he pushed his tray back. There was a lot of work waiting for him at the office, that he figured he would go do, before he checked out and went to the moon for a day of recreation. Picking up their trays, he headed for the recycling station to turn them in.

Willy was a few yards ahead of Sydni, shouting for everyone to clear the way as they ran down the crowded halls. He stopped at an access tube and opened it. Sydni knew with the crowds that could form at the lifts and carrier tubes, it would be quicker to use the engineering access tubes to go up a couple of floors.

Willy's feet disappeared. Sydni crawled in and reached for the first handhold. Willy was rapidly climbing and Sydni followed. She caught up with him as he was opening the portal in the hall with the Dojo. Willy helped pull her out before they started down the hall.

They stopped at the door before they opened it. A couple of students were in the first room, getting ready to leave. Sydni looked at one and asked, "Class over early today?"

He was only a yellow belt, and he looked scared as he glanced over his shoulder and then back at Sydni. "Yes, Ma'am. It was interrupted."

They walked into the back part of the dojo where the mat was. Tanya was on the mat facing Vladimir, who was poised to spar. Willy shouted, "Lieutenant Williston, come here."

Tanya looked over at her commanders and then ran over to them. "Yes, Sir!" she said, standing at attention.

"Thank you for filling in today, but if you remember, I asked you to help Sergeant Diego today. You do not have time to spar right now."

"Yes, Sir. Sorry, Sir!"

"Dismissed."

She looked at Willy and mouthed: thank you. He nodded and she left the mat. Vladimir stood in the center of the mat shaking his head. Willy took off his sneakers and socks and then bowed before he stepped onto the mat. He glanced at Sydni and shook his head.

"Major, I want you to listen carefully. I order you never to spar with any of the scouts. In fact, I am barring you from use of the dojo until further notice."

Vladimir shot his head back and laughed. "You are barring me from the dojo? You have no right."

"Vladimir," Willy said, lowering his voice. "You are not good at playing this game. Not only do I outrank you, it is in the charter of the dojo, signed by the captain and the ambassador, that I am second in charge of the dojo. Now, I order you to leave the dojo now, or I will report you for insubordination."

Squinting, Vladimir shook his head and crossed his arms in defiance.

Willy nodded and growled. "Sydni, would you please notify security that I need some assistance."

Sydni did not reply, but out of the corner of his eye, Willy could see her punching in the code for security into her scanner.

"Ha, the mighty Commander Colton is afraid to spar with me."

Willy smiled and said, "No, Major, not afraid. My commission is important to me, and I will not allow you to foul that up. I will have security come down here. I will have them cart you off in humiliation through the halls. I will make it so Ambassador Gallagher will come down and have to release you in person. I will...."

Vladimir lunged at Willy, grabbing for his throat. Willy grabbed Vladimir's wrists and fell backward. He put his feet on Vladimir's abdomen and flipped him over his head. Willy flipped and landed on his feet, turning calmly as Vladimir came at him slowly. "You can walk out of here now, Vladimir, before security arrives. This is my last warning."

Vladimir threw three punches that Willy swatted away and swept Vladimir's feet out from under him. As Vladimir was falling, Willy grabbed his arm and wrist, twisting until Vladimir lay still on the mat, groaning. "Fight me," Vladimir said.

"I could break your arm and leave it useless for a week or two. I could cripple it for months, but I will not let my anger get the better of me. I think the world would be a safer place if right now I put you in the hospital bed next to Chief Su, fighting for your life."

"Are you implying that I attacked Chief Su?"

"You're the investigator. You tell me." Willy heard the door open and Sydni say, "Bob, glad you responded quickly. In here."

Bob came in followed by three other Marines. "What is the problem here?"

Willy looked up. "Bob, Vladimir here attacked a superior officer after he was asked to leave the dojo. The tapes will show that. I am pressing charges."

The Marines surrounded Vladimir and Bob said, "You can let him go, Commander. We will take over from here."

Willy let go and stood up in one quick motion. Vladimir stood up, shaking his arm that Willy had twisted. "Major," Bob said to Vladimir, "place your hands behind your back."

Vladimir reached out for Willy again, but the Marines were well trained in subduing large prisoners. Two of the Marines hit Vladimir with stun sticks, sending a lot of voltage through Vladimir, who hit the mat with the sound of wet clothing hitting the floor. Bob and another Marine were on Vladimir. Bob had his knee pinning Vladimir's head while the other one locked Vladimir's hands behind his back with a pair of manacles. As his mind cleared, he started to fight. "Don't make us use the stick again, Vladimir," Bob said. Looking up, Bob said, "Set the sticks higher. If he tries anything else, I want him out."

Vladimir stopped struggling and they dragged him to his feet. Two of the Marines stayed on either side of him and held him as Bob said, "Let's go. Wait in the hall while I get the tape."

Willy picked up his sneakers and socks and slipped them on. When Vladimir was outside, Sydni said, "Thanks, Bob."

Bob, who was grinning, said, "Are you kidding? I really enjoyed that. Thanks for calling us. It looked like you had the situation under control." Bob opened a panel at the front door and hooked his version of a scanner up to record the last hour's worth in the dojo. "Got it," he said. "Good footage. Please be careful. When he gets out, he will be mad as hell."

"Thank you, Major," Willy said.

Bob smiled at Sydni and said, "Good day, Commanders."

"What do you think he would have done to Tanya?" Sydni asked.

"That answer scares me. We probably would be visiting two people in sick bay, but we don't have to."

"I will need to go write up a formal report and send it to Gallagher and Bucky. Apologize to Conrad for me."

"He'll understand. But I am serious. I want to meet your new love, and I want you to sit down and tell me about her."

Willy sat down along the wall and Sydni sat down next to him. "Maybe in a few days I can send a message and we can arrange a meeting. You, Conrad, Dekonal and I."

Sydni placed her hand on Willy's arm. "That's perfect!" she exclaimed. "I know Conrad would be intrigued as well."

"You saw her picture before, from my scanner."

"Right."

"Her eyes are lavender with silver specks, like mine are marked with gold specks. Her light brown skin is accented with stripes. She can run with me, and she has an intoxicating scent that drives me wild when I am near her, but the most important thing is that besides her physical beauty, there is something about her spirit that draws me to her, as if all this time it was meant to be."

Sydni did not need more of an explanation. That, word for word, was how she would have described Conrad to Willy. Sydni touched her brother's cheek and said, "I am so happy for you, Willy."

Willy looked at her, and her voice had trailed off as if she had more to say. "But what?" he asked.

"I just wish Mother and Father could be here to see this."

"See what?"

She stared into his eyes and said, "That light shining in your eyes, the smile on your face as you describe her, and the happiness that has filled your heart. Love wears well on you. I wish they could have seen the little boy inside, the man waiting for happiness to find him."

Willy shook his head. "They'll never know," he said. "I will never go back now. I can feel it, Syd. I can tell. The UWC could break out into a tri-world revolt, but I am not leaving this planet."

"Hopefully they can put a spaceport nearby that will not affect the Hingandu life."

"History does show us that there is a spaceport everywhere they find Coppertroid, but I do not know if the Hingandu will allow it. The Jolabwe may allow it, but do we owe anything to the Hingandu? They are human, too.

Sydni shrugged. "How about if we just let things continue for now and see what happens from there." She was looking at Willy, and his forehead was deeply creased; that only happened when he was in deep thought. So she ran her hand across his brow and asked, "Willy, what is it?"

He looked at his sister and said, "Dekonal says she has visions, that much I have told you. What I did not tell you was that she says there is going to be a war. From what she describes," he paused long enough to take a deep breath and sigh. "She describes me leading them into battle."

Sydni smiled. Willy had seen that smile a million or more times, usually when she was about to comfort him for some indiscretion handed down by humanity. She said, "You have always believed in making the world suit your needs. Just keep being Willy Colton, and the rest will fix itself."

"I did not realize that your scout ship had so much storage capacity," Conrad said, as he secured a crate with web straps in a small cargo hold in the side of the craft.

"Can you tell me what I will be carrying and to where?" Sydni asked.

"Surprise."

"I will need to be flying there soon." She tugged on the strap he had just secured. Then she ran her hand up his arm and said, "Pretty please."

"Okay, one hint. First we are going to the moon to stop and off-load these supplies, but that is all I am telling you."

She stared at him for a while and said, "Okay. I take it that you have sent the coordinates to my ship." He nodded.

"All taken care of. They will be moving into the sunny portion of the planet, and their beacon will be on."

"Well, we are fueled. I ran a level three diagnostic on the water floatation system, and it is working." She grabbed him by the flight suit and said, "Did I tell you how sexy you look in that flight suit?"

"No."

"You are absolutely the most sexy man to ever zip up a flight suit." She pulled herself up to him and they kissed. "Now climb aboard and we will get out of here."

Sydni kept her flight tame, knowing that the 3D of space flight could be disorienting to somebody who was not a flyer, and she did not want to make him sick. The moon came up fast, and Sydni switched over her computer and picked up the beacon. She eased back on the throttle when the makeshift boat came into view. It was two shuttles moored together with a set of lounge chairs set up on the top, and along the backside of both shuttles where the bay doors opened. There was a platform that made a dock. Someone appeared through a portal on top and began waving. Sydni waddled her wings back and forth as she flew past.

"Hold on," Sydni said as she banked around and headed back toward the boat. As she lowered down, she turned on the water mode. Her ship clicked several times and she throttled back even more, until she was bouncing along the small swells. As they pulled up, two men, wearing only shorts, and a woman in a bathing suit ran out to help secure the scout ship. Sydni cut the thrusters and drifted in.

"Do you get seasick, Sydni?" Conrad asked.

"Not hardly."

"Well, we are staying here for a day of sun, swimming, and a good old-fashioned cookout. Followed by an evening of stars, wine, and stars."

Sydni popped the canopy and unbuckled so she could turn and see Conrad. "You made these arrangements? You don't even like open spaces."

Unbuckling and standing up, Conrad said, "You are worth braving the open sky."

She slipped off her helmet and leaned over her seat to kiss Conrad. When she stopped, the three-crew members were clapping. When they both were on the deck, Conrad said, "Okay, in the two side cargo decks I have two cases of real beer, a case of Synth-wine, a case with food, and one case marked personal, and that is for me."

The crew members started unloading cheerfully and Andrea appeared on the upper deck. "Welcome aboard the UWC Mayflower."

"Mayflower?" Conrad asked. "Knowing you, Andrea, that has some sort of significance."

Although Andrea was silhouetted by the brilliant blue sky, Sydni thought she saw a smile. "Good call, Admiral. It was one of the first ships of colonists to land on North America Earth, and one of its second incarnations was the first ship to land on Alpha One."

Conrad nodded. "Good name, Andrea. I believe you already know my companion, Commander Colton."

Andrea waved. "Hello, Sydni."

"Hey." Sydni said back with a wave.

"Come on inside and I will give you a tour." Andrea said. "Anything you ask for I will try and provide."

*　　*　　*　　*

Willy was packing his larger backpack and planning a longer stay on the planet. He would only return soon only if Vladimir kept proving to be a pain or if the scouts turned up vital information in their investigation. He thought one of the *tests* that Quistqui might try would have something to do with hunting, so he packed enough ammunition and his favorite hunting rifle, the 7 mm Magnum that his first Scout Leader had given to him as a present after he had saved two other scouts in the Skalkanian Bush Skirmish. Jean-Pierre Degaul had given it to him and said, "William Colton, this will make an honest hunter of you. To be a true scout, you must be a true hunter, and to be a true hunter, you need a traditional rifle."

Willy laughed. He thought he had known a lot about scouting until Jean-Pierre had instructed him. He ran his hand over the wood stock and looked at the well-oiled action. He missed Jean-Pierre, who died during the last days of the Doreea Star War, and in death he taught Willy even more. His will had left all his hunting gear and weapons to Willy, and a simple message: "Willy, my friend. Do not let them judge you by your looks. Only let them judge you for being a scout. Good hunting."

The 121st Scout Squad resembled a Jean-Pierre scout squad, because they knew the ship inside and out. Jean-Pierre had taught him to use the air ducts and engineering access tubes to move about undetected, and they constantly trained. "Jean-Pierre, what would you say I was about to do?" Of course Willy didn't really need an answer, he knew the answer already.

Jean-Pierre would have supported his mission. He had seen how people had treated him, and even had suggested the cloak as to keep him mysterious instead of a sideshow attraction..

His door beeped, and he looked over his shoulder as he said, "Enter."

The door slid open and Tanya stood there, dressed in a bright blue jumpsuit. She forced a smile and asked, "Can I come in?"

"Certainly, Tanya." After leaning his rifle against his pack, he picked up his bottle of beer. "Can I offer you a drink?"

She nodded. "Anything will be fine, thanks."

Willy walked over to the kitchenette and opened the refrigeration unit and pulled out a bottle of beer. He twisted off the cap and said, "Glass?" She shook her head and took the bottle from him. "What's on your mind?" he asked.

After three long gulps she said, "I wanted to thank you, sir. I left the dojo today like nothing ever happened, and then I ran into Bob. Do you know Bob?"

"Security?" Willy asked.

She nodded and continued, "He told me about you taking Vladimir down and then how they had to stun him once just to subdue him."

"Correct."

"Sir, then I got to thinking just what would have happened had you and Sydni not shown up today, and I will tell you outright, it scared the hell out of me. I tried to work out and shake it off, but I couldn't. I went and talked to Chief Su, and that just worried me more. I thought I better thank you."

Willy smiled, and so few times had she seen him truly smile it eased her mind a little. Then he sipped his beer and said, "Tanya, you are Sydni's and my responsibility, and I required you to obtain your black belt for my squad. I will not allow anything to happen to you. Sydni could probably take out Vladimir. If it happens again, keep your students there. Several lower black belts should be able to deal with him. However, to put you at ease, not only am I pressing charges, he is also banned from the dojo and from sparring with any of you."

She nodded and leaned against the counter, relaxing a little. "That is a relief, Sir."

"I want you to know something else," Willy said, lowering his voice. "Had he injured you or one of the others, I would have dealt with him severely. He would die a slow and painful death."

The tone Willy used made Tanya shudder, but deep down it gave her a warm peaceful feeling. Knowing that revenge would be taken, she could go into a fight with confidence. "Would I have stood a chance against him?" Tanya asked.

"Doubtful, if he is the one that took Chief Su out, however he must have hit Chief Su off guard. If he ever comes after you again, though, try getting him mad. Insult him. Once he is mad, he is not much of a fighter. The cooler head usually prevails."

"Well, thank you again," she said. "You are by far one of the best commanders I have ever had."

"Thank you. It has been difficult for me to maintain leadership for reasons you may or may not understand, but it helps that I have always had your respect."

She raised her bottle and said, "You lead and we'll follow."

He clinked his glass to hers and said, "I like that attitude."

They both drank. "Sir, if you don't mind me asking, I know you and Sydni hand-picked this squad. I know that she served with Gordo, and that you served with Barkley, but why me? I wasn't even in your squad for two months before you got your command. Why me?"

"Who trained you?" he asked.

"At the academy?" Willy smiled and shook his head. "I was a rookie during the Doreea Star War...oh, you mean Commander Degaul."

Willy's smile broadened. "He told me that you were a hunter the last time I saw him. I remembered that when you joined my old squad before I came here."

She was nodding. "You and Pierre were friends?"

Willy took a long draw on his beer before he said, "Yes. I knew Jean-Pierre a long time. Almost my whole professional career." He looked at Tanya and paused. "He was a hunter, and I was a hunter. He used to say that our hearts had been molded by the same god, and that our bodies didn't matter."

"Now that I think about it, both your styles of leadership and training are a lot alike."

"On purpose," Willy said. "He molded one of the finest squads I have ever worked with. I was proud of that squad and I am proud of this squad."

"Well, we'll have to go hunting sometime soon."

"I want to form a hunting party, but I have to find out more about the boundaries of the Hingandu land and whether or not we would be encroaching on their territory."

Tanya slipped the bottle into the recycle tube and said, "Thanks for the talk and the beer. I am going to get going so you can finish getting ready for planetside."

"Anytime. I will be in close contact in case Vladimir tries anything else, and I may be calling a meeting on the surface in a few days."

"And you will get the first report on your possible crash-site. Good-bye." Tanya opened the door and left.

* * * *

The chaise lounge was set up on the front end of the makeshift deck. Sydni sat between Conrad's legs as he sat in the chair. The stars were brilliant, and the planet didn't yet show in the night sky. Faintly, over the sound of the small swells crashing against the hull, they could hear the laughter and splashing of the crew members swimming near the dock below. They had set up sonar and sensors so if any fish drew near, that could possibly be dangerous, they would have ample time to get up on the dock. Sydni was impressed at how much Conrad cared about his subordinates. He really let them party down, not to mention that he partied with them; she'd had no idea Conrad even knew how to dance, let alone that he was a good dancer.

The boat pitched and rocked a little, and somewhere nearby a bird called. "I didn't know this moon had birds," Sydni said.

"Yes. I asked Andrea about that today when I saw one. She said that in the shallow waters there are colonies of plants growing that provide enough cover for the birds to nest and lay eggs."

"Aren't you just full of trivia?"

"Only to serve you, ma'am." He kissed the back of her head. "Isn't it lovely out here tonight?"

Rubbing his hands that were clasped around her, she said, "I have seen billions and billions of stars from in space, boats, mountains, from forest treetops, but none have been better than the ones I am seeing from right here with you tonight. I understand how difficult it is for you to be down here, out from the closeness of your walls, and it makes me love you even more."

"As I said when we arrived here, you make me forget my anxiety. Besides, at night, like this, I cannot see the vastness of the planet and it does not seem nearly as bad." There was a long pause between them, and there was a shriek of laughter followed by a large splash. Sydni figured that they were using her ship as a diving board. Conrad hugged her tighter and whispered, "You must know, I would do anything for you. Anything."

Chapter 8

Before four a.m. Willy headed down to the flight deck to leave for the planet. He had completed his transcription of Dekonal's reading and sent it on to Sydni and Conrad. When he got down to the flight deck and saw that Sydni's ship was not back yet, he started to get nervous, but when he checked with the bridge, they told him that she had stayed on the moon, moored to the science vessel. He stowed his gear and was ready to take off when an idea struck him. He could at least give them a morning fly-by and a burst of speed to wake them up. Everyone else on board might not appreciate the noise, but he did owe Sydni for the past couple of practical jokes.

Willy computed his flight plan to the bridge and listed a moon fly-by as a shipment drop. The bridge commander usually could care less what the flight jocks did as long as they kept the space clear around the ship and the chatter off the main channels. The moon was just fading on the horizon of the planet in the path of the Orion. So when Willy's ship was free, he computed a path back along the trail of the Orion.

He began scanning for the boat's beacon as soon as he could see the entire moon. It did not take long for him to locate the boat; Sydni's scout ship was moored to one side of the boat, and it was floating just within the touch of morning's light. Cloaking his ship, he made a high pass in the atmosphere, then he started his dive. He figured he'd swoop in and just as he passed, he would hit his boosters, but his scan told him that two people were up on the top deck. He zoomed in, and could just make out Sydni and Conrad asleep on a lounge chair. He turned off his microphone and started laughing. His laughter grew as he drew nearer the boat. Adjusting his flight path a little more, he dropped down so he was skimming the tops of the nearly calm swells. Glancing over his shoulder, he could see a plume of water rising fifteen feet above his tail.

His ship was on a direct course at the boat. At the last moment, he banked his ship and kicked in the boosters. He cut in a tight curl around the boat and continued to laugh as he watched Sydni and Conrad jump from their chair when a wall of rain splashed down over the upper deck. After a few more turns, slowly increasing the diameter of his turns around the boat, and seeing two more people appear, he straightened out and headed into the upper atmosphere.

Once the stars surrounded him, and he was on his path to the planet, he typed in a message to Sydni: "Good Morning, Sis. Tell Doc I am sorry he got caught in the middle of revenge. Remember the eggs. Willy."

For a moment he wondered what kind of revenge she might try and extract from him. He knew it would take her a while to top that bath, but when she did strike, she would likely embarrass him. He glanced back at the moon over his shoulder and started laughing again.

* * * *

The morning was coming on in small increments with the changing color of the sky. Conrad did not stir as he did not want to wake Sydni from where she lay, and with her there, the open space was not yet causing him distress. It had been years since he had seen sunrise planetside. The color of the water was as spectacular as the color in the sky. The water lapped gently against the boat, and there was almost no breeze. He thought he could hear something else, but when he strained his neck to look around he couldn't see anything.

Suddenly the world around him erupted. He knew the sound of a ship flying by, which made both Sydni and him jump from chaise lounge, but then there was the wall of water he saw coming at him as if in slow motion. A moment before the water hit, he thought how cold the deck was to his bare feet. He was drenched. Curses were on his lips, but before he could say anything, he realized that Sydni was laughing.

Dripping wet, she turned and looked at Conrad and saw the anger on his face, which made her laugh even more. Andrea and one of the other crew members climbed onto the deck asking, "What was that?"

Sydni looked up; she could hear the scout ship with its boosters kicked in circling above them. "I would say a cloaked scout ship, kicking in its boosters as it swooped by, sending a wave of water at us."

"Which scout would do that?"

Sydni hugged Conrad for a moment, and a chill ran down to her toes in the cool morning air. "I would say that was in return for the last practical joke I played on my brother. I replaced his fresh eggs with those about to hatch from a planetside farm. It was at the end of a very long cruise and he was craving real food. I definitely apologize for you getting caught in the middle of it."

"I think my heart is settling down," Andrea said. "Although, I would have to say, that is not my idea of a wake-up call."

"Me either," the other crewman said before he headed back down.

"Rest assured," Sydni said, looking up to where she had last heard Willy's ship, "he will be repaid for his visit here."

"Some brother-sister relationship," Andrea said, turning to go back down into the boat. "I don't think I would want to have to watch my back that much."

Conrad had started to smile, and he even started laughing before Sydni asked him, "Why are you laughing now?"

"Because, I may not be much of a psyc doc, but you are," Conrad said. Sydni shrugged and Conrad continued, "Willy never had any friends that would just goof off and play jokes on him, so you wear many different hats with him. You play sister, huntress, mother, friend, and jokester."

Sydni smiled. "I always had to, but he would have nothing of my mothering him."

"I can see that."

"When we were five, and he started staying out all night in the woods, it frightened me. My twin, my brother, who looked no different to me than the back of my own hand, but I saw him being torn apart by his separation from humanity. So before I ever knew about psychology, I started playing all those parts, and have continued to do so." Sydni turned and looked at the orange sky and the water that had settled back down and looked as if it were on fire. "Everyone always thought that I was the one who was on top of things, but I was so scared."

Conrad hugged Sydni from behind. "I can't imagine you being scared."

"Oh, but I was. I was scared that Willy would step into those woods one night and disappear forever. Quadra Three is still undeveloped enough, compared to Earth and even Alpha One, that he could do that. I fought to keep peace in my family and keep Willy grounded." She spun in his grasp so she could see his face. "Don't get me wrong, for the most part I had a happy childhood, but there were times. That's all."

"I never would have guessed."

"Not even my parents would have guessed. They still believe that I could come home someday and have a family on Quadra Three and settle down."

"And you can't?" Conrad asked.

"I can settle down and have a family; I just cannot go back to Quadra Three. Not with Willy staying here." She used her finger to move some of Conrad's matted hair off his brow and she stared off for a moment. "I hope you understand when I tell you this. I never want to be far from my brother, I need to have him nearby as much as he needs me to be nearby."

Conrad dipped his head and kissed Sydni. Then he said, "I have a large family. That was because my parents refused to follow the Earth Family Guidelines for religious reasons. Since I left the New New Delhi Academy, I have only been back when my parents died. My sister is now a CSO on the UWC Challenger, so I see her from time to time. Despite all that, I am not nearly as close to my family as you are to Willy, and I am envious of that sibling relationship, because I do not have one. I have fallen in love with you, and I will go wherever that love takes us."

Sydni stepped back and said, "Do we have time to let our clothes dry, or do you need to get back right away?"

"I guess we have time. Why?"

Sydni unzipped her flight suit and shimmied out of the wet and clinging suit. Underneath she wore only a white, tank top tee shirt and panties. Conrad glanced back at the portal where the others had come up and then back at Sydni. "Do you really think they'll be back up after the amount they drank last night?" she asked.

Grinning, Conrad unzipped his flight suit, stripping down to a tee shirt and underwear. They both threw their wet flight suits over lounge chairs to dry, and Conrad dragged two other chairs and covered the portal. Giggling, Sydni said, "That does not look like it would stop them."

"No, but they should get the hint." He shrugged. After taking off his tee-shirt he said, "Maybe it will give us a little warning."

Sydni took off hers and they wrung them out. As water dribbled to the deck, Conrad said, "I will have to look into taking a little revenge of my own."

Laying her panties and shirt over another lounge, Sydni said, "If I didn't know any better, I would say that you planned all this with Willy just to get me naked."

Conrad, who was moving closer, tossed his underwear at a chair, and they just caught an arm and hung there. To him, her body was perfect. A surge of excitement coursed through him, and Sydni could tell. She felt the same about Conrad's body. Although he was a bit older, he had not let his exercise slack off, as had many of the CSO's she had met. With a quick laugh, Conrad said, "You're cold."

He placed his hands on her waist, and she pushed her body up against his. Laughing even more, she said, "Hmmm. So are you?"

"Hey..." he started to protest before she smothered him with a kiss.

Reaching down, she said, "Look, I am starting to warm you up already."

Kissing down her neck, he said, "You keep that up and you'll overheat me."

"Don't worry," she said, "I know how to control your heat."

✶ ✶ ✶ ✶

Gallagher walked through the halls of the Orion with two of his armed guards walking behind him. He was grumbling to himself. They had called him the day before about Vladimir, but he had not had the time to mess with it, so he had told Security to keep him. Maybe cooling off in the brig for a day might change his attitude.

Once at the brig, Gallagher motioned for the guards to stay outside. He passed inside and through the security scanner. Bob sat at the Duty desk with another Marine when Gallagher approached. Both Marines stood up and saluted the ambassador. Gallagher nodded and said, "I am here for Vladimir. I would like him released into my custody."

Bob, in his best stern Marine voice said, "Sorry, Sir. I am unable to release the prisoner." Inside, Bob was jumping for joy, but the ambassador couldn't tell.

"Why not?"

"Sir, the Acting Constable, Lt. Commander Juarez, has reviewed the case and is holding him over until a hearing today at fifteen-thirty."

"Lt. Commander Juarez. He would be a...."

"Nursing Corps, Sir."

"Nursing Corps, yes, and the Lt. Commander is qualified to make such decisions?"

"When he is Acting Constable. They are especially careful when the offense is something of a violent nature."

"Yes, yes. May I see the evidence against him?"

"I may show it to you on my visual, but I cannot release a copy of it pending the investigation."

The ambassador sighed. "What about to his legal counsel?"

"It is a military matter; he has been assigned J.A.G. legal counsel."

Gallagher moved around behind the counter, and Bob keyed-up the tape he had entered into the evidence files. He showed from where Vladimir disrupted the class. After a few minutes of talking to Tanya, he had her back out on the dojo mat ready to fight. Gallagher watched as the scene played out, and Bob amplified the voices so the ambassador could hear the direct order from Willy. When the tape finished, the ambassador stood there shaking his head.

"I can allow you to see the prisoner, but all conversations will be recorded."

"I am the UWC ambassador on this flight. Any and all of my business is confidential…."

"I get my orders directly from Captain Dollinger, and I was told that if you had a problem with this, you should take it up with him."

The ambassador was beet-red and his ears starting on purple. Bob was ready for him to throw a fit, but the ambassador took a deep breath and then let it out, calmly saying, "Okay, you win, Major. I would like to see the prisoner."

Bob motioned for the other Marine to the help the ambassador.

The brig was divided into four corridors, two to the left and two to the right, while directly behind the counter were the security offices and quarters that held one division of Marines out of the four that were aboard the Orion. Vladimir was housed in corridor A, cell 11.

Gallagher was led to the cell door and the Marine said, "Do you want in with him?"

"No," Gallagher replied. "I won't be long."

From where he sat on the bunk in the cell, Vladimir looked up, but he was not hopeful. He had seen that look on Gallagher's face before. "Our conversation is being recorded, so I will be brief. I still need your services, but you screwed up. I have no recourse in this action against you, it is a military matter. I will put a word in for you and my need for your work, but it is out of my hands." Lowering his voice, Gallagher added, "If they let you out of this place, you report to me immediately."

As Gallagher turned to leave, Vladimir said, "Sir?" Gallagher turned and looked at Vladimir, who was standing at attention. "I apologize for failing you, Sir."

"If they let you out, I will deal with you."

Vladimir stayed at attention, but did not respond to the threat. Once Gallagher was gone, he slumped back onto his cot, holding his head in his hands. He promised himself that if he slipped out of this one, he would not let it happen again.

Gallagher left the brig without speaking, and his two guards just fell in behind him as he walked down the hall. He was trying to decide whether or not he should put a call into Chancellor Chambers, or should he just wait to see how the proceedings went aboard the Orion first. If the UWC Council had people aboard, which he believed they did, they would make the report soon if they hadn't already. He'd better put in a word to the Chancellor, just to be on the safe side; all Gallagher knew is that he didn't want to disappear as he had heard other ambassadors had. He thought he'd better tell the Chancellor straight up and let the him decide what was important.

* * * *

Dawn was starting to lighten the mountains in a firestorm of color, and the birds were busy conducting a symphony unique to this section of this world. A group of large scavenger birds rose in an early thermal and were circling, resembling more a funnel cloud than a flock. Small mammals that ranged in color from black with brown circles on the tail to a pale gold with black circles, grouped in fruit trees and chattered loudly, as if competing with the birds. Willy took all this in as he hiked from the clearing where he had landed his craft toward the hill where he'd first met Dekonal singing. His large pack was across his back, and he carried his rifle. Three times since he had left his ship, a feline-like call had erupted into the morning behind him. For a little while, he stepped off the path and waited in a tree, but nothing had passed below.

So he had continued his way, remaining vigilant. He made the hill as the morning sky was turning golden, the fiery colors fading as the sun rose higher. Circling the lower part of the hill, he detected no sign that Dekonal had been there yet that morning. Something had told him to go there. Maybe it was just that she had been there before in the morning, singing. He wished he would see her there again.

He shimmied off his pack and set it down and then sat cross-legged on the crest of the hill. His gun was across his lap and his hands rested on his knees. As he sat there meditating, he thought about praying; it had been a long time since Willy had prayed. His parents were part of the Unified Church, and he had gone on Sunday mornings for much of his life, but he had found even rejection in the place that taught about not rejecting people and how people were equal. The only person who had seemed to care about him in the church had been the preacher, Boris Takalov.

Willy smiled at the memory of the short stocky man, who was athletic, but not comfortable in the woods, coming out and searching for him one Sunday afternoon. Willy had heard him calling, and had gone down to see him.

"I missed you in church this morning, William. Have you been out here?"

"Since yesterday," Willy answered.

"Yesterday. Why do you hide in the woods?"

Willy shook his head. "I do not hide out here, with the exception of Sydni, this is the only other place I am accepted."

"You are accepted in church," Boris said.

"By you."

"Everyone."

Willy shook his head again. "You are an optimist, Boris. You see the good in everyone, and you believe that God can cure anything or solve anything." Boris tried to speak, but Willy continued, not giving him a chance, "I know you accept me there in church, and I even believe that God does, but that is partly because it has been taught to me from childhood. The other churchgoers are no different than others in the community, or their children. God just cannot or will not fix everything. I am living proof. It would put your precious followers at ease if I just disappeared."

"God's plan is not often easy to understand, if we ever do while we are in this body. I do know this much, William. God made you special, you are faster and stronger than other children your age, you are smarter..."

"I am only smarter because all I have of a social life is with my sister and studying."

"Nonetheless, you are smarter, and one day you will look back and realize that you are here for some reason, and that you are special, and that God did not abandon you. He gave his only Son's life for you."

Willy and Sydni had gotten word while they were in the academy that there had been a scandal with Boris and another woman, and that Boris was no longer their preacher. Boris had committed only one crime, he had been a man, who fell to temptation. The very next time Willy and Sydni went home, Willy overheard a few hushed conversations about Boris and his abhorrent behavior, and it became too much for him to bear. So when the new preacher started in with the service, Willy stood up, and said, "This congregation makes me sick. You claim to be followers of God and you claim to want to spread his word. Does your God not forgive? Does the Bible not say that every man sins? Does it not say, 'Ye without sin cast the first stone.'? You placed Boris Takalov on some pedestal that no man or woman should be on, and when he fell from your precious pedestal, you cast him out." At this point three deacons and two young men were moving up the outside aisles to force him to leave. Willy snatched up a Bible from a pew and held it up. "If you have no place in your heart for forgiveness, and you consider yourself higher judges than God, then this is worthless." He threw the Bible over his shoulder, it landed on the organ, which made a foreboding deep note that echoed in the room.

As the men came across the front of the sanctuary, Willy's father stood and said, "Gentlemen, there is no place for violence in this church, let him have his say."

Willy flexed his claws, ready to fight off the men if he had to. "I won't take up any more of your time this Sunday morning, but I will say this; if the God you worship is like this, I want no part of him or you." Turning to his parents, he said, "I apologize for the embarrassment I know I have just caused you."

Willy remembered it like it had just happened. It was one of the few times he had bucked the system and stood up and challenged the system that had caused him so much grief. He had sought out Boris Takalov, and found him one day teaching religion and philosophy in a school in a newly formed outlying jurisdiction. When Willy saw him after school, he asked Boris, "What are you doing, hiding here?"

Boris laughed and said, "They accepted me here." They sat on a bench in front of the school and Boris said, "I heard what you said in front of church. I am sorry I let you down."

"If you heard what I said to the congregation, then you know you did not let me down, your followers let you down. We all make mistakes, Boris. It is what is in your heart that counts. Your followers failed you in a time of need. They only saw the sin and not the man who made the mistake. For that I will never go back into that church. They did not listen to what you taught us all along, and I think it will serve me better the rest of my life to live with what you taught me of God and not what they think."

"If I can forgive them, William, can you forgive them?"

"I can forgive them, but I do not have to worship with them. Just like you."

Boris was laughing again. "You have me there. Just remember what I have said, and don't give up on God, he will never give up on you, that I promise."

That had been the last Willy had ever heard of Boris Takalov. So, sitting on the hill in a faraway land, happier than he had ever been, he thought that maybe Boris had been right all along. He offered up a short prayer, hoping that Boris had found peace, hoping that all would work out for the best on this planet.

Through all of the chatter in the nearby trees and over the slight breeze, Willy heard something that sounded like a deep rumbling. A growl. His eyes were open and he was instantly alert. Moving slowly, he looked to his right, and stalking along the stream where he had sat the other day, under the tree, was a Gyod like he had seen when Quistqui had followed him. It was not looking at him, however. Something else held its attention. Willy followed its line of sight; Dekonal was crouched at the stream drinking. The Gyod flicked its long tail and crouched even lower.

Grabbing his rifle, Willy rolled over on his stomach, taking the safety off . Willy took a second to judge the distance and wind, and at that second, the Gyod rushed Dekonal with a heart-stopping scream. Willy had it sighted in. He followed it in his scope. He squeezed the trigger. The rifle sounded loudly, hushing everything nearby but the wind and stream. Willy slid the bolt deftly and was ready to take another shot at the Gyod, but it had already dropped in the stream.

Dekonal was sitting back with her knife pulled from its sheath, ready to defend herself. She was stretching her neck to look down in the creek at the Gyod, and then she slowly turned and looked at Willy, who was walking toward the creek with his rifle still trained on the cat. Dekonal was getting to her feet and Willy could see that the cat was no longer breathing. Dekonal adjusted her long, white tunic with a v-neck, cinched at the waist by a maroon and white sash. She was wearing maroon pants that reminded Willy a little of sweatpants. It looked good to him.

"I am happy you were here," she said, running up to him. She threw her arms around his neck and he embraced her with one arm. They kissed for several minutes before she plowed her face into his shoulder, still hugging him. "Do you realize the thrashing I would have taken, if it didn't kill me."

"I am happy I was here, too. I think it may have followed me here." He looked at the cat and said, "Something was following me this morning, but it made a different sound."

Dekonal nodded. "If it is just finding a scent, it makes one noise. The Gyod makes a loud scream, as it just did, to freeze its prey." Glancing down at the cat, she said, "That is a beautiful pelt, it will gain you some respect among the hunters of the village."

Willy asked, "Will you hold this?" He held out his rifle and she took it. He walked down to the creek and grabbed the seven-foot-long cat by the hind legs and hauled it out of the water. He checked the bullet wound in the cat's head, and he examined the cat for a moment before he dragged it most the way up the hill. Black spots around the shoulders and neck and black markings around the eyes and muzzle marked the tawny-colored hide. The giant paws were light brown, and the underbelly was light brown to white. He pulled back the felines lips, exposing the giant white teeth. Glancing up at Dekonal, Willy said, "A very impressive animal. Too bad I had to shoot it."

"I am not offended." She smiled at him. "Nice shot."

"Thanks." He ran his hand down the dry part of its fur and he asked, "Is there anything special you do with this animal?"

Shaking her head, she said, "No, but the pelt is rare and worth a lot because the Gyod is difficult to find, not to mention the respect it will earn you as a hunter."

Taking his rifle back, he reached out and took her hand. Looking into her eyes, he said again, "I am glad I was here."

"Why were you here?"

"Hoping that you would be here."

They kissed again and walked to the crest of the hill. "I came to give a prayer of thanks."

"Is that what you were doing here the day I met you?"

"Yes and no. That day I knew you would be here, so I was also thanking God for your arrival."

Willy held up his hand and repeated the word she had used for God and shrugged. Dekonal thought for a minute and then said, "The Master." She tapped her chest. "Spiritual leader. The Creator of all."

Willy nodded. "I understand who you are talking about. You believe in a single god, one powerful being?"

"God." She nodded. "Do you believe in God?" she asked him, looking into his eyes.

He wondered how she would react if he said no. Then he thought of Boris again and smiled. "Yes I believe in God. I will be interested to hear the stories of God."

"And I will be interested to hear your stories."

Willy set his rifle down across his pack. "You picked a beautiful place to pray."

Dekonal looked around and said, "My great-grandmother used to bring me here when I was a little girl, and she always told me that, to her, this was the most beautiful spot in the forest. She thought that God had touched this place. So I sing here, hoping that not only God will hear me, but that she will as well."

Willy, still holding her hand, looked around. He thought that Boris would like this spot too, but then again, Boris had found God everywhere. He kissed her cheek and said, "I am certain she will."

"Will you stay while I sing?"

"A voice that makes the birds fly away with jealousy. I would not miss it for the world." She blushed and looked away. He wasn't certain exactly what kind of compliments were customary, so he would just have to improvise. Little did Willy know that Dekonal's heart was pounding faster and now more than ever she loved him. She looked at him and wondered if he could know how few men had a gift for words.

"Thank you," she said. She wanted to touch him, run her hands through his hair, kiss him, and make love to him there on the hill, but she hesitated. They had time, and she thought maybe she should offer thanks for him, since that is why she had shown up there. "I do not require long."

"Take your time," Willy said, sitting down with his back against his pack. "Will I bother you sitting here and watching?"

"Not you."

She turned away from Willy, and looked out over the rolling hills that could be seen through a break in the trees. She let the beauty engulf her and took deep breaths. The song began with her faintly humming, and slowly she raised her arms at her sides. She picked up a steady cadence and her humming grew stronger and stronger. Suddenly her voice broke onto the hill in what sounded like a chant, reminding Willy of some ancient folk music he had heard. At first it seemed more like a chant, not words exactly. Then the tone and rhythm changed and she sounded more like she was singing a song, but still Willy couldn't understand it.

Finally, her song shifted once again, and this time he could understand her as she sang to God, thanking him for everything. She stopped singing, and her last words died out. Slowly she dropped her arms back to her sides, and with her eyes closed, she raised her face to the sky. Willy was watching her and he thought her lips were moving, in what he guessed was prayer. He was still in awe of her song; it was beautiful.

As Dekonal turned to face him, the sun broke over the trees and bathed her in sunlight. Her hair seemed to glow and her smile was even brighter. She almost looked like an angel. He stared at her for a minute, before he reached a hand out to help him up. "What is it?" she asked.

"You," he replied. "You are so beautiful."

Looking him in the eyes, she held his attention. He waited to see if she was going to speak, and after a few moments she did. "You constantly give me words of praise, that I hardly feel I deserve."

Willy smiled and said, "You deserve it, and if I did not feel that way, I would not say them." He kissed her.

"But I do not give you such praise...yet..."

He cut her off with a kiss, running his hands through her hair. "Your eyes do." She looked down, and Willy noted the color change in her face; she was blushing. "Shall we start back to the village, and there I can take care of the Gyod?"

"I think we better," She said.

Sydni brought her ship in for an easy landing, and upon shutting down the power, she said, "Thank you, Conrad. That was a most delectable diversion."

The cockpit cover popped with a hiss of air and noise from the busy landing bay. Conrad couldn't resist smiling. The trip to the water moon had proved relaxing. Now that her ship was firmly back on the deck of the Orion, he breathed even easier; the drab gray bulkheads of home.

They climbed out of the cockpit and crawled down the ladder, and when Sydni turned, there was a crewman sent from the deck commander. He snapped to attention and saluted her. Saluting back, she said, "Easy, Crewman, don't strain yourself."

"Yes, Ma'am. Good flight, Ma'am?"

She hooked up her scanner to the crewman's electronic clipboard and transferred her ship's log into it. "Very nice, thank you." When the scanner beeped, she unhooked it and the crewman saluted again before turning to run back to his station.

As she unpacked their packs from a hatch, Conrad asked, "Have you always had to sign in your log like that?"

"Only since Gallagher went on his kick. Before we just logged it into the computer at a convenient time." She slung her pack over her shoulder, handed Conrad his, and closed the hatch again. "It doesn't bother me any, but the crewmen under the deck commander are running themselves ragged."

They had just made it to the relative quiet of the level two corridor, leading to the officers' quarters when Conrad's scanner paged him. "Not even on the ship two minutes and they're after me." He read the message and raised his eyebrows. Looking at Sydni, he said, "Engineering says it's important."

"Let's stow our gear and get going," Sydni said.

Conrad replied that he was on his way and jogged down the hall to catch up with Sydni. They threw their bags into Conrad's cabin before proceeding toward the Engineering Room. A Marine stood guard as usual at the center hatch to main engineering, and he snapped to attention as Conrad and Sydni passed. Conrad threw him a quick salute as he passed.

In the outer section, a dozen techs constantly read readouts and checked the computers, one looked up upon their entrance and jerked his thumb toward Chief Yamamora's office. "He's waiting for you, Sir."

Conrad did not even miss a beat, turning in mid-stride; he aimed towards Chief's office, with Sydni a step behind. Conrad clicked the arrival button and it was returned by a gruff voice, "Enter."

Conrad pushed the hatch button and it slid open, revealing the Chief Engineer sitting behind his console, with a cup of coffee in one hand and an electronic clipboard in the other; his eyes were riveted on the clipboard and after he sipped the coffee, he said, "What is it now, seaman, can't you even read a damn monitor?"

"Actually, I cannot," Conrad said, laying his Indian accent on thicker than usual.

Chief Yamamora slammed down the cup and clipboard simultaneously, and, as he stood up, his chair flew out from behind him, striking the wall behind with a clatter. Chief saluted Conrad and Sydni, standing at full attention. "Sorry, Sirs. I did not realize you had arrived yet."

"At ease, Chief." In one swift motion, Conrad came to attention and saluted back to the Chief.

The chief slumped his shoulders and stood at ease. "I am sorry though, if a few more of my seamen could work without having a baby-sitter along then I could finish up my reports. But where are my manners." He made a motion toward a long leather couch that was to the right of his desk along the wall. Conrad wondered how the Chief had managed to get it through the narrow corridors of the engine room. "Please have a seat. Can I get you some coffee, tea, or anything else?"

"Coffee would be great," Sydni said, sitting in the middle of the couch.

Sitting to her right, Conrad said, "Tea, if it's not any trouble."

Chief pressed a button on his console and said, "Canterbury. Tea'n coffee, ASAP."

Through the speaker, Canterbury responded, "Aye, aye, Sir."

Walking around the front of his desk, Chief clasped his hands behind his back and paced. "Working with your techs, Sir, I found that the device discovered sent out a signal. We tracked that signal, and since it was not one usually used in this ship's day-to-day work, it was not that difficult to find. Up in the forward array, the nose of the ship, just below the upper missile launching hatch there is an access tube." Sydni nodded. She knew it well. Motioning to her, Chief said, "You know what I am talking about?"

"Quite well."

"Okay, that hatch is chock-full of communications wiring to the forward array and dish, so it was easily hidden unless you know what you're lookin' for. We found the receiver, and it is all hooked in with the ambassador's private channel. If you hadn't found the emitter on your scanner, it would have gone unnoticed. We hooked a bypass up to it and a small monitor so we could read what it was receiving and had your techs play with it. I could see the message your techs sent you."

Conrad shuddered. "The ambassador's private channel, that bloody, little...."

Sydni put a hand on Conrad's arm and said, "We cannot jump to conclusions. He does have Vladimir working for him, maybe he's behind all this."

"That son-of-a..." Chief choked off his comment and finished with, "Sorry, Ma'am."

"I agree, Chief."

"I have to sit on the board of inquiry in the matter of the attack on your brother." Chief said, shifting his position. "Twenty years ago we'd a just hung 'em."

"Who's presiding as acting constable?" Sydni asked.

"Commander Juarez, and at least this time he saw fit to keep him in the brig until the board of inquiry resides. If they left it up to me, I'd throw his arse in the brig until he rotted away."

"Gallagher has a lot of pull," Conrad said.

"True," Chief said nodding. "All too true."

The door buzzed and Chief reached over his console and pushed the entry button. Canterbury, a lanky seaman who had to duck to enter the hatchway carried a silver tray with two silver pots, creamer and sugar bowls, and two porcelain cups with saucers. He poured one with tea and the other with coffee, and looking up he said, "Cream and sugar?"

"We'll fix them ourselves," Conrad said with the wave of a hand.

Canterbury turned and faced the Chief, and while standing straight at attention, asked, "Will that be all, Sir?"

"Dismissed."

Sydni took her coffee black, and Conrad added a spoon each of creamer and sugar to his tea. Once they sipped their drinks, Chief picked his cup back up and added more coffee to it. Holding up her cup, Sydni said, "Vintage porcelain from New Japan, Alpha one. Takanora pattern, right?"

Chief smiled and nodded. "It was made in the early days of Alpha one, and my great-great-great grandfather worked in the plant. This set dates back to one of the first batches in the plant."

Sydni turned to Conrad and said, "Willy knows his wines, and I know my porcelain."

"I would like to document everything you have found so far, Chief, and I would like to do a bit more investigating as well." Conrad said.

"My men are at your disposal, Sir. Confidentially, of course."

Conrad's grin beamed as he repeated, "Of course."

"Are you in a rush on that?"

"At your convenience, Chief. Even on short notice."

"If I may so suggest," Sydni said. "My scouts know that area well. I think if we did a little snooping with a maintenance crew as cover, neither of you would be implicated if there were a problem."

Chief's voice grew gruff as he growled, "That'll be the day I am scared of the likes of Jasper Gallagher. I'd just as soon throw him out an air lock, the little..." Chief looked down, "Beggin' your pardon again, Ma'am."

Sydni smiled at the Chief's remarks. "You're too kind, Chief. I did not mean to suggest that you would fear of retribution. My scouts and I could disappear in a heartbeat up there, but if you or Conrad were found, it would be irregular."

"Irregular for me to be checkin' my ship?" Chief asked.

Sydni nodded. "How often do you have time to be checking out access tunnels?"

Chief frowned and gulped his coffee. "All right. I'll have a team of my trusted techs on standby to assist whenever you make the call. Leaning forward, he squinted and grumbled, "An' don't be afraid to call me just because it's three in the mornin'." Sydni and Conrad both nodded and he added, "Now, can I interest you in a second cup?"

During a cruise, the captain was the ultimate power among the crew, and his word was law. The gray areas crept in from where the ambassador stood. In any case, Bucky was perfectly creased and polished in his dress whites, and he was just as clear on any policy that dealt with disregarding orders; it was his territory. From behind the raised judge's desk with just enough room for three officers, Bucky looked down at the empty seat where the prisoner would be chained to the post in front of him. Gallagher and his secretary sat in the front row, and Bucky nodded curtly when they made eye contact.

Commander Juarez walked in dressed in his whites and saluted, before taking a seat to the left of Bucky. Then right behind him the XO, Commander Alexandra Cho stepped into the room, taking a seat to the right of Bucky. There was not much room for onlookers in the room, but every seat was taken. Chief Yamamora sat in his place as a non-com observer. Some of the attendees were Vladimir's subordinates in the Ambassador's personal guard, some were ship's personnel from varying departments, and Sydni Colton was sitting in the back in her dress whites. Bucky had seen her in the observation video, and knowing that Willy was planetside on assignment, she would speak for him. Bucky pressed a button that sounded a bell, bringing the room into silence. "Bring in the accused," Bucky said, his voice stern.

Two Marine guards brought Vladimir in with his hands and feet shackled, and he was wearing the orange and blue jumpsuit of a prisoner. The Marines attached Vladimir's shackles to the post in front of the chair. Bucky hit the button for the bells again and said, "The prisoner will identify himself."

Vladimir stood at attention with his hands in front of him on the post. Major Vladimir Karlov of the UWC Ambassadorial Marines, Sir. Serial number five-four-one-oh-one-nine-two-two-seven-oh-oh-six."

"Major Karlov, do you realize the trouble you are in?"

"Yes, Sir."

"The board has gone over the statements of those involved in the incident and we have reviewed the tape." Bucky flipped up a computer console embedded in the desktop and scrolled through Vladimir's military record. "Your record shows a flagrant disregard for orders, and twice you have been busted for striking another officer." There was a short pause as Bucky read the screen imbedded into the desk. "This latest offense shows you disregarding a direct order from a superior, attacking a superior, and resisting arrest. Do you have anything to say for yourself?"

"If I may, sir," Vladimir said. Bucky nodded and groaned inwardly, he did not feel like listening to the lies a prisoner would say, but he listened. "I have been under a lot of pressure, while investigating the injuries to Chief Su, and in the meantime I have had no one to spar with. In an attempt to get a decent workout, I was stopped by Commander Colton, who ordered me to not participate in dojo activities. It was more than I could bear and I resented him for the orders. I wish now that with a clearer head, I would have thought before I acted. I apologize to those involved and to you and the other board members for taking time from your regular duties."

Bucky wanted to sigh, yawn, or even laugh, but he had to contain himself and keep the authority on his ship. "Do you deny these charges against you?"

Looking down, Vladimir examined the post in front of him. "No, sir."

"In that case, the board has gone over the evidence and..." Bucky's voice trailed off as Gallagher stood up silently. Bucky had thought he would get through the proceedings without interference from Gallagher. If Gallagher had not interfered, the board was ready to court-martial, Vladimir and leave him in the brig for the duration of the cruise. However, Bucky had warned the other two that they might have to settle for a deal of a harsh rebuke with repercussions that if he repeated the offense, nothing would save him. The board trusted the Captain's judgment, and they knew the need to placate the Ambassador.

Gallagher was playing it quiet. He knew that if the Captain was so inclined, he would not have to listen to objections or even consider a plea from the Ambassador. So Gallagher just waited for acknowledgment.

Bucky motioned with his hand for Gallagher to step forward and when Gallagher stood facing the board, he cleared his throat and said, "Thank you for taking time to listen to me. I need Vladimir's services, and I do not have time to train another aide. I will do as you wish in this matter, but I implore you to release him into my custody. I will promise you his complete and utter obedience."

Bucky sat back and shook his head. He would not let the ambassador have his way so easily. "I don't know, Jasper. He attacked some very important personnel. You yourself are dependent right now on Commander Colton's assistance, yet that is who Vladimir tried to harm."

Jasper looked down and sighed. He would have to negotiate for Vladimir, and looking at the hopeful face of the chained prisoner, he wasn't certain that he was worth it. "I will concede the order for around the clock patrols and place the flight crew back on regular status."

The reply was more than Bucky would have asked for, and he would still get to place Vladimir on the strictest probation. "You can have him back, Jasper, but I am still going to have to be hard on him."

"I wouldn't have it any other way. I need him, but punish him as he deserves."

Gallagher walked back across the floor to his chair. Once he was seated, Bucky rang the bells again. "The prisoner will stand to hear his punishment."

Vladimir stood again and waited to hear the worst. Gallagher had not looked too happy.

"Vladimir, with the charges against you confirmed, I will now sentence you. You are stripped of the rank of major to the rank of Lieutenant First Class. You are docked three months pay. You will still function as Aide to Ambassador Gallagher, but during your off duty hours, you are now restricted from ship access unless you are escorted by Ambassador Gallagher." Bucky stood up and leaned forward on the desk and his voice grew softer and colder, "I want to make certain you are perfectly clear on this next part, Lieutenant Karlov. You are on probation for the rest of this cruise. I will not tolerate actions such as yours on my vessel, and I will not tolerate any sort of insubordination. You will obey commands and you will not lift a finger against anyone on or off this ship. I don't care if fifteen Marines start a bar fight with you, if I find out that you touched one of them, I will see you punished to the full extent of my law. I am releasing you on Ambassador Gallagher's promise that you will act as an officer in the UWC Armed Forces." Standing straight, Bucky tugged at his coat and said, "Is that clear?"

After swallowing hard, Vladimir softly said, "Yes, Sir."

"What?" Bucky shouted.

"Yes, Sir!" Vladimir said loudly.

"And just as a reminder to you, you will serve on two hull cleaning details when the ambassador does not need you. I will expect you to make the arrangements and take those shifts in the next two weeks." Turning to the Marine guards, Bucky said, "Remove him." Bucky looked at Gallagher, who nodded his approval before he rang the bells again, signaling the end of the inquiry.

CHAPTER 9

The sun was filling the courtyard to Dekonal's house. Next to where the fire pit was, Doqui set up a drying rack used to tan hides. Doqui was very excited about the Gyod when Willy and Dekonal had returned with it, and he insisted on helping Willy take care of it. He was impressed by Willy's ability to skin the animal, and then he went through the process of cleaning the excess from the hide. "This is a fine skin you brought back. The thick fur and the coloring of the coat, and the fact that you did not ruin it with a shot in the body, but to the head."

"Thank you, Doqui."

Doqui smiled. "Do not thank me, Willy. You honor me by asking for my help. I am proud to help you."

"So you do not share in your brother's beliefs that I am unproven."

"Especially not now. First you have proven a worthy adversary by fighting him, now you save my sister from being attacked by this animal. No, I believe you are proven." Doqui stopped stretching the hide on a rack and looked at Willy, "Undoubtedly, Quist will still believe you unproven."

Willy nodded and continued with their work. "When will he be back?"

"You never know with him. It could be today. It could be tomorrow. Only Nurian ever knows."

They applied a couple of liquids that Doqui pulled out of a cabinet. Willy looked at the brown glass container and asked to examine it.

Holding it up to the sky, Willy looked through it. "Clear and clean," he said, in English. "Glass."

"What?" Doqui asked.

Extending a claw and tapping the bottle, Willy asked, "What do you call this container?"

"Bottle."

"Bottle," Willy repeated in their language.

"And the substance it is made of?"

"Glass."

"Glass."

"You look amazed, Willy. What is wrong?"

"Nothing," Willy said shaking his head. "Nothing at all. So we use this to fix the hide."

Nodding, Doqui pulled out a cloth and as he poured the brown liquid on the hide, he rubbed it around with the cloth. "After this has dried, we have another substance to apply before it is finished."

"How long until this is dry?"

"Between midday meal and evening meal."

Dekonal walked out into the courtyard, now dressed in a simple sleeveless dress made of forest green cloth and sandals. "How are you two coming along?"

"We are finished for now," Doqui said, recapping the bottle. "You two go on, and I will take care of the body of the Gyod."

"Thank you," Willy said.

Taking Willy's hand, Dekonal said, "Let's take a walk."

He offered no resistance and allowed himself to be guided out into the streets of the village. "You seem to have some sort of plan in mind."

Stopping, she turned and kissed him deeply. Willy didn't stop to think where the impassioned kiss came from, he just responded. His hands were roaming her body, and had they not been in the streets, he would have been removing her clothes; suddenly he stopped, holding her waist. Their lips still touched, and each of their breaths were only raspy whispers. There was a group of people not far away, many of them were shouting. "Angry voices," Willy whispered, his lips brushing against hers.

"Yes, let's go see."

They ran down the street hand-in-hand, and took the curve into a central plaza where a crowd had gathered. Seeing Dekonal, people moved aside to let her and Willy pass. A man stood in the center with his one hand gesturing wildly and the other holding the reins of a Brotu that sat on its haunches while it drank from a bucket of water. Douka stood facing the man, and turned as Dekonal and Willy walked up. "Tell her your story, Hanst, slowly," Douka said.

The man panted and then started speaking as if he were picking his words with great care. "I was flying with Quistqui and Bokta when a bird appeared in the sky. It was a very funny bird that did not flap its wings. Then when it landed in the clearing of the Shrine of Halkala, the tail opened and strange beings appeared." He pointed at Willy and said, "Dressed like you, but their face and skin was strange."

"Damn!" Willy said more forcefully than he would have liked.

"Do you know what is going on?" Douka asked.

Nodding, he said, "I think so."

"They cannot harm the Shrine of Halkala. It is a sacred religious place that has stood for generations. Can you make your people leave that place?"

"I can try."

"I will have to assemble a party to repel them. Do you need your weapons?"

Willy did not understand the meaning of Douka's word party, but he understood the general meaning. He would assemble warriors to attack. All Willy had with him was his scanner and knife, shaking his head he said, "I will not need weapons. What is the fastest way for me to get there?"

Douka looked at Hanst and said, "Can you take him?"

Hanst nodded, turning to his Brotu that was stretching like a cat and had spread its wings. Turning to Dekonal, Willy kissed her and said, "I will return as soon as I can."

"Be careful," she said in not much more than a whisper.

Hanst was sitting in a saddle that was positioned just behind the wings. He looked over his shoulder at Willy and said, "Sit here and hold the straps." He patted the animal's back just behind him. Willy climbed on. No sooner had he settled on a spot and grabbed the straps on the back of the saddle, than the creature rose quickly into the air with its flapping wings.

The crowd stayed around the plaza until the Brotu was out of sight. Dekonal could see in Douka's face that he wanted to speak with her, but was waiting until many of the people left. Klisk and Watkil were in the crowd and moved forward as it dispersed. Douka asked, "How will this turn out?"

They all turned to look at Dekonal, who was still looking in the direction the Brotu had flown, and she said, "You need not assemble warriors this time, but something tells me that this is the beginning of the war we have discussed."

Douka looked at the ground and sighed. "I do not want war. We have had peace for so long."

"Yes," Dekonal said. "Maybe it will not be a long war."

Turning and shuffling away on his staff, he studied the ground and said, "If any of our people die, it will have lasted too long."

* * * *

Willy recognized the terrain, as he had passed over it many times in his ship, but this time he was cruising along at the tree top level. Suddenly the forest broke into rolling hills with clumps of trees. Hanst guided the Brotu along the tree line and then headed toward a thick clump of trees that formed a little valley. The flying was exhilarating, and Willy made a mental note to ask for lessons so he could fly on his own. The Brotu's legs began pumping when they were only inches off the ground, and soon it folded its wings against their legs and was running across the open area.

Willy could see two other Brotus lying in the thigh-high grass along the trees. The other two Brotus stood to greet the third. As Hanst vaulted from the saddle, he motioned for Willy to follow him. He whispered, "This way."

Quistqui and Bokta were crouching with their backs against the trees, a long shoot of grass protruded from Bokta's mouth. "You?" Quistqui asked with obvious rancor. "Why are you here?"

"Douka sent me to avoid a battle."

Quistqui frowned. If he made a scene about Willy, who was there with Douka's approval, it would not look good.

"Come on." Willy said. "Just don't show yourselves to the strangers." Willy didn't wait, he just spun on his heel and started running through the grasses. With a grunt, Quistqui followed. Hanst and Bokta looked at each other. Bokta shrugged before he spit out the grass and followed.

Willy stopped just before the last rise and looked at Quistqui. "I cannot explain this to you very well, but you need to stay out of sight."

Grumbling something Willy couldn't understand, Quistqui nodded.

The shuttle had settled down twenty yards from the rock formation where Willy and Sydni had first shown the Coppertroid fuel to Conrad. Four techs had already started to assemble a small extraction table, but luckily they had not yet taken apart any of the rock formation. He wondered why Conrad would have ordered this extraction team without clearing it first, he knew the rules that applied. Willy waited until he was within a few yards of the crew when he shouted, "Just what the hell is going on here?"

Each of the techs jumped, one tech fresh out of the academy even let out a frightened yelp. Slowly they recognized Willy. "Commander William Colton, UWC Armed Forces, 121st Scout Squadron. Report."

The techs snapped to attention and one sergeant said, "Tech First Class Ollman, Sir. We have been sent down to extract thirty kilos of raw Coppertroid fuel and set up a permanent siphon station."

"On whose orders?" he snarled at her.

"By order of Ambassador Gallagher during Lieutenant Admiral Singh's absence."

"Shit! You idiots are not even monitoring your sensors. There is a small group of Hingandu warriors on the other side of that hill, and if it wasn't for me, more would be showing up in order to remove you from one of their places of worship."

The techs lost their color, and the one that had yelped looked like he was about to throw up. "The only way for me to stop them is for you to pack up everything, on the double, and get the hell out of here."

Tech Ollman cleared her throat and said, "Sir, the orders from the ambassador are very explicit."

"Check your damn sensors, Ollman."

She ran over to a table and picked up her scanner and after adjusting it she looked at Willy. "Okay, you heard the commander, pack it up, double time. This is your ass on the line." They all moved at once. Hooking her scanner on her belt she looked at Willy and stepped closer. "Thank you, sir. We appreciate your warning. Any word for the ambassador?"

"Tell him I just averted a war and not to try this again without talking to me first. This site, by UWC Colony Expansion article six, fifty-seven is off limits due to religious reasons of the inhabitants of the planet."

She snapped a salute and once Willy saluted back, she hustled with the others to replace the equipment in the shuttle. Willy watched for a while, glancing from time to time at the top of the hill, where he could just see Quistqui and the others peering through the grass.

Once they were moving the tables back into the shuttle, Willy said, "Good day," and did not wait for their response. On the far side of the hill, the Hingandu's looked at him and nodded. "That scared them."

"Good," Quistqui said, heading back toward the Brotus. "I would have just killed them."

"Starting a war with a people you do not know?" Willy asked.

Quistqui did not respond, and the others took his lead with their silence. The Brotus stood and sniffed as they approached. Quistqui looked around and then looked at Willy, asking, "Where is your ride?"

Willy pointed at Hanst's mount and said, "That is how I came."

Quistqui shrugged his shoulders, looked at the others and said, "I guess you will just have to run back." The other two did not look at Willy; they just mounted their rides and walked them past him into the plain. Willy would never beg for a ride, nor would he ask if that was how they were going to behave.

For a moment, he thought about calling in his ship and flying back to the village, but there was not much room to land near the village. Besides, if he did not return until long after Quistqui, then Quistqui would look like the idiot with his pettiness. Hanst met Willy's eye and looked down when Quistqui shouted, "Get moving."

Willy watched as they prodded the Brotus with their feet and a quick snap of the reins. With the deep thud of their wings, the Brotus launched into the air. Before they even were ten feet off the ground, Willy was running toward the village.

* * * *

A horn blared from the cliff above the village and echoed down through the valley; it signaled the return of Quistqui, Bokta, Hanst, and Willy. Douka had ordered the ancient signal so he could be summoned for a report. The elders of the war council met with Chakdon and Dekonal under the cliff where the riders would descend. Although it was still light outside, several large lights hung from the walls lit the area.

Dekonal saw her father shaking his head as they waited and she placed a hand on his forearm, thinking that maybe she had read the situation wrong. "What is it, Father?" She asked in a whisper.

He glanced at her and continued to shake his head. "I am certain everything went fine, just as you said, but Quistqui has made another judgment error. Willy is not with him."

Dekonal's grip tightened on his forearm as she asked, "What do you mean?"

"He left him to run back," he said, patting her hand in a reassuring gesture. Dekonal was about to curse, but her father shushed her.

Quistqui stopped short when he ran into the knot of people waiting for his return. Hanst and Bokta nearly ran into him. When they saw who was present, their eyes started searching the ground at their feet. Quistqui smiled and asked, "What are you doing here?"

Douka pushed him aside with is staff and tried to get a view behind them. "Where is Willy?"

"The stranger?" Quistqui asked. At Douka's gaze through squinted eyes, Quistqui swallowed hard, realizing his error. "We left him to run back."

"You what!" Dekonal shouted.

Douka smacked his staff against a wall and said, "Quiet." Dekonal knew she had spoken out of line, so she bowed her head and waited; she would have her chance to run her brother through the wringer later. "Are you telling me that you left him in the plains at his request?"

"No, Douka."

"So you left a guest of this village out in the plains to run here, without his weapons." Douka's voice was growing louder, and his knuckles were white as he gripped his staff. "I sent him to help save the Shrine of Halkala without bloodshed and you felt that you could deny him a ride here." Quistqui felt his heart beat against his ribs and he was at a loss for words. He was trying to say something, but nothing would come out. Douka filled the silence. "Is the shrine still standing?"

"Yes, sir," Quistqui answered, finding his voice.

"Was there any blood spilled, or did Willy deal with it on his own?"

"Willy sent them away."

Douka shook with anger, while Klisk and Watkil whispered to each other. Quistqui, like the other two, continued to look at the ground. Douka's anger overflowed and he smacked Quistqui in the face with his staff. The resounding crack caught everyone's attention, and under Quistqui's hand a large red welt was forming on his cheek. "Look me in the eyes, you inconsiderate whelp. If something happens to him while he is out there without his weapons, I will hold you responsible as if it happened at your hand."

Quistqui looked at his sister and father, saying, "I am sorry. I was not thinking."

"That is correct," Douka shouted. "You never stop to think. I spoke your name in the last meeting to enter you into the war council, and I guarantee that if he does not return safely, it will never be. Now, you get out of my sight and think about what you have done."

Quistqui walked past them, but stopped when Klisk added, "Maybe you should seek out Tyuk and see why this hatred burns in your heart." Quistqui had not spoken to their spiritual leader Tyuk in a long time. He walked away, wondering where he might find him.

"What about these two?" Watkil asked. "They are no better."

"Listening to their leader is to be commended, but their stupidity is not," Klisk said.

Watkil and Klisk looked to Douka, who still shook with anger. "Hanst, seek out the elder of the guards and tell him to let Willy pass when he arrives unaccompanied, and to summon me afterward. Bokta, gather up as many riders as you can and form a search that you and Hanst will lead. Ride out and see if Willy can be picked up still."

Hanst and Bokta ran off the way Quistqui had gone. "Damn his stubbornness," Dekonal said.

"I wish I knew what to do with him," Chakdon said, still patting his daughter's hand.

"I will have to remove his nomination if he does not change his attitude soon," Douka said. "Maybe you are right, Klisk. Maybe he needs time with Tyuk to see what is in his heart." Turning to Dekonal, Douka said, "I am sorry that I sent him out there without express instructions for them to return with him."

Dekonal forced a smile. "It was implied. Willy enjoys running, he will be fine."

Releasing his grip on the staff and leaning it against the wall, he flexed his hand. "For your brother's sake, I certainly hope he is."

* * * *

Conrad stood in front of the techs who had reported to his office with their story of being sent away by Commander Colton. Shaking his head, Conrad said, "Not only do you disregard all safety precautions that are set up to keep you from getting killed, you go based on orders given by the ambassador. I am the only one authorized to give such an order. If you had continued on, and that is a religious site for the Hingandu, you could have started a war. Do you not have any common sense? It is an academy mistake, not one for a Tech Sergeant First Class aboard a UWC flag ship."

Tech Ollman stammered, "Sorry, sir.... it...won't...."

"No excuses! Dismissed."

At the door, the techs stepped aside as the ships Captain, Bucky, walked in. They stood at attention and saluted, as did Conrad. Bucky saluted them back and said, "As you were." The techs scurried out the door and it slid shut. "You look infuriated, Conrad. What's wrong?"

"The ambassador is now seeing fit to send my techs out on missions. Even disregarding the fact that according to my contract, I am the only one allowed to authorize such, he sent them to an uncleared area and nearly got them killed. If it was not for Commander Colton, they probably would be dead and a war would be brewing planetside."

Bucky sighed. "I take it that the ambassador is on his way here."

As an answer the door chimed. "That should be him now. Enter!"

The door opened and Gallagher walked in, saying, "What the hell is so urgent, Dr. Singh?" Gallagher then noticed that Bucky was impatiently standing there. "Captain? What is going on?"

Conrad looked at the Captain, who said, "It's your show, Admiral."

Gallagher knew that Bucky out-ranked Conrad during a cruise, but a Lieutenant Admiral should not be scoffed at. He needed to become the diplomat in a hurry, but Conrad started. "Mr. Ambassador, it is not your right to send techs planetside! You nearly got one of my best teams killed today. Do you realize that? You sent them down to an uncleared area, one now identified by Commander Colton as a religious site. In fact if my team had succeeded in finishing before Commander Colton stopped them, and had he not been present to intervene, you would probably have a war on our hands, or should I say, your hands." Gallagher cursed to himself at his impatience. If Chambers heard about it, he would not be pleased. "I am placing this matter on report, and if you try and order any of my techs again, I will bring you up on charges."

Gallagher's face was turning red, and he cleared his throat before he said, "I am sorry, Dr. Singh. I did not realize..."

"I don't care what you realize! Are we clear, Ambassador? Do you want to read my contract, or maybe you would like to see my Lieutenant Admiral contract?"

"We are clear, Dr. Singh. I will not interfere again with your work or your department."

"Once we have compiled more data, we will choose a site that is acceptable to all parties before we set up a collection site."

Bucky had clasped his hands behind his back and watched with what some could misconstrue as a grin. He didn't think Conrad had that kind of fire brewing in him. In the tense silence, Bucky said, "Well, I think that clears up this matter." Turning to Conrad he asked, "Anything else, Doctor?"

"Yes. Two scouts spotted something planetside and began an investigation. I have dispatched a team to assist, but the preliminary report is a crash site."

"Crash site," Gallagher gasped.

Raising his eyebrows, Bucky asked, "Something new we missed?"

"Not one of ours," Conrad said. "It is still being determined.

"I need more information, Doctor. What kind of..."

Turning on him again, Conrad said, "I have had enough of you for one day, Mr. Ambassador." He nearly spit out the word 'mister'. "When more information is available, I will compile a report and submit it to both you and the Captain."

"I want to visit the site, firsthand," Gallagher said eagerly.

Nodding toward Conrad, Bucky said, "Not until he gives the word."

"I look forward to your report, Doctor. Please let me know when I can go to the site." He turned and headed for the door. "Good day, gentlemen."

Once he was gone, Bucky said, "Conrad, I am impressed. I didn't think you had that kind of dressing-down in you."

Shrugging, Conrad said, "He needed it or he wouldn't have backed off."

"Probably. Are you going to report him?"

"I have to, not only because I said I would though. He almost got four people killed. I can't just let that go."

"I can witness it for you since he admitted it in my presence."

"Thank you, Bucky."

"Now, what about this crash site? Any speculation?"

"I know this much, it is not a UWC ship."

✶ ✶ ✶ ✶

The sun was going down, and in the deep forest it was darkening. At a small stream trickling along, Willy stopped to take a drink. His scanner beeped, indicating that he had a message; the scanner was also set to buzz if it detected any creature the size of a dog or larger. Unlike the techs he had run off earlier, he had no wish to get caught off guard while he was concentrating on making good time through the forest. Twice he had heard the beat of a Brotu's wings, but since he was already in the forest he decided not to bother looking for a way to see who it was.

As he reached for his scanner to look at the message, it beeped again. Looking at the readout, one message was from Tanya and one was from Sydni. Tanya's message read: Sir, Site you gave us is a crash site of a non-UWC ship. No overt markings. No passengers evident. Tech team is going over it now, we have returned to ship for the night. Attached are the preliminary findings.

He replied his thanks and to continue to observe the tech team. His message from Sydni read: Willy, Vladimir punished, but Captain had to make concessions to Gallagher. Probation, docked pay, stripped down ranks to Lt. and he is unable to go around ship off duty unless Gallagher present. Any further occurrences and he will be brigged for the duration. Captain reamed him good. Conrad reamed Gallagher over tech incident and is reporting it. Glad you were there to intervene. Miss you as usual. Need to see you soon. Love, Sis.

Willy and Sydni always had a catch phrase for information they could not send for security reasons and it was her last sentence. Willy knew they had found something out, but what it was he couldn't be positive. He replied that he would have to set up a meeting planetside, but was unwilling to leave at this time. Once he sent his messages back, he drank again from the stream before he moved on. He figured he only had about another hour before he made it to the valley where the village was.

He had not gone very far when his scanner buzzed again. He figured it was someone else flying over still looking for him, but old habits died hard. He glanced at the screen to see something moving on the ground. It was man-sized, but the mass was larger than the average Hingandu and Jolabwe. Other old habits die hard. He reached for his rifle and it was not there. He remembered Douka asking if he needed a weapon, and he had declined.

Instantly, Willy began moving in his hunter mode, and, after silencing the buzz, he continued on his path, moving at a slow pace so that he would not make a sound. Whatever it was moved in a perpendicular course to him, but would cross his tracks back near the stream. Another scan of the creature showed it to be a new entity that he had not crossed before. The computer made several similarities to the Jolabwe, but it was still quite different. It showed a long neck, heavy jaw muscles, and a skin of scales. Flashing on the screen was the word: Unidentified. Under his breath, Willy cursed. He pulled out his knife and continued to move away from the creature.

Adjustments could be made to the scout's scanner to turn it into a mini stunner and also so a high-pitched shriek could be emitted. He set the adjustments and paused as the creature reached where his tracks should be. A screeching roar filled the night, and a covey of birds scattered and several smaller animals scurried off through the underbrush. Willy wondered if he should just cut and run. Was it calling in other creatures, or was it hungry and now had a path to follow?

Willy turned the scanner up to its full distance and noted no other creatures within the set parameters, but the one had now turned and was following his path. He decided to wait and confront his attacker and see if he could run for it when it was closer; the last thing he ever wanted to happen was to be dragged down from behind while running. When he could hear the creature moving through the trees and brush, he flipped on the record and transmit button. It always made him feel better knowing if he died, everyone would know what happened to him, and maybe learn from him.

With the stunner ready, he crouched, half behind a tree and dimmed the light from his display so as not to obscure his vision. Light was almost non-existent down in the trees, but the remaining rays of daylight were enough for Willy to see by. The creature moved into view with its head gliding back and forth on its long neck. It reminded him somewhat of an alligator from Earth. Its stocky body came into view. The creature had short arms and legs, and its tail was about half its body length. It stopped and looked at him. His judgment told him that from the size of its legs, he could outrun it.

The creature growled, and the growl shifted into a roar as its mouth widened, showing two rows of gleaming teeth. It made a clicking sound as it snapped its jaws open and closed. It rushed forward a few feet and stopped, but Willy held his ground. Stamping its feet, it snorted and growled again.

In general animals had many of the same reactions as did intelligent species, and from what he gathered, this creature was building up to an attack. Willy tried to use some of his own tactics. Growling, he waved his arms and hit the sound button on the scanner. The sound from the scanner made the world around him silent. Then he flipped it into a hearing range far above humans', and then even above his own hearing range.

Crouching back down, Willy had observed the creature backing away shaking its head. As it came forward again, he hit the sound button, this time using only the sound frequencies above his own hearing. The creature shook its head furiously and growled. "Don't make me get violent," Willy said aloud when he shut down the noise again. The creature stared at him intently and blinked.

When the creature rushed forward again, Willy hit the noise emitter and then the stunner. White energy sparkled in the air and connected with the creature, sending it to the ground in a fit of seizures. Willy cut off both functions when the creature hit the ground shaking. The stunner would drain the scanner's energy the fastest, especially with everything else running. He waited while the creature shook, and when it snapped its jaws shut and twisted its head in his direction he hit it again for three seconds. He could see that it was still breathing, but after a minute it did not move.

Then, with speed that even surprised Willy, the creature in one swift motion jumped up and was rushing Willy, who barely had time to dodge the snapping jaws of the mobile head. As he flipped on the noise, the creature's tail struck his arm and knocked his scanner several yards away. He didn't have time to worry about it as the creature rounded on him, snarling.

Willy placed a kick, connecting with its head, snapping it back, and he followed with a second kick to its scaled neck. It wailed and flailed its arms at him, but he twisted, landing a roundhouse kick to the face as its head came toward him.

In the dark, he didn't see the tail coming at him, striking him in the ribs. He could hear the material of his flight suit rip as his head hit a tree. Ignoring the pain, he spun around, with his knife ready to strike at its head. He could see the creature ten yards away, head swaying like a willow in the breeze. Blood trickled down his face from where he had hit the tree, stinging his right eye.

It rushed again, a blur in the darkness, but Willy slid to his left as the creature's teeth slammed into the tree. He jammed his knife into the creature's neck at the base of the skull and wrapped his arm around the creature's neck, holding it against the tree. Warm liquid spilled over his hand as he dug his knife around, searching for some sort of nerve cluster or spinal cord. The creature wailed and clawed at his right arm, but when Willy hit a place that crunched under his knife, the creature ceased to resist and its mouth only issued a gurgling sound.

After pulling out his knife, he dropped the limp body and leaned hard on the tree. Scanner, he thought, where is the scanner? He got his bearings and searched the area, finding the scanner in functioning order next to a tree. Once he shut down the noise emitter, he stopped the recording and transmitting. A quick check of the area showed no other creatures nearby. He scanned the body of the creature, which still showed some brain wave activity, but all bodily functions had ceased, the spinal cord was severed.

He sat at the base of the tree and turned the scanner to himself. There was a bloody but non-urgent laceration above his right eyebrow, multiple abrasions and lacerations to his arm. He would be sore later, but for now it was nothing to keep him from moving forward. One thought alone was enough to make him hurry: Dekonal.

After wiping off the knife blade on his pant leg he resheathed it and was about to hook his scanner back to his belt when a message chimed in. It was Sydni and read: You okay, bro? Scan shows wounds and blood.

He replied back that he was tired and sore, but nothing serious.

* * * *

The table in Chakdon's house was quiet. While the food was in bowls and drinks poured, no one touched them. The steam was long since gone from the once-hot food. Chakdon sat with his fists clenched on the table and eyes fixed on Quistqui, who stared at his plate. All Chakdon had said at the beginning of dinner was, "We will eat when Willy is present to eat with us."

Dekonal fiddled with a cloth napkin, unable even to look at Quistqui without foul words coming to her mouth. Doqui shyly smiled when his stomach growled.

In the outer room there was the sound of a shutting door, and then Willy appeared in the doorway of the kitchen. Dekonal shrieked when she saw all the blood and moved to get up, but Willy held up his hand, saying, "Please wait."

Blood stained his face and clothes, and both the sleeve and side to his flight suit were shredded. "With your permission Chakdon and Madak, I would like to speak freely in your home."

Chakdon and Madak both nodded. Willy looked at Quistqui, who met his eye, and asked, "Quistqui, I do not know what I have done to make you dislike me. I understand the need to look after your sister, and I myself have had to prove many men unworthy of my sister's love, but what else must I do for you to approve? What is left in your test?"

Quistqui smiled faintly. "What happened to you?"

"I was attacked on the way back, just at sunset. What else?"

"The hunt. You have to prove yourself worthy in the hunt. To prove that you can protect my sister, my family, and provide for them."

Doqui smiled, which caught Willy's attention, and Willy asked Doqui, "Would that count?"

"I don't see why not, it is only one of the fiercest creatures in the forest," Doqui replied.

"What are you talking about, Doqui?" Quistqui asked.

"Follow me," Willy said. "I have something to show you." Everyone followed Willy and Doqui out of the house and into the courtyard.

Doqui headed for the shed attached to the courtyard saying, "I'll get it."

"Get what?" Quistqui asked.

"This morning, while I was drinking from a stream where I pray, a Gyod was stalking me. Had Willy not been present, I would have been mauled."

Doqui, running back with the rack in the dim light from the lantern by the door, said, "It was a great shot, Quist. Right in the head. The pelt is perfect."

Quistqui examined the pelt and nodded. "Even I have to admit, that is a great shot and nice pelt."

"It is yours."

"What!" Quistqui shouted.

Doqui and Dekonal laughed. Chakdon put a hand on Quistqui's shoulder. "Son, you have scorned this man, and he gives you one of the most prized pelts a hunter could bring home."

"I want you to have it to always remember this day."

Quistqui looked down and softly said, "I am sorry..."

"No!" Willy said. "I am not done with you yet. If hunting is important to you, I want you to see just what attacked me on my trip home." Willy jogged toward the exit of the courtyard and bent down, just outside of everyone's vision and groaned as he pulled something along. "I apologize for bringing this in your courtyard, Chakdon, Madak, it is ugly and it stinks. I carried this back because I thought hunting might play a part of your unproveness."

Willy dropped the body and stepped aside so the light would hit the creature. Madak screamed and buried her face in Chakdon's chest. Doqui and Dekonal looked at Willy in amazement, while the color went out of Quistqui's face. "What did you kill this with?"

Pulling out his bloody knife, he held it up. "This mostly, but this gave me an advantage." He also held out his scanner. "It stuns it and hurts its ears."

"A knife."

Doqui looked at Willy and said, "It is unheard of."

Chakdon, who rubbed his wife's arm and cooed to her, said, "Pay attention, this is what legends are made of."

"Legends?" Willy asked.

Dekonal moved over next to him and touched the wound on his face. "A hero. Someone everyone looks up to and stories will be told about for years to come."

"I am no hero," Willy said.

"But you are." Quistqui said, with some color returning. "You will be. No hunter has survived an encounter with a Gaza-Kan without a higher powered weapon."

"That aside," Willy said, handing his knife and scanner to Dekonal, "I have one last thing to do. I will apologize in advance, Chakdon, but I have one last score to prove to myself."

The tone of Willy's voice caught Quistqui's attention. "I want another chance to prove myself to you. So there are no future doubts."

Everyone backed away, and Quistqui held up his hands. "You are in no condition..."

"Oh but I am, Quistqui. I would go do the run all over again if I had to. But you left me in a land that is not my own without a weapon, and for that, we are going to go at it again."

"I concede, Willy. You are proven."

Flexing his hands, Willy took a karate stance and said, "But I already knew that. I am going to pound it into your head." Willy smiled a bloody smile. "So you won't forget."

Quistqui moved to speak, but Willy's fist beat him to it and shut him up, sending him sprawling in the dirt. Even if Quistqui conceded, that hit had made Willy feel better. After he raised himself up to his knees, Quistqui rubbed his jaw. He said, "Please forgive my behavior, Willy. I have wronged you, and I will work hard to make it up to you. I give you my word." A trickle of blood ran from his nose.

Boris Takalov's voice came to Willy, telling him to forgive those who cross him. Quistqui had just been trying to protect his sister. Willy glanced at Dekonal who nodded. Willy relaxed and said, "Okay."

* * * *

"I think he's hiding something, and if he's the one that is receiving the information, then he is clearly in violation of the privacy act." Sydni pulled herself along the tube, using the handholds, with Barkley following close behind.

"Even though it was a military device and used to discover military information?" Barkley said, straining his voice as he pulled himself along.

"Doesn't matter. Any recording device installed must be there only under the permission or knowledge of the user."

Without even a pause, Sydni dove headfirst into another tube, using both her toes and hands to descend the hand holds. "Where are Tanya and Gordo?" Barkley asked as he followed Sydni down the tube in the same manner.

"They were on that recovery detail until sunset, and since they were returning with the recovery team tomorrow, they've been given the evening off."

Barkley grunted. He was great at using the ship's access tubes and ventilation shafts but it was not his favorite practice. Sydni peeked her head down into the tube they were looking for and saw two engineers about twenty yards away, right where they were supposed to be. That tube was lined with electrical, fiber optic, and hydraulic lines. It was one of the few access tubes large enough for a person of average height to walk upright and barely wide enough for a service cart the width of a hatchway. Three techs lined the hall, and down the access to the hall, Seaman Canterbury stood watch.

The tech in charge, Tech First Class Inovani said, "Attention!" and all four saluted Sydni.

"As you were," she said, flipping up her hand in a salute. "Okay, Inovani, work your magic and tell me what you found."

Inovani opened up an access plate and said, "These lines here are incoming from the dish. It is not easy to see, but there is a connector added to this bunch of optics, and that connector is attached to the receiver that we found here." He traced a tiny fiber optic line to a gray box only an inch square, tucked behind a clump of other optics.

"Very elaborate, yet so simple," Barkley said.

"After we found this, I was asking Chief if I could look into this some more, and I followed each of these optic groupings."

Sydni looked at Inovani, and the dark circles under his eyes proved that he had stayed up well past his shift working on this. "Did you find out who is behind all this?" she asked.

Nodding, Inovani said, "Well, that is why I took off the next panel down." He pointed down the access tube a little further and everyone scooted down the hall a little.

"Another one," Barkley said.

Sydni found another breaker, and it was in a much smaller group of cabling. "This batch of strands belongs to someone in particular?" she asked. Inovani nodded again. "The ambassador?" Inovani nodded again.

"What is the secondary coupling behind it?" Barkley asked, fingering another tiny fiber optic strand.

Inovani held up his hand and in it there was a small receiver antenna cord with a three-prong plug that would adapt to a scanner. "This is a way of proving that what Dr. Singh sends on his scanner is recorded by the ambassador. If you feed data or send a message on the tainted scanner, you should be able to see it pass to you as it goes to the Ambassador. Record and verify and you will have your case against him with my testimony."

Barkley chuckled. "You don't like the Ambassador?"

"Nothing personal. I don't like anyone who tampers with my optics and electronics."

"Fair enough, Inovani," Sydni said taking the receiver. She pulled out her scanner and plugged the receiver into it and flipped it on.

"Now, we were sent here to help you tap into his. The receiver was my idea. We can still plug into it now if you would like." He motioned toward an anti-gravity cart one of the other seaman leaned against.

"Can I just leave this running?" Sydni asked.

"Yes, ma'am."

"Then we can get out of here. No sense in pushing it."

"Agreed, ma'am."

Barkley leaned against the wall and yawned. Inovani looked at him and said, "Sergeant, may I ask you a question?" Barkley's nod was barley visible. "How do you know about optics?"

Barkley grinned and then laughed. "I was in engineering school at MIT Alpha One, but wasn't very good at keeping my grades up, so I joined the UWC Navy. I was taking optics and electronics, which I already knew from school, when a slot opened in the Scout School. I couldn't pass it up."

"Impressive." Inovani was awed. Someone who had actually gone to one of the three MIT's, the hardest schools to get into throughout the UWC planets.

"Naaa," Barkley said waving off Inovani. "They're just a bunch of snobby geeks. I feel it is an honor to serve in the Scout Corps."

Sydni laughed, "You are dismissed, Barkley. You could have just asked to be dismissed."

"Besides my Commander's disbelief, I love scouting. Ninety percent boring, but that ten percent of excitement is a rush." Barkley was holding Inovani's attention.

"I am going to dismiss myself," Sydni interjected.

The seamen, including Canterbury down the hall, came to attention with salutes. Sydni replied with a salute and inched past Barkley saying, "Good day, gentlemen."

She heard Inovani ask, "How would you like to go get a drink, Sarge?"

Quistqui had insisted that they use his bed as a place to work on Willy's wounds, so Willy stripped down to his shorts with a little tender help from Dekonal and lay on the mat with a clean sheet over it. Madak brought in a bowl filled with water and a glass bottle with a clear ointment in it. As they cleaned his wounds, Doqui stuck his head in and asked, "Shouldn't he see the healer?"

Madak smiled at her youngest son, appreciating his concern over Willy, but she shook her head and said, "No, none of his wounds require greater attention. Although that was a dirty animal and we may have to look for signs of infection."

Not understanding the word for infection, Willy repeated it. Dekonal was washing off his face and the now oozing laceration on his forehead. Leaning over him, she looked down and said, "When a wound is dirty and fills with liquid and does not heal correctly."

Willy nodded, and closed his eyes to focus on relaxing. He was fatigued from carrying the creature that Quistqui called a Gaza-Kan and also from the adrenaline rush when he had been ready to fight Quistqui. Dekonal and Madak's hands were gentle as they washed each scrape and cut. He wasn't worried about infection; in his backpack was his usual mini medkit that had an anti-infection booster that he could take to ward off any problems.

Chardon's voice broke the silence. "How long until you are finished?" he asked.

"A while," Madak said. "Why?"

"He has an audience in the courtyard. War council, council, hunters."

"Who's to say if he will even feel like speaking to them tonight?" Dekonal said. "He has had a long day."

Willy couldn't suppress the smile and opened his eyes enough to see Dekonal. He reached up and touched her face. "I will be all right, and I will talk to them."

Leaning into his hand, she continued to clean his wounds.

It only took half an hour to apply the ointment, bandage his wounds and give him his shot from the medkit. Dekonal rummaged through Willy's pack and pulled out a black pair of BDU pants and a gray tee shirt from the 99th Scout Squadron with the insignia on the front. She ran her hand over the shirt as he was pulling up his pants and asked, "What does this mean?"

"Our warriors are split into groups and the people in my position contact other races and see if a place is hostile or friendly, and that is the symbol that explains what group we are."

"We have a similar word among our warriors. It is called a war party."

Willy recognized the word as the one Douka had used earlier in the day, and he had a better understanding of the word. He was starting to get sore from his fight so he stretched out his arms a little before slipping his shirt on. Dekonal pulled the shirt down and helped him tuck it in. He was watching her closely as she helped and when she looked up at him, he pulled her in and kissed her. "Thank you," he whispered.

She could feel his warm breath on her face, and it smelled like the cup of Grakan root and leaf stew he had eaten before they started patching him up. "For you, anything."

"Shall we go get rid of all these people?"

Taking his hand, she said, "We could only be so lucky. The hunters will want to spend hours going over your story." They had headed toward the door, but she stopped. "Oh, they will want to see this." She picked up his still bloody knife from where she had put his clothes.

"You are making fun?"

"No. What you have done is literally unheard of. Search parties have gone out looking for people in the days when the Gaza-Kan hunted this far north, and they found very little remains of hunters better armed than you were."

"Okay, let's go."

From the kitchen, the bustle in the courtyard could be heard, and Madak was preparing a tray with cups and a pitcher. She looked at Dekonal and Willy holding hands. For a split second she examined the stranger, in the even stranger clothes, although she had tended to his wounds and knew he was just like themselves. Tears welled in her eyes. She knew her daughter loved him, and hadn't Quistqui proven him? She blinked away the tears as Willy smiled at her and said, "Thank you, Madak. I appreciate your care."

Picking up the tray, she said, "You are most welcome. You have quite a following already."

"Can I take that?" Dekonal asked.

"No, but please come outside to appease this crowd."

Madak walked into the doorway and stopped. "Excuse me," she said in a loud and authoritative voice that sounded like a mother speaking to her children. A hush moved through the courtyard and everyone looked. "May I present to you Willy, the killer of the Gaza-Kan."

She stepped aside, and Willy stepped out, still holding Dekonal's hand. All eyes turned to him, and he recognized a few people; Douka, Klisk, Watkil stood with Chakdon and Quistqui. Doqui was standing with a group of younger Hingandu near the body of the Gaza-Kan, which had been laid out next to the fire pit.

Douka started raising his staff and hitting the ground with it, making a dull thump. Others started clapping. Doqui started a cheer, which quickly rose through the small crowd.

Not very often in his life had Willy been thrust into the center of attention, and not knowing what to do, he smiled and walked out amongst them. He looked at Dekonal, who seemed proud to walk hand in hand with him. As they made a straight line for Douka and Chakdon, the crowd parted and let them pass.

He stopped in front of Douka, who was smiling in return. When Douka spoke, the crowd stopped cheering and clapping to listen. "You have achieved a great thing, Willy. Will you ever stop impressing me?"

"I hope not." A couple people laughed.

"We were just discussing what to do about our young friend Quistqui, who has shown such a discourtesy to you. What do you say?"

Quistqui, who had been studying the ground, embarrassed to look up, shot Willy a glance. Willy studied him for a moment, still smiling. The moment must have been killing him. How long had Willy spent as an outcast of his people? He would not send anyone into that punishment. "If it was not for Quistqui, I would not be nearly as popular as I am right now." A couple of people laughed again.

"But he left you without a weapon, and you quite possibly could have been killed."

"Douka, I have heard that you are angry at Quistqui, but I wish you would not judge him. Quistqui and I had a disagreement. I am not certain how you deal with things in your village, but Quistqui and I have already solved the problem between us."

"Is this true?" Douka asked Quistqui.

"Yes, Douka, it is true. I declare in front of everyone, that Willy is proven."

Squinting, Douka stepped toward Quistqui and said, "Truthful. No more antics?"

"I am ashamed at what I have done, and it will never happen again."

"Okay," Willy said, trying to change the subject. "Besides he didn't leave me weaponless, I had this." Out of the long pocket on his thigh, he pulled the bloodstained knife. A shout of surprise went through the crowd. "Isn't this what everyone hunts Gaza-Kan with?"

This time everyone laughed. A woman, maybe a little older than Madak, made her way through the crowd and stopped next to Willy. Chakdon stepped up and said, "Willy, this is the leader of the council, Alar. Alar this is Willy." Her long graying black hair was pulled back into a ponytail. When she smiled, her long white teeth gleamed. The first thing Willy thought of was a politician.

"Welcome to our village, Willy." She bowed a little.

He bowed back. "Thank you for accepting me into your village."

"I think that this is a clear sign that we may have a long difficult summer of Gaza-Kan moving about the hills. No hunter should hunt alone in the lower mountains or plains."

"Enough," someone shouted from near the courtyard door. "Let him tell his story."

Alar looked up and frowned. "Okay, okay, you'll get your story."

A small cheer rose through the crowd and Willy squeezed Dekonal's hand and whispered, "They want me to tell a story?"

"That is what hunters do, right? Tell them your hunting story or they'll never go home." Willy sighed, only enough to let Dekonal hear. She, in turn, squeezed his hand and said, "Just make it a short story."

They all turned to Willy and he glanced around at the eager faces, and cleared his throat. "I apologize if I have difficulty with your language, it is new to me." He glanced around, still holding on to Dekonal's hand and he said, "I was running through the foot hills, and had just crossed a creek when..."

Chapter 10

Gallagher had waited as long as he could before he called on the secured line to Chancellor Chambers' office. It would take a while to connect, so he just waited, looking at the initial report of the team investigating the crash site. It was a lead in the direction that Chancellor Chambers was looking for. Although the preliminary report couldn't show much, it was definitely something interesting. He looked at the vid recordings from the scout ship and then from scanners on the ground. The scene was mostly overgrown, so there wasn't much to see, but the metal and charred rocks were evident.

His screen blinked and Chambers' secretary appeared on the screen. "Ambassador Gallagher, how nice to hear from you. How is the cruise going?"

"Ups and downs, Diane. Aggravations and idiots, but then if I wasn't on the cruise, I would have to deal with it at home."

Diane winked and said, "Tell me about it. You want to speak with the boss man?"

"Yes, thank you."

"Hold on."

The screen blinked to the UWC insignia and music played. It wasn't more than a minute before Chambers appeared, saying, "Gallagher, great to hear from you. Any improvements?"

"Well, sir, we have had a couple of things happen here since I spoke with you." Chambers' smile disappeared. "We have found a crash site on the planet today, and the preliminary report shows that it was an old and non-UWC ship."

"Really," Chambers said.

"I will transmit the report to you now." Gallagher transmitted and continued, "Vladimir was nearly court-martialed here again. He has been demoted to Lieutenant and cannot move about the ship unless on duty."

Chambers looked down, shaking his head. "Has he jeopardized the mission? Do you want me to alleviate the problem?"

Gallagher shook his head, "No I think that we have solved the problem and I don't feel like breaking in a new person now."

"Very well," Chambers said. "What about the collection site?"

"Well, sir, that is the main problem. I had a chance and ordered the team down like you said to, but Commander William Colton, who is studying the forest-dwelling people, stopped them."

"Why?" Chambers demanded.

"It was a religious site, and if they didn't pack up, they would have been slaughtered by the forest people."

"Damn! I should have known not to rush it. What repercussions?"

"I was read the riot act by the CSO, nothing I can't handle."

"Sorry, that was my fault."

"How are you getting to know the City people's leader, what did you call him?"

"Zartig."

"Yes, that was it. Zartig."

"He is coming along perfectly, and it doesn't hurt that he is greedy and hates the forest people. If we decided to help Zartig battle them then that religious site just won't matter."

"I don't think I am ready to start a war, but if that satellite doesn't show an alternative site soon, we will have to aid Zartig so we can move this project forward. Keep up the search and keep me informed. Continue to bait Zartig until we know what we want to do."

"Yes, sir."

"Shall I look forward to another coded call twenty-four hours from now with an update on the crash site?"

"Yes, I may go planetside to get a look at it myself so I can give you a first-hand report."

"Very good, Jasper. If you can prove that there are or have been space travel life forms there, then XenoTec could get their grant. That would benefit not only me, but those who have helped me."

Gallagher smiled. He knew that he would be rewarded handsomely for any extra work he did for Chambers, and he was eager to please. "I will do what I can to expedite the process, sir."

"Okay, Chambers out."

The console blinked and Gallagher clicked off his screen. He pressed a button for his secretary's voice mail. "Please arrange a shuttle down to the crash site during the day and inform Vladimir that he will accompany me."

Smiling through his yawn, Gallagher would go to sleep with dreams of kickbacks from XenoTec.

* * * *

Sydni sat up in bed, swinging her arms at an unseen attacker and shouting. Sweat matted her brow and she was breathing hard when she realized that she was sitting in her bedroom. She had been dreaming that she was fighting some unseen monster. She realized now that it must have been leftover anxiety from watching the scanner relay Willy's fight the night before. She hated the feeling of helplessness she had as she watched. By the time she could have been in the launch bay and powering up, the battle would have been decided.

She sighed and Conrad, who was wearing only a pair of silk boxers, came running into the room, glancing around wildly, "What happened."

Nearly laughing, she waved her hand, saying, "It's okay. It was just me."

He sat on the bed next to her and ran his warm hand over her shoulder. "Are you okay, Sydni?"

She looked into his eyes and took his hand. "I guess I was dreaming about Willy's fight last night. I have only had to watch something like that one other time since the scanners were improved to record and transmit. But this creature was quick and worried me."

"You think you dreamed about it because you are twins?"

Sydni laughed. "No, I doubt he dreamed about it. He lived through it, but I felt helpless and that bothered me more than you know."

"I think I understand." He kissed her. "You are close to your brother. Even among twins, you two are unique. If I had a sister that I was close to, I would worry." He smiled and said, "Are you kidding? I am starting to worry about both of you." Standing up quickly, he looked away. "Wait here a moment," he said, heading back out the way he came from.

A tear welled up in her eye. He really did care about Willy, too. She wondered for a moment when she started getting so emotional. She laughed. What would she do next, have children?

Conrad reappeared, carrying a tray. Orange juice, toast, synth eggs, a red carnation, and her scanner were placed on the tray. "I thought you might like this luxury."

"Why my scanner?" she asked.

"I saw the message light blinking and thought you might need to respond."

He laid the tray across her lap and moved around the bed to sit next to her. She set the scanner aside, saying, "It can wait until after breakfast."

It didn't take long for her to finish breakfast, and leaning over the bed, she lowered the tray to the floor. The covers fell away, revealing her body down to the hips. As she leaned back up, Conrad scooted closer to her and placed a hand on her thigh as he leaned in to kiss her. She was returning his kiss and leaning toward him, allowing his hand to explore, when with her free hand she clicked on her scanner to listen to the message. As the message began to play, she threw aside the covers and thrust her leg over Conrad and was quickly straddling him. It took a moment before she realized that it was Gallagher speaking. When she lifted her head to listen, Conrad's lips and tongue followed down her neck, until she said, "I don't believe it." Conrad's kisses slowed and Sydni reached for her scanner. She had no vid, but their voices were there.

The scanner beeped when the message was done, and Sydni was sitting there with her mouth ajar, not believing what she heard. Conrad was staring at her, shaking his head. "That is borderline treason," Conrad whispered.

"Borderline nothing," Sydni said. "The UWC charter itself does not allow us to shape or change a world, or assist one culture over another for either personal or UWC gain. Secondly, if Chancellor Chambers is involved with XenoTec, that itself is a violation."

"What, are you an lawyer, too?"

"Willy's and my motto, always know your contract to the letter, and always know the regs and laws. That way you can manipulate them as well."

"You are amazing."

"I try." She paused, and smiled a wolfish grin that nearly alarmed Conrad. "Sometimes." From the look in Conrad's eyes he was hungry again, even after a voracious night, so she kissed him and said, "I have to send one message, then I am all yours, for the morning."

"Undivided attention?" He asked.

She winked at him. "Undivided and attentive. That is, unless you have work to go do or something."

"No, you go ahead, I can wait until you are done with your message."

Glancing down and then back into his eyes, Sydni said, "Are you certain you can wait?"

Willy couldn't decide whether the throbbing in his forehead and aching arm or, some unidentified noise had roused him from his fitful sleep.

He strained to listen in the silence, waiting for any kind of movement in Quistqui's darkened room, but there was nothing. Suddenly there was a clicking sound at the door. Willy tensed. He was ready to leap up and fight. He wondered, though, who would be sneaking around Chakdon's house in the middle of the night.

Moments later, Dekonal's scent filled the room and the door clicked shut. Willy relaxed himself and breathed deeply, wondering why she would choose a nocturnal visit. He felt her kneel on the sleeping mat, then her hair brushed over his chest and neck just before she lowered her lips to his. After a long kiss she moved so she had one knee on either side of him.

"Hello," he whispered.

"Hello." She ran her hands down his bare chest and back over his shoulders and leaned down for another kiss.

His hands searched up her thighs to her hips, and he could tell whatever she was wearing was barely enough to cover her. "This is a pleasant surprise," he said.

"Willy, when you told me you could be happy here, in our village, and that you loved me, did you mean it? Me and you forever?"

He could barely make out her face in the darkness, but he reached up and cupped her cheek in his hand and rubbed his thumb under her eye. It came away wet. "Yes. I meant it. You and me forever. As soon as I can leave my assignment at my home in the sky."

"I have never cared for anyone the way I care for you, and now with this proven silliness out of the way, we can stop worrying about Quistqui and start concentrating on us."

"I cannot prove to you how much I love you other than to tell you that I do."

She smothered him with another kiss and untied her gown. Willy felt the wisp of air as her gown slipped away. Her smell was more intoxicating than ever, and one last thought crossed his mind before passion took him completely. Forever wouldn't be long enough.

* * * *

Dawn came swiftly through the window, and Dekonal lay cradled in Willy's arms as he sat up against the wall. Their breath was the only thing that stirred until she said, "We should get up, or I should go back to my room."

"Then let's get up and go get something to eat."

"There are going to be more people who want to see the great Gaza-Kan killer. You should get some rest."

Staring at the brightening window, he said, "I am rested enough. If you need sleep..."

She patted his forearm. "No, I am fine. I am happy."

"I need to clean up," he said. "Then I will need assistance with my bandages again."

She leaned to look at his arm in the light. His wounds had oozed a little and the bandages would need to be replaced. Sitting up, she turned to look at the bandage on his forehead. In the center of the bandage was a darkening red spot. "We opened a couple of your wounds," she said with a smile.

"Maybe we can try and open them again later."

She stifled a laugh. "Not if I don't get out of here and come back under the pretense of cleaning your wounds. I may be old enough to do what I want, but our coupling would be frowned upon in my father's home since we are not mated."

"I understand."

She glanced around and picked up her blue gown as she stood up. For the first time he saw her naked. A darker stripe went the length of her spine and split across her buttocks and down the back of each leg. Stripes started from there and went around the front of her body. She spun, her gown flaring out as she started to put it on. Stopping, she saw Willy staring and asked, "What is it?"

"You."

She looked down at her nakedness, and blushing, she covered herself. "What?"

"You are beautiful."

Her face darkened even more as she tied her gown at the top and in the middle. "Thank you." She listened at the door and after a moment, she opened it a little. With a quick look back and a wink, she disappeared into the hallway.

Willy stretched in bed for several minutes before he stood up. He kicked the shorts he had been wearing over next to his pack. Nothing was new on his scanner, but the power was lower than he liked to operate with, so he opened a small panel with solar collectors and he set it in the sill of the window. In the bathroom he took off the bandages and folded them so the blood would be on the inner side. After an examination, he turned on the shower and adjusted the warmth before he stepped in.

By the time he stepped out of the shower, dripping wet, he felt even more refreshed. He picked up a towel and as he dried himself, he stepped into the bedroom. His scanner was blinking. He took the scanner and turned it on. An urgent message from Sydni read: Willy, Cannot wait to see you, I will come planetside for the meeting. Very important. Send me coords and a time. Love Always, Sydni.

He wondered what news she might have. He wondered if Sydni would want to meet Dekonal while she was planetside or if Dekonal would want to meet Sydni. He typed out a message back: Sydni, Coords attached. Try for 1600 hours. I have idea. Would you be interested in meeting with Dekonal while you are planetside? Please confirm as soon as possible. Love, William.

He laughed as he sent the message. She had always thought it funny when he called himself William. It had been her idea to call him Willy, saying that he seemed more like a Willy than a William.

There was a knock at the door. "Who is it?" he asked.

"Dekonal."

"Come in." he said, setting the scanner back down. Dekonal entered. Her dark hair was still wet and hung past her shoulders. She wore a simple dress like she had worn the day he had met her, cinched at the waist by a thin belt. She was carrying more bandages.

"I see I dress quicker than you," she said, looking him over.

He finished drying, and she helped by drying his back. She studied him as he crouched down and rummaged through his pack. He pulled out a pair of underwear and slipped them on, and then a pair of socks. The pair of BDU pants he had worn the previous night were neatly folded, and he picked them up and slipped them on.

"Can I put your bandages on now?" she asked.

"Oh, is that why you are here? I thought you came in to watch."

"Well, it was fun to watch, but now you have clothes on, so I should at least bandage you up."

He sat down on the sleeping mat and waited patiently as she bandaged his arm, side and head. When she was finished, she said, "That ought to last you most of the day."

"I have to ask you a question," he said. "Would you like to meet my sister?"

Her eyes widened and she said, "Really? Where? Up in the stars?"

"No. Nearby. She is coming here to give me a message, but I want you to meet her."

"That would be wonderful." Tugging at his hand, she said, "Come on. I will make you some breakfast."

* * * *

Tanya groaned when the next shuttle down opened up to reveal Vladimir and Gallagher arriving to examine the crash site. Gordo, absorbed in a scan a tech had just shown him of a section believed to be the engine looked up and said, "What's wrong, Tanya?"

Rolling her eyes, she jerked a thumb in the direction of the new shuttle and said, "Another headache."

Gordo laughed. "There's no way he'd try something now. Capt'n Dollinger reamed him from one side of the hull to the next. Besides, if he tried anything, I would be forced to take drastic measures and blast him back to Orion in pieces."

Batting her eyelashes, Tanya spoke in a soft tone, "You would do that for little old me?"

"Well, only partially for you, the rest for the Chief."

She lowered her hand to her holster and let her gaze drift back to Vladimir, who was now helping Gallagher out of the shuttle. "That's fair enough, Gordo. Fair enough."

Studying the scan again, he said, "Look at this, Tan. Yesterday they said this could not be a UWC vessel. I do not make any claim to engineering, but this scan looks a lot like a scan of one of our engines. There seem to be some differences, but the basic structure looks the same."

Tanya leaned over his shoulder and studied the readout for a minute. "I am impressed, Gord. I know you're no engineer, and that does look like one of our engines. Although look at the unidentifiable materials showing."

"Ha, ha," Gordo replied looking up at Tanya. When Gordo realized that Vladimir was picking his way through the cleared sections of the crash site in their direction, he stood up and closed the image on his scanner. "Here he comes."

"I wonder what the hell they are doing down here now?"

"Same as us, I would assume, checking out the sight firsthand," he whispered. Then out loud to Vladimir, in as even a tone as he could muster without laughing, he said, "Good day, Lieutenant. Nice day for a shuttle ride."

Vladimir tried his best not to scowl. To keep his job and possibly his life, he had to be cordial at least. "Good day, Sergeant. And you, Lieutenant." He paused and straightened himself out and said, "I first must apologize for my behavior the other day in the Dojo. I want to be the first to tell you there will not be another incident in the future."

Tanya nodded. "Very well. Anything else?"

"Yes, ma'am. Ambassador Gallagher requests that you join him over by the shuttle, if you have a moment."

Gordo looked at Tanya, who in turn motioned to Gallagher and said, "After you."

They followed Vladimir over to Gallagher, who dabbed at his brow with a white linen handkerchief embossed with his initials. His face was scarlet and he squinted to see in the sunlight. "Ahh, Lieutenant Williston and Sergeant Diego, just the people I wanted to see." He swept his hand across the crash site and then held it over his heart. "You don't know what this means to the UWC or to me personally. This could be the discovery of the century."

Neither Tanya nor Gordo were impressed with his theatrics. "Thank you, sir," Tanya said, forcing herself to be diplomatic. "It didn't look like much from the sky."

"Well, your names will go down in the annals of history with many other great explorers." Gallagher felt elated with the find, as well as being feet away from the action as the teams combed through the debris. "Anything new today?" he asked.

"They found what seems to be an engine, and are in the process of moving it. If they can get it to the Orion intact, then they can study it further and see what is going on or what its origin is."

"Excellent news," Gallagher said, shoving his handkerchief back in his breast pocket. "Well, I must thank you again. I appreciate your loyalty and devotion to the UWC and your work, and it will be duly noted in my report." He barely listened to their uninspired thanks before he asked, "Now, can I walk around?"

Tanya motioned toward the staked off area with ropes sectioning off the wreck and said, "Stay outside the ropes so you don't disturb anything they might be looking for."

"Of course, thank you,. Vladimir, come along please."

Gallagher tottered off, muttering, with Vladimir walking close behind him. When they were out of earshot, Gordo said, "What a pair?"

"You said it. We better send that report off to Willy before Gallagher gets his hands on it."

"It is a matter of public information now. Do you think he knows something we don't?"

"Willy always knows something we don't," Tanya said. "He may look different and even act different for that matter, but he is one smart Commander."

"I am glad he's on our side."

"Amen."

* * * *

The afternoon sun filled the little clearing and warmed Willy and Dekonal as they sat leaning against his pack. His scanner and rifle were only inches away in case of trouble. They stared into each other's eyes and had not said anything for several minutes. Somewhere nearby, a songbird sang its tune, and in the distance, another bird answered its reply.

"You say she will be able to find us here?" Dekonal asked in a voice barely even a whisper.

"Yes. My recorder sends her a signal so she can locate me."

She leaned closer and ran the bump of her nose up from the base of Willy's neck to his cheek and he turned his face so their lips met. As he pulled her closer, his scanner buzzed. Dekonal jumped at the unexpected noise. Willy was out of her arms and crouching over his rifle and scanner in an instant. He glanced at the scanner, and then adjusted it to examine its readings. It was human and the size of Sydni. She was walking in their direction, and her scanner suddenly sent a confirmation code to his signal. Setting his scanner back down, he said, "Don't worry, it's just my sister." He pointed in the direction that she was coming from and continued, "She should be here in a couple of minutes from that direction."

Dekonal was glancing over his shoulder and said, "Is that light her?"

"Yes. We would be here in the center." He pointed to the center of the grid.

"Is this what you meant when you said it told you the Gaza-Kan was coming?"

"Yes."

She ran her hands down the length of his back and then up again. Gently she started massaging his shoulders. "When it took you so long to get back, I started worrying."

"Worrying?" Willy said, twisting around to see her. "I thought you could see us having a future together."

"I can," she said, "but that does not stop me from worrying. My visions could change or I could be misreading them." She paused and said, "I can hear your sister coming now."

Sydni emerged from the wood line with a smile, carrying her daypack on her back. Holding up her hand, she said, "Hello," in Dekonal's language.

Willy stood up and looked at Dekonal who was staring at Sydni with a blank expression and her lips parted. This was her first contact with an alien who looked different than anything on her world. Willy didn't know that Dekonal was having one of her visions. She caught a glimpse of Willy fighting side by side with Quistqui and this stranger who appeared in the glade. When the vision passed, she snapped out of her stare and returned the smile.

Sydni looked over Dekonal, and then stared into her eyes. Dekonal said, "Hello."

Speaking in Dekonal's language, Willy said, "Dekonal, this is Sy-dni." He said his sister's name slowly. "She speaks some of your language, but not very well." Then in English, "Sydni, this is Dek-o-nal. I told her you do not speak her language well."

Dekonal squinted as she looked at her, saying, "It is good to meet you, Sydni. I hope our friendship grows like the trees."

Sydni smiled. She did not understand it word for word, but she understood the meaning. "If what Willy says is true, I am certain we will become friends." She looked at Willy and raised her eyebrows. He nodded and Dekonal's smile widened.

"She has a spectacular grasp of our language."

Reaching out, Sydni touched the bandage on Willy's head. In English, she said, "How bad are your wounds?"

"Not bad. You want to join us for a late lunch?"

"Sure," she said, but her smile went away. "I do not mean to be disrespectful, but we have to discuss something first."

Turning to Dekonal, Willy took her hands and said, "She will eat with us, but first she has to speak with me about my work."

Dekonal kissed his lips. "Okay. I will start getting ready."

She turned and started opening Willy's pack, and Willy turned back to Sydni. "What was so important?"

"With help from Chief Yamamora and some of his trustworthy men, we found where the information from Conrad's scanner was going. So, we placed another transmitter to prove this, and you won't believe what we found out."

"What?"

She unhooked her scanner and punched several buttons before handing it over to him. "Listen carefully."

Willy's expression didn't change as he listened to the taped message, but when it was over, Sydni could read the anger in his squinted eyes, his set jaw, and the wide flaring slits of his nostrils. He looked up at Sydni and a low growl issued forth. "That arrogant bastard, when I get my hands on him..." Willy's claws fully flexed.

"Wait a minute, Willy. We just can't go barging in there making demands and allegations. The way we obtained this information is highly illegal. We need to proceed slowly and with caution."

Willy stopped and retracted his claws. He breathed deeply and sighed. "Of course you're right. If we keep recording, he may hang himself, and in the meantime, we can search for alternatives."

"Now you're thinking, bro."

"Those bastards would start a war over Coppertroid fuel and exploration. Money. How many people would they kill for money?"

"However many would gain them the most. When do they need to know that the Hingandu are human, too?"

Willy nodded. "I guess sooner than I wanted and before I reach any conclusions."

"How about if we ignore everything else and have a nice time this afternoon with Dekonal?"

Dekonal looked up at the mention of her name and Willy smiled at her. "Okay, in a couple of hours, there will be more than enough time to worry about it."

"She is gorgeous, you know."

Willy looked at her. "You think so?"

"Using you as a judge." She smiled and nudged his ribs. "Those stripes are very interesting, but more importantly, what do you think?"

"Next to you," Willy said in a soft voice, staring as if a million miles away, "I think she is the most beautiful woman in the galaxy. I'm in love." Coming back from the distance his mind had traveled, Willy glanced at Sydni and noticed her glistening eyes. "Don't tell me you're sad."

"You know better," she said, jabbing him again in the ribs. "How long I've waited for you to say that. But what will you do if...well.... you know, Gallagher?"

Willy sat down next to Dekonal, who had spread out several small containers and an animal-skin bag with some water in it. Smiling to reassure Sydni, he said, "No ambassador has been able to get their hands on me yet. I have no intention of letting Gallagher thwart my happiness."

"Well, either way we have to be careful," Sydni said, sitting down across from them. "We need to find alternatives to his plan."

"Or like I said, let his own plan hang him."

Then, forcing herself to use Dekonal's language, she said, "I am sorry for speaking my language in front of you."

Dekonal shook her head and held up a hand. "No. Do not worry. Our food is ready."

They spent the afternoon speaking, Willy translating when necessary. For a while both Willy and Sydni forgot about their possible troubles and their problems and just enjoyed the day. Near nightfall, Willy asked, "Would you like to come back to the village tomorrow, if it is all right with the council?"

"I would love to see it," she said.

"I will send a message tonight, after I ask for permission."

Willy took his sister's scanner and copied the ambassador's message. Then Sydni gave him the receiver attachment and said, "I'll let you sort through all of the Ambassador's mail, if that's all right with you."

"Sure." He plugged in the receiver to his scanner.

"I should get going," Sydni said, standing up. "I have late dinner plans with Conrad."

"I wish the four of us could have dinner sometime."

Shrugging, she said, "Well, he spent the night out on the Water Moon with me, but I think he would be hard-pressed to have fun eating like this."

"True, and we can't go to the ship."

Sydni winked. "You never know what Conrad is capable of if he is properly motivated."

Willy smiled. "Come on, we'll walk you toward your ship before we get going."

* * * *

A small fire burned in a small pit encircled by large stones. The flames danced, casting wild shadows about the meeting room. Chakdon, Douka, Alar, Dekonal and Willy sat in a circle close to the fire. Chakdon threw several large dry leaves on the fire, and instantly the fire glowed blue and there was a sweet aroma in the air. Alar was the first to speak, "So you wish to invite a stranger into our village, Willy?"

"Stranger to you, yes. She is my sister and can be as trusted as I am."

Alar looked at Douka to her right and in a flat tone said, "You are to identify any threats. What do you say?"

Douka squinted as he looked across the fire at Willy. "You say this is your sister, but she looks different?"

Willy had explained to them what he had explained to Dekonal that night in the cavern above the village. It took a while, but he finally made them understand. Douka trusted Willy, and he understood what he was saying, but for the sake of his position, especially in front of Alar, he had to make it look good. He nodded. "I say there is no threat, we let her come in as we did Willy, no weapons."

"Chakdon, do you see any problems with this?" Alar asked.

Chakdon shook his head. "No. I sense both Willy and his sister being a benefit to our people. I have not pinpointed how, but that is what I see."

"What of the war your daughter sees?"

Chakdon lifted a leaf to his nose and sniffed. "I see it, vaguely. I do not see it as a war in the sense of the War of the Rolling Hill, but there will be some sort of conflict. I see our hearts saddening because of it, but not perishing from it."

Alar trusted Chakdon and nodded as he spoke. He had been a great advisor to the tribe and to her. Alar looked over at Dekonal, who stared into the fire. "Dekonal, I know that where Willy is concerned you may be clouded by feelings for him, but I have never known you to cloud your reports. Anything to add?"

"I have seen Willy and his sister helping us, even in battle. I have seen great sadness as a result of the war, but I cannot see why."

Alar had heard enough; she stood up and cleared her throat. "I speak for the council when I say that we trust your judgment, and I leave the decision in your hands, Douka. Thank you for consulting with me, and I will now take my leave." She bowed slightly, breathed one last deep breath, and turned to leave the meeting hall.

Once she was gone, Douka looked from Chakdon to Dekonal to Willy. "I consent, but I would like to meet her before anyone else, as I did with Willy."

Chakdon nodded and Dekonal said, "That is fine. Tomorrow then, we will let you know when she is coming."

Douka stared at the fire for a while before he forced himself to his feet and picked up his staff. He bid them goodnight and left.

Chakdon threw the leaf on the fire and looked at Dekonal and Willy. He was lost in his thoughts when the vision came to him; it was quick and simple, but it was a mating ceremony between Dekonal and Willy. He saw a gorgeous day on the hill where Dekonal liked to pray. Giant clouds moving along in a lazy breeze and the whole family was there. Willy was right for his daughter; he knew that now. Realizing that he had been staring at them, he smiled.

Dekonal knew her father had a vision, anyone that knew him could tell when it happened. She just waited it out and then he looked away and threw several large sticks on the fire. "I will take my leave now. Will you take care of the fire?"

Dekonal nodded. "We will watch it."

With a quick motion of his hand, he said, "Good night."

The fire crackled and popped as the wood burned, and Willy held out a hand to Dekonal. She interlaced her fingers with his and squeezed gently. Willy unfolded his legs and stood up, still holding onto her hand. He stepped behind her and brought her arm in front of her; then he sat down with a leg on either side of her and he took her other hand, crossing her arms in front. She leaned her head back and sighed. "Comfortable?" he asked.

"Very."

He pressed his nose into her hair and breathed deeply, and involuntarily, he squeezed her tighter. "I am glad you met Sydni."

"You love your sister very much, don't you?"

"I grew up in a world where I was very different, but she was always there for me. She always loved me."

"The difference between you and your sister is great, but your own people did not accept you?"

"Not very often. Most people could not see past the differences in my face, hands, teeth, and eyes, but there were some who could see past my skin to my heart and knew who I was."

"That is very sad."

"Just say, for purpose of argument, that you had a child who looked like my sister. What would you do?"

Dekonal smiled, because she understood what Willy was trying to ask, without being so obvious or presumptuous. "I would love it, no matter what it looked like. Your sister is different, but if God sees fit to give me a child that looks different, then it is up to me to love and care for that child."

Her answer made Willy love her even more than he thought possible. If it were not for his obligations to the ship and to get to the bottom of what Gallagher was up to, then he would ask her to mate with him now, and he would stay with her forever. He wasn't certain how his children would turn out, more like Sydni or more like himself, but to him it would never matter. His parents had taught him just what acceptance would mean to a child.

"You know, we are alone. No one will come in here until morning. Even then no one might come in here."

"Really? Then what are you trying to say."

Loosening her hands from his, she stretched over to the small pile of wood and leaves. She threw a couple more logs on the fire and then a leaf. As the fire glowed blue, she twisted to look at him and said, "If you don't know, I'll just have to show you."

Chapter 11

"Why did you erase it?" Conrad asked, rubbing Sydni's bare back as she lay in bed.

Sydni moaned with the pleasure of having the stiffness between her shoulder blades removed. "Common practice."

"What do you mean?"

She laughed, shaking the bed gently. "You would not make a good intelligence agent, my love, and please stay just as you are. I can be cynical enough for both of us. However, since Willy and I have been old enough to know what people are like, any time we have incriminating evidence, only one of us will have it in possession. When he took the receiver and data, it was a given that I would erase it."

"It must be incredible to have someone who knows you that well. I am envious."

Sydni reached around and patted Conrad's arm. "Give us time, we will be that way. Willy and I have had a long time to practice."

"So you are going to let me into your little clique?"

She twisted underneath him and faced him. Smiling, she said, "Your application is in, and if you would like, I can put in a good word with the board member that oversees applications."

"Oh," he said, raising his eyebrows. "Just what do I have to do to gain such a favor?"

"Well, I take bribes. And I have just about an hour before I have to be down to pre-flight to go over my ship."

"Only an hour," he said. "I will try and limit myself."

Sydni laughed again. "What happened to those massive amounts of work you had to get done?"

"Blessed relief. Andrea came aboard last night and said she would be in to resume her regular duties this morning. I think she's taking pity on me, and once things are running smoothly, I will make certain she goes back down to the moon again."

"You're such a good boss."

"Yeah, yeah, enough talk already," he said leaning over her. "If I only have an hour to work with, I don't want to spend it discussing my job." He kissed her.

* * * *

The Jolabwe city smelled pungent, but as much as Gallagher tried, he could not put a name or a substance to the source of the stench. He was being escorted through the bustling city streets in what almost looked like an ancient golf cart. He was relieved that he did not have an irrational fear of snakes as he did with spiders, or sitting this close to creatures that bore an uncanny resemblance to snakes would have driven him insane. Their scaly skin glistened in the sunlight and their voices were soft and almost slurred to him.

His translator, Sandra Donaldson, was sitting next to him, dressed in a beige jumpsuit and wearing a green jacket. She had short blonde hair and kept her eyes darting around the city. It was her first cruise, and once the Colton twins had made contact, she had been working on learning the language with the other scouts. Gallagher had almost requested Willy's assistance on this trip, since he had not only learned the Jolabwe language, but the Hingandu language as well. For a moment, Gallagher wondered why they had sent out a translator who didn't learn languages fast. With a sigh, he remembered it was her first cruise, and probably nerve-racking for her.

She grabbed his arm and said, "Sir, look."

Gallagher looked where she pointed at a group of Jolabwe beating on another one that struggled wildly. "Ms. Donaldson," he said, looking down at her hand. "You will kindly not point."

"But they are beating on that poor creature."

"You know neither the circumstances nor reasons, so you will kindly mind both your manners and your business."

"Sorry, sir." She took her hand away. "You are correct, of course. I will try and control myself."

Gallagher looked over at Vladimir, who was on the other side of him. Vladimir smiled and shrugged. Turning back to Sandra, Gallagher said,

"Look, I understand this is your first cruise, and your first time off Alpha One, but while we are here, planetside and among a race we hardly know, you must conduct yourself in a professional manner."

She glanced up at Gallagher and nodded. "Yes, sir."

The caravan of three carts stopped in front of a building with rough-cut, stone pillars and a short staircase. Two guards stood in front and held their crude firearms at the ready. Sansanal, the Jolabwe who had met them at the landing site, motioned for them to follow.

The two guards glanced at them, but let them pass without words. Sansanal led them through a sparsely decorated foyer, up another flight of stairs and then he stopped where two more guards were standing outside of a set of double doors of smooth, polished wood. In a very soft voice, Sandra said, "They asked who we are, and Sansanal responded that we are the outsiders who had an appointment with Zartig."

Gallagher nodded. At least she was paying attention to her duty now. The guards stepped aside and Sansanal opened the door. The humidity struck them before they were even close to stepping in the room, and the smells that assaulted their senses were unidentifiable.

The room had a low ceiling and was only as wide as the double doors. Tapestries hung on either side of the walls depicting other Jolabwe and gatherings of Jolabwe. The room ended in a wider circular part, with a mound of pillows, in the middle of which, sat Zartig. He was wearing a gray robe, stained with food and drink, that could not hide his girth, and in one hand he held a large mug.

His antennae vibrated as he spoke, and Sandra translated the conversation back and forth. "Welcome again to my home, Ambassador. Please come in and sit."

He motioned toward a small cushioned chair facing him. Gallagher took a seat, while Vladimir and Sandra stood behind him. "Thank you for seeing me, Zartig."

Waving a hand, Zartig said, "No, no. I am glad you could come see me. Some days get boring here. This is a pleasant diversion. Can I offer you or your officers anything?"

"We are fine. Thank you."

"What does Gallagher of UWC want to see Zartig for?" Zartig had difficulty with the initials UWC.

"I want to make certain that the friendship between Jolabwe and UWC is strong."

Zartig stared at Gallagher with is black eyes and seemed to smile. "Of course our friendship is strong. Is there something you need from Zartig?"

"Not yet. However, if we were to need something, I would want to know if the UWC could ask Zartig."

Zartig had not risen to his position without negotiations or implied promises. He understood why Gallagher was dancing around his meaning without getting to it. He made the motion that he had seen many of the aliens use to imply that they were correct; he nodded. "Yes, I feel that you could ask me for help if you so chose."

Gallagher relaxed as much as he could with Zartig eyeing him with those black eyes. "Thank you." He did not have anything else to discuss with Zartig, and he was starting to feel foolish for going through the bother of coming planetside.

Zartig gulped his drink and asked, "Is that all the business you came to discuss?"

"Yes."

"Have you seen much of our city?"

"No."

"Well, then maybe with business out of the way we should go around the city so you can understand us better. Maybe it would make you feel more at ease if a time comes to ask us to help you."

Gallagher smiled and rubbed his hands together. He was at home with a diplomat, even if the room stank.

* * * *

Sydni tracked down Willy's ship and landed next to it. She pulled out her laser rifle and slung it across her back with her daypack. Because of Willy's warning, she flipped on her scanner so a Gaza-Kan would not be able to sneak up on her. It was a picture perfect day with a brilliant blue sky and a gentle breeze. She had changed out of her flight suit and into camo BDU's and a black squadron tee shirt.

The forest loomed ahead of her, but Willy had given her specific directions and coords to reach them. She would have to meet some of the War Council before she could be admitted into the village, which in her experience was not unusual.

As she ran, she found her pace and fell into a steady rhythm, figuring she would meet up with Willy and Dekonal within the hour.

After she had run about twenty minutes, her scanner beeped, and without slowing down, she unhooked it from her belt and examined it. There were two life forms on either side of her, paralleling her path. Each one was about fifty yards on either side. She scanned them, to see if they were the same creatures that Willy had fought just days before, but she recognized the readings as being members of the Hingandu people. She breathed a sigh of relief, knowing that if they decided to confront her, she could at least speak with them.

The two Hingandu kept their distance for the duration of the run, although twice they veered in closer, but stayed out of visual contact. Two more life forms appeared ahead of her, and she knew that those were waiting at the coords that Willy had given her; then Willy's scanner gave off a transponder signal.

She slowed to a jog and then to a walk before she came into view of Willy and Dekonal, who stood hugging as they leaned against a large tree. Dekonal saw Sydni first and waved, a greeting Willy had taught her just for this time. Sydni waved back and said, "Hello, Dekonal, Willy. Did you two arrange for the escort?"

"What escort?" Willy asked.

"Two Hingandu have been following me over halfway here."

Willy snatched up his scanner and turned it on. He saw the two readings moving toward them very slowly. Dekonal looked at him, and, shaking her head a little, she shrugged. "I did not know anyone would be out this way."

"Probably just out hunting and came across you and decided to follow."

"Fair enough. They should be close enough to see, though."

Dekonal cleared her throat and in a rising voice, she said, "Show yourself. I am Dekonal of the Mountain Village."

There was a brief pause, and then two Hingandu stood up, within twenty yards on either side. Willy recognized them immediately as Bokta and Hanst. "What are you doing out here?" Dekonal demanded.

Hanst was staring at Sydni and he said, "We are patrolling."

"Do you not patrol from Brotus?" she asked.

Bokta, who was also staring at Sydni said, "Yes, but we were not allowed to patrol from Brotus for a full moon. Until we learn manners."

"Bokta, Hanst, this is my sister, Sydni."

Both Bokta and Hanst stood motionless with their mouths agape. "S-sister?" Bokta asked. "But she looks so different."

"Yes, but she is my sister."

"That is enough," Dekonal said. "You two have duties, this is not a matter for you."

Hanst bowed his head and said, "Yes. Sorry, Dekonal. We will leave you alone, now that we know the being we followed is with you."

"Our apologies," Bokta said, backing away.

Hanst and Bokta headed back down the path that Sydni had come. Once they had disappeared into the woods, Sydni said, "I only caught part of what was said, "What was that all about?"

"Remember when I said that Dekonal's brother, Quistqui, left me in the plain to run back?" Sydni nodded and Willy continued, "Well, those two were with him and Douka was furious that they did not help me."

Sydni nodded. "Makes more sense now. So I have to meet with some of the War council?"

Willy nodded, "A formality that I went through. They want to meet you before you are allowed to go into the village."

"Great. Let's go meet them."

Dekonal turned and started hiking down the path, as Willy picked up his rifle and slung it across his back. They were very close to the mouth of the valley, and it did not take long before they were moving down into the valley that led to Dekonal's village.

About halfway down the valley, there was a small contingency of Hingandu waiting along the path. Chakdon leaned against a tree, while Douka leaned on his staff talking to him. Sitting in a small circle, were Alar, Klisk, Watkil, and Tyuk. This was a significant day for their village, with the arrival of an off-worlder that was different than any of the races known to them, yet in many ways very much like them. The group scrambled to their feet.

Chakdon, not surprised by their visitor's visage, looked at Dekonal and Willy. He saw complete happiness and utter despair, but the brief vision did not show him why. There was no stopping what was to be; all he could do was be there for them both.

Douka stared at Sydni. Her skin was bright and smooth, and her round eyes were clear blue, like the sky reflecting in a lake he had seen once as a child, high in the mountains. He glanced at Dekonal and then to Willy, who nodded. "Douka," Willy started, gaining everyone's attention. "This is my sister, Sydni. Sydni, this is Douka of the War Council."

"Hello," Sydni said. She smiled her warm and pleasant smile that had charmed many a heart.

Nearly in awe, Douka said, "Hello."

"She speaks your language, but has some trouble with it, so I will translate only when necessary."

Willy slowly introduced her to everyone except Tyuk, who was new to him. Dekonal stepped up and said, "This is our holy man, Tyuk. Tyuk, this is Willy and Sydni."

Sydni looked at Willy and shrugged, and in English he said, "Priest or some sort of holy man." She nodded.

Douka stepped up so he was nearly nose-to-nose with Sydni and looking in her eyes, he asked, "Do you intend us any harm?"

"No."

He nodded and looked back and forth, between Willy and Sydni. "You say that you have the same mother and father? You say that you are twins?"

"Yes." Willy and Sydni answered in unison.

Douka nodded. "You have tried to explain this to me, Willy, and I think I understand. I have no problem with your sister going into the village." He turned to the others, who were all intent on watching Sydni. "Anyone else have any reservations?"

They shook their heads, none would disagree with Douka, since he was not asking for their opinion. Turning to Sydni, he said, "You are free to roam our village. You are very different from everyone, and as a precaution, you may want to remain in the company of Dekonal or Willy. We are not a violent people, but you are new to us and it is difficult to say how everyone will act."

"I understand and I will be careful," she said.

Alar stepped up and cocked her head a little as she looked at Sydni. Then glancing at Willy, she asked, "So you say we have the same ancestors, you, she, and I." She motioned toward Sydni.

"Yes. A long, long time ago. Maybe before your history began."

"That is why you wanted to see the Hut of the Past."

"I was trying to see what your history said about where you came from."

Alar looked at Douka, who had lost his smile. Alar then looked back at Willy and asked, "Is it a possibility that you came from here?"

"I thought about that, but on my home, they have proof of our growth from the sea to us." He wondered if they understood what he meant; there were no other words that he could think of to convey evolution better.

"We have always been like this," Alar said laying her hand on her chest. Douka shuffled forward and laid a hand on her shoulder. She turned and looked at him. Willy was trying to understand what was passing between them, but neither spoke for several seconds. Finally Alar said, "I will convene the council of the villages. Turning back to Willy, she said, "I would like both you and your sister to be present at a meeting late this afternoon. Would you?"

Willy glanced at Sydni, who nodded her consent, and then he looked at Alar and said, "So be it. We will come to your meeting."

Alar nodded and looked at Sydni again. Hesitantly, she reached out, and then withdrew her hand. "You seem so different from us, but very similar."

Sydni stepped closer to her and held out her hand. "Do you want to touch my skin and hair?"

Alar's eyes widened and Douka, Klisk, Watkil, and Tyuk crowded closer. Alar reached out again and paused before she touched Sydni's light skin. She rubbed her fingers over the back of Sydni's hand, and then the back of her hand. "Soft," she said. "Very soft." Then she took Sydni's hand and examined her fingernails. She held up Sydni's hand so the others could see the fingernails.

Sydni's laughter made them all look up. She could see Willy's question in his look and she said, "All my life it was you that was the different one. You were the one everyone wanted to touch and examine. Now I guess it is my turn."

That made Willy laugh. He had not thought about it in that way, but she was correct; the tables had been turned. Dekonal held Willy's hand as the examination turned to Sydni's hair. Dekonal turned to Chakdon and asked, "Are you not curious?"

Still leaning against a tree, he shook his head. "You forget that I too have seen the strangers, and her countenance is not new to me."

"Of course," Dekonal replied.

Chakdon pushed himself off the tree and stepped up next to Dekonal and Willy. "Very fascinating, though."

Dekonal smiled. She had thought the very same thing when she first met Sydni. "This is a very significant happening for our people."

Chakdon nodded. "Very. That is why I invited Tyuk. He of all people will assimilate and predict what this means to us as a people."

"What do you see, father?"

"Many things, as you described. Happiness, despair, hopelessness, and joyful times."

"Why so vague?"

"That is all I see. I believe that your mind filters what it sees and does not allow you to see the very horrible things that would incapacitate you with fear. Think about the hours you would spend, trying to change the outcome of something you have seen, only to have it happen anyway."

"An interesting theory. It sounds correct. I, like you, have never seen someone's death, just the repercussions of that death."

Once Alar and the others had satisfied their curiosity, they backed away, thanking Sydni. Alar, speaking to Watkil, said, "Send out the riders when we get back. The meeting will be here tomorrow." Then to everyone, she said, "Good day."

The council members started down the path with Alar. Tyuk bowed in Chakdon's direction and said, "Thank you for inviting me. I too will take my leave now."

Tyuk turned and ran to catch up to the others. Once he was out of earshot, Willy asked, "Chakdon, that means that Sydni must stay here for tonight, do you...."

Chakdon held up his hand and said, "You need not ask, Willy, for I will offer." He paused to make certain that he pronounced Sydni's name right. "Syd-ni, I will offer you my house as yours while you stay in the village."

"Thank you, Chakdon."

"Shall we show your sister the village?" Chakdon asked of Willy.

"Yes, that would be a great place to start."

* * * *

Sydni examined the skull of the Gaza-Kan, which had been encased in some sort of clear lacquer that was supposed to be a preservative. "Very formidable-looking creature," she said, passing it back to Willy. "Skill or luck?" she asked, her eyes betraying her amusement when her lips did not.

Willy shrugged and looked into the eyes of the Gaza-Kan. "A little of both I guess."

That brought a laugh from Dekonal, who said, "I doubt that. Only a highly skilled warrior could kill a Gaza-Kan with only a knife."

Turning to Sydni and holding the skull in one hand, Willy shrugged. "They keep saying that about me, but...."

"You are too modest, brother," Sydni said, cutting him off. "We all know you are the greatest hunter, so just give it up."

Quistqui and Doqui were standing in the doorway and they caught Sydni's eye by the way in which they whispered back and forth. Ever since they had been introduced to her they had been talking like that. She turned her back to them and asked, "What's going on with Quistqui and Doqui? They have been whispering together ever since I got here."

Willy looked at Dekonal, who shrugged. "With my older brother it is difficult to say just what goes on in that head of his. As you know, he was very suspicious of Willy, and he looks like us. I can only imagine what he thinks of your fair, soft skin and light eyes."

"He promised to cooperate with me, but that does not say anything about including you."

"True," said Sydni.

"My brother has never gone back on his word, but he could very well twist it if it suited his needs."

Willy shot Quistqui a quick glance, and Quistqui caught his eye and nodded. Willy nodded back. "We'll have to keep an eye open."

"So what did you think of our village?" Dekonal asked, trying to shift the focus away from her brother.

"This is a great setup for the town, using the face of the cliff for both protection and tunnels and as access to the top of the cliff. Those Brotu as well, what majestic creatures."

"I agree," Willy said. "I had the opportunity to ride one, and they are gorgeous."

Dekonal smiled and said, "Most people know how to ride and even have Brotu, but some people are afraid to be that far off the ground."

Sydni laughed and said, "Remind you of anyone?"

"Yeah," Willy replied. "How about you, Dekonal? Do you fly?"

"Only in an emergency or if I need to travel far away. I like my feet to be on the ground."

Madak pushed her way past Quistqui and Doqui, saying, "Dekonal, Willy, I have prepared a midday meal."

"Coming, Mother."

Willy hung the head of the Gaza-Kan back on the door of the courtyard and closed it. Madak turned and went back in and her sons followed close behind. Dekonal was several paces ahead, and Sydni asked in English, "What is it about the head on the door? Isn't that kind of gross?"

Willy shrugged, and speaking in English, he said, "A status thing. They made a very big deal of it when I returned with that thing's body. I think hunting ability plays an important role in the males' status."

"And female status?"

Willy grinned. "I only know so much. I have not met any female hunters. Their council leader is female, and Madak seems content to manage the home. Most of the males I have met were very concerned with hunting and strength."

"So if Madak manages the home, how is her food?"

Speaking in Hingandu, Willy said, "Delightful."

Dekonal dropped back and held her hand out to Willy, who took her hand and kissed it and then held it at his side. "What is delightful?" she asked.

"You, of course."

Sydni could see the color change in Dekonal, as she had in Willy for so many years when he was angry or embarrassed. Willy's compliment had embarrassed Dekonal, but by the shy grin, it was obvious that she enjoyed the compliment. She watched the two look at each other, and deep in her soul, she knew that Willy was home. She wondered if she and Conrad could be that happy here. Would there be a station here that they could live on? Suddenly she realized that both Willy and Dekonal were looking at her, waiting for her to proceed inside.

"Sorry," she said as she scooted past them.

*　*　*　*

Conrad examined the report three times while Andrea stood at attention in front of his desk. His mouth lay wide open and he looked over the vid attached again. He let his scanner drop into his lap and he looked up, realizing that Andrea was still standing at attention. "At ease. Sorry, Major. Did you read this?"

Andrea stood at ease and nodded. "Yes, Conrad, I did."

"The implications are phenomenal. This could be a link to those people who first gave us interstellar travel."

"If you believe we were given interstellar travel and did not retrieve it by total blind luck."

Conrad frowned. There were two standard theories among the science community. One side believed that some unknown people, who wanted humans to expand, had aimed the uninhabited interstellar ship that drifted into Earth's solar system. While the others thought that blind luck brought that derelict ship into the solar system. Humans had only met one other race with interstellar travel, which had been named Broadarians, due to their multi-eyed, wide-face. Their propulsion system was based differently. Their engines worked on different physics.

"Okay, either theory aside, this could be the most significant find in our lifetime," Conrad said.

"Undoubtedly. I brought this straight to your attention, but might I suggest that Ambassador Gallagher be informed. He has been hounding the team since they boarded the engines."

"Agreed. Maybe I can get him off our backs for a while."

Leaning over his keyboard, Conrad typed in a message and sent it to Gallagher, marked with a level one priority and copied to the captain. "He should be here soon. Can you make three copies of this report?"

"Yes, sir." She took the scanner and removed her mini memory card, on which the report was taped. "Anything else?"

"No, but you may want to take notes and save a copy for yourself. You can maybe get a couple of articles out of this." Andrea's jaw dropped. She needed some sort of edge to get her next contract as CSO, and such publications would be the key, even if the publications were pure speculation as to the existence of the engines on this planet.

"Don't worry, I will write something too, but you deserve it with all the work you've done on this voyage."

Her slack jaw pulled together into a grin. "Sir, I mean, Conrad, that could very well make my career."

"I know, and you have a fine career ahead of you. Just remember me when I am an old and teetering fool, babbling about the old days."

She pulled into a quick salute and stood at attention until Conrad saluted back. As she left for her office, to copy the report, Conrad leaned back in his chair and swiveled around to look out of his portal. His mind drifted to the engines and the possibility of a culture nearby that could be well beyond their abilities. Then Sydni's long range scan flashed in his mind. Was that what Gallagher was looking for? Had he known what might be found? A chill ran down Conrad's spine as he realized they might be closer to something than anyone suspected.

* * * *

Bucky showed up first, wanting to get the upper hand on Gallagher, and he was halfway through the report when Gallagher walked in with Vladimir trailing a few paces behind. Gallagher shook as he read the report, and when Bucky finished, he looked up at Conrad and said, "Do you realize the connotations and implications? This could change the whole face of our mission out here, not to mention extend it and even add another Star Cruiser Class ship along for the fun."

"I know," Conrad said.

"No!" Gallagher almost shouted. "This is confidential information, and I will deal with this."

Bucky smiled, his white teeth gleaming. "Gallagher, this is bigger than you. There is no way that you can suppress this. My superiors need to know this not only for the safety of the ship and crew, but for the government."

"I-I cannot let..."

"Ambassador," Bucky said as if he was talking to a child accusing a parent of being unfair. "You have no power over this one. Not only do I have a right and duty to report this, I am certain that Doctor Singh must report such a find through the proper channels as well." Bucky looked up to Conrad, hoping for a quick backup.

"Indeed, Captain. A find of this nature must be reported to the Earth Science Admiralty immediately."

Gallagher was about purple by now, and his nostrils flared rapidly. He took out the mini memory card, and holding it up, asked, "I presume that this is intended for me?"

"Correct," Conrad said.

Gallagher tossed the spare scanner down on the desk. He whirled around and stumbled as he bounced off Vladimir, who rushed to assist him. After smacking Vladimir's hand away, Gallagher straightened himself and exited Conrad's office.

"Bucky, that was just too simple."

"What? You mean flustering the poor little guy? He has been trying to railroad this whole cruise, and now it is just a little payback for him." Bucky pulled out the mini memory card from his borrowed scanner and set the scanner down on Conrad's desk. "I have read stories of days where such ambassadors were sent on separate ships, and when the captain cruised, he or she was the sole authority."

"I would bet that he knew something about this before it happened. The way he has had long range patrols, dropping off sensor beacons, the constant solar system patrols. I bet this is why he has been acting so strangely recently."

"Surely if he or the council had known about this, I would have been informed."

Conrad shrugged. "I am just a CSO, I don't even want to begin to fathom the thoughts in the head of a politician."

Bucky laughed and slapped Conrad on the back. "What do you say I buy you a drink, Lieutenant Admiral Singh, and we can discuss the idiocy that makes up the council, while I wait for a connection to UWC Admiralty and see what they have to say about all this."

* * * *

"Yes, Sir, I do understand the implications, especially coupled with the vid you have shown me, but this was under the direction of the CSO. Legally he and Captain Dollinger are on solid ground." Gallagher drummed his fingers on his thighs as he looked at a red-eyed Chancellor Chambers, who he had awakened in the middle of the night.

"Damn!" Chambers said. "The ESA will be all over this, not to mention the media, and if they leak this to the vids, they may very well be sending another cruiser."

"Sorry, after that mistake with the extraction team, I could not demand they give me first look at the report. Lieutenant Admiral Singh had his people well trained and versed. He received first report."

"Well, we can't stop that now..." Chambers voice dropped off and he rubbed his eyes. After clearing his throat again, he said, "Look, we are just going to have to act before the rest of the council decides how to respond to this. It is now a foregone conclusion that we will need a station there, but I want to act swiftly no matter what the UWC decides. If you can't find a new suitable site for collection, we will have to take action. Is Zartig ready to proceed?"

Gallagher nodded. "I think we have him right where we need him. He is interested in any technology we could give him in order to start aggressions."

Chambers smiled through his sleepiness. "Good to hear. Let me know if you can find another suitable collection site."

"Yes, Sir."

Chambers had started to turn away, but he stopped and faced the camera again. "And, Ambassador Gallagher..."

"Yes."

"This is a fine piece of work. It will not be forgotten."

"Thank you, Sir."

* * * *

The oblong meeting hall had one fire burning in the center of the room. Hingandu sat shoulder to shoulder along the walls. In the far back corner from the door sat Willy, Sydni, Dekonal, and Chakdon. Sydni was wearing a cloak to hide her, and several people nearby glanced at her, but did not say anything. Sydni noticed that far more than half of the attendees were female.

As Alar stepped into the middle of the room, next to the fire, a hush fell over the room, leaving only the sound of the crackling fire. She looked around the room, nodding and smiling. Finally, she cleared her throat and said, "Thank you all for coming. Your quick response is very much appreciated, for what I have seen very well may have changed life as the Hingandu know it." She paused as a murmur went through the crowd.

A woman with stark white hair spoke up, "What proof do you have?"

"You all know Chakdon and his daughter, Dekonal. They foresee a strange war that may include off-worlders, and definitely include the Jolabwe."

Another murmur went through the crowd, and Willy wondered about her use of the words: off-worlder. The implication was that they had seen other races before; he knew that the Broadarians had visited generations before, due to a couple of old Broadarian satellites, but would this generation know and remember them? Were there other races that visited them? He would have to ask Dekonal later.

Alar was holding up her hand and said, "Wait, please before you jump to conclusions." She had recaptured everyone's attention, and she signaled to Willy and said, "Willy, would you come here please."

Willy stood up and walked over to the fire. For the first time, many people realized that he had no stripes, which caused a whole new round of shouts. Again the white-haired woman spoke up, but she stood and moved forward, keeping her eyes on Willy. She pointed a crooked finger at Willy and said, "You are not from our tribes. Where are you from? You a rogue?" She was now within an arms length and squinting, her nostrils widened as she sniffed at him. Walking behind Willy, she continued to sniff, and the hair on the back of Willy's neck rose. Next to his ear, she whispered, "Off-Worlder."

Spinning, Willy looked at her and smiled. "Yes."

"You smell of other foods and off-world."

"Yes," Alar said. "He is from off-world. Right now, another race of people circles the world."

This time the shouts erupted and people stood up. "Borsha, listen to Chakdon and Dekonal before you jump to conclusions." Borsha, the white-haired woman, took her eyes off Willy and looked at Alar. "If my pleas do not work, then I order it."

Taken back by one of the few direct orders she had ever heard Alar give, Borsha knew it must be important. Nodding, she turned around and walked back to her seat; many others took note when she sat back down, and they started to settle back down. One older man, whose dark stripes stood out against his paler skin, shouted at Borsha, "Why do you just sit back down? Alar has brought an off-worlder into our midst."

He had gained the attention of almost everyone in the room, and as Borsha spoke in a whisper, everyone strained to hear her. "Histab, you are a great war council leader. You repelled the Jolabwe as a young man in the three-river attack, but Alar is the council leader, by our own vote. We will hear what she and Chakdon have to say before we condemn her act."

Histab jerked his head back as if he had been brutally rebuked by Borsha. Bowing his head, he mumbled, "Of course, you are correct." He crossed the room and took his seat.

As the others followed suit, Willy relaxed a little. The council had started sounding a bit hostile. He glanced at Sydni, who had remained seated with Chakdon and Dekonal on either side. Alar placed a hand on Willy's shoulder and said, "Can you talk to them first? Before Chakdon does."

"Yes. My name is Willy Colton, and I come from a light in the sky, far, far away. I have come here in peace, and as you can see, I even look like you." Willy started walking around the fire, looking at the various attendees as he spoke. "Our ancestors are the same. I cannot explain in your language how I know this, but it is true. There is something you will have a difficult time understanding. The city that is circling your planet is full of my people, but they look very different from me." He knew by their murmurs that they were having a difficult time with his explanation, so he redirected. "Alar asked me to be here with my sister, my twin sister, so you could see that the off-worlders are different, yet the same." Willy motioned for his sister to stand up, and with her, Chakdon and Dekonal approached.

In English, Willy said, "Are you ready? This crowd looks a little uptight."

"It's now or never," she said, readying herself for their reaction.

Dekonal cocked her head a little, questioning his English words, and he shook his head, "Just seeing if she is ready."

Sydni showed her pale hands for the first time and unhitched her cloak, letting Willy pull it away. "I am Sydni Colton." Willy smiled; Sydni was a show-stopper.

Willy continued, "We are brother and sister, born from the same mother at the same time. Yet where I am from, I am the only one who looks like this and the rest look like her."

Sydni slowly turned around so the awed crowd could all get a look at her. "Willy and I come in peace. We want to learn more about you. We want to be able to help you."

Chakdon moved to her right and Sydni looked at him, giving him the floor. "Council members, elders, and fellow Hingandu, I know how wary you are of off-worlders. Our history is still fresh from when the strange ones came from the sky and had to be repelled, but these two are different. I know what I have seen, and what my daughter has seen, and I have taken them into my home." Several people gasped. "The oncoming war would seem to be unavoidable. We must be prepared."

Borsha stood up, bowing to Chakdon. "Please excuse my interruption, Chakdon. I would speak with Alar."

Alar walked over to Borsha and said, "Yes."

Whispering in Alar's ear, Borsha said, "I believe in Chakdon, he has never led us down a dismal path. However, I would like to hold the rest of the council without the off-worlders, if you wouldn't mind."

Pausing to look around and seeing many people talking in hushed tones to themselves, Alar said, "You may be correct." Turning to Willy and Sydni, Alar said, "You have been a great help and I thank you for coming, but I feel it would be better to hold the rest of the council meeting without your presence, so the others will feel at ease."

Sydni looked to Willy, who had become their spokesperson. "We will do what you wish, Alar. We will wait back at Chakdon's house for word from you."

Alar bowed ever so slightly and said, "Thank you."

Dekonal placed a hand on Willy's forearm. Patting her hand, he said, "We will wait for you at your house."

"We could be a long time."

"I understand. We'll wait."

They turned to leave, and Histab stood in front of Willy, squinting his eyes and staring. After a moment, he asked, "Is what they say true? Did you kill a Gaza-Kan with nothing but a knife?"

Willy nodded. "What they say is true."

"You have my respect for that much, off-worlder, but your test will come."

Histab stepped aside and Willy and Sydni exited. Once outside, they were certain someone was watching them from the door, but they did not turn around to look. Instead they headed for Chakdon's house. "Test," Sydni said in Hingandu. Then in English she continued, "What do you think he meant by that?"

Willy shrugged. "I just don't know. The only test that I have heard about is the thing Quistqui called Unproven. What that man meant, I do not know. I am almost afraid to ask."

* * * *

When Histab turned away from the door and said that they were gone, the council broke into bedlam again, until finally, fed up with their unruliness, Alar shouted for quiet. "I will not tolerate this behavior in my council chamber. If you have something to say, you will have my permission first." Several members raised their hands, but she shook her head. "No. I give no such permission at this time. Wait until you hear what visions Chakdon and Dekonal have seen about these visitors. Then, and only then will we discuss this." Turning so that all could see the anger on her face she spat into the fire and said, "Now sit and be patient."

Everyone who was not already seated moved quickly to their place and remained silent. Alar looked around again, once everyone was seated, she turned to Chakdon and Dekonal, who still stood by the fire. "Chakdon, Dekonal, if you would."

They both nodded as Alar took a seat in the place where they had sat with Willy and Sydni. Dekonal looked to Chakdon to begin, and Chakdon said, "Since Dekonal was the first one to see a vision with the off-worlders, I will let her begin." Then, in nothing more than a whisper, Chakdon said, "Don't be nervous. Tell them all."

Dekonal cleared her throat and glanced around the meeting hall before she spoke. "I saw war coming for a long time, but I see it loom even closer now, a strange war, unlike any we have seen before. We are facing a war with a race from the sky, a war with the Jolabwe, and a war that will cost us many things. But in this war, I saw strangers, who at first I thought were fighting against us, but now realize that they are fighting for us. They have come to our aid, and these strangers are Willy and Sydni. I do not usually speak of my personal affairs, as my father taught me that it is best not to let others know what is to directly happen, life, death, love, but I must share with you today, so that you will see what is in the hearts of these strangers." The fire cracked and sparks rose into the air. Dekonal was uncertain if the warmth she felt was from the fire or her own feelings.

"Willy is a kind soul, a fierce hunter, and a fearless warrior. In my vision, I have seen great happiness come into his life, and overwhelming sadness. But you must know this of him." She pointed around the room as she paused. "He not only fights for us, hunts for us, and cares for us, he and his sister become one of us."

"I have foreseen that day in which I take him as a mate. The day of our ceremony is a perfect summer day, and the night when our child is born the stars cover the sky. He is destined to be one of us." She bowed her head and looked into the fire. "You must know that I already love him, but that happened long before he ever came to meet me."

Dekonal did not enjoy opening up to the council, many would say she saw only that which her heart would see. They did not understand the way of the visions, and that one had no will over them. She sat facing the fire, not wanting to meet their eyes; she could hear the murmurs run through the crowd, which halted abruptly when Alar cleared her throat.

Chakdon bent down and placed a hand on his daughter's shoulder and squeezed. He knew her well enough. She did not feel like talking, but he wanted to reassure her. "Members of the council, I have not seen as much of the off-worlders as my daughter, but I have seen plenty. I have accepted both of them into my home to eat at my table, talk with my family, and sleep under my roof. This I assure you would not happen if I had not seen them as anything other than friends. I have seen disturbing pictures of war, and of many great losses. The Jolabwe will move against us, and something tells me that we may have to revert to old ways to put an end to this. We may have to call upon the ancient to secure our future, but in the end I still see the off-worlders living among us as family.

"We have lived in peace for many, many years. Some of the off-worlders are not friendly as the two that are here, and their greed sends them after our mountains' lifeblood. I wish my words did not sound of doom and despair, but some hard times will visit us. Of these two, you must see goodness. If you spurn them and send them away, our lives could follow a more drastic path."

Chakdon looked around the room silently and stopped at Alar, who he told, "That is all I have to say."

Chakdon then sat down next to Dekonal and tossed a few more logs on the fire, as Alar stood and walked around the circumference of the room. "You all know how wise both Chakdon and Dekonal are, and how correct their visions have been ever since they were children. Do you remember the tale of Chakdon's grandfather and his visions? Remember when the wise council pushed aside his visions and pursued their own plan? Histab remembers, for he is one of the few who heeded the advice of Chakkan. Histab remembers the rivers running red with Hingandu blood."

Alar looked at Histab, which he clearly took as a symbol to speak his mind about that day, so he did, "I remember it well, and still I can see it in my dreams. I trusted old Chakkan, as my father, his friend, did. I took my war party aside and waited above, on the cliffs of the three rivers, knowing what Chakkan had told me. Had I not been there, to rain deadly attack down on the Jolabwe, surely many more would have died. I trust not only Chakdon, but his daughter, Dekonal. I suggest everyone else listen as well."

Alar nodded to Histab, who nodded back. "We will not listen to arguments today, but we will vote. A show of hands for all those in favor of accepting Willy and Sydni into our village and listening to their counsel."

CHAPTER 12

Madak made Doqui bring chairs out into the courtyard, into the warm evening air, with the sky still lit from the fading day. She had squeezed a pitcher full of Gombo juice and gave Willy, Sydni, and Doqui each a glass. "The council could take a long time, or they could be done soon."

Willy said, "Tastes like a cross between kiwi and pineapple juice." Turning to Madak, he added, "Kiwi and pineapple are fruits back on our home."

Sydni looked at the lime-green juice and then sipped it. "The juice is excellent," Sydni said. "Thank you."

Madak smiled at her and said, "You are welcome. I am glad that you feel comfortable in my home. I know how Dekonal feels about you both, and Chakdon trusts you more than he trusts some Hingandu."

Willy smiled. "I know that we are different, but I thank you for allowing us into your home and treating us like family."

Madak looked at Doqui, who had been staring at Sydni, and she said, "Doqui, mind your manners. Do not stare at our guests."

Doqui looked down and said, "Sorry."

"Really, I don't mind," Sydni said. "We have gone to many worlds and seen many people, but it takes time to become used to them." Pausing, she leaned a little closer to Madak and spoke a little softer, "What I don't trust is when someone watches from afar and will not approach."

"What?" Madak said.

Sydni pointed to a darkened window, where Quistqui could just be seen within, watching Sydni. Madak saw him just as he disappeared. "I apologize for him. He has been acting strangely ever since you arrived, and we had just made it past a point where he had started to trust Willy."

"He will come around," Doqui said.

Snapping Doqui another quick look, Madak demanded, "What has he told you?"

Doqui shook his head and said, "Nothing. We discussed how different she looked, but that is all."

"Well, I apologize, Sydni. I just don't know what he thinks. I think the stress of his mating approaching is getting to him."

Sydni glanced at Willy, but he was staring at the door of the courtyard. A moment later the door burst open, with Dekonal running toward them. Willy, moving faster than Sydni remembered that he could, jumped up and met her halfway.

Dekonal nearly leapt into Willy's arms and without a word started kissing him. Willy held her. Their kiss turned into a hug, and Willy wondered what was wrong, because he had seen tears streaming down her face. Her voice was raspy and thick with emotion as she whispered over and over, "I love you."

Running one hand down through her hair, he said, "I love you, too. What is wrong?"

"Nothing, Willy. They have accepted you and Sydni. The whole council, with a unanimous vote, voted to accept both of you into our tribe." She pulled her head back so she could look into his eyes. "I had to tell them about us and what I saw and how I felt, and when they released us after the vote, I ran all the way back here because I had to see you."

Willy smiled and chuckled. "So you cry because your heart is full of joy?"

"Yes, now nothing can stop us from being together." She wiped away some tears, and Willy set her down. "But having to tell all of them has made me realize just how much I really do love you, and exactly how long I have loved you." Suddenly she stopped herself, afraid that she would scare him off, but then she looked up, and he was staring at her, his head cocked to one side.

She did not need to worry about scaring him away, his heart was beating faster at her confession. Speaking softly, Willy said, "I have loved you since the day I first saw you, and you are correct. Nothing can stand in our way of coming together, and we will be together forever."

They hugged again, and for several minutes they were in their own world and time stood still. They each saw the possibilities stretch out before them and the happy life that awaited them; neither wanted to let the moment pass or the other one to let go, but the approaching footsteps broke into their world. When they parted, they realized that several people were there, watching them. Alar was standing at the front, smiling. "You and your sister are free to come and go, but we will ask for your counsel on how to deal with your people coming to our planet."

Willy nodded. "Of course."

"We will not bother you now," she said, nodding toward Dekonal. "But as time goes by, I will want to ask you some questions."

"Let me ask you this. Is there a place where my people can take some of the liquid that is at your ceremony site?"

Alar looked at Douka and several others before she turned back, saying, "No. That is forbidden."

"Forbidden?"

Douka was shaking his head. "We cannot allow your people to destroy the land to take that. We call it Arzimin."

"My people use this as our fuel already. They mine it on other planets."

"Then they do not need ours," Klisk said.

Willy let his shoulders drop. "They need a place to mine it. Our home is very far away."

Alar stepped forward and placed a hand on Willy's shoulder. "We do not have time to discuss this right now. Your people do not have such a pure source of Arzimin, and they cannot be allowed to have it."

Willy was flabbergasted and left speechless. How did they know what his people had, or even what their source could be? How could they know about the purity of their source? Finally he found his words and started to ask, "How could you..."

Alar, sounding a bit impatient, said, "Willy, as I have said, we do not have time to go into this. Given time we will discuss it at length."

The contingency turned to leave, and to their backs, Willy spoke in a very low tone, "They will end up fighting you for it. It goes against what we believe, but there are those who are evil."

Everyone had paused at his words, but continued to file out of the courtyard. Only Chakdon turned around. He looked very sad and he nodded. "We know this already, but we will be prepared. In time you will understand as well." Then looking past Willy and forcing a smile, Chakdon looked at his wife and waved. "I will be home later, do not wait to eat."

"Should I come along, too, Father?" Dekonal asked moving forward.

He smiled what Dekonal would have called a fatherly smile. "No child, you stay with Willy, I will represent us for the rest of the day."

"Thank you."

Chakdon retreated with the rest, leaving Willy still somewhat speechless. Willy turned to Sydni, who was walking up. "Did you hear that?" he asked her. "They don't understand." Then he turned to Dekonal, "You don't understand, Love. The city that floats in the sky has powerful weapons. The council cannot just let a fight begin."

Dekonal smiled, and tiptoeing, she kissed his cheek. "They do not patronize you, Willy. We are just prepared to stop off-worlders. Trust me on this, I will explain, or Douka will, in time."

Looking into her eyes, in which there was no fear of the mighty UWC Orion or its vast arsenal and battalions of troops, Willy knew he would have to wait and see what had them so confident. "I trust you." He paused and glanced at Dekonal. "And because I trust you, I also believe in you and I will wait."

Willy's scanner started to beep in his pack. Sydni asked, "Didn't you put it on silence before the council meeting?"

"Yes. It must be a priority message." He went to his pack and pulled out his scanner, and as he examined the screen, he said, "Huh, two messages." He read through the initial report that Conrad had sent top priority. Then raising an eyebrow, he said, "Interesting."

Sydni's scanner beeped and she started reading the message as Willy flipped to the second message. As he listened to the chatter back and forth between Gallagher and Chambers, his hands started to shake. "Son-of-a-bitch!" he shouted in English before he realized it.

"What is so wrong?" Sydni asked, moving closer. "This is quite interesting."

The report from Gallagher stopped and Willy replayed it and handed it to Sydni to listen. She too cursed, but mumbled it under her breath. "We need to talk to Bucky," she said as she handed back his scanner. "Soon."

Still speaking in English, Willy said, "They have to be told now that the Hingandu are human. We cannot let them be attacked." Willy dropped his head and said, "I would have to fight on the side of the Hingandu."

"Let's just hope we can stop it before it gets to that point. I cannot lose you, brother. No way! No how!"

"What is wrong?" Dekonal asked.

"The changing of the world."

"What?"

Shaking his head, Willy said, "Nothing, Dekonal, but I must return to my home. There are problems brewing that need to be attended to." Leaning close, he kissed her.

* * * *

Once Willy and Sydni were on the deck, Willy tossed his helmet in the compartment behind him and removed his scanner from its docking station.

His anger had not abated, as he had hoped it would, but Bucky would know how to proceed and how to contact the correct people at UWC. As he climbed down, he cursed to himself. He needed time to cool off, but more importantly, he needed time for the Hingandu people.

Sydni met him and they turned in their flight report to the officer on the deck before they left. As they turned a corner, Sydni stopped short, but knew there was no way to turn back without causing suspicion, Gallagher had already seen her. Willy came around the corner and stopped next to his sister. Vladimir saluted as Gallagher said, "Hello, Commander Colton."

"Ambassador," Sydni greeted him.

"I am interested to know what you have learned of the Hingandu people."

"We need more time..." Willy started.

"To complete any studies," Sydni finished.

"And to find a decent collection site. Ambassador, you cannot force these people to give you a collection site."

"Easy, Commander. We'll give them enough time. I was over-eager when I ordered the other team down. I will not make the same mistake twice."

Willy grumbled something under his breath as he pushed past Vladimir. "What was that?" Vladimir asked.

Spinning back, Willy said, "How come I keep getting the feeling that we are not being told everything?"

"What do you mean by that?" Gallagher asked.

Holding up his hands, Willy said, "Nothing," before he turned and continued down the hall.

Sydni walked past Vladimir and Gallagher. "Good day, gentlemen. You will have our report as soon as possible."

Sydni caught up with Willy two corridors away and matched his stride. "Do you want to give us away?" She lowered her voice as two sailors, passed them. "Why don't you just tell him what we know?"

The elevator to the bridge was several decks away, and Willy stopped. "I am sorry, Sydni, but that bastard is way out of line. It was all I could do to not throttle him right there."

"And where do you think you are going now?"

"To see Bucky. Captain will know how to handle this."

Sydni laid a hand on her brother's arm. Her voice softened as she said, "Look, Will, we can't just run to Bucky until we have thought this out, maybe even talk with Chief Yamamora. If we don't have a plan or some back up, Bucky might just be obligated to arrest us for spying or treason. Think about what we have, and what you are going to say."

A growl emanated from deep within Willy; his claws flexed and he closed his eyes. Several deep breaths later, he said, "You are correct. We can't just barge in."

"And you need to cool off."

Nodding, he said, "Yes. I need to cool off."

"Go clean up, take a shower, and then meet me in my room and we'll go over things." Willy started smiling at her as she back-pedaled down the hall, motioning for him to follow her. "Come on."

Willy followed her as they headed for their quarters.

* * * *

Willy took a long, steaming shower in his attempt to relax, and it was starting to work. Sydni had been correct that rushing into Bucky's office and demanding that Gallagher be removed would not help their cause. He had been so blinded by hatred and his love for Dekonal, that he had almost committed a fatal judgment call. For that matter, his manner with Gallagher had been wrong. If Gallagher suspected anything, he could blow the lid off of everything. If it was exposed that they had been illegally listening in to Gallagher's calls, they could be court-martialed.

A court-martial would start with a jail sentence, if not worse, and Willy could never be pent-up in a cell, especially not now, when he was so close to realizing a dream he had never even dared to dream, that there were a people like him in the universe. As he turned off the shower, he took a deep breath, breathing the recycled air, longing for the fresh, fragrant air of the Hingandu forest. Soon he would be back there, living as a Hingandu.

As he toweled off, he walked into his bedroom, and instantly he knew something was wrong. A smell. What was that? He grabbed his BDU pants and was slipping them on as he leaped into the living room, heading for a weapon. He came face to face with a UWC Ambassadorial Guard, who Willy inadvertently knocked over. Smoke from the over-ridden door hung in the air, and Vladimir aimed a pulse pistol at Willy. "By order of the UWC Ambassadorial command, you are under arrest, Commander William Colton," Vladimir said with a smile. "You can come in, Ambassador. We have him."

Willy glanced around him, looking for an escape or a weapon, but Vladimir gestured with the gun by flicking it side to side, saying, "Go ahead, Commander. Try and go for a weapon, because I have no problem with frying you on the spot."

Gallagher walked in and said, "Good work, Vladimir."

"What the hell are you doing in my room, Ambassador?"

"Looking for evidence, Commander. Did you find it, Vladimir?"

"On the counter, Sir."

Willy was fast, but he knew he had no chance of beating a pulse pistol, especially when the person holding it hated him. His only consolation was that Sydni would have erased the information from her scanner, and he would be the only one who would be implicated. Gallagher picked up the scanner and looked at the antenna and asked, "Is this what you meant, Vladimir?"

"Yes, sir. It can be used to extend range on a scanner, forward messages to another scanner, or intercept calls, if the correct hardware is in place on an optical line."

Gallagher looked up and said, "Do you have anything to say for yourself before I turn on this scanner, Commander?"

Willy stared at Gallagher and said, "You are a cowardly dog, who would sell out his government to gain an extra paycheck from the likes of Chambers. What you are doing is not only morally corrupt, but illegal."

Gallagher powered on the scanner and quickly found the files of his and Chambers' conversations. He did not play them long, but his face went ashen before it flamed into a bright red. "Treasonous, arrogant, bastard," Gallagher sputtered. "I will hang you out to dry."

Vladimir talked into a headpiece, "Unit two, this is Vladimir. Status?" He listened intently for several minutes and then looked at Gallagher, who was awaiting word. "Commander Sydni Colton's room is clean. No listening devices. No files in her scanner. Nothing. She is demanding to know what is going on."

Turning to Willy, Gallagher said, "So you acted alone on this, Commander? That is why you were an ass in the hall this morning and your sister was cordial."

"I know what you are, Gallagher. I will see to it that the whole galaxy knows what you and Chambers are up to." Then turning on Vladimir, Willy said, "I know what you are too, Vladimir, and Chief Su's injuries will not go unpunished the next time I get my hands on you."

"Shut up, Colton. Hands behind your back. Wilson, put the restraints on him."

The guard Willy had knocked over moved behind Willy, carrying a stun stick. He clamped on hand braces and then leg shackles as he held the stick to Willy's back. "Secured, sir," Wilson said.

More guards showed up at the door, and Sydni pushed past them, wearing a now-wet jumpsuit. She had been in the shower too. "What the hell is going on here?"

Shutting down the scanner, Gallagher turned to Sydni and said, "Commander Colton, your brother has been spying on me, and due to your closeness with him, we couldn't take the chance that both of you were not. That is why we invaded your privacy."

"Is it true, Willy?" she asked turning to him, knowing she was his only chance. Willy just looked past her, not meeting her eyes and remaining silent. "Look at me," she said softly.

Willy looked into her eyes, and he felt like a pent-up animal heading for slaughter. She could see the near panic in his eyes, and she knew that somehow she had to do something, but for now she had to keep up the charade. "Why?" she asked. "Why didn't you tell me?"

"I-I," Willy stuttered and glanced at Gallagher, straightened out and said, "I have nothing to say. I am truly sorry, Sydni."

"Get moving," Vladimir said again waving the pistol.

As Willy started shuffling out the door, Gallagher turned to Sydni and said, "I trust you will secure your brother's door for us. I am truly sorry that it had to come to this."

They left Sydni standing there, wondering how this had happened; they had been so careful to avoid detection. She turned back into the room and glanced around, making a mental note of just what Willy would want if all he could have was what would fit into his ship.

* * * *

Sydni's room was dark and quiet, with music playing softly in the distance. After half an hour of arguing with Bucky's secretary, Sydni had given up and went back to her room to think, lying on the couch with her arm across her eyes. Bucky was in his monthly meeting that took place via long distance vid. This would take him all day, and he had been given orders that short of an all-out attack by some unknown space source, he was not to be disturbed. But what could she tell him? She would just have to take action herself, and by herself alone.

Several times they had played war games that involved a riot in the brig, or a hostage situation, and she was starting to formulate her plan to break out Willy. It was the only solution she could think of, and the action would ban her to living on the surface with the Hingandu, without Conrad the rest of her life. Willy would risk everything had it been she who had been captured, even his own freedom, so it was all she could do. When third shift came around she would start loading his ship and hers with the essentials that they would need.

Her door slipped open, spilling light from the hallway in a line across the room. A shadow crossed the doorway and the door shut. She could smell Conrad's cologne and she began to wonder what she could tell him. She felt his weight on the couch next to her. Removing her arm, she scooted up a little to get a better look at him.

"What is wrong, Sydni?"

She reached up and touched his cheekbone, just under his eye, and then ran a finger across his eyebrow. "You know that I love you, Conrad."

"Yes."

"Then what I am about to tell you must never leave this room."

"Of course," he said, his accent thickening a little.

"Gallagher had Willy arrested today. Willy was caught with the tapes of Gallagher's conversations with Chambers."

"Oh, my God," Conrad breathed out. "Is there anything we can do?"

"No, not we, but me. There is something I can do."

"What?"

She pressed her index finger to his lips and shushed him. "I am going to break him out," she whispered.

Grabbing her hand and removing it from his face, he said, "To where? Don't you think that they will assume it was you and come looking for you?"

Sydni nodded and said, "I have thought a long time about it all, and I don't like the answers I have come up with, but Willy will go insane in the brig. Can you see him in a penal institution?" She sat up more, to look into his eyes. "My brother has been there for me all my life, and I have been there for him all my life, and if it means escaping to planetside and living among the Hingandu for ever and ever, I will do it." Conrad went to speak again, but she shook her head, stopping him. "No, I do not like the idea of separating myself from the rest of my known galaxy, and especially not from you. I do not ask you to like what I am going to do, but you must understand."

Conrad shook his head and held both her hands tightly. "Is there no other way?"

"Not that doesn't endanger you, me, or the other scouts, and Chief Yamamora."

"Do the other scouts know about this?"

"Lord, no! I cannot ask or involve them." Sydni replied

"It would seem that they would lay their lives down for you."

"And Willy and I for them, but we cannot ask them to give up their family and home for our personal safety."

Conrad sighed audibly and leaned his forehead against hers. "It pains me greatly to say this, my lovely Sydni, but I understand, and I will not stand in your way."

Sydni's chest tightened; and if her love had been a swimming pool, it would have just spilled over the sides. Her lips found his and for a long time they just held each other and kissed. When he pulled his head up, he whispered, "How can I help?"

Focused on his lips, it took her a moment to realize what he had said, and then she just shook her head, "Just love me. I cannot risk your future for me. Stay clear and act like you know nothing."

He brushed his lips across hers and whispered, "I must. I have to. I love you and Willy is my friend. Please."

"Run any kind of interference you can, but do not be associated with us when we go. Do that for me, Conrad, I cannot allow you to be caught up in this."

"That is all?" He asked, his voice almost full of desperation. The one woman he could truly say he loved, was planning on asking to marry him, and all he could do was watch her go.

Just for a moment, he felt an enormous weight on his chest, but Sydni lifted it off and set it aside when she said, "Make love to me." He knew his choice was already made. He crouched next to the couch and scooped Sydni up in his arms. She clasped her hands behind his neck and held on as he carried her into the bedroom.

They made love and held each other all through the evening, until finally, between ten and eleven, as Conrad was dozing off, Sydni got up, kissed his forehead, and whispered, "Goodbye, Lover."

Once she was gone, he got up and went to his desk. Once his computer was powered up, he began an inventory search.

* * * *

Sydni was exhausted, and she would have felt better if she could have Willy by her side working this mission, especially since so much was riding on it. It had taken her several trips, but she stuffed both of their ships with gear and clothes. She routed several hanger functions through her scanner so she could control them. Now she was lugging a bag of gear through the access tunnels. As she crawled along, she tried to remember a saying Willy had picked up from Jean-Pierre. With a smile she whispered, "Strike fast and hard, before they have time to blink."

Once she was in position, she brought her pack up alongside of her and fished out the pinpoint laser drill. It was mainly used for fine detailed work and craftsmanship work, but the scouts had learned that the ship's sensors did not register the small intrusion on an inner wall. Sydni had done the exact procedure before, when trying to disarm several Marines who had taken the brig hostage during a battle simulation. She knew where to drill without disrupting any ship functions. Once the pinhole of light shone into the access tube, she pulled out a breathing mask and slipped it over her head.

Her heart pounded against her chest. Never before had any mission brought forth such a reaction. However, her brother's life hinged upon this mission. Out of the same pack she pulled a bottle of gas that had a name longer then ten crewmen's names put together, but the slang term used for it was migraine in a can, because when you woke up, you had one hell of a headache. They always had some on hand; after all, it was a scout's mission to be prepared. She placed a small suction cup over the pinpoint hole and marked the time on her watch. It would take exactly two minutes through that size hole to affect the guards.

Taking the other mask she had brought and Willy's flight suit, she left the bottle fully opened and shimmied back down the tube to the grate, leading to the hallway. When the two minutes were up, she scanned the hall, and slid out of the tube with a pulse pistol in her right hand, flight suit over her shoulders and the extra mask in her left hand. Glancing both ways she saw nobody. She ran to the door, took a deep breath and prayed she didn't have to shoot anyone.

Willy had been sitting in his cell for hours. A UWC Ambassadorial Guard had brought a meager meal for dinner, which Willy had left untouched next to the power cell door. He sat cross-legged in the center of the floor meditating. He prayed that for Sydni's sake she would not try and break him out. She deserved to be happy with Conrad, but he knew he needed to get out; he needed to help the Hingandu, who just did not understand what they were up against.

It was about three-thirty in the morning when he first heard the noises, and wondered just what was going on outside in the main control room. He figured that Sydni was on her way. The light on his door went out and he stood up and breathed deeply.

Sydni ran in through the doors tossing him a mask. Once he slipped it on, she tossed him his flight suit. He slipped it on over his pants and zipped it up. "Come on, she said, "we have an express flight holding for us, heading planetside."

"Syd," he said as she turned to go back out. "Thanks. I know what a sacrifice you are making."

"It would have been more of a sacrifice to see you rot in here."

That was all she said before she turned and ran. He was on her heels, only stopping at the main door to check the hall again. Empty. They tossed the masks in the brig door as it closed and they headed down the hall. Soon they were in the access tubes again, where she had hidden another weapon and two cloaks. "Wear it. It may cause just enough confusion to let us slip away. I don't think Gallagher has told anyone that you are under arrest, and Bucky was in the two-day meeting."

Willy took point and sped through the access tubes with the speed of a man possessed. She stayed close behind, knowing that he was now a very motivated man, who would stop at nothing to get his ship free of the Orion and bound planetside.

* * * *

Vladimir was up early; the excitement of having Willy Colton in the brig left him unable to sleep and restless. He was walking the decks and for the first time in a while, he was actually in a fantastic mood. His stride was long and fast, but ahead he saw a cloaked figure cross the hall he was in, and his heart started pounding into his throat. Shaking his head, he said aloud, "It can't be. If he had broken out of the brig, alarms would have sounded, calls would have been made."

Moments later, Vladimir found himself running down the hall. There was one unmistakable place that hallway led to, the hangar. Vladimir slowed himself down, not necessarily wanting to run full tilt into a very angry Commander Colton. He had to respect his speed and agility. Vladimir cursed himself for not being armed.

The hatchway to the hangar was just closing as it came into his view. He walked up and peered through the thick, distorted glass, and there he was in his unmistakable cloak, striding toward a scout ship that was ready for takeoff.

He punched the hatchway access button and walked straight after the cloaked figure, who seemed not to hear or notice him. Vladimir caught the cloaked Commander Colton just as he reached for the short ladder to the cockpit, and Vladimir spun him around with his fist flying to cold-cock him, but the female features and voice stopped him just short of punching Sydni Colton. "What the hell is going on?" Sydni demanded. "Is that some new sort of salute?"

"No Ma'am. I, well, I thought that you were the other Commander Colton." Vladimir snapped into a salute and stood arrow straight. "The cloak, Ma'am. I thought it was your brother."

"You son-of-a-bitch, you have him locked up in the brig, don't you?"

"Yes, Ma'am."

"Well I need to think, and I do that best from the cockpit while dodging asteroids and satellites. Any problem with that?"

"No. I am sorry."

Then a ship on the far side of Sydni's fired up its engines, and Vladimir looked up, as if he could see over the nose of the ship. "Wait a minute," he said, realization crossing his face.

Sydni knew their time was up, so she struck hard, and she struck fast. As her foot came full into his crotch, Vladimir blinked. As he doubled over, she brought her knee up into his chin, sending him backwards.

Before a groan escaped his lips, she was climbing into her cockpit and firing off her engines. As she slipped her scanner into her docking station and pulled her helmet on, she heard a voice in her earpiece say, "You do not have authorized flight plan, power down your engines now." She glanced at Willy, sitting in his cockpit, and he gave her the thumbs up.

The code she had to bring their systems to a halt was so simple, it would boggle the techs' minds, but with one access number typed into her scanner, the retention beams were off-line, and the safety shield to the outer door opened. Changing frequencies, she said, "Scout two ready."

Willy, laughing on the other end and said, "Scout one ready. Ladies first."

Lights glowed red in the hangar. Scramble alert had been called, and a quick glance showed several Marines charging in the hanger door. Sydni punched her engines and shot down the hangar and into space. She flicked on her ship's cloak before she was even out of the hangar. Her ship wavered in front of Willy and was gone.

Willy did the same as she had and said, "Break Beta two, now!"

As the ships emerged from the hanger, Sydni broke to the left and straight up over the top of the ship, while Willy broke right and angled down toward the nose of the ship. They each set their frequencies to bounce off of nearby satellites so that the Orion could not hone in on their communication signal.

"This is XO Cho, who has left the ship? I order you to return immediately." Then they could hear her in a muffled voice call for the captain.

Neither Sydni nor Willy responded. They were maneuvering to head planetside using the moon and two passing satellites as cover. Sydni had removed the transponder modules so the Orion could not track their ships. That would have proved fatal; two smart missiles would have stopped them from ever making it to the moon.

From the chatter of the open channel, they heard techs try to explain why they couldn't spot them to the XO, who was ready to start firing blindly into space to stop those that exited her ship without permission on her watch. They heard another tech try and explain that there were no transponder codes answering the computer's commands.

Then, as Willy and Sydni were halfway to the water moon, Bucky's commanding voice came over the radio. "What the hell is going on here?"

"Two ships took off without permission, they left one man down, who is on the way to the infirmary and they shut down functions in hanger C, and all retention beams are down."

"Where are they?" Bucky asked.

"Cloaked."

"Scout ships. This is Captain Dollinger, I order you to respond immediately. Who the hell is in my sky?"

Willy couldn't resist. Bucky was still his captain and a friend. "Bucky, it is me."

"Who? Willy?"

"Yes, Sir."

"What the hell are you doing?"

"Kind of hard to tell you everything right now, but you will find out soon enough. I have just escaped from the brig, where Gallagher and Vladimir were holding me."

"What for? This is insane."

"Bucky, you said find proof. I had it, but they caught me with it."

"What was it?"

"Conversations between Gallagher and Chambers."

Willy maneuvered around a satellite, putting it between him and the ship. "Aw, piss and vinegar, Willy."

"Yeah, well, they are planning on taking that which the Hingandu will not freely give them."

"Coppertroid?"

"Yeah. They are going to start a battle between the Jolabwe and Hingandu, to move the Hingandu off some land that is perfect for an extraction site."

"That is a tall accusation."

"You don't know all of it yet, Bucky. The Hingandu, they are like me. Bucky, the Hingandu are Human, mutated like myself, and brought here a long, long time ago."

"You must be joking."

"No joke. I cannot let Gallagher interfere with their lives. I will not let Gallagher interfere with their lives."

"Look, turn back, Willy, Sydni, and we will work it all out."

"Yes," Gallagher's voice crackled over the speakers. "Turn back."

Bucky nearly screamed, "Get off this frequency, Ambassador."

"I have evidence that Commander Colton illegally tapped into the Ambassadorial secured line and taped conversations that were classified."

"Shut the hell up, Gallagher," Bucky said.

"See, Bucky, he already has had time to doctor up the evidence. I don't have a case against him. I am gone."

"And you would condemn Sydni to life on the planet too?" Bucky asked.

Sydni said, "Don't play that game, Bucky, I am not doing anything I have not considered thoroughly. Life among humans that look like my brother holds no fear for me."

They heard Bucky sigh into the mike. "Willy, I will look into this, and see what I can do. Hang on. How can we contact you while you are planetside?"

"Don't try, I will contact you."

Bucky's voice then commanded the bridge as he left the mike open and said, "Stand down. Cancel red alert and recall any ships that made it out during the scramble. Send a HAZMAT and medical team to the brig, and tell that slimeball ambassador I want to see him immediately."

The frequency went dead. "Well, we are fugitives now," Willy said. "How does it feel to be an outlaw?"

Sydni was unsure about that feeling, but she did feel like someone had parked a shuttle in her stomach. All she said, was "It feels more like I tore my heart out and left it on the Orion, lying down next to Conrad."

In the excitement, Willy had forgotten all about it, and all he could muster to respond was, "Sorry." And then after another minute, he said, "Maybe Bucky can fix things for us." After that, they flew on in silence.

Chapter 13

Because the mountains where the Hingandu lived were enshrouded by darkness, only hours from dawn, they used their infrared and landed in a small clearing, leaving their ships on cloak. Willy didn't bother looking to see what all his sister had brought of his belongings, because as of now, his past was gone and soon he would be Hingandu. But his first thoughts were of Sydni, who he could not see yet. Suddenly she appeared as a dark shadow as she stepped away from her ship. He leaped down from the ladder and ran to her, hugging her as they met.

"As I sat in that cell, half of me hoped you would not take action, but try and go through Bucky."

"I tried, but when I couldn't get through, I knew I had to act. It also seemed like the most logical time to do it. If I had given Gallagher and Vladimir enough time, Lord knows what they would have done. So I took Jean-Pierre's saying to heart and acted."

"Very effective. What was it they said about a man down and heading for Sick Bay?"

Sydni smiled and shrugged. "Not so much a man as an ass. Vladimir tried to stop me, and he was starting to realize what was going on when you fired off your engines. I hit hard and fast and dropped him in his tracks."

Willy winced, and in the starlight, Sydni could see his face. Then he looked around and sniffed the air. "Freedom," he said. Then turning back to her, he said, "It is too bad about Doc, though. Too bad he could not be comfortable in the wide open. He would have made a great addition to our expedition."

Sydni pictured him lying there in the darkness, peaceful and content. She wondered if he was awake yet, knowing she was gone, or was he still peacefully sleeping in the silence of the morning. A tear welled up in her eye and spilled down her cheek. She turned away and said, "I couldn't have asked him to come, to run with us, give up all he has worked for." The sadness in her voice was evident to Willy, and he placed a hand on her shoulder. She continued, "They will hunt us, you know. Bucky will not be able to stop Gallagher and Chambers for long; they have had this planned all along."

"That is why I had to be here. That is why I had to escape. I have to be here to help them fight for their beautiful land. Maybe we can hook you two up..."

"Not right now," Sydni interrupted, patting his hand. "Look, I just need some time to assimilate the severity of what we have done. I don't even want to get my hopes up right now, I need some time."

"Fair enough."

Sydni pulled out her scanner and flipped it on. She ran several scans before she hung it on her side with the detection system running. She motioned toward a tree with her thumb and said, I am going to sit down for a few, do you want to do anything before dawn?"

"No. I'll stand guard while you rest up. We'll hike into the village when you wake."

She walked over and curled up at the base of a tree. Totally overcome by emotion and exhaustion, she was asleep in moments. Willy quietly checked his supplies and compartments, seeing what all Sydni had stuffed into them. He turned on the scanner she had plugged into the docking station; it wasn't set up like his, but he could fix that over several days. From behind the cockpit, in the passenger compartment, he pulled out a case that held a rifle. He found his 7mm magnum and opened and closed the bolt. He loaded it and flipped the scope from regular to night vision. The new scanner would have informed him of any intrusion, but he scanned the tree line anyway.

He would move all of the supplies to a safe haven once they had established a base camp, but he doubted now that they could stay at the village. That would be putting too many of their people at risk for just two off-worlders. Dekonal would not like the separation, but she would be able to see him whenever she wanted and as often as she wanted. He tried to picture Conrad living wild among the Hingandu, and he had to stifle the laugh that came to his lips. He remembered Conrad's first day planetside when he and Sydni had brought him down to see the Coppertroid site, and how skittish he had been.

Willy leaned back and stared up at the stars. He had grown up memorizing the skies above his forest, now he had the same stars, just a different configuration. A satellite slowly made its way across the maze of lights. "What have I done," he said softly. "I was so arrogant. Forgive me, Sydni."

The remaining hours passed quickly, with Sydni sleeping against the tree and Willy staring up at the sky. Once, as the sunrise started to lighten the sky, the Orion passed overhead, just another star among the millions. Willy paced around the clearing as he was growing restless, but he knew that he must be patient and could not change the course of things in a day. Finally he sat cross-legged where he could watch Sydni sleeping.

It started with one bird singing, soon the air erupted with chatter, and finally streaks of sunlight filled the sky and brightened treetops. The flutter of wings brought birds across the open sky, one white and yellow parrot-sized bird came down only inches in front of him. It nervously looked around before it started rooting through the grasses. It found something to eat and continued searching the grasses. The bird jumped and then flew away. Willy looked up, and Sydni was sitting up, looking at him.

"Wow," she said. "I guess I was tired." She stretched her arms and arched her back and said, "I take it that it is not a dream I had last night, and we've not returned to the Orion." Willy shook his head. With a yawn, she continued, "I didn't think so. I need to loosen up."

Setting down her scanner and pistol, she began to stretch, and having nothing better to do, Willy set his new scanner down next to his rifle and started shadowing his sister's moves. Once they had stretched out, they ran through several sets of calisthenics. The morning was shaping up to be warm, and Willy stripped off his flight suit between sets. After an hour of working, they stopped and started stretching again.

"So what's your plan?" she asked.

"We need to make some kind of base camp. I figure we take just what we need for now and go see the Hingandu and explain. We will ask them where we can make a camp so when we become hunted, they will not come to any harm."

"Sounds good. Just like an extended camping trip."

Willy smiled at her. "Look, I know that you don't want to talk about it, but when you do, I am here. My arrogance and my mouth got us into trouble, I will do anything I can to make it up to you."

Sydni grabbed her pistol and scanner and moved over next to Willy, who was staring down at the ground. She sat next to him and put her arm across his shoulders. "Will, all my life there has been one constant: you. From womb to crib, from school to academy and all through our career so far, you have been there for me. We have fought together; we have worked together, watched each other's backs and covered one another. How many heartaches have you sat through with me? And you pushed me to be what I am today. You were always so determined to be the best, the fastest, the strongest, the smartest, and I had to try and keep up."

Glancing at her sideways, Willy said, "You did damn good for all those distractions you always dealt with."

"You adjusted damn well for not having any distractions."

Willy laughed and it prompted Sydni to laugh as well. "I had distractions," he said, looking up into the sky. They were just different."

"Not to mention Phyllis Donnelley."

"Not to mention." Willy pictured Phyllis as he had last seen her on graduation day. They had a secret relationship for almost nine months their second year of high school, when her father accidentally found out. He had forbidden them to see or talk to each other. Her father had even threatened Willy with his life. Fred Donnelley had a long-standing prejudice against Willy, for no other reason than fear. "Given time, she forgot all about me."

"I doubt any woman would ever truly forget about you. Maybe she moved on, but no woman would be able to forget a man as distinguished as you." She patted his shoulder as she said that.

"I hated Fred Donnelley, and probably still do, but when we broke up it was because of him. Now I have become the reason that you have broken up with Doc."

"Stop it!" She said. "Never compare yourself with the likes of Fred Donnelley, and when you count it, I only just started dating Conrad, you have been with me much longer. I will deal with the loss, and I will ask for your help when I am feeling down or lonely, but for the first time in your life you have a chance at being truly happy. Concentrate on being happy."

"I will," he mumbled, still feeling sick over her situation.

"Promise?"

Never before had he gone back on a promise to her, and she knew he wouldn't now. He took several seconds to answer, but he said, "Promise."

"What the hell are you doing arresting one of my senior officers without consulting me first?" Bucky yelled. He was standing behind his desk leaning forward on his fists. "Look at the mess you have caused now."

"The mess I have caused?" Gallagher asked, his face starting to flush. "Your senior officer was listening in on my scrambled calls to my superiors."

"Let me hear them. Let me see your proof."

"They were of a sensitive nature, and they were erased."

"How convenient for you. If his allegations are correct, then it will be you and Chambers who are in trouble, not him."

"He himself admitted it, Captain. He told you that he was listening in on my conversations."

"I will start a full inquiry as of now, do not try and stand in my way, Ambassador. You are a long way from home and it is very, very cold outside."

"Are you threatening me, Captain?"

"No, I am letting you know where you stand on my ship."

"You best start a search for them, so they can be brought to justice."

"If that is who needs bringing to justice. And what do you know about the Hingandu being human? How about the link between the engines found on the planet and the fact that there are humans this far from our own civilization?"

"Humans," Gallagher spat the word out. "It was a last-ditch effort to throw us off his trail and divert our attention. There are no humans here, that is an impossibility. I will take this up through the UWC, Captain. You can trust me on that."

Bucky lowered his voice and said, "Trust me, Ambassador. I will report this to brass and I will get to the bottom of this, and if you and Chancellor Chambers are trying to pull a fast one while you are aboard my ship, I will hang you from the yard arm."

"Good day," Gallagher grumbled as he turned to leave.

"Good day." Then Bucky shouted out the door past Gallagher, "Sergeant, get me Admiral Oats, and get him ASAP."

Gallagher nearly ran through the halls to his office, and as he huffed and puffed his way into his office, he tried to say, "Get me Chambers, now."

All his secretary heard was Chambers, and she could guess the rest by his reaction. He almost never spoke with anyone else, so she connected to the Chancellor's office and waited.

Gallagher was pacing the length of his floor, wringing his hands. "How did this get out of hand? We have to stop this. What is Chambers going to say? Damn those Coltons, they could blow this whole operation up."

"Chancellor Chambers' office, Ambassador."

Gallagher ran around his desk in time to see Diane's image fade out as Chambers stepped in front of his camera. "Jasper, good news I hope."

"No, Sir. We have a problem." Gallagher paused and took a deep breath before he continued. "We have a serious problem."

"What happened?"

"Commander William Colton has found a way to cut into our scrambled line, and he was recording our messages. He had some of our more damaging conversations. Vladimir and I both became suspicious, so we arrested him, brigged him, and confiscated the scanner."

"So what's the problem?"

"Chancellor, during the night, his sister, Commander Sydni Colton broke him out of the brig and they escaped, putting Vladimir in Sick Bay for a couple of days. Now he did not have a recording of our messages, but he did talk to the Captain as he was fleeing, telling him what he knew."

"Is the XO Commander Cho?"

"Yes."

Chambers rubbed his chin and hummed to himself. "Go on."

"Well, the Captain is starting an inquiry, and he is not believing me, he is leaning toward Colton's story. Then Colton threw out a tidbit that the people on the planet, the Hingandu, are human, but I believe this was a ploy to throw us off."

"Why wasn't Colton tractor beamed?"

"They disabled it before they left."

"Why didn't ships stop them or weapons fire?"

"Their ships were cloaked, the transponders removed, and they bounced their communications off of satellites so we could not pinpoint them."

"Damn! This is not good. Contain it as much as you can on your end and I will work on stopping Dollinger from getting anywhere. Let your secretary know where you will be at all times in case I have to call you. I may have further instructions for you."

"I will await your orders."

"Do that. And you say Vladimir is out of commission for a couple of days? Commander Colton finally got tired of him, eh?"

"It was Commander Colton, Sir, not William but Sydni."

"She took him out?"

"A kick to the groin and a knee to the chin. Laid him out like a baby."

"I'll have to make a note of that."

"Anything else I can do to help from this end?"

"No, as long as the tapes of us were destroyed, just try and keep the rumor mill from getting out of hand, or start your own rumors about the Coltons committing treason."

"But that is no rumor. It is true."

"Gallagher, let's not be naive, okay. If he had those tapes and could prove what we had said, the court would overlook his indiscretion in favor of the even larger indiscretion, ours." Chambers leaned in closer and spoke like he was scolding a child, "So let's not forget what we are involved in. I want hunting parties sent out for them immediately. Your own guard."

"Sir, have you looked at Colton's dossier?"

"The usual First Scout stuff, right?"

Gallagher's lips twitched up in a bit of a smile. "No, not exactly." Gallagher punched it up on his computer and sent it to Chambers. "Here it is. I have highlighted several parts."

After a few minutes of reading, Chambers cursed loudly before he said, "Not him. Son-of-a-bitch, I did not realize he and his sister were First Scout on this cruise or I would have had them reassigned." He looked up into the screen and paused. "Nonetheless, send two parties to start looking for them. Maybe we can entice the scouts to help us. Send me their dossiers as well."

As Gallagher brought up the other scout records, he asked, "And if the two parties never return?"

The smile that crossed Chambers' face was one of his best politician's smiles, and with a shrug, he said, "We'll recruit more."

* * * *

Conrad gave the list to one of Andrea's assistants and said, "I want this packed and secured into shuttle 31. That will be all."

The tech left and Conrad sat back down behind his desk. Andrea had gone back down to the water moon, and the research there was going superbly. He absentmindedly picked up an electronic clipboard and started signing off on the various forms that would usually take him half a day to sort through, but today he didn't really care. Once they were signed, he picked up an inventory sheet and signed off on two requests by the research team. As usual, he left the two clipboards on the front corner of his desk where they would be picked up and taken care of later. With everything else taken care of, he began the tedious process of downloading files from his computer to a scanner that he had rigged up to hold three times as much memory. The same techs who had caught the chip that was used to spy on his scanner were more than happy to show off for him.

He picked through his files and it took him a better part of the morning to complete the task. By then, the same tech that was loading the shuttle had returned and picked up the clipboards. He paused and stutter-stepped and finally, when Conrad looked up at him, he said, "Sir, that list you gave me to put in shuttle, well, it is a very odd grouping...."

Conrad stood up, sending his chair back, tumbling across the floor. "What, Tech? Have you been promoted to rank high enough to start questioning your superiors?"

The tech snapped to attention and saluted. "No, Sir. I was just thinking..."

"That's enough! Do your duty and I will tell you when and what you can think."

"Aye-aye, Sir."

"Dismissed." The tech, now white with fright, turned and nearly ran out of the office, but what he didn't see, or Conrad couldn't let him see, was just how pale he was, and how his stomach was tight with knots at the tech's questioning. The feelings he had for Sydni beat down the anxiety that welled up within him, and when it boiled right down to the bones of the matter, he wasn't certain he could abandon the safe confines of his quarters shipside forever. His heart pounded faster and faster at the thought of giant expanse of sky and the towering trees, the open rolling plains.

Conrad leaned against his desk and picked up a glass of water he had poured earlier. As he sipped it, he thought of the ways he had always fought his panic attacks when he was forced to go planetside, for then he always could use the thought that he would be returning soon. This time, he had no such safety net.

The door chimed, and Conrad straightened himself out and took a deep breath. "Who's there?"

"Conrad, this is Bucky, with Chief Yamamora. May we enter?"

"Please, come in." Conrad's mind raced. Why was Chief here? Had he told Captain about the tap on the ambassador's private channel and their discussions? No, not only did Chief hate Ambassador Gallagher, he would never implicate himself, it could mean his contract. Another deep breath and another sip of water before they walked in. Conrad motioned toward the chairs in front of his desk and asked, "Will you have a seat?"

"Thanks," Bucky said. Both Conrad and Chief Yamamora waited for Bucky to sit before they did the same.

"This is an interesting trio for a meeting, how can I help you two?"

"Well, honestly, we're worried about Willy and Sydni. This whole fiasco is getting out of hand, and quickly it is tying my hands. But you can help to clear up a couple of things. First, because I know how close you were with them, did you have any idea this was going to happen?"

"No, sir. It is making my heart sick just to think about it."

Bucky nodded. "I know how close you were with Sydni especially, but I want you to know that I am trying everything within my power to alleviate the situation. If I could prove what Willy said was true. If I only had those recordings, then I could blow the whole lid open on Gallagher and Chambers and resolve this whole mess."

"What can be done without those recordings?"

Bucky slumped a little and shook his head. "I am afraid that there is not much that can be done. The ship has a recording of Willy admitting what he did, but nothing to implicate Gallagher, and the First Chancellor of the UWC. Keep your eyes and ears open."

"And second," Conrad prodded.

"Willy's claim that the Hingandu people are human, what is that all about?"

"That is what he believes, and some of the evidence back's him up, but he wasn't quite done with his thorough examination of them as a whole culture and people. From what he described and based on his scans, they are human."

"Damn. If that is true, it just backs up Willy's story even more, but I need to know what the hell Gallagher is up to." For a moment, Bucky looked like he wanted to hit something, but with a long sigh, he let it go.

They were all silent for a moment, then Conrad glanced at Chief Yamamora, who slowly was shaking his head. "And you brought Chief because, why?" Conrad finally asked.

Bucky, sitting up and glancing at Chief said, "Right. I almost forgot. We are a bit puzzled by the manner in which Willy and Sydni escaped. Within seconds the safety door was open, the retention beams were off-line, and several systems were a mess, causing all kinds of confusion. Chief can explain better than I."

Yamamora cleared his throat and then said, "The systems affected are all on separate lines and each one has precautions from being overridden by a remote access. So I need to know how they tapped into the system."

Conrad shrugged. "I will look into it, and I will have my best team look into it, but Willy and Sydni both majored in Computer programming, computer engineering, and basic systems engineering, so for them to come up with a program of that sort isn't all that unlikely. It was a long flight out here for a group of Scouts."

"Well, if you'll look into it, then that covers everything I came to discuss." Bucky stood up and straightened out his jacket. "Thank you for your cooperation, Conrad. Please contact me when you find out anything."

"Yes, sir."

Chief Yamamora stood up and saluted Bucky, who returned it and said, "Good day, gentlemen."

"Good day, Sir," they said in unison.

Once Bucky was out the door, Chief said, "Looks like a backfire."

Conrad nodded. "One hell of a mess."

"I know and could tell how close you and Sydni were becoming. It may be out of line for me to say so, sir, but you were one hell of a couple, and it is a crying shame."

"You're not out of line Chief, and thanks. I will get a team on that and give you a report as soon as I can."

"Thank you." With a nod, Yamamora headed for the door as well.

Once he was gone, Conrad slumped in his chair and slammed his fist on the desk. The life he had envisioned with Sydni would never exist, but he knew one thing, life without her would be more unbearable than life with her planetside. In his early days, the psyc docs had told him that he could overcome his fear of open spaces by confronting them and living in just that situation. He just hoped he could get in that shuttle and flee after them before his panic overrode any chance of them being together.

* * * *

Willy carried a large pack, and attached to its back was his military issue pulse rifle and his 7mm magnum. Sydni carried the same pack, but only her military issue pulse rifle was attached. When they neared the village, their sensors beeped, and they ran into a small hunting party, carrying sacks; long black and green tail feathers were sticking out of one bag, and Willy recognized the feathers of a pheasant-sized bird. The hunters watched Willy and Sydni carefully, but did not try and turn them back.

The scanners blinked out at the head of the valley. "Right here," Willy said. "There must be some sort of energy field, or some sort of polar field, when our scanners stop working, except as a communication device."

Sydni was examining hers and shaking her head. "I have a lot of questions about the Hingandu. Their power, their hot water, their lighting, their weapons are all curious, and we cannot get a scan of anything to examine."

"I know. Maybe now we can stay long enough to investigate, or just start asking some very direct questions."

"And why were they so adamant about not letting people get their hands on the Coppertroid?"

Willy started moving down the path, and over his shoulder, he said, "Hopefully given enough time, we'll find out."

Sydni reattached her scanner to her belt and started down the path behind her brother.

It was early in the morning, but the village seemed unusually quiet. They stopped at the edge of the small stone fence and glanced around. "What's going on?" Sydni asked.

Willy's pack moved as he shrugged and glanced up and down the fence line. Willy sniffed the air and then he looked up to the sky just in time to see a Brotu glide over the top of the cliff above. "I don't know, maybe this is some sort of Holy day or a holiday. Maybe they had a really big celebration last night."

Hitting the back of Willy's pack, Sydni laughed. "Yeah, they struck me as real group of partiers."

"Well, to the untrained eye, you look like a relatively non-partying individual."

"You're just jealous that you cannot hold your liquor."

This time Willy laughed as he continued into the village. He caught a glimpse of a young boy, who ducked around a building, running. "Strange," he said aloud.

"What," Sydni asked.

"I've got a funny feeling that something is going on, and that we are being watched."

Sydni cursed under her breath. She had been in more than one situation where Willy had thought he was being watched, and each time he had been right. "Something bad?"

"Let's just say we meet back at the clearing with the ships if something happens."

"Okay."

They slowly made their way into the village, heading for Chakdon's house, hoping they would find someone there. They walked by a fire that was still smoldering, the smoke curling up in long wisps. After exchanging a glance, they continued on.

Once they were close to Chakdon's house, Willy whispered, "I can hear voices now. It sounds like there may be some people in Chakdon's courtyard."

Sydni listened intently and she could just barely make out a faint murmur. The voices grew stronger, but when they neared the door of the courtyard, a hush went through the voices. The door was ajar, so Willy just pushed it open and stepped inside with Sydni close behind.

The courtyard was packed with people, including the war council, Alar, Chakdon and all his family, and many others they did not recognize. Dekonal pushed her way forward with a smile and a bounce in her step. She kissed him, and shifting his pack, he hugged her the best he could. "Hi," Dekonal said. "What kept you?"

"What kept us? What do you mean? You expected us?"

Dekonal glanced at Sydni and gave her the same smile. "Hello, Sydni."

"Hi." Sydni found Dekonal's smile infectious and she smiled through her confusion.

Willy helped Sydni remove her pack, keeping an eye on Dekonal and hoping she would answer his questions. "We were expecting you earlier, that's all."

"For what?" Sydni asked.

"The ceremony."

"Ceremony?" Willy asked. "A ceremony celebrating what?"

"Your acceptance into the Hingandu tribe. Tonight you and Sydni become one of us."

"We cannot stay here," Willy said. "We are on the run from my people, and we cannot stay. They will soon start to hunt for us, and we cannot let you or your people get in the way of that."

"Willy, we are not afraid. We are ready for you to become one of us."

Sydni could tell Willy was becoming frustrated with Dekonal, but she wasn't certain if she should speak up yet. She helped Willy remove his pack and leaned it down against hers. He nodded at her, but turned back to Dekonal. He lowered his voice and continued, "You don't understand, Dekonal."

"No, I don't," she nearly shouted.

"From that city in the sky, my people can sense where I am and they have weapons they can fire from up there and destroy your whole village. Granted, they usually don't fire at a planet."

Douka, who had been listening to the last part, stepped forward. "Willy, you don't understand." He turned and motioned for Alar to step forward. Once Alar was there, he asked her, "Can I tell him now? He doesn't understand and wants to run and hide." Turning back to Willy, he said, "He does not understand that we can protect him."

Willy started to shake his head when Alar said, "Tell him."

"Tell me what?"

"Our word for it is technology." Willy didn't understand Douka's word, but he listened intently. "You have only seen our simplest things, because we, as a people, choose to live simply." Douka bit his lip and mumbled to himself, he was becoming frustrated at his lack of words to express himself. He smiled to himself and pointed at Sydni's scanner. "That does not work in its full function, within our village, right?"

Willy glanced at Sydni, who replied, "Right."

"There is a cover over our village that protects us from off-worlders and their technology so they cannot look down on us and see our strength, weakness, or us at all." Douka's smile turned into a grin. "If it becomes necessary, then we have something each person can wear to protect himself while out of the village."

Willy was amazed if he understood correctly. He looked a Sydni who laughed and said, "I think they have outsmarted us."

"Or we did not give them enough credit."

Dekonal grabbed Willy's arm and squeezed. "Both my father and I saw the trouble that led you back down here, and we knew the course you and Sydni would take. We are ready to accept you into the village as one of us."

Willy shifted his arm so he could hold Dekonal's hand, but he turned to Sydni, and speaking in English, he said, "We have been through a lot in under twenty-four hours. Do you feel comfortable becoming Hingandu?"

Sydni looked around at the faces of people in the courtyard, and then for a moment, she glanced up at the sky. She knew that their chances of returning home were slim, and in the meantime, what would it hurt to be a part of the Hingandu community? Speaking in Hingandu, she said, "I think we should become Hingandu."

The crowd cheered at her reply and Dekonal was nearly jumping for joy and kissing Willy. Alar let the crowd cheer for a minute as many people pushed forward to be close to the newcomers, but then she started to hush the crowd. Both Willy and Sydni took note of Quistqui, standing next to Chakdon and Madak; he was cheering. Willy and Sydni looked at each other and shrugged.

"Come then," Alar said, holding her hands up in the air as if to shush everyone. "Come to the meeting place and all who care shall watch Willy and Sydni become Hingandu."

Another cheer rose through the crowd and Alar headed for the door. Chakdon and Madak flanked Willy, Sydni and Dekonal, with Doqui and Quistqui following close behind. Out in the street, they turned toward the mountain and wove their way back toward where Willy and Dekonal had climbed into the mountain to talk in the cave. However, at the entrance Willy knew about, they turned left and followed along the cliff. Then both Willy and Sydni saw the glow from the torches and lanterns. Between two pillars there was an elaborate entrance to the part dug up under the cliff, and they realized that it was a giant meeting hall. Torches lined the cliff along the entrance. Inside there were many of the small lanterns glowing with golden light. The murmur from the crowd was very loud. Dekonal, who had been holding onto Willy's arm, squeezed it with excitement as she said, "Most of the village is here, and a few people from the other villages."

"I did not expect this many people," Sydni said.

"Once everyone understood you and listened to my father and myself, they realized that it would benefit not just me, or our village, but the entire Hingandu nation to have you as part of our people."

The meeting hall was deep and slanted, so that everyone in the back could see over the heads of those in the front. He was amazed at the structure. Near the front was a small stage-like structure where Alar, Douka, Klisk, Watkil, and Chakdon walked up on, and Dekonal motioned for Willy and Sydni to follow. Everyone from the courtyard moved in front of the stage and sat on some blankets that were laid out on the ground.

Once everyone was seated in front, the war council and Chakdon and Dekonal stood along the back of the stage. Alar stepped between Willy and Sydni and held up her hand, as if to command silence. The crowd immediately obeyed, and a few mothers and fathers could be heard hushing small children.

"Today is a great day for not only the Hingandu under the cliff, but for all Hingandu. Today we accept two newcomers into our midst, and, a historical note, they are the first two off-worlders ever to be accepted into the tribe. They need a place to live, and come from another tribe that lives far away at another star. Although one of them may look different, she is of the same tribe and in fact the off-worlders are brother and sister."

Voices broke out in the crowd, but were quickly followed by a hush. Alar paused only long enough for the hush to silence most of the people. "They will, as of tonight, have full privileges as any member of our society. They have been graciously given a home next our beloved advisor Chakdon, donated by Chakdon." Willy shot a glance at Dekonal and Chakdon who were both looking forward, but were both smiling. Then he looked across Alar and looked at Sydni, who was looking at him as if to question the remark, but Willy could only shrug and listen to Alar. "War, as most of you know, is coming to our land, and we expect that Willy and Sydni of the Colton Clan will be able to help us and advise us through such a difficult time. Now, before we move forward, Douka has asked me to relay a message to all of the people. Willy has advised us that his tribe can see us from above and detect us as we move outside the protection of the village, so it will be known that no one will leave the village without their amulet of protection."

Neither Willy nor Sydni understood the word amulet, but both understood the concept. There existed a device that would render their scanners inoperative and hide them. Willy smiled and thought of many advantages that they would have in an upcoming battle with the Jolabwe, even if the Jolabwe had technological help from Gallagher.

"Now, Willy and Sydni of the Colton Clan, do you swear that you and your clan, from this day forward, will assist the Hingandu, live among us peacefully, never betray us to your old tribe, and if it comes down to it, fight for our tribe? Do you swear to be loyal to the Hingandu tribe?"

The hall was silent. Willy raised a hand and said, "I do swear, upon all that I love, that I will be a loyal warrior to the Hingandu tribe." He smiled and looked at Sydni.

She cleared her throat, and knowing as she raised her arm that soon she could be fighting the same ship where her love was, she said loudly, "I do swear, upon all that I love, that I will be a loyal warrior to the this Hingandu tribe." A single tear escaped the corner of her eye and glided down her cheek, but as her words faded, the crowd stood up and cheered. The sheer noise was deafening, making Sydni and Willy blink. They shook hands with Alar, and then the war council moved forward to congratulate them, then finally Chakdon and Dekonal.

Over the noise, Willy shouted in Chakdon's ear, "How will we be able to repay you?"

Chakdon nodded and grinned. Then, shouting back into Willy's ear, he said, "You never have to. Be a good member of our society and prove to them, what I already know is true." He motioned toward the cheering crowd.

Willy mouthed the words "Thank you," to him.

Then Dekonal embraced him. Ignoring her whole tribe, and his sister, and her family, he kissed her for a long time. That was when a thought struck him: Something he knew was right from the first day, and that he knew he wanted more than any other thing, next to his sister's happiness. Taking her hand, he stood at the front of the stage. Looking at Alar, he shouted, "How do I get them to listen again?"

Waving her two fists in front of her, she shouted, "Raise your hands." She motioned moving her hands up in the air.

Willy turned to the crowd and raised both his hands, and much to his surprise, they quieted down for him. He paused, and cleared his throat as the crowd hushed, and he took Dekonal's hand. He looked at Sydni, who through another rush of tears was smiling and nodded. Turning back to the crowd, he said, "I am uncertain how this is done properly in our tribe." Several people chuckled when he said, *our tribe*. "I do not know if I am to ask permission of her parents," With his free hand, he motioned toward Madak and Chakdon, and continued, "or her brothers, or of the war council itself." More laughs came from many who understood what he was about to say, when he turned to Dekonal. "Or if I am only supposed to ask her in private." He looked into her lavender eyes, with their silver flecks, now wide with anticipation of his words. "But I know one thing is for certain." He took both of her hands and got down on one knee. "My love for you is greater than the sky over the plains and stronger than the rock of the mountain and more precious than any wealth a man could gain in a lifetime. Will you be my mate?"

"Yes," she shouted as she dove into his waiting arms. He stood up, holding her, and their lips met in a fury of passion. The cheer that ran through the crowd was stronger than before, and Sydni was glad that everyone was watching Willy and Dekonal as she used a black bandanna to wipe tears from her face.

Douka had a smile that would lead anyone to believe that he knew about it all along, and as he leaned on his staff, he nodded and cheered with the crowd. Madak rushed forward meeting Chakdon in front of the stage, and they hugged one another as Madak was wiping at tears of her own. Quistqui and Doqui moved forward clapping and cheering at the news.

Willy could feel hands patting him on his back, and people shouted at both he and Dekonal, but he only heard that in the back of his mind. Right now, in front of him was Dekonal, who was commanding most of his attention with her mouth. They stayed locked in the embrace until the roar from the crowd faded to a low buzz. As she stepped back, again taking his hands, he could see tears running down her face.

Again everyone on stage came forward to pat them on the back and wish them well. Douka grabbed Willy's shoulder in a tight grip and said into his ear, "Son, you have just made it very difficult for every man among this village."

Glancing at him sideways, Willy asked, "Why?"

"Now every woman will expect such a beautiful proposal."

They both laughed. That was when Willy spotted Sydni, standing at the back of the stage, facing the other direction. He held up a hand to Dekonal and said, "I will be right back."

Dekonal nodded and jumped off the short stage to where her family was standing, watching her. They crowded around her and were all wishing her congratulations. She turned to Quistqui and asked, "Do you really mean your congratulations?"

"Yes, Dekonal. He will make a great husband and addition to this tribe and most of all, I think he will be a great warrior of the Hingandu nation."

She stared into his eyes as he spoke and could tell he was speaking the truth. Then she asked, "What of his sister?"

Quistqui shrugged. "I have been watching them both together, and although she is strange to us, they are very familiar to each other and have many of the same mannerisms. It will take time to become used to her, but if she is half as worthy as Willy, then the Colton Clan will be great among the Hingandu, and I will be proud to have a sister who has gone into that clan."

Dekonal smiled, and as she hugged her brother, she said, "Thank you."

Willy stood next to his sister and looked out along the row of torches. He put an arm around his sister's shoulders. Sunlight moved in patches outside the line of the cliff, but in the shadow of the meeting place, the torches danced. Sydni turned into her brother's arms and speaking in English, she said, "I am so happy for you, Willy. I truly had begun to worry that I would never see this day for you. Yet here we are and I am so selfish that all I can think of is Conrad."

"I understand," he said just loud enough for her to hear. "There is nothing I can give you to repay such an honor and sacrifice you made to bring me down here and to give me such happiness. I know you do not want to get your hopes up, but I personally guarantee that you will see Conrad again. If I know him well enough, he will make trips planetside hoping beyond hope that you will find him, and if not then I feel confident that Bucky will solve this conflict and expose Gallagher and Chambers so that we will not be fugitives."

Looking into his eyes, she replied, "A personal guarantee? I have a personal guarantee from the new leader of the Colton Clan that I will see him again?" Willy nodded. "Then how can I mourn for something that is not yet lost? And because I see such happiness in you and all these people, how can I not keep hope that all will work out?"

"See," he said with a grin that exposed his sharp teeth. "Now you are starting to think like a member of the Colton Clan again."

"Then let us rejoin your celebration."

"Our celebration," he corrected.

"Yes, Willy, our celebration."

* * * *

Conrad searched the logs in the equipment room for nearly an hour until he found what he was looking for. There was an equipment log in record signed by one of the ambassadorial guards, and the piece of equipment was a scanner. He then went to the equipment room and requested the article. The sailor in the checkout window did not dare question a Lieutenant Admiral on his need for the equipment, especially since Conrad was the CSO, who always needed equipment. When the sailor handed it to him, he examined it and recognized the weathered and scratched piece as Willy's. Conrad signed for it and left.

Once in his office, he started examining the scanner. Most of the recorded files were deleted, but the functional files were all intact. It took him several hours through the morning to find the program, but there it was. With a simple keystroke, this scanner could shut down not only the retention beams, but also weapons systems and the outer shield so they could escape quickly.

The command codes to disarm everything were high-level, and Conrad suspected might even have been from the top three command line. "Why would they be so paranoid to set up such a function in the first place?" he mumbled. "Had they been planning something all along?"

Every file was dated, and the dates from the creation of the file were from the onset of the cruise. Conrad knew that it was impossible for them to have predicted the need for such a command, but it would help him, and he could always ask them later. They usually had some sort of explanation for their behavior, when their behavior was unlike most people on the cruise.

After memorizing the keystrokes to work the command, he carried the scanner to his quarters and placed it in a large pack he had prepared to take with him. He pulled out an electronic clipboard and ran item by item through his list of necessary items. Everything was accounted for and packed on a shuttle, now he only had one thing he wanted to do. He wanted to walk through both Sydni and Willy's rooms to see if they had left something that might have been of importance behind. Then all he would have to do was act normally until it was time to head out. He gulped down his growing anxiety and closed his eyes tight.

He had started to find a way to quell his anxiety and fear. He pictured Sydni in his mind, and he knew everything else was worth it.

Chapter 14

The celebration of Willy and Sydni's acceptance into the tribe lasted well into the afternoon as people came forward to announce their congratulations for both occasions. Willy and Sydni were introduced to so many people; there was no way they could ever remember all of their names. Food was brought out, as most people had brought their own, and then a group of musicians gathered in the center of the hall and began playing music that reminded Sydni of ancient folk music from Earth. Ten Hingandu men and women made up the band, and their equipment ranged from stringed to wind instruments. One woman had a pair of four-foot bongo-like drums.

As the music played, many people began to dance and laugh. Children ran around in groups, dancing in and around the adults. During a lull in well wishers, Willy leaned against the stage hugging Dekonal from behind. He watched the scene in front of him and felt content. He felt like he was home.

Dekonal had been rubbing his arms in a slow motion as her mind wandered. She looked at Sydni, who was talking to Doqui and Quistqui, and from their motions, it seemed they were talking about hunting, which Dekonal knew would gain Sydni much respect from her brothers. Leaning her head back against Willy's shoulder and said, "Your sister is very sad."

"You can tell?" Willy asked.

"In her eyes. Although she talks animatedly with my brothers, I can see the sadness in her eyes."

"The man she loves is far away at our home in the sky."

Immediately Dekonal understood and she nodded. She had understood when her visions told her that Sydni would free Willy from the small room that Sydni would have to give up so much of her own life. She nodded and thought of other visions she had seen Sydni in, with another person who looked more like her. She saw the smiles and knew that this scene had not yet happened in their lives.

"She will be happy," she half said to herself and half to Willy.

"What do you mean?"

"It is best that I do not say, for things do change, but I do see her being happy, here, and maybe sooner than you might think."

Willy did not push her for an answer. He thought it might be better to not know what was going to happen in the near future. He just nodded, although she couldn't see it, and he whispered, "Okay."

The music faded, and after a brief lull, a new song began. Dekonal stood up and turning toward Willy, she took his hand. "Come dance with me."

Willy stood up, and said, "I can't dance."

Leaning in and placing a hand against his chest, she said, "I have seen the grace you use when you run, and I know you can dance." She paused and grinned. "Or I can teach you."

She turned and ran toward a group of dancers as Willy let himself be pulled behind her. They stopped close to the musicians and Dekonal faced him. She took both his hands and started to move her feet. Willy watched her for a second and started to imitate her. He was awkward for a moment, and glanced around at the crowd, which was quickly forming around them and he nearly tripped. A few laughs echoed around them.

"No," Dekonal said. "They are not here. It is only you and me. Watch me and relax."

Willy concentrated on her feet, and slowly as they started to move around at the fast pace, turning and turning, Willy started to understand the movements. Soon he looked up into her eyes, and tried dancing without looking at her feet. He didn't trip.

A large space was cleared for them to dance and a circle formed around them. People started clapping in time with the music as they moved, and what laughter there was, had been changed into shouts of encouragement. Sydni, Doqui and Quistqui entered the edge of the circle to watch. Sydni, who had danced all her life at parties and formal dances, started to move her feet as she watched, beginning to understand the steps quickly. Doqui looked at her feet and then to her and asked, "Would you like to learn as well?"

Sydni looked at him as he held out his hand from the other side of his brother. "I don't know…"

Doqui smiled, reminding her of Willy when they were at the academy, and he said, "We are to be family, and it would be an honor to teach you this dance."

Sydni looked at Willy smiling and dancing, and then she took Doqui's hand and said, "I would like to learn."

So Doqui faced her and took both of her hands and waited for the music to hit a certain point. Then he began to move, and quickly Sydni followed his steps until they were dancing around in the circle with Willy and Dekonal. Soon Quistqui and his mate-to-be Nurian and Chakdon and Madak joined them.

They danced into the evening, stopping to drink and eat, when the small band needed a break. As the evening wore on, slowly the crowd dispersed, until the band, finally tired, packed up to leave. It was then that the small group still celebrating moved back to Chakdon's court.

Once the party was down to just family, and Quistqui left hand-in-hand to walk Nurian home, Chakdon and Madak led Sydni and Willy over to their new home. From the front door, there was a set of stairs leading up and a hallway leading to the back. Immediately to the right, in front of the stairs was open archway into a room with three wooden chairs with cloth-padded seats, and a long couch with padded seats and back. At the far end of the room was a small fireplace and a little stack of wood. Along the left wall of the little family room was another open archway. They followed the hallway further to where there was another archway that led into a dining room with a long wooden table twice as big as the one in Chakdon's house. "This was the original clan house for my clan," Madak said. "I was from the Horkan Clan before I married, and when my parents died, the house was left to me, since I was the only one left from my family that still lived in the village. Since you two are starting your own clan here, it is only fitting that you have such a grand house and table."

"Thank you," Willy said.

Sydni had walked over to it and ran her hand across it. "It is a beautiful table, and room and house."

Madak walked past them and into the kitchen, which had an entrance from the dining room and the hall. The kitchen took up most of the back wall, and had a small round table and a counter separating the table from the food preparation area. On the left wall, behind the table, there was another small fireplace and another stack of wood. Willy walked along the food preparation area and looked at the sink with running water, and then a tall wooden cabinet with a large handle. When he opened it, he felt a burst of cold air. "That is for keeping food edible for a long time." Dekonal said, and Willy understood it would be a freezer. Then he opened the next one down and it was not as cold. "That keeps food ready to be cooked," Dekonal added.

Willy nodded and then saw the stove, with square stones set in it, which he figured would act as heating coils of old stoves, and under that was what looked to be a conventional oven. Before he examined it more, he realized that there was a door leading to what would be the back of the house. He opened it and looked out. "Wow," he breathed out between his teeth, which brought Sydni close behind him.

Lights set in the ceiling of an overhang led out into a courtyard almost twice the size of Chakdon's. He stepped out and looked around. The others followed. Madak did something and more lights clicked on along the wall of the courtyard. Pointing up, Madak said, "The rest of the house is a little bigger than the downstairs. Split into two sections, so more than one family member could live here with their families."

Willy and Sydni stepped out past the overhang and looked around. Toward the back they could see a fire pit and another long table with four benches. "This is…" Willy paused looking for words.

"Too much," Sydni finished for him.

"Yes, how can we accept such a gift? We have nothing."

Chakdon put a hand on Willy's back and said, "Now you do. We could not give this to one of our sons, because our clan would be insulted at giving away such a clan house when they already have one. Years ago, Madak and I decided we would give it away to someone who needed a clan house. God watched out for you, and now he has given you a home. Bless it with happiness and children and laughter."

"I have never had a home," Willy said half to himself.

Madak looked at him and shrugged. "Where did you grow up?"

It took several seconds for Willy to realize what he had said, and then he looked at Sydni who shrugged. Before Willy said anything, though, Sydni answered. "We had a home, with a mother and father, but it was not always a happy one. As different as I am to you, Willy was different where we lived, and he was not always accepted. It is too difficult for me to explain in a manner in which you would fully understand, but Willy has always lived as one outside of the circle looking in. Our parents did not know how to handle the situation and it made life for them difficult. Your acceptance of Willy, and me for that matter, into your tribe has made him feel more like he belongs than ever before."

Madak looked at Willy, who had been watching Sydni. He turned to Madak and said, "It is true. Here I feel like I belong. It was like all my life I have struggled to come here."

"Then you are home," Madak said. "You will always be welcome here."

Soon after Chakdon left with Madak and Doqui, Willy and Sydni saw the two sides of the upstairs and how there was a master-like bedroom suite and three bedrooms to each half of the upstairs. They had taken sides and found beds and bedding ready for them along with towels for the bathroom. Sydni kissed Willy's cheek and hugged Dekonal, saying goodnight and saying she was too tired to stay awake any longer. Willy set his pack down inside the doorway to his new room and stretched.

"Tomorrow will be a busy day," Dekonal said. "We will bring your things here, and we will find food to supply your kitchen."

"Can you stay? Tonight I mean?"

Dekonal nearly blushed, but her smile betrayed her. Nodding, she answered, "Yes. No one will care now that you are to be my mate."

"Great," Willy said, stripping off his tee shirt. They kissed and she examined his belt buckle. He showed her how it worked and as his pants dropped, he looked down and said, "Well, I will have to take my boots off first."

As he bent down though, he stopped. Dekonal's gaze had become fixed and she was staring far past him. He had seen sleepwalkers aboard ships do this before, and he realized that she must have been having a vision. He pulled his pants back up and watched her intently. Her head tilted to one side and her brow furrowed. Nearly a minute later, she snapped out of it and looked at Willy.

"Was it a vision?" He asked.

She nodded. "One you care about is in trouble. You must go to him."

"Him? Who him?"

"You must fly." She ran out the door and headed down the steps.

Willy stepped after her, but paused, wondering if she meant fly his ship. He stooped and unzipped his pack and quickly, as any well-trained UWC pilot would, dressed in his flight suit and grabbed the replacement scanner Sydni had put in his ship. He took the stairs four at a time and saw that the door was open. Outside he found Dekonal pointing up at the sky. "What is it?" he asked.

"There," she said pointing. "Someone needs your help in the stars. If you do not go to him…it may already be too late."

"Who?"

"I do not know him and I have never met him, but he is your friend, I see him with you and you are happy. Your sister is happy with him."

"Conrad?"

"Run! If you do not go now, he may not make it."

That was all Willy waited for. When she said run he was already bolting down the street, punching in codes to his ship in his scanner. He would start it by remote control and bring it in closer to him.

✶ ✶ ✶ ✶

Conrad sat in the pilot's seat of the shuttle and slipped on the headset. The engines were primed. He flicked on the frequency for flight control and said, "This is shuttle two-four-three, ready for takeoff and clearance."

"One moment, shuttle two-four-three," the flight control officer said.

"Is there a problem?" Conrad asked, trying to hide his nervousness.

"I am checking flight authorization, shuttle. Who authorized this flight?"

"I did. The is CSO Lieutenant Admiral Singh, I am carrying supplies down to the moon exploration team."

"Please stand down, sir. Cut your engines. You do not have authorization to leave the Orion."

"Who the hell gave that order?"

"The captain did, sir. Please cut your engines."

"Aw, hell," Conrad said as he reached for Willy's old scanner.

"What, sir?"

Conrad didn't answer, he just keyed in the code and smiled as the lights in the flight deck changed and the outer door opened up. He throttled forward in the shuttle, and the minute he had enough clearance, he hit the launch thrusters.

"What?" the flight officer said. "Shit, not again. Get the captain on deck! Shuttle two four three, you are in direct violation of UWC command. Stop this instant or face severe consequences."

As the ship disappeared from around him, Conrad breathed a sigh of relief, before he hit a new button he himself had installed on this shuttle. Instantly the shuttle disappeared and he changed directions.

The flight officer sounded even more frustrated as he said, "What, the shuttle just cloaked on us."

Conrad was smiling and he relaxed a little as he made a course change to head for the moon before he headed to the planet. Only seconds later, he nearly panicked when the radar alarms sounded. Once he shut them down, he looked at the screen and saw a squadron of fighters heading on a path that looked like an intercept path with him. He decided to burn his thrusters and change direction again, but quickly the fighters responded.

Turning off the voice of his radio, he said, "How the hell can they find me? I'm cloaked."

"Shuttle two-four-three, this is Jackson Jeffries, commander of the 21st squadron, turn back now or face the consequences."

Conrad cut away and spiraled, as much as he hated to do evasive maneuvers, he would try anything to get away at this point. "You are out-numbered, out-gunned, and out of time, sir. Turn back now," Jeffries said.

One of the ships fired and the green energy pulses filled his view screen as they passed the front of his ship. As he maneuvered again, a shot hit the left side of his ship. The seat belt kept him in place, but alarms sounded and the ship rocked like it had been rammed.

He was desperate and out of moves when a new voice came over the radio. "The next ship to fire on the shuttle will be destroyed." It was Willy. The ship directly behind Conrad's shuttle was suddenly struck by an energy pulse and tumbled out of line. "That was my only warning shot."

Over the radio, the XO Commander Cho shouted, "Destroy the scout ship."

Willy's laughter filled the radio and he started gaining position to follow the other fighters until they backed off. "Call off your dogs, Jeffries or I'll start frying them."

Jeffries cursed a long string of curses. "XO, he has us."

Ignoring their chatter, Willy asked, "Doc, how did you manage to bypass their systems and tractors?"

Conrad looked at the scanner and said, "Your lost scanner proved most helpful. I just figured out how you and Sydni did it."

"You have my old scanner?" Willy said, suddenly excited.

"Why, yes I do."

"Quick, Doc, key in alpha-two-alpha-nine."

Willy slowed his ship and keyed in a message to his old scanner, telling Conrad to key in a flight pattern he would know but the others wouldn't. The transponder signal stopped and Conrad turned to follow Willy's directions. To his relief, the fighters did not follow, but stayed on course.

Now Cho was cursing from the bridge of the Orion. "Colton, you will pay for this if I have to send down every Marine to bring you home."

"Belay that," Bucky said as he entered the bridge. "What the hell is going on?"

Willy had heard it before, so he turned off communication with the Orion, but kept his earpiece on low, just in case they said something that would help him. He continued to give Conrad directions via the scanners, and he couldn't resist sending Jeffries one as well, taunting him a little and signing it: the ghost.

They landed in the same clearing that Willy and Sydni had landed in before. Willy gave very distinct instructions as to where Conrad should land so he would not damage Sydni's ship and he could land and not damage Conrad's shuttle.

Willy wanted to get the transponder out of the shuttle so that the Orion could not track them. He stepped away from his ship at the same time Conrad stepped away from the shuttle, instantly becoming visible to one another. "You showed up in the nick of time, Willy. I think they were going to let me have it."

They shook hands and Willy smiled, "I think they were trying to let you have it and just could not visualize where you were. Did they hit you?"

"One shot did on the left side somewhere, if I ever take off in that thing again, I will have to examine it closely to see what kind of damage was caused."

"What the hell are you doing down here?"

Conrad stopped and shook his head. "She could not let you rot in the brig, and I could not see something that simple and so right come between us. I love your sister, and if it costs me my career, my good standing as a UWC citizen, my pension, and my wealth, she is worth it."

"What about your sanity?"

"If I have to live in a cave, or in a room I construct out of natural materials, or even this shuttle, she is worth it."

Willy smiled. "Not until I met Dekonal would I have understood what you are thinking, but now I can say I understand."

There were some sounds in the woods that made Conrad jump. Willy pulled out his scanner and turned on the stun. Just as he was starting a scan, he heard Sydni say, "Willy, are you okay?"

"Sydni, you are never going to believe what I brought you."

"What?"

Dekonal, who walked close behind Sydni, turned on a lantern, showing Sydni carrying her pulse rifle. Sydni stood in the bright light blinking, first focusing on Willy and then on Conrad behind him.

"Conrad!" she said. She rushed past Willy and into his waiting arms. They were deep in a kiss when Dekonal walked up to Willy.

After kissing Dekonal, Willy said, "Thanks for the warning, I made it just in time. Not much longer and they would have killed him."

Sydni pulled away long enough to ask, "Is that true?"

Since Willy and Sydni were speaking in Hingandu, they had to translate for him. Once Conrad understood, he nodded. "Most certainly. In fact, my ship is most likely damaged from the hit I took before Willy rode in as the proverbial cavalry."

"When you offered your personal guarantee, I did not know you were ready to go fetch him."

Willy shrugged. "I told you whatever it takes." Then he looked back and forth from Dekonal to Conrad and said in English, "Conrad, meet Dekonal." Then in Hingandu, he said, "Dekonal, meet Conrad. He is the love of my sister's life." Conrad extended his hand and Dekonal shook it. "Doc, Dekonal is my mate-to-be, or I guess I could call her my fiancé."

"Fiancé? What? Congratulations, my friend. I am very happy for you both."

Turning to Dekonal he said, "He is happy for us that we are to be mated."

"Thank you," Dekonal said.

"That means, thank you," Sydni said.

Dekonal reached in a pocket of her pants and held out two amulets, which were copper-colored stones set in a dark metal setting with a pin on the back. "This is the amulet that will make us invisible to the eyes of your people. They must now be worn at all times outside the city."

Willy pinned his on as Sydni explained it to Conrad and pinned it on him. "So they are advanced?" Conrad asked.

"Quite," Sydni replied.

"Look," Willy said. "I will let you two reacquaint yourselves while I remove the transponder." Then he motioned for Dekonal and asked, "Can you come with me?"

Dekonal handed Sydni the light before she took his hand and followed. "Where are we going?" she asked.

"You understand how we fly, right?" She nodded. "Well, three of them are hidden here, and I am going to take you inside one to make it so the others cannot find it." Willy felt along the space where he could feel the energy from the shields until his hand pushed through and disappeared. "In here."

Dekonal was amazed as Willy disappeared, and with a pull, she suddenly was standing inside the shuttle next to Willy. The cargo door was sealed, but what Willy wanted was in the cockpit. Dekonal lagged behind him as she stared at all the equipment in the strange room. Once she walked into the cockpit, she found Willy setting aside a panel and opening it to reach inside. She watched the concentration on his face, but soon he smiled and pulled his arm out, holding a computer chip.

"What is that?" Dekonal asked.

After thinking about it for a minute, Willy said, "It is something my people put in these flying things to keep track of where they are."

"Even though they can't see it?" she asked.

"Yes, they can't see it, but they can find it with this." Willy dropped it on the floor and pulled out his scanner. Using the scanner's stunning ability, he fried the chip. He examined the control panel as he replaced his old scanner with his new one. "Holy shit." he said softly, examining the readout from the ships computer.

"Holy shit," Dekonal mimicked. "What does that mean?"

Smiling, Willy looked at her. "When someone is angry or surprised, they say words that they would not like their children to say."

"Oh, I understand that," she replied. "We have many such words."

"Well, according to what the…." he paused, realizing he did not have a word for computer or machine. "This says his flying thing was nearly destroyed." He led her out of the cockpit and he had to manually override the emergency lock on the cargo hold. Once he opened the cargo hold, he just stopped and stared at the gash in the side of the shuttle.

Willy knew that Conrad was lucky to have survived his ride to the planet. Had the warning shot been back several feet or down several feet, it could have very well destroyed the shuttle. Willy found himself saying a quick prayer of thanks and then decided to leave it alone until the next day.

After a quick stretch and a yawn, Willy said, "It has been a long couple of days. I need a long nap curled up in your arms."

"Then we are ready to head back."

Nodding, and leading Dekonal back outside, he said, "Yes, that was more than enough excitement for an evening."

As they reappeared, Sydni and Conrad were talking, holding each other. Conrad looked up first and said, "Sydni was just telling me all about your induction into the Hingandu tribe. Very impressive."

Willy nodded. "Doc, you have the grace of God flying with you."

"What do you mean?" Sydni asked.

"I mean that warning shot that hit you was within feet of destroying you, and if you had forgotten to seal your cargo hatch, you would have depressurized and could have been killed."

"Hull breach?" Conrad asked.

"Two footer. Some of your equipment may be lost, but most is intact."

"Well, I just stocked the shuttle with everything I could think of, hoping it might come in handy down here."

Sydni looked at Dekonal and asked, "Is it a problem to bring Conrad to our new home? Do we need to get permission to bring a stranger into our village?"

Dekonal laughed. "Did you hear what you asked? Already it is a home to you."

Shrugging, Sydni asked, "What?"

Willy had caught the phrase she used and he repeated it to her. "You said, our village. Already accepting it as your home."

"I guess I did."

"No, I don't see why Conrad cannot come into the village with us. He will be under your strict supervision all night, right?"

"Oh, yes. He won't get out of my sight."

Dekonal smiled. Even in the shadowy light from the lantern, she could see just how much the two of them loved one another. "We will set up a meeting with Alar and the war council in the morning."

Conrad, finally unable to stand it any longer, asked, "What are you all saying?"

"We were talking about what a cute butt you have," Sydni said, kissing him on the cheek. "Don't worry, I will tell you later."

"Doc, we have a lot to start teaching you," Willy said. "And if you still don't know it, the first one is not to believe everything she says." He pointed at Sydni and winked. Still looking at Conrad, he said, "Now if I could only remember which way the village is."

"That, my friend, is not even funny."

"Come on, let's get going so we can actually get back before it's light out."

* * * *

Bucky sat in his office chair that looked out over the bow of the ship, and he poured scotch straight from a bottle. It was real scotch that an old friend had given him on his commission to the Orion. "Someday, Bucky, you may want to celebrate or someday you may just need a friend. Drink to your health and my health, is all I ask."

Today the scotch represented an old friend, and with the desertion of his third officer in two days he thought he might have to find himself a second bottle. Ice clinked in his glass as he raised it to his lips and gulped; it burned a path to his stomach. Three of his most trusted officers were now living planetside, one of which he knew by the psych reports did not like living in open spaces or solitary. He himself did not like the wide openness, except for the reaches of space, which was his job to go explore, but even then he was watching out of a porthole with his thick walls surrounding him. Half aloud, he said, "Why did you go, Conrad? What infection is aboard my ship that has three of my best officers running away?" But he already knew. Ambassador Jasper Gallagher was somewhere at the heart of the infection, and he was certain that if he could clip Gallagher's wings and get at the truth, then his crew could rest easy and his officers could come back.

"I'll get to the bottom of this, Gallagher. Trust me. If it takes the rest of this cruise, I'll expose you and that damned Chambers."

The door chimed and he knew it had to be someone important to get past the yeoman sitting in the outer office. He steeled himself to see Gallagher's face as he said, "Enter."

Chief Yamamora filled the doorway when it opened, and he stepped in. With a crisp salute, he said, "Chief Yamamora reporting, Sir."

"At ease, Chief. What have you got?"

"We figured it out, Sir. How the Coltons escaped, and how Admiral Singh escaped too."

"Drink?" Bucky asked, holding up the bottle.

"No, thank you."

"How did they get out of here?"

"They had an elaborate program that somehow hacked into your command codes and gave authorization codes for emergency shutdown of retention beams, weapons systems, and shield, while giving the override code to the outer hull door to the hangar. My programmers say it is a beauty of a program."

"How did you find it?"

Chief smiled. "I received a delayed message from Admiral Singh. He sent a copy of the code, and said that it was the last order you gave him, the least he could do was carry it out."

"Fine work, Chief. I will change the codes and nullify the program. Make certain that any copy you have is destroyed."

"Yes, Sir. Is that all, Sir."

"Dismissed, Chief. Good day."

The Chief spun on his heel and headed back out, and as he did, Commander Cho passed him, returning her salute without losing her stride. "Can I speak with you, Captain?" She asked saluting him.

Saluting back, Bucky said, "By all means. Please have a seat."

Alexandra sat and he held out the bottle, saying, "Care for any?"

"No thank you. I just came on duty."

"What's on your mind, Alex?"

"It's that pest Gallagher. He has been calling the bridge every five minutes asking for you. I told him that if he called the bridge one more time, I would have him in the brig waiting for an appointment. He is quite an irate little man." Bucky nodded and sipped his drink. "I will say that you should schedule an appointment soon."

"Thank you. I will have the yeoman call and set up one for this afternoon."

"Permission to speak freely and off the record, Sir."

"Always granted to you, Alex. What's on your mind?"

"If Gallagher is following Chancellor Chambers' orders, then we best step carefully, Sir. As you know, I was aboard the UWC Chancellor One, from Chancellor Hildebrandt through the election when Chambers was voted into office. That ship is privy to much information, and it was well known that Chambers was quite underhanded, corrupt, and rumor had it he was dirty."

"And you are telling me this because…?" Bucky let his sentence fade off.

"Because I don't want to see you end up shoved out an airlock late some evening, with some witness who said you were drunk out of your mind. We need to play all our cards during this deal very carefully."

"Very carefully," the Captain repeated. "We will be very careful, but I need proof against the Ambassador. Some solid evidence that he was acting out of UWC regulations and that he and Chambers were up to something illegal would let us shut down his operation and toss him in the brig. Until then, our top scouts are fugitives, and our CSO is with them of his own free will."

"Who is to be appointed interim CSO?"

Bucky looked at the electronic clipboard on his desk and read aloud, "That would be Major Gubani."

"Only a major?" Alex asked.

"She must have some good qualities, she is hand-picked by Singh. Will you please inform her? I need to call in the scouts and talk to them."

"Yes, Sir. If that is all, I will return to the bridge."

"Certainly. Dismissed."

Once Alexandra left and the door was closed, Bucky sent out a message to the other scouts, telling them to report immediately to the captain's office. Then he put away his scotch and swallowed the rest that was in his glass. Chief and XO seeing him drink was one thing, but the other's in the crew were different.

He straightened out his uniform and then stood motionless with his hands behind his back up against the porthole, which was twice as tall as he was and four times as long. He could just barely see the planet off to his left and the moon stood out as a bright spot in the vast background of stars.

His door chimed and he said, "Enter," using his deepest tone. The three scouts lined up and simultaneously saluted and in turn, said their name and that they were reporting to duty. Bucky waited for a moment before he turned around and returned their salute. "As you were," he said, stepping toward them. They all stood in the at ease stance. He knew the training they each had logged during the long and tedious cruise from Quadra Three, which was their last port of call. He thought of how proud Willy and Sydni would be of them.

"Rumors are flying around the ship faster than this ship can fly, and I want to know where you guys stand in all this. I will not even insult you by asking where Sydni and Willy are, because I hope that you are loyal enough to them that you would not even tell me. The Ambassador charged Willy Colton with treason and brigged him. Sydni broke him out and they escaped in their scout ships shortly thereafter." Bucky noticed that Tanya tried to hide a smile, but was failing. "Do you find that amusing, Lieutenant?" he nearly shouted.

"No, Sir!" she snapped back. "They just always said that if they wanted to they could leave the ship without permission, or escape from any locked-down section. We always thought they were bragging to stay on top of us and push us."

"Very well." Bucky started pacing in front of them. "Not long ago, CSO Singh pulled the same stunt and left the ship in a shuttle. Personally I think the charges against Willy are true, but I am certain that he has extenuating circumstances." He stopped and faced them. "I know that I could send down two divisions of Marines and twelve science vessels to cruise along and look for them, and I know they would escape detection." All three nodded in agreement. "So what I want you three to do is set out to find them, not to bring them in, not to spy on them, but to take messages to them and bring back word from them."

Tanya, Gordo, and Barkley were shocked and the looks of surprise almost made Bucky smile. "Yes, Sir!" Tanya said enthusiastically. "We will start immediately, Sir."

"Belay that. Start tomorrow. Give them some time to come down from this rush of activity. Let them settle in just a little, wherever they are, and whatever you do, don't spook them. Lieutenant, you are now Scout One for the interim. I will stay in contact with you, Sergeant Diego and Sergeant Billings; you will take your cues from her. Understood?"

"Yes, Sir." They said in unison.

"Okay. Just make contact and tell them what I have told you. Dismissed."

They all saluted again. When Bucky saluted back, they turned and left his office. As the door closed behind them, he thought that there went the last link to his officers and friends, and he hoped that they would be successful.

* * * *

Willy had slept unusually long into the morning hours when the smell of food woke him from a dream about Quadra Three. He had been dreaming that he was sitting on an outcropping far up in the mountain range behind his home. The summer air was just warm enough at that climate to go without a shirt. The only other thing he saw at that altitude was a few longhaired mountain sheep and several predatory birds circling lazily in the sun. For one last moment, while he was lying there in bed, he was up on the mountain, stretched out under the high cirrus clouds and the sun. That had been a place even Sydni had not known about. It was a place where he went for absolute solace from the universe. The mountains had always made him feel at peace, and as he sat up, he realized that was where he was now. The Hingandu village was his place of peace.

He stretched and stood up before he slid on a pair of shorts and went downstairs to the kitchen. Conrad's laughter mixed with Sydni and Dekonal's, giving him an even greater feeling. No one noticed him at first; he just leaned in the doorway listening to them talk about the house and the previous night.

Finally Conrad looked up and saw him standing there. "Willy! Good morning."

"Good morning, Doc." Willy said in English. Then in Hingandu, he said, "Good morning, Dekonal, Sydni."

They were all seated around the table, and Willy walked over and placed his hands on Dekonal's shoulders, kneading them gently. He kissed the top of her head.

"You've taken up sleeping in." Sydni said with a hint of amusement in her voice.

Willy, faking a yawn and stretching, said, "That's what happens when I have to run out and save your boyfriend in the middle of the night."

"Boyfriend," Sydni said. "You mean fiancé."

"Really," Willy said. "He asked you?" Sydni stood up and she hugged Willy. "I am so happy," he said.

"She asked me, though," Conrad said.

Willy laughed. "She always did go straight for what she wanted."

"Give him credit," Sydni said. "He brought up the subject first, and he was trying to ask me, so I just gave him the punch line."

Reaching out a hand, Willy shook Conrad's hand and said, "Congrats, Doc. Welcome to the family." Then looking at Dekonal, he said, "They are to be mated as well."

"They told me. If I may make a suggestion, we could have the ceremony on the same day if you don't mind."

Sydni sat back down and leaned over toward Dekonal saying, "You really wouldn't mind sharing your ceremony day?"

"Our day," Dekonal said. "We are all part of the same clan now, it will be a very special day to mark the beginning of our clan."

Willy repeated what Dekonal said in English for Conrad. "What a perfectly splendid idea. What exactly do you mean by clan?"

After thinking for a minute, Willy said, "The old Scottish of Earth and Alpha One used to have clans, their family name. It would seem that there are clans here. Sydni and I have started the Colton Clan. This is to be our clan house and we can raise our families here. Can you live with that?"

"Sounds good. I have never been part of such a tight-knit family group."

Sydni was relaying what Conrad was saying into Hingandu for Dekonal.

"The first thing we need to concentrate on his teaching you the language, Doc. Once you are speaking Hingandu, life will be easier here," said Willy.

"Agreed," Sydni said. "This can be tiring."

Dekonal stood up and made Willy take a seat while she dished up what looked to be a sort of egg omelet with meats and cut up vegetables or roots in it. The smell was enticing. Before he started eating, though, he stopped and thought of Boris Takalov, who stopped and prayed before each meal, no matter how meager. So Willy, realizing that all his life he had endured what he had, to come to this planet, in this village, at this table, to create a new life and family here, he saw God's hand at work. Closing his eyes, he said a small prayer of thanks. So it was from his first meal in his new home that every time someone in the Colton Clan sat down to partake in a meal, they said a prayer of thanks for their meal.

After they met with Alar and Douka, obtaining their permission to have Conrad in the village indefinitely, they started out for their grueling day of humping equipment back to their new home. Conrad's Hingandu lessons started that day, as they took four trips to the ships and back, pausing for a meal in midday. They finished in only four trips because Conrad had the foresight to pack a gravity sled with him.

The hikes to the ships were terrifying for Conrad. His moments back in the house were his comfort zone, where he had solid walls surrounding him. Once they were back, Doqui brought two fresh birds.

Dekonal started preparing them for the oven when she stopped and wiped her brow with her sleeve. "Tomorrow we need to start picking up some things to make the house more livable. We need some seasoning for the kitchen, not to mention food supplies and fresh fruit. We need to start growing some food in the courtyard."

"I guess I need to ask your brothers to teach Sydni and me how to hunt and what to look for," Willy said. "Then we can bring back some fresh meat for the table."

Dekonal nodded. "That is the spirit."

Willy was watching Dekonal, and he realized that he could help her prepare the birds. He had prepared many birds in his days on Quadra Three, not to mention many hunting trips since then. He picked up the second bird and started plucking it.

She elbowed his arm, not losing her rhythm as her hands pulled feathers away, and said, "You go get cleaned up and I will take care of these. You carried twice as much as me today."

"I will never have it said that in our clan one does not do their share of work. I know how to make birds ready for the oven, I will help."

"As you wish," Dekonal said.

"And then we can go get cleaned up together."

Slowly a smile grew from Dekonal's stern look, and she said, "Oh. I think I like this clan already."

Once the birds were free of feathers, they washed them thoroughly in the sink. "What did your brother do with the insides?"

"Oh, he loves a stew made from the inside meats. He keeps a store of them until he has enough to make stew and then makes enough to feed everyone he can invite."

"Does he make it?"

"Yes, and it is really very tasty."

Dekonal looked around in a couple of cupboards and found a stone dish that looked like many meals had been cooked in it. She retrieved a small jar from the refrigerator and smeared a brown greasy substance around the pan, and then she greased each bird and set each one in the pan. Willy took the jar and smelled it. It had a lard smell, mixed with some sort of herbs or spices.

She searched the refrigerator and Willy placed the jar in a slot on the door. Then she pulled out a small packet of spices and mumbled to herself, "Mother must have been over here and left some things. This will work." She held the cloth packet to her nose and inhaled. Then she held it up for Willy to smell, and he did. It was a peppery mix that hinted of mustard and something else that he couldn't place. "It is not the best mix for these birds, but it is a general mix and will pretty much work with anything we have."

"Great. It is making me hungry already."

Dekonal opened the pouch and sprinkled the contents over the birds, dumping the extra around the greased pan. Then she added some water to the pan and placed it in the oven. After turning a dial, she took Willy's hand and said, "Now, in this new clan thinking, we go get cleaned up together?"

"That was the plan."

"Let's go," she said, pulling him toward the stairs.

And so several days passed as the Colton Clan adjusted to life in their new home, and they settled into a routine, giving Conrad Hingandu lessons over breakfast, learning to hunt with Quistqui and Doqui until midday while Conrad worked on setting up a lab with his equipment. Then, in the afternoons they practiced using the Hingandu crossbow, using a sharpened arrow for killing bigger game and a blunt arrow for small birds. Willy showed Doqui and Quistqui how to use his rifle and pulse rifle, but he knew that he had a limited supply of ammo for his 7 mm. He made a mental note to ask Conrad to come up with a solution using what was available on their new home. Then in the late afternoon and evening, they would walk the streets of the village and meeting people, and ending up at their house or Chakdon's for dinner. Then they would sit in the courtyard as the sun went down, again teaching the already tired Conrad more Hingandu. They knew that the only way to have Conrad speaking Hingandu fluently was to saturate him with it.

Chapter 15

Willy was following the fresh tracks of the Muntaka, and although he had yet to see the creature, he was told that it was fierce, and could gore and trample a man without even a thought. Judging by the size of the tri-cloven hoof print, he knew that it had to weigh as much as the famed Bull Moose from Earth. He had never had the chance to hunt the moose on Earth, but it had been an aspiration. The odor coming from the creature smelled like wet fur mixed with rotting grass. He glanced to his right, and saw Sydni poised with her pulse rifle, while he was holding his 7-mm. Doqui had fanned out on his left, and Quistqui was directly behind him, ready for a follow-up shot.

Sydni did not want to use her pulse rifle, but it was the only weapon she had that she could use proficiently. Doqui had remarked how quickly she was picking up their crossbow, but still she took the pulse rifle and saying, "Willy, I will just give you first shot, and I'll back you up."

A finger came past Willy's head and pointed to a tall area of grayish-green grasses just within a thick stand of trees where a stream gurgled. Willy nodded, and glanced at Sydni, who looked at him. She saw Quistqui pointing and glanced into the woods. She then realized that they were saying the Muntaka would be in the grasses.

Their advance was slow and silent. Sydni had hunted with her brother since they were young, and she loved the anticipation. She didn't care much for the butchering and hauling back to camp, but her brother's cooking when they were at camp or aboard ship could not be rivaled when it came to game meats. That was another reason why she liked Willy's mentor, Jean-Pierre, because he had added a touch of style to Willy's cooking. She had not picked up as much from her scout leaders, but she had picked up a lot from Willy.

Suddenly the forest erupted to her right with a snort-like trumpeting sound and a crashing of underbrush. She stepped back as the creature's large brown head with two short spike horns and a long snout curled up in the air exposing large flat teeth broke through the underbrush. Its neck was long and as it reared up on two hind legs, it kept its head aimed at Sydni.

She brought her rifle to bear, and she shot without aiming, striking the animal at the base of the neck. The creature's trumpeting turned to a screech, and before its front hooves touched down, Willy's shot struck it right between the eyes. Its legs buckled, but before its trumpeting quieted, a second beast rushed forward with its head down. Two glowing crossbow bolts hit it, one in the back of the neck along the spine and the second one between the horns. The second Muntaka burrowed face first into the ground, and as its horns hit, it flipped over on its back; it snorted and softly tried to trumpet.

When Sydni looked over at the others, she saw that both Doqui and Quistqui had already rearmed their weapons. She slowly moved toward the downed Muntaka's, keeping her muzzle pointed into the underbrush from where they had rushed out. She wished she had her scanner with her, but she knew that with the amulet of protection that was given to her, she would not be able to use it. She watched intently, looking for signs of life, but when there was none, she crouched down and stroked the dark smooth fur.

"Great reflex shot, Syd," Willy said, crouching down next to her.

"Thanks for the follow-up, though. These guys look pretty formidable."

Doqui moved past them, edging his way slowly toward the trampled underbrush, looking for any other Muntakas. Quistqui stopped and crouched down, keeping his eyes on his brother, and his crossbow ready. Glancing quickly, he said, "These are two wondrous creatures and will help feed our families. We can give the horns to the healers, the fur to the clothes makers, and the bones to the builders. These creatures will serve our needs well.

"So you give away these things?" Sydni said. "What do you get back?"

Quistqui shrugged. "What you need you get. When you need clothes, you go to the clothes maker, when you need something built you go to the builders. Our resources go towards the good of the people."

"That works?" She asked. "No fighting over materials? No shortages?"

"When we have a shortage of one thing, another village may have what we need, or we take a war party on Brotu to another part of the mountains. We have a simple life, but it works."

Willy laughed. "Wouldn't the Multi-World Communist party like to hear that. They could have a whole new model for their culture."

"Write the book and you could make millions in credits," Sydni said, nudging her brother.

"Make millions writing a book about communism. That does not sound right. Not to mention we are already on the top ten most wanted list, this wouldn't help us with the UWC big-wigs."

"A renegade writer, inciting the tri-world area to convert. Could you just see Father's face?"

"He would blow an artery." Willy shifted and said, "I wonder if he and Mother will hear about all this."

Sydni shook her head. "I don't know. The way the UWC works, who knows how this will play in the media, or if it ever does. Chambers could try and sweep it all under the rug, knowing that bastard."

Doqui walked back, his crossbow strapped to his pack, smiling. "No more. It would seem that there was a herd along the stream over there," he pointed to the grassy area, "but they headed toward the lake." Then pointing at Willy, he continued, "I would say it was probably when his weapon fired."

"Probably," Quistqui agreed. "At least we won't have to watch our backs as we are preparing them for transport."

"True."

Quistqui slung his crossbow on his back and pulled out his knife. Willy leaned his rifle against a tree and followed suit, with his knife. "If Doqui and I prep this one, then he can show me what you save and how you do it here." Willy said. "And if you and Sydni do it, then she'll know."

Sydni was nodding and Quistqui said, "Great idea."

They worked on the Muntakas and Doqui provided a sack with a moist lining to hold the heart, kidneys, and liver. They skinned the giant animals and quartered them, and once they were prepared, Doqui ran off for the Brotu.

Quistqui looked around at their work and said, "Since we were hunting Muntaka, I took the liberty to ask Bokta to meet us here with two pack Brotus to haul our catch back to the village."

"No argument here," Sydni said. "I can live without packing one of those back to the village."

Doqui came running back faster than he had run away and his crossbow was unsheathed, he was pointing back behind him. "Jolabwe, ten, maybe twelve. They are following someone."

Quistqui pulled off his crossbow and Willy and Sydni picked up their rifles. "Show us."

Doqui headed back the way he had come, but he went slower, once again going into hunting mode. They sprinted through the open edge of the plain to a clump of squat trees. They crawled in the trees and watched out the far side. Willy spotted Tanya first as she walked between clumps of trees about one hundred yards out. Then Doqui motioned toward a group of Jolabwe just starting to show, following Tanya at a great distance.

Another group was following the Jolabwe though; it was a group of Hingandu, all armed and trying to out-flank the Jolabwe. Sydni pointed them out, and Willy knew that Tanya could be in trouble. He whispered, "Look, give me a minute to get into position. I want to protect the human."

Quistqui furrowed his brow and asked, "You would help one that would cage you?"

As Willy slipped away, Sydni whispered, "She would not cage us, she is our," she paused, not knowing how to describe the relationship, so after a few seconds, she finished, "our friend."

Quistqui nodded. "You shoot well, so I do not have to worry about you hitting any Hingandu, but if this breaks out into a fight, the Hingandu may be standing in our crossfire with the Jolabwe."

Sydni looked over and saw movement on the far side of some squat trees, and by the gait she judged that it was Tanya. She waited for any sign of Willy, but she couldn't see him anywhere. Doqui tensed and raised his crossbow in reaction to a Jolabwe bursting ahead and stopping, as he raised his weapon in the direction of Tanya. The rest of the Jolabwe dashed towards some trees as three turned and raised their weapons in the direction of the following Hingandu. Quistqui raised his crossbow and said, "Doqui, we will not be the ones to break the peace."

"Quartainian's group, they will be ambushed."

"Look, already he has moved his group to react to their position. Target a Jolabwe, and if they fire, kill them."

Tanya knew Jolabwe were following her, but after all her contact with them, she couldn't figure out why they were following her. She could almost feel the hostility in them. Soon they might break to catch her, and she was ready to sprint into the trees and duck for cover. She was keeping an eye ahead of her too, just in case some of them tried to out-flank her. As she cut around a large tree and she went to pull off her weapon, her feet went out from under her. She was pushed to the ground and a voice whispered in her ear, "Stay low or you're dead." It was Willy's voice she heard through her pounding heart.

When she looked up, Willy was crouched with his back to the tree and his rifle in his hand. "One of them was readying to fire at you. Get up."

Just as she righted herself, using the tree as cover, the ground where her head had been exploded, leaving a four-inch gouge. The resounding crack from the Jolabwe rifle shattered the otherwise quiet day.

Willy leaned around the tree and fired at the rushing Jolabwe, striking him in the chest and sending him tumbling backwards. The world erupted with the sound of Jolabwe fire, and faintly, Willy could make out the sound of the crossbow bolts swishing through the air. With a quick motion hand signal, Willy left her at the tree to cover that side, and he went around the far side of the trees. He moved slowly, knowing the Jolabwe party was not too much farther ahead. Then he saw them nestled down behind a group of trees, firing on the group of Hingandu. Further behind the Hingandu, he saw where Sydni, Doqui, and Quistqui were firing.

The 7mm was not quite as loud as the Jolabwe rifle, so Willy knew that he had a chance to get an edge, but he needed to see more of the Jolabwe party without exposing himself. An older, thicker tree was nearby in the center of the trees where he was now hidden, so he made his way to it and climbed up about forty feet before he found a little three way split. Once worked in the crotch of the tree, he readied his weapon and aimed at the Jolabwe. Over half of the group was lying on the ground dead or dying, and they continued a fierce barrage against the Hingandu. Trees were snapping as the Jolabwe fire hit them, and one medium tree keeled over into the open plain.

Willy targeted four of the Jolabwe he thought he could get before they realized that his attack was coming from behind them. He shot the first one, and as that Jolabwe slammed face first into the tree he was hiding behind, Willy was firing at a second one, and before that one hit the ground he was firing at the third. The fourth one he had targeted slid around his tree, realizing where the shots were coming from, but he quickly fell with a crossbow bolt protruding from his neck.

The last one yelled out his hiss-like scream and fired up at Willy, but Tanya had moved forward slowly and was in position by then. As several shots struck the tree around Willy, Tanya fired.

After reloading, Willy climbed down and walked over to Tanya, who stayed hidden from the rest of the Hingandu. "Thanks," he said.

"Nothing you didn't teach me."

"I don't know what the other Hingandu will do or say, knowing that I am an outcast from my people, so I will make this short. What the hell are you doing out here?"

"Captain sent us out in shifts to look for you. He wants to know if you are all right and pass on what is happening or get any information."

Willy looked over his shoulder to the cautious Hingandu, tentatively moving from their positions. "We are okay, we will be okay. Tanya, this may be hard for you to believe, but we are happy here. Look at those people just coming out of hiding and tell me what you see."

Tanya peered through the leaves and then shot a quick glance back at Willy before looking again. "Except for those stripes, they look like you."

"Tell Bucky," he paused and cleared his throat. "Tell Captain that there are humans down here, just like me. Tell him I know I am in a heap of trouble, but if he keeps looking for Gallagher to screw up, I will do the same."

"Captain says he's trying."

"Tell him I understand." Willy placed a hand on Tanya's shoulder. "You do this at personal peril, and do not let on to Gallagher that we have talked, or he will drum up charges against you."

"How can we contact you?" she asked, shouldering her weapon.

"I will send a message to you, scrambled, from my cockpit."

"Standard twelve hours later?" Tanya asked.

"Yes."

"I am sorry about everything, sir. I wish we could have helped you."

"You are. Now we just have to concentrate on fixing the problem. Keep your eyes open when it comes to Vladimir. As a personal favor, go see Chief Su. He needs company and encouragement."

"Yes, Sir."

Willy glanced at the Hingandu now searching through the area where the Jolabwe were strewn about. "Dismissed, Lieutenant. Run with the wind."

"Likewise, Commander. Tell Sydni we all miss her too."

"Done."

Tanya turned and ran back along the clump of trees, and then she sprinted toward the plain, hiding behind more trees as she ran. The first Jolabwe Willy had shot was only a few yards away, so Willy grabbed him by the arm and dragged him toward the others. Quartainian looked up from one of Willy's victims and saw Willy approaching. He said, "Nice tactic, Willy. You probably don't remember me, but we met on the day of your induction to the tribe."

While Quartainian looked familiar, Willy couldn't be certain if he remembered him. "Thank you. I just had a great vantage point and took advantage of it."

"Very effective. You may even have saved us a casualty or two." He turned to a woman standing beside him and said, "Bring in the Brotus and we can send the wounded to the healers." Turning back to Willy, he said, "They are not seriously wounded, but I want them transported back quickly."

Quistqui and Sydni joined them and Doqui held back talking to some other men. Quistqui nodded to Quartainian and said, "Sorry to rush into your little war here."

"Quist, your crossbow is always welcome in my battle. Were those first two responses from you and Doqui?"

"Yes. I guess this is the beginning, then. They broke the treaty that has spanned nearly a lifetime."

Quartainian bit his lip and nodded. "I would say so. Who was the female they were following?"

"A friend of mine that came looking for me. To give us news from our old home."

"Is she safe?"

"Yes, I sent her on her way so there would be no more trouble."

"You trust her."

"With my life," Willy said.

"And mine," Sydni added.

"Good enough for me. Bokta is hanging back with our rides, he should be here momentarily."

* * * *

Conrad sat down after finally setting up a lab in one of the bedrooms on his and Sydni's side of the upper floor. He had brought down a portable solar collector with a power converter and rechargeable power packs for everything. The slight breeze coming in the open window made him a little uneasy only because it reminded him that he was not in the confines of a ship or spaceport or even one of the major cities of Earth, but his solar collector was giving better readings with the window open.

Quistqui tried to explain the amulet that he wore, using Sydni as a translator. Conrad had a feeling that he was missing something in the translation, but the general idea was that the scanning ability of the scanner did not work while they were near an amulet or in the village. Many of his devices did not work, but his mobile computer did, which would serve as a whole network for a remote site, like the one Andrea had set up for the floating workstation. Now that he had a power source, he could reconfigure the scanners so they could send messages, using the computer in his new lab as a home base, and the Orion could not read them. He would change the frequency modulation so they could not get a fix on it even if they happened to come across it.

So with the computer up and running, he started to pull up several different frequencies, to study the difference between the scanning ability and the messaging capability. He wanted a way to make his scanner available to him, so he would have to find a bypass solution. The solution would take endless hours to adjust the scanner's frequencies until one worked in the environment, if it ever worked in that environment. He wanted to speak with Hingandu engineers or techs or whoever worked on their equipment, but until he could truly understand the language and its nuances, he would have difficulty.

First he created the three scanner accounts for their scanners. He collected Sydni's and Willy's from their bedrooms where they had left them. Then he calibrated them with his computer. This would give them their usual messaging features and he could easily contact them from the main computer. Then he gave each one a fake name so if the computer aboard Orion happened to pick-up any transmissions, they wouldn't stand out as any of theirs.

He took the extra scanner that they had and opened it up, to work on it, trying to make it work in the Hingandu village. He spent a couple hours working on it when Dekonal walked in with a little tray. On the tray was a bowl of spicy smelling soup and a glass of water. "Lunch," she said.

Conrad could not carry on a conversation with Dekonal, but he was starting to pick up several words. He smiled at her and said in Hingandu, "Thank you."

"You are welcome," she said before she left. Dekonal wanted to sit down and talk to him too, but she knew that it would only frustrate them both. So she left him to his strange equipment spread out on the dresser, the bed, on a table they had brought in, and strewn across the floor.

Conrad turned back and worked on the scanner a little longer before the smell of the soup made his stomach growl. After eating, he went back to work, consumed by his task.

* * * *

Tanya nearly ran through the halls to the bridge, and she ran full tilt into Vladimir, who was pacing in the waiting area outside the captain's office. The yeoman stood and saluted and once Tanya returned it, he sat down at the watch desk. "What is your hurry, Lieutenant?"

"That would be none of your business, sir." Turning to the yeoman, she said, "Will you please inform the captain that Lieutenant Williston is waiting."

"Yes, Ma'am."

"What is so special that you are running to the captain to report it?"

"I think you forget yourself, Lieutenant." Tanya said loudly. "We are equals and under different commands." The door to the captain's office swung open as she was speaking. "If the captain chooses to have me and the other scouts report to him now that our officers are not aboard ship, then maybe you should take it up with him."

"What's going on here?" Bucky said in the loudest voice he could muster without shouting. Both Tanya and Vladimir snapped to attention and saluted. "Gallagher, if you cannot keep him in check, I will throw him in the brig for the duration of the cruise. Vladimir, get the hell off my deck."

"Captain, I assure you that the other matter we were discussing is not finished."

"I am certain you are correct, Ambassador, but I have had enough of it today, and I have other duties to attend to. Good day." Gallagher stalked off after Vladimir, who had already left. "In my office, Lieutenant."

Tanya had never heard the captain raise his voice, and she stole a sideways glance towards him as she rushed past. He looked like he hadn't slept very much in the past few days. Once inside, she again stood at attention. When his door shut, he said, "At ease, Lieutenant." Tanya stood at ease. "What was going on outside?"

"Sir, I hope I was not out of line, but Vladimir was questioning me about why I was here to see you and why I had been running. So I was informing him that it was none of his business."

Nodding, the captain said, "Good work. Just stick with the story that I have been acting as your commander in the interim. Quick thinking, that was inventive."

Tanya smiled and said, "A product of the Colton School of Scouting."

"They do think fast on their feet. Do you have a report for me?"

"Yes, sir. Contact was made, although I thought I was dead there for a minute. I was being followed by a group of Jolabwe along an area that is part plain, part forest. I was trying to make my way to a point where I could lose them in the forest. Without warning, I was pushed down to the ground by Commander Colton. A skirmish was fought between Hingandu and Jolabwe. The Jolabwe must have thought I was with the Hingandu, because they fired first and tried to kill me."

"Did you speak with Willy?"

"Yes, sir. He said keep watching for Gallagher to screw up and he would do the same. He also said something else that I have been thinking about all the way here. He said he was happy down there. I also got my first look at the Hingandu."

"And?" Bucky asked.

"Sir, with the exception of some pigmentation patterns on their skin, they look exactly like Commander Colton." She paused as the captain slowly recovered from his astonishment, closing his mouth. "He said they were human."

"Damn, that would mean that he was right. Tell me you got a scan of them."

"Sir, that was the weirdest thing. I did not know Commander Colton was there until he was standing beside me. It was like a ghost appeared next to me. As I left, I tried to scan the whole Hingandu group, but could not detect any of them on my scanner."

Bucky scratched his jaw and stared past Tanya, as if he were trying to see down to the planet's surface. "Ghost, you say. That is how he signed a message that he sent to Commander Jeffries. I wonder what it means." Then, bringing his attention back to Tanya, he asked, "When are you to contact him again?"

"Sir, respectively, it is a scout thing, and I would feel more comfortable if you would not ask that of me."

Bucky wanted to know, but he had always given his scouts a lot of leeway, so he let it pass. He nodded. "Very well. Just remember I want full updates when someone talks with him, and check before you go, just to see if I have any information."

"Yes, Sir," she said again, snapping a salute.

He saluted back and said, "Dismissed." Tanya was heading out when Bucky said, "And good work, Lieutenant."

Tanya hid her smile until she was out the door. She keyed in a general call to all scouts to meet in her quarters as soon as possible. She shared the room with two other lieutenants from the medical corps and one lieutenant from the bridge. However, she had checked their schedules, and by some happenstance, they were all on duty right now.

Once back in her room, she changed from her flight suit into her standard black jumpsuit with the Orion insignia on her right shoulder and the 121st scout squadron on the other. She sat at the shared terminal on the one desk in the small living area and signed on. She checked her mail, but there was nothing other than a request for a date from a marine flyer she had met while drinking one night. She decided not to reply when someone chimed at the door. "Come in," she said.

The door slid open. Gordo was in mid-stretch and yawn, wearing only shorts and a tee shirt. "This is just a meeting right? Not a drill?"

"No we have to deploy by the ambassador's orders within fifteen minutes. Snap too it, Gordo." Gordo snapped awake and alert, turning to run back out the door when he realized that Tanya was laughing. "Good morning," she said through her laughter. "Or should I say afternoon."

Yawning again, Gordo walked to the small couch and flopped down on it. "I don't care what you call it when I just got off a graveyard shift on the planet searching for Commander..." His voice trailed off and he looked over at Tanya. "Why aren't you planetside looking for them?"

She raised her eyebrows and asked, "Where is Barkley?"

"I haven't seen him since he got off his shift."

"I wanted to tell you at the same time, but you look like you might bust if I don't. I got caught up in a Jolabwe-Hingandu skirmish today, and right before it started, I was dragged out of harms way by none other than Willy."

"Details. I want details."

Tanya turned her chair around to face Gordo and described the skirmish to him along with what she had seen. She told him how Willy or Sydni would contact them and that she had already reported it to the captain.

Gordo had leaned forward, listening, and when she finished, he sat back and said, "Commander told you that they were happy there? Diós mio. I hate being away from my home on a cruise, if I didn't know I would get to see civilization within two years that would kill me. How can they be happy down there?"

"Maybe being among people that are like him is easier, and with Doc Singh having taken off, I bet Commander Syd is pleased."

"Yeah," Gordo said, "I forgot she told us that they were seeing each other. I bet they are happy. And if they are like Willy then maybe they have accepted him and he truly will be content."

"Where the hell is Barkley?" Tanya asked, turning back to her computer to send another message.

"Who knows?"

The door chimed. "Come in." Tanya said, her voice not covering her annoyance.

Barkley stumbled in and caught himself, saying, "You rang?"

"Geez, Barkley, you're hammered."

"Yes, Lieutenant Williston, I am drunk. I do not need to be sober until tomorrow morning." He staggered to an overstuffed chair and sat down with a sigh. "I am sorry it took me a few minutes to get here." He smiled and looked at them, finally saying, "Well, what?"

Tanya started, "I can't believe your drunk. Our commanders are in trouble and what do you do, but go pickle yourself."

Barkley slammed his open hand down on the chair as he sat up and said, "What am I supposed to do, ma'am? Willy and Sydni were the first ones to trust me and give me a shot at something good. Now they've been banished planetside until we can clear some things up. You may deal with that how you want to, but I dealt with it by drinking. Don't you think that if I could do something about it I would? What would you have me do?"

Tanya was speechless; she had never heard Barkley speak so passionately about anything. He eased back into his chair and slumped like he had exhausted every last ounce of energy he had. After she apologized, she started in with the story she had just finished telling Gordo. To her even greater surprise, he seemed to sober right up and paid close attention. When she finished, he smiled and said, "I knew he was up to something. Son-of-a-bitch. Humans here and engines that match our current configuration found at a crash site. Doesn't that just boggle the mind? This will have the anthros and techs going bonkers back at home when it is released."

"If," Gordo corrected. "The way Gallagher and Chambers are running this whole thing, you'd think they would rather just eradicate them. If Willy's accusations are true, then this skirmish is just the beginning."

Barkley moaned and covered his eyes with his hand. "Man-o-man. So what are our current instructions?"

"You're not going to like it, Barkley. We wait until Willy contacts us. He will send the scrambled message and we go twelve hours later and meet him. Still keep your eyes and ears open and we need to visit Chief Su. Give him hope to live."

"Hey, that man has taught me some good moves," Barkley said. "I'll go see him."

Tanya lowered her voice and said, "Watch out for the asshole Russian. Vlad is mad."

Gordo grumbled. "Not that it takes much, but what did you do that pissed him off this time?"

"He was getting nosy about our business and why I was seeing the captain." Tanya Shrugged. "I told him to back off."

Barkley smiled and said, "I bet you used your most polite manner and softest voice too."

"Let's just say all of us should steer clear of him, and if you get a page from me, come running and bring the biggest division of marines you can find."

Gordo chuckled. "In full battle gear."

"Look," Barkley said, pushing himself to his feet. "I did not even think about staying sober to help you guys out if something happens with Vladimir, and that was just wrong. Remember, both Willy and Sydni always said that our teamwork can beat anything on this ship. We don't need marines to take him out. We just need teamwork. I am going to go sleep this off and I will be ready when you call…if you call."

"Take it easy," Gordo said.

"Don't dream anything too wild," Tanya added.

✶ ✶ ✶ ✶

Before dawn, Willy climbed through the tunnels to the top of the cliff, where they herded the Brotu, and for the first time he realized that it was a well-protected place for their village, due to the sharp rise in the mountain behind. He also realized that there were more houses up along the second level and up into the mountain. The Brotu were dispersed along the grassy and tree-lined ridge. Three men, two younger and one older, nodded to Willy as he walked out of the entrance. He walked to the edge of the cliff, where there was a small fountain and several stone benches. He sat down and faced the direction of the sunrise off to his right. The sky was spotted with high cirrus clouds and the horizon was starting to brighten. He wasn't certain what had made him wake up so early, but something about the meeting the night before was nagging him. They obviously had abilities to help hide them from the Orion and the scanners, but a conventional war with the Jolabwe could prove to be costly to them.

He unconsciously shook his head. War could be stopped, but not without evidence. Although he tried to explain this to his new people and leaders, they held no ill will toward him. They told him that only the inevitable was happening and all he could do was to help them win.

Something brushed his shoulder like a feather, and he realized that a Brotu had walked up to him and had brushed its tail past him. Holding out his hand, palm open, Willy waited to see what the Brotu would do. It sniffed his hand, flaring its nostrils and then stepped closer nuzzling his chest. Uncertain what he should do, Willy began petting the Brotu, scratching particularly behind the ears. The large creature moaned, and from the way it looked, Willy figured that it was enjoying the attention. Its fur was a dark auburn color, with a black mane and tufts along the backs of its legs.

The Brotu picked up its head and looked past Willy. Turning, Willy saw the old man standing behind him. His stripes were thinner and he had about double the amount of stripes as most Hingandu. He had a long dark scar that ran from his right ear to his upper lip. His long gray hair waved in the breeze. His bony hand reached past Willy and rubbed the main of the Brotu. "You are the stripeless one I have heard of," he said in a soft, scratchy voice.

"Yes."

"Ah, the leader of the new clan. I hear great things about you."

"I'm just a man, and I don't pretend to be anything more."

The old man moved around where he could face Willy. "I see more."

"You sound like Douka."

At that, the old man started laughing. His laughter turned to a roar and his one hand clutched his belly while with the other he kept smoothing back the mane of the Brotu. "Willy," he finally said through his laughter. "It is Willy, right?" Willy nodded. "I should sound like him. We grew up in the same clan. He is my cousin. We shared a drink at the same table last night, and he sees much caring in you. He tells me of a battle where you protected the village."

Willy nodded, but he did not want to talk about it, so he hoped this man would let it go. Trying to redirect the conversation, Willy asked, "What is your name?"

"I am Gonnaktu, head keeper and trainer of the Brotu."

"This one certainly does seem friendly."

"He likes you." Gonnaktu paused and said, "I will give you that Brotu because of your bravery yesterday."

"I cannot…." Willy stopped in mid sentence when he saw the frown on Gonnaktu's face. "Thank you, but I do not know how to ride one yet."

"You can be taught, and you need to be taught. I will even give you a harness." Then Gonnaktu pressed his lips together tightly and hummed for a second. "Your sister will need a Brotu as well. I will cut a second one from the herd and bring a second harness."

Willy glanced at the colors forming along the horizon, as the sun was about to rise. "Thank you, Gonnaktu. You are too kind."

"Nonsense, it is my job, and judging from the warriors you and your sister are, you will each need a Brotu." He whistled at the two men who were nearby and motioned toward the creature. Willy didn't understand what he was motioning about, but the two men were off and running. "It is very simple to command even a difficult Brotu. Be firm and do not be afraid to use your feet. They respect authority, but from how much this one likes you, it will not take you much to guide it." He made a clicking sound with his mouth, gaining the creatures attention. "Now listen closely," he said to Willy, "and I will have you riding this morning."

For the next half-hour, Gonnaktu explained the basics in guiding a Brotu, and Willy listened intently, forgetting any of the turmoil that had sent him up there to watch the sunrise. The sun was now a giant orange ball in the sky. Gonnaktu and his two grandsons, Gonnak and Tunnak, showed him how to harness the beast, which it accepted without fidgeting. Willy also noted that the reins did not affect the creature's capability to bite down, and he wondered if this was used during battle.

Finally, Gonnaktu stepped back and swept his hand toward the open valley before them. "There is nothing more spectacular than your first solo ride."

"Right now?" Willy asked, standing up.

"Would you rather wait until later when you have time to forget what I told you?"

"No."

"Then go, and bring your sister back so we can show her as well."

"How long can I ride before he needs a rest?" Willy ran his hand through the mane.

"He is very young," Gonnak said.

"But he should last until dark if necessary," Tunnak added.

Gonnaktu smiled and said, "They are smart grandsons, yes? Well, in half a year's time, this Brotu will be able to fly for a day without rest. You will be tired before it will be."

"How much will it carry?"

Gonnak looked at Tunnak and said, "He asks many questions."

"You, Dekonal, a child and a pack." Gonnaktu said with a smile, nudging Willy.

Willy sat on the seat of the harness and positioned his feet in stirrups that had been adjusted to fit him. The massive wings of the creature pressed against his legs, and he could feel the power. Using the reins, he steered the Brotu toward the cliff and urged it forward with his feet, like he had seen with the horses back on Quadra Three.

"Should we tell him that it is a jumper, not a winger?" Tunnak asked.

Willy understood the basic words, but not their implication in this instance. Gonnaktu shook his head and smiled. "He will see."

"See what?" Willy asked.

"Nothing," Gonnaktu said, "just go."

The creature stopped at the edge of the cliff, roared, and jumped. Willy's stomach leaped into his throat as they plunged downward, and he felt just like his ship were dropped into the emptiness of space. The Brotu's wings unfolded and while it was still far above the village, it leveled off, and then shot upward, reminding Willy of a ride at the newest Disney that his family had visited when it opened on Quadra Three.

The wind was refreshing and cool, and the colors of the morning had spread halfway across the sky. As often as he had flown in his scout ship, and as fast as he had gone, this was, by far, the freest he had ever felt. He tried several simple maneuvers, and the Brotu responded quickly each time. Once he was a little more comfortable in the harness, he stopped circling the city and headed into the sunrise, giving a quick wave to Gonnaktu and his grandsons.

Out past the last house, he saw fields spotted throughout the rugged mountain terrain where there were herds of animals, and faintly he spotted Hingandu among them, sitting at small fires. They had domesticated herd animals throughout terrain where no attack could be successfully mounted. Far off to his left, out toward the plain, he saw another Brotu and rider, but whoever it was didn't seem to see him.

Then he gradually shifted so he was flying along the treetop level, looking into the early morning shadows. He followed a stream along one valley that ended in a large lake that filled the bottom of a valley. Along one marshy side of the lake he could see a giant herd of Muntaka, and at the far end of the lake a flock of water fowl with red heads and black and white bodies, scattered with a cacophony of honking at the sight of the Brotu.

Willy was intoxicated, wishing only to share this ride with Dekonal, but unwilling to turn back yet. Then he turned and headed out toward the plain, having passed by in his ship enough times to know there would be miles and miles of forest before the plains started. He rose higher and higher into the air, to gain a better look, noting several rivers and streams that he had sped past so many times, but never had seen properly. When the air started to get cold he stopped, uncertain of how high he could take a Brotu. Something off to his left and behind him caught his eye, and he turned to look, seeing the sun glint off ice and snow in the high peaks of the mountains.

Everything seemed so new and beautiful. He realized that he was no longer seeing the world through the objective eyes of a scout, trying to figure out the land, but as someone who had moved to a new homeland and was discovering it all for the first time.

The plains rolled out ahead of him spotted with small clumps of trees; the plains seemed to breathe on their own as the grasses moved in the breeze. Then he saw two giant herds of animals out on the plain, and he closed in to get a better look. One herd was the fast moving Saka, while the other herd was a larger animal that resembled the Muntaka, but had shorter necks, longer horns, and their brown fur was accented with white stripes. He did not want to get low enough to scare the herds, but he went down a little for a closer look, not even wanting to try and count the thousands that spotted the plain almost as far as he could see, with a high concentration along a river that were cutting their way through the grass.

A large pride of Gyod was milling around a group of three trees that were near a turn in the river and provided an area of shade. He saw at least ten to fifteen of the animals. There were other smaller creatures that he could not see very well, some in small packs or herds, some larger and some smaller. Then he saw something move where the river widened into a pool almost like a lake, and he veered toward it. He swooped closer and saw what had to be the largest creature that he had ever seen in all of his travels. It walked on four legs and reminded him of a creature that had roamed Earth, called the elephant. There were only a handful of elephants still alive on earth through genetic reproduction and cloning, but Willy had never seen one before. It was massive and had two short trunks and one long one, with two giant black horns that started just in front of the ears, dropped toward the ground and curved way out in front of the creature, past the trunk. Its body was covered with long brown and white fur. As he flew past, the creature raised its three trunks and trumpeted a deep tone from the long trunk and shrill tones from the smaller trunks. As he maneuvered the Brotu to circle, he realized that an answer to the creature came from the water, where he now could see many trunks lifted above the water line. Another giant lumbered out of the water, shaking its frame as it cleared the water and whirled around, looking for danger, until it spotted Willy and the Brotu. Many of the creatures started coming out of the water, some were much smaller and had smaller horns, and then Willy spotted several that were so small they were probably yearlings or younger.

After two more passes, Willy figured he had done enough to frighten them, so he directed the Brotu up and back toward the mountains. He steered clear of the Jolabwe and their outlying settlements, not wanting to stir up any trouble; he also knew that if Gallagher was trying to help Zartig and his people, then ships would probably be moving to and from the planet.

The ride back to the village was uneventful, but as beautiful as his trip out, and he couldn't wait to show this to Sydni. He knew she would love the ride as much as he had. During the flight, Willy leaned forward and patted the massive neck of the creature. As they closed in on the village, flying down towards the valley where he knew it was, he could not see it until he was close, and then he started looking for his house. It took him a minute, but once he spotted it, he directed the Brotu to set down in the courtyard. As its wings folded up, Willy took his feet out of the stirrups and dismounted.

"Good, boy." Willy said in a soft tone as he knelt on one knee in front of it. He was petting the creature's face and scratching it behind the ears when Dekonal ran out. The Brotu hummed and moaned.

"That Brotu likes you very much. When did you learn to fly?"

"This morning, I walked up to the cliff," Willy pointed up as he spoke. "This Brotu walked up to me and started nuzzling me, so Gonnaktu gave it to me, and he taught me to ride." Willy kissed Dekonal.

"It is a magnificent animal, and very young. What is its name?"

Willy shrugged. "They did not say."

"He will need a name, but that can wait. So you have been riding?"

Willy grinned, trying to find the words to describe his ride. He pointed toward the cliff and then along the mountain range and then he paused. "It was as beautiful as you," he said looking into her eyes. "As beautiful and magnificent and breathtaking. I only wish you could have been there, but I..." He stopped and kissed her.

"I remember my first ride as a child, and how it was one of the most grand and intense scenes I had ever seen."

Sydni came out of the door followed by Conrad, who did not look so certain that he wanted to be outside. Sydni walked up and said, "Is that where you sneaked off to?"

"Well, it started as a walk up to see the sunrise and ended with a flight on this guy, here." Willy again ran his hand through the Brotu's mane. "Douka's cousin, Gonnaktu has one for you and said I should bring you up to learn how to ride."

"Sounds great." Sydni said, stepping up to the Brotu and holding out her hand. "We just finished breakfast, you want any first?" After the Brotu sniffed her hand, Sydni petted it. Then in English, she said, "Magnificent. Come see, Conrad."

"Respectfully, I will keep my distance, if you don't mind."

Willy laughed before he spoke, "No, I am too excited to eat right now. I want you to learn so I can go for the same ride again. I saw wonderful places and new things and new creatures. You've got to learn."

"Well, I told Quistqui that since I couldn't find you, we would not go hunting this morning." Turning to Conrad and speaking in English, she said, "Willy said that there is one of these for me and that I need to go learn how to ride it. Do you mind?"

Conrad smiled and said, "As long as I don't have to ride it, certainly."

Sydni looked up at him and pouted just a bit, saying, "You wouldn't even go for a ride with me?" She placed her hand on his chest and leaned in close. She pushed her lip out a little further and batted her eyes, and whispered, "For me?"

Conrad was shocked and speechless as she turned around and looked at Willy, saying, "Let's go."

Willy sat in the harness and Sydni sat behind him, holding onto his waist. Looking at Dekonal, Willy said, "My love, we will try and be back for lunch."

"Don't worry about it, if you are not, enjoy your first day on the Brotu. Have a good time, Sydni."

"Thanks Dekonal. Bye Conrad."

Conrad, still staring with his mouth open said, "Bye."

Using his feet, Willy urged the Brotu to fly, just as Gonnaktu had shown him. The Brotu unfolded its wings, and in seemingly effortless movements, propelled them skyward. They spiraled up in a corkscrew maneuver that had them at the ridge level in no time, and Willy used the reins to guide the Brotu over to where he had left from earlier that morning, where several Brotu were milling around Gonnaktu.

As they landed, Gonnaktu smiled and said, "I was worried that you might never come back. But I see you have landed, picked up a rider, and taken off again."

"Yes, I have. Sydni, this is Gonnaktu, keeper of the Brotu. Gonnaktu, this is my sister, Sydni."

Gonnaktu nodded his head and never lost his smile. "A pleasure to meet you, Sydni. Have you come to learn the art of riding a Brotu?"

"Yes. Willy said you would be giving me a Brotu. You are too kind to a new clan."

"Fresh blood in the village is usually good, especially when they can shoot and hunt like you two. I have picked out a Brotu the same age that will not only serve you well, but prove to be a mate for this one." Gonnaktu patted the nose of Willy's Brotu. "Then as your clan grows, so will the Brotu for your clan."

Willy looked bewildered at the thought of trying to mate and raise Brotu, and as he asked, "How do we...." Gonnaktu held up his hand.

"My grandsons, my son, my youngest daughter, and I take care of all of that. You just exercise them, treat them right, and love them, and we shall provide the food and help with the mating and care of the little ones."

Willy was relieved. "What is this one's name?"

Gonnaktu shook his head and said, "He has not been named. At that age, they learn quickly, and many of the people teach them certain tricks, or how to hunt, or how to make them come. You call him a name and he will learn it soon enough." He turned toward the trees where there was a hut and whistled shrilly. Tunnak looked out and then disappeared.

Willy led his Brotu over to the fountain, but before he got too close, he looked at Gonnaktu and said, "Can he drink from this fountain." Gonnaktu nodded and Willy let go of the reins.

"So what are you going to call him, Willy?" Sydni asked.

Willy looked at the creature as it lapped up water and said, "We have never owned a pet before, I don't know what a good name would be."

Tunnak came out of a stand of trees, guiding a chestnut colored Brotu with dark auburn colored accents. It was a little smaller than Willy's Brotu, but not by much.

Willy sat on the bench again, as Gonnaktu and Tunnak introduced Sydni to her new ride. His Brotu walked up to him, sat down facing him, and laid its massive head in his lap, looking at him with golden eyes. "You need a name, my friend. You need a name to honor your strength and speed." Willy ran through names he remembered people always named their pets, but he did not remember liking many of the names, and this was no pet. Then it struck him; he knew a name that he liked. He whispered, "I shall call you Remington. It is the best rifle that I own, and I shall name you for it."

He watched the rolling hills and a flock of birds flying as Sydni was given the same lesson as Willy had earlier that morning. Once Sydni was sitting on her Brotu, ready to fly, she called out to Willy, who was looking out into the valley, "Are you ready to ride, or what?"

Willy looked at her and smiled. "I am ready." As he stood up, Remington stood up and faced the edge of the cliff.

"Did you name him?" Gonnaktu asked.

"Yes, it is a word from my native language; Remington."

Tunnak cocked his head and repeated it, "Rem-m-ming-tin."

"Close," Willy said. "Remington."

Sydni was laughing and Gonnaktu asked, "What does this word mean?"

"Douka told you how I killed the Jolabwe, right?" Willy asked, and Gonnaktu nodded. "The weapon I used is called Remington, because it was made by Remington." Willy wasn't certain that he could explain companies and that they had been making weapons for centuries, but by the smile on Gonnaktu's face, he thought Gonnaktu had caught the reference.

"You honor him," Gonnaktu said. "Ride well."

Sydni urged hers up to the edge of the cliff and paused. Willy looked at Gonnaktu and said, "I understand now, jumper or a winger. Hers?" He nodded his head toward Sydni.

With a broad grin, Gonnaktu said, "Jumper."

"What?" Sydni asked.

"I'll tell you later."

Sydni urged hers forward, anxious for the flight, and her Brotu jumped over the side, plunging downward before it opened its wings. Willy urged Remington on and he gave a shout as they dove over the edge, quickly chasing after Sydni.

Chapter 16

"This is very serious, Captain Dollinger." Admiral Oats said over the vid screen, which would convert back to the massive window once a transmission was over. "Both the Ambassadorial staff and Chambers' office are saying that both Commander Sydni and Willy Colton are directly responsible for and involved in the hostilities planetside. This is hurting our chances of gaining access to the Coppertroid fuel supply."

"Sir, frankly speaking, the ambassador and Chancellor Chambers are full of shit. They are the ones up to something, and Willy was trying to stop them."

Admiral Oats shook his head and looked down. "Look, Buck, I personally pinned their promotions on Willy and Sydni for their heroics at the Doreea Star War. I know you think highly of them, but there is a pile of proof against them, and none in their defense. There is a push to bring them in for a court-martial."

"Proof." Bucky sighed out, knowing he had nothing in their defense. Then he mumbled, "Sir, let the media in on it. Call their bluff, because I can tell you one thing, they don't want the media digging into this, but I can tell you that Willy and Sydni both wouldn't mind."

"Hmmmmm," I will see how he reacts. "There is a matter of Willy firing on a ship, nearly destroying a fighter pilot."

"Yes, Sir. Those ships were firing on a shuttle that was leaving, and Willy was making a point that they were at risk if they fired on the ship again."

"Oh, that was when your CSO defected."

"Correct. Sir, he also claims that this other race, the one he is living with, are human. I have an eyewitness that has confirmed that there is a race of people that look like Willy."

"I want a scan of them, stat," Oats ordered.

"One of the scouts tried, but something was interfering with her scanner."

"Then use the ship's scanner."

Bucky raised his hands up and shrugged. "Sir, we have been trying to, but we find absolutely nothing."

"That is impossible. If there is a race of people down there then they cannot escape detection. Find them. Look, it has been weeks since this happened, and I need you to take some kind of action, even if it is in vain. At least make it look like you have some sort of plan, and I will get back to you soon."

"Yes, Sir."

"Oats out."

The image of the admiral faded and left the stars visible again. Stepping up to the window, he looked down over the front of the Orion, lights sparkling where others had portals as well, only much smaller. He could faintly make out a troop of Marines training in their full battle suits, and a squadron of fighter jets passed by. He sighed audibly and slammed his fist into the window. "Damn you, Gallagher, I will see you rot in my brig before I see Willy and Sydni Colton there."

The door chimed, and Bucky leaned his head against the window and asked, "Who is it?"

"Yeoman Brothers, Sir. There is a Lieutenant Williston here to see you."

Bucky straightened up, ran his fingers through his hair, tugged on his jacket and clasped his hands behind his back. "Let her in."

Bucky heard the door open and close, and he could picture Tanya standing stiffly, saluting him as she said, "Lieutenant Williston reporting, Sir."

He didn't turn around; he just stared out at the stars and said, "At ease, Lieutenant. You may approach." Tanya walked up next to him and looked out over the ship. "It is a spectacular view, is it not?"

"It is, Sir."

"Do you have any news?"

"Yes, sir. He contacted us and it is Gordo's...I mean Sergeant Diego's slot, so he is going down to meet him."

"You trust him?"

"Yes, Sir." Tanya said emphatically. "I trust everyone on my team. There is a strong loyalty to the Coltons."

"That is a good thing indeed and it may very well be tested before this is over. I want you to be clear about one thing, Lieutenant, I believe in their story, and I believe in their innocence, and no matter what happens over the next couple of months, you need to stick with them, regardless."

Tanya looked at Bucky for a moment and then nodded and said, "Yes, Sir."

"Now, have Sergeant Diego tell him that I am getting heavy pressure from Admiralty, and that we are running low on time. Tell him I need a scan of the Hingandu, or some solid proof against Gallagher."

"Aye, aye, Sir. Is that all, Sir?"

"Yes, dismissed."

Tanya saluted and then left the room, as Bucky still stood there with his hands clasped behind his back. Deep down in his heart, he feared the pressure from Chambers might overwhelm the admiralty back on Earth, and he worried about his command if he did not follow their orders, and start actively searching for Willy, Sydni, and Conrad. He knew that that search could lead to a private war he was not ready to fight.

* * * *

For Willy and Sydni time passed quickly as they continued to hunt, use the native weapons, and teach Conrad the language. Conrad could now hold his own in a very casual conversation, which gave him the freedom to roam through the village somewhat easier than before. Every day they worked with their Brotu's, teaching them verbal commands and hand signals. They finally met some engineers and technical Hingandu who knew the secrets of the Hingandu village. Conrad grilled them for a whole day, and he was asked many questions by them, the result of which, Conrad made several friends, who were now helping him to work on the scanners. They also showed him the basis of their technology and energy. Willy also found out how to make more bullets using comparable materials, and he set aside a part of each afternoon, when he could, to make an ample supply for his rifle.

One weapons expert, named Azia, took a particular interest in Willy's weapon and he stripped it down for her and showed her how it worked. She took notes on a clipboard and some flimsy paper, as he explained it to her. He gave her a bullet at her request, and when she left she was extremely happy.

They were all happy at the progress of their new clan as time passed. Quistqui was mated in a small ceremony to Nurian. Quistqui and Nurian started coming over to dinner or just to spend some time in the evening, sitting out back, sipping a drink that Quistqui introduced them to, which rivaled some of the finest brandy made in some of the oldest breweries back on Earth. Willy, Dekonal, Sydni and Conrad all discussed their mating ceremony, and decided that they would have it on the hill where Willy first met Dekonal. They had waited until after Quistqui and Nurian were mated, but they all agreed that they were ready and would be mated in several more days.

It was early in the morning when Willy woke to find that Dekonal was gone. He had to meet Gordo in several hours, so he got up and dressed, taking his scanner. Conrad had the messaging functioning through his computer in the house, and he had several other functions working, but still no scanning ability. Conrad had told them that he understood much more, now that he had spoken with the engineers and he was working on that solution.

Willy walked into his room where he had fashioned a loading bench and displayed the guns Sydni had secured for him, and there he picked up his 7-mm and a small pack of ammunition. Then he went downstairs where he smelled a hot liquid that Dekonal had brewed, that reminded him of an herbal tea that an old scout in the academy used to drink. He poured himself a pungent cup and looked around. Quickly he realized that Dekonal was standing out back with a shawl draped over her shoulders holding a steaming cup in her hands. Light from the kitchen spilled out just to where she stood.

It was a quiet morning; the birds had not even begun to sing yet, so he remained silent and walked up next to her. She was looking up at the sky, watching stars through the patchy clouds. He sipped his drink and she looked at him. "Good morning," he whispered.

"Good morning," she whispered back.

"You are up early. Is everything all right?"

"I do not know how you will feel about this, nor how to even tell you."

Willy turned to her and rubbed her shoulder. "I promise you this, you can tell me everything and anything. I am here and I am not going anywhere. You can tell me whatever you want to."

"I am pregnant," she said softly, staring into his eyes and looking for a reaction.

Willy did not understand the word she had used and he shook his head and said, "That is a new word. I don't understand."

Reaching down with one hand, she rubbed her abdomen and said, "I have a child growing inside of me. Our child."

It took Willy several seconds to realize what she said, looking down at her abdomen and back up to her eyes. He repeated her word, "Pregnant." She nodded, still unwilling to show emotion, trying to read what he was thinking. Slowly Willy started to smile as the realization hit him. "You are pregnant with our child. You, no, we are going to have a child?"

She nodded again. "Yes."

He shouted out before he realized what time it was, and then he said, "That's wonderful. That's great. Spectacular. If I had more words to exclaim in your language, I would use them."

Dekonal was grinning now, and as he hugged her, they nearly spilled tea all over themselves. With both of them laughing, Willy took their cups and set them on the ground and then embraced her again. He picked her up and swung her around, kissing her.

"Can we tell everyone? Can we tell anyone?"

"Some, but after the mating ceremony, you can tell everyone. This happens to many couples when they are to be mated. Some have a child before they are mated. You took this news better than I expected."

"Better than you expected? Are you joking? I have lived in a world where I thought I would never have a child so he would not have to grow up isolated like me, and now here I am going to have a child. It is the second-best news I have ever heard."

Tears rolled down his face and he didn't realize it until she reached up and wiped away a tear. "What was the first?" she asked.

"That you said you would mate with me."

A shadow crossed the doorway, and both of them looked up to see Sydni standing there. She was wearing a pair of shorts and a tee shirt. "I heard shouting," she said, running her hands through her hair. "What's up?"

Willy looked at Dekonal and asked, "Can I? I have to." Dekonal nodded. "Sydni," he started, looking at her again. "Dekonal and I are going to have a child. She is pregnant."

They could not see Sydni's face very well, since she was in the doorway, but she said in English, "Does that mean pregnant?"

"Yes."

She ran out and hugged Willy, and then Dekonal. "A child. The first child born into the Colton Clan. I never thought I would be an...." She paused, not knowing the family prefixes for Aunt or Uncle.

Dekonal filled in the word, "Aunt. You would be Aunt Sydni and Conrad would be Uncle."

Sydni repeated the words and then asked, "When will you have the child? How many months from now?"

"In four months. The month of the hottest days."

Willy and Sydni looked at each other and then back to Dekonal. "Four months," Willy said, holding up four fingers. "It takes eight or nine to have a child."

Dekonal looked shocked and laughed. "Eight or nine months? You are kidding. It takes four or five and I have been pregnant for about a month."

"Now that is evolution," Sydni said. "Dekonal, it would take me eight or nine months to have a baby. That is why we were surprised."

"I understand," she said, smiling. Then patting Willy's chest, she continued, "Then you would be worried about who the father is." She picked up the habit from Sydni and winked at Willy.

Leaning a little closer, he said, "Are you certain it is my child?"

Dekonal slapped him on his chest and said, "Don't get me started. Sydni must be freezing, let's go inside and have some more tea before you have to go see your friend."

Willy picked up the cups as they went inside, but he stopped and looked back up at the sky and paused. He thanked God and he thought he would never forget this day as long as he lived.

* * * *

Gallagher paced back and forth, rubbing his hands together and mumbling to himself. He had been up all night and on line with Chambers, who was angry. Although Gallagher had done nothing to infuriate him, he still respected that fury and did not want to end up on the wrong end of Chambers' wrath.

The outer door opened. Vladimir walked into Gallagher's office, adjusting his uniform and then straightening his hair. He scratched at a dark stain on his sleeve like it would disappear. "Vladimir reporting, Ambassador."

"Tell me you have something to report, Vladimir."

"Well, sir," he said lowering his voice. "I picked the two that you said we could get to, and one of them broke." He erupted into a grin and nodded. "Just like you said."

"You certainly do appreciate your work. What about the other one?"

"He won't talk."

"Vladimir, one man is lying in sick bay at your doing, and if he talks, there will be hell to pay."

Vladimir held up his hands and shook his head. "Not like that, Ambassador. I swear. I just scared him real good, I think he would be too embarrassed to say anything."

"Tell me there is no proof that you even threatened him."

Vladimir smiled again, and said, "If there is one thing I am good at it is not leaving evidence. I found out one of them is going down to meet with the Coltons, today. Our scans have shown no signs of the Coltons, Singh, or the Hingandu, but we can track the scout by homing in on his scanner."

Gallagher resumed pacing and rubbing his hands. "Pick the best of the UWC Ambassadorial Guards and send them down."

"I will tend to it myself, sir."

"No!" Gallagher nearly shouted. "No, you have personal reasons for wanting to get your hands on Willy Colton, and I do not have the time for you to screw it up."

"Sir, I am the best qualified..."

"I said, no!" Gallagher was in Vladimir's face and pointing. "You have cost me too much already. Set it up, and stay the hell out of the way. If you don't obey me, I will not only have you busted in the brig, I will have Chambers deal with you."

Vladimir looked at the ground and mumbled, "Yes, Sir."

"I am through trying to coax you, Vladimir. This is your last chance. Now get the hell out of here."

Vladimir stood straight and turned and walked away.

Gallagher watched him go and resumed his pacing, shouting after Vladimir, "Have them keep an open channel and report back during the mission."

"Yes, Sir."

The outer door opened and Vladimir was gone. Stifling a yawn, he knew he would not be able to rest until after the mission was over.

* * * *

Willy wanted to stay and talk with Dekonal, Sydni and Conrad, but he had contacted Diego, and it would be too late to call it off. He needed to go and see if there was any news from the ship or Bucky. So he stood up and said, "I have to get going."

"You want me to go with you?" Sydni asked, still dressed in her tee and shorts.

"No, enjoy a lazy morning, and maybe this afternoon we can go out and find something for dinner."

"Sounds good. Tell Diego I said hello."

"Certainly. Do you think our new trick will work?"

"Oh," she said standing up. "I hope it will. We should try it."

"Try what?" Conrad asked in Hingandu, after catching only a portion of the conversation.

"We have a way of calling the Brotu, but we don't know if their hearing is good enough to hear us at this level," Willy said. Willy walked out carrying his harness and his rifle slung across his back. "Come on. Let's see."

They all walked outside, and spread out along the overhang as Willy stepped out and punched a code into his scanner, setting off an ultra-high pitched sound that was out of Willy's range of hearing. Then he and Sydni looked up into the sky. "It did nothing," Dekonal said.

Conrad looked up and asked, "Ultra-high frequency?"

"Yes," Sydni said.

Willy looked at Dekonal and said, "I created a sound that is out of the range of our hearing, but not out of the Brotus'. I am trying to teach Remington to respond to the sound and come to it."

"There!" Sydni nearly shouted, pointing up in the air.

Willy and Dekonal looked and watched as the plunging creature opened its wings and then began a slow steady spiral, gradually heading straight toward them. "I have never seen anything like this," Dekonal whispered.

Remington flapped his wings several times just before he landed in front of the group. Willy stepped forward, saying, "Good, Remington. That was perfect." He scratched behind Remington's ears and chin. Remington moaned. As he started putting the harness on Remington, Willy said, "Gonnaktu said he could be trained to do many things, and so far, he has proven correct."

"I have seen Brotu trained to do many things, but that is definitely something new." Dekonal commented, stepping forward and sticking her hand down to Remington's muzzle. Even though Willy's meeting was with one of his friends, she was very uneasy about it; she had not seen any visions about it, but it was nagging her.

When the harness was finished and secure, Willy checked for his scanner, knife, bullets, and rifle. Then he turned and said, "I don't have much to talk to him about, so I won't be very long." He stopped when he looked Dekonal in the eyes. "What is the matter? You look worried."

"Something is bothering me about your meeting. I know he is your friend, but be very careful."

Willy smiled his most reassuring smile and said, "I am always careful. I'll be fine." He kissed Dekonal before he sat in the harness and nudged Remington, saying, "Go."

With a few long, graceful strokes of his wings, Remington rose above the level of the houses and quickly was gone. Sydni stepped up to Dekonal, who was still looking up in the sky, and asked, "What is it you're worried about?"

Dekonal shook her head and said, "I don't know. Just something in the back of my mind bothering is me about today."

Sydni looked back at Conrad and said, "Maybe I ought to get ready just in case he needs some back-up."

Willy was moving out past the village quickly, and Remington was gaining altitude. He wanted to be well in place and hidden before Diego touched down. Willy had been taught that the best way to hide a Brotu was in a low thicket where the trees were not so binding that it couldn't fly straight up. Willy had already picked a spot and led Remington in there and crouched down with him, waiting and listening for Diego's ship to fly over.

A scout ship passed over, and Remington's ears perked up. Stroking Remington's muzzle, Willy said, "Don't worry. That is just a ship, nothing you need to worry about." Holding up his open hand, Willy said, "Stay here."

He slipped out of the thicket and moved through the woods like a spirit; silently he moved from tree to tree, from bush to bush, making certain all the way that there was no trap set for him. He waited as he neared where Diego had set his ship down. He also kept an eye on the openings to the plain as he passed by, since the Jolabwe had increased their attacks, almost in an effort to see how good the Hingandu defenses were.

The wind was blowing through the woods and Willy could smell first the burned Coppertroid fuel, and then Diego's scent. There was a stand of trees that were much like spruce trees with soft needles and space between for someone to walk through that he had targeted for the meeting.

Diego was walking quietly, but somewhat casually in a direct line through the woods, his eyes darting back and forth. Willy moved so Diego could see him and then motioned towards the spruce trees. Diego nodded in approval and changed his course.

Willy arrived first and lay down under a tree to look for other feet entering the spruce trees, but he saw none other than Diego's feet. A stark red bird squawked loudly at the intrusion and flew off with a high-pitched flapping of wings. Willy moved in behind Diego, who was frantically pushing keys on his scanner.

"Diego," Willy said softly.

Diego jumped and spun around looking at Willy. "Willy. Geez, I couldn't find you on my scanner. You shouldn't sneak up on me like that."

"How goes everything shipside?"

"Same. Tension is high, especially between the command and the ambassadorial group." Diego was looking around and his fingers tapped his scanner.

Willy was beginning to feel uncomfortable with the way Diego was acting, so when Diego looked away, he switched on his messaging system so Diego would be recorded and Sydni could listen. He hit a key so her scanner would produce a loud noise to alert her. Willy calmly said, "What's wrong, Diego? You seem very nervous."

"I've just heard that there are a lot of skirmishes down here between the Hingandu and the Jolabwe and Tanya said she almost was killed."

"We shouldn't have anything to worry about, here. If the Jolabwe show up, all we have to do is melt into the woods, only a few of them are very adept at traversing the woods."

Diego breathed out a heavy sigh and relaxed a little, which eased Willy's concerns. "Where is Sydni?" he asked.

Willy shrugged. "I left her at camp. She didn't feel like coming today."

"You'll have to tell her everyone says hello. Captain says things are still the same, nothing new. Gallagher is still an ass, but Capt'n has not been able to scare up any proof."

"Well, I hope that Gallagher makes a mistake...." Willy stopped mid-sentence and held up his hand demanding silence from Diego. He heard a troop shuttle overhead, and he turned away, looking toward the sky. "Troop ship," he said. "We better get out of here. They may be following your transponder, thinking you would meet up with us."

And then the hair on the nape of Willy's neck stood on end as he heard the distinct sound of a pistol being drawn from its holster. Before he could even turn halfway, Diego said, "Put the rifle down, Willy, or I will fire."

Willy's heart dropped into his stomach. Out of the corner of his eye, he could see Diego pointing his gun at him. He set his rifle down, and raising his hands, he faced Diego. Willy had never expected Diego, or any of his scouts to turn on him. "Diego, you're holding a gun on me, Willy, your friend."

"Don't come any closer."

"On whose orders are you holding me?"

"It doesn't matter, Willy. It just doesn't matter."

Willy shook his head. "It does to me, Gordo. I want to know why one of my hand-picked, specially-trained soldiers would hold a gun to my face."

"It was Vladimir, and Gallagher, and Chambers." Diego's eyes turned pleading, "They didn't threaten me, Willy. They threatened my girlfriend and daughter. They are so far away, and I have no way to protect them."

"So how many are on their way to bring me in, or did you think you could do this alone?"

Diego shook his head. "A squad of Ambassadorial Guards and a squad of Jolabwe. They will be here any minute now."

"That is a lot of people to capture one man and one woman." Willy said.

"They have started calling you the ghost because they can never find you on the scanners, or in your ship."

"I never would have believed it. Gallagher himself could have warned me and told me, but I thought you had more loyalty."

"Believe me when I say I am sorry. The things they said they would do to my girlfriend and daughter before they died, I-I..." Tears rolled down Diego's cheeks, but he still kept his eyes on Willy.

"You could let me go. Say I overpowered you and escaped." Willy tried. He wanted to get away without hurting Diego, for once in his life he understood where he was coming from, now that he was to be married and a father. But he wouldn't allow them to take him so easily.

"I can't. I am on an open channel. They can hear what's going on."

Willy smiled. "I am a ghost, Gallagher. I will slip in one night and slit your fat belly open, and as for you Vladimir, I am down here waiting for you, I will teach you what Hingandu hospitality is." And then Willy laughed, which made the ambassadorial troops shudder along with Gallagher.

"Don't even think about it, Willy," Diego said. "You can't out move a pistol."

Willy did move, though, and he moved so fast that Diego's wrist was in his grip before he could pull the trigger, searing the spruce trees. Willy slammed a fist into Diego's face, twisted the pistol free before he hit him in the solar plexus, knocking the wind from Diego. "Don't come after me again, Diego. Next time you are a dead man."

Willy picked up his rifle, pushed the pistol in his belt, and jumped to the edge of the trees toward the plains where he saw five of the guards slowly picking their way through the woods. He would try and lose them before he had to hurt them. He ran back past Diego, who was moaning and rolling on the ground. "Leave me my pistol," Diego said.

"Not a chance," Willy said without stopping. "Your new friends are here."

Willy waited only a second, looking closely for other guards or Jolabwe before he dashed through the trees toward, deeper, thicker forest. A shot from an Ambassadorial Guard rifle struck a nearby tree, snapping it. Willy ducked and dodged until he hit the thick underbrush. He turned around against a large old V-shaped tree and readied himself to fire. He saw several guards go into the spruce trees, but he lost the others.

Willy's blood ran cold when he heard Diego scream, "No, I did what you said..." He was cut off by the sound of rifle fire. The first soldier came from the right, moving out of his hiding place to gain an angle on where Willy had entered the thicker part. Willy fired, dropping him in his tracks. A second one popped up to fire at Willy, but never even got his shot off. The sound of Willy's two shots brought more guards into sight, and the first two who appeared in the spruce trees were shot down as well.

Jolabwe showed themselves in the distance, moving rather clumsily through the low brush. With them backing up the remaining four guards, there was a sudden rush toward Willy. He melted back into the forest, reloading his rifle.

Knowing his rifle was too loud and they would hone in on him quickly, he slung it across his back and pulled out his knife. The four guards plunged into the thicker part and stopped, while the Jolabwe stopped at the edge. Willy watched and waited until he realized which one was the leader of the guards. As his remaining men spread out, Willy crawled on his belly to get close to him. Then he waited until the officer stepped right next to him. Willy dragged him down. The officer screamed until he was unable, and two Jolabwe shots whistled overhead.

"Captain," one of the other guards shouted. "Captain's down."

That second guard was too close, and he too went into the underbrush screaming. Then there was an uneasy silence just before a resounding crack from Willy breaking the guard's neck.

Shots sizzled all around Willy as the guards fired blindly at him, and he jumped aside and ran hunched over. Several of the Jolabwe saw him and started firing until he went out of sight.

He sat at the base of an old tree, and he typed in a message to Sydni telling her roughly where he was and what was going on. Then he heard more hushed voices as the two remaining guards conferred with someone else. He crawled along toward them, realizing that the Jolabwe were still hanging back, giving him the opportunity to sneak toward them.

Willy pulled out the pistol and inched his way right up to the two guards as they crouched over the body of their captain. "Yes, Mr. Ambassador, but he has kicked our buts and we have no way to tell the Jolabwe to get in here and search for him." There was a pause and he continued, "Damn it all, Ambassador, we are in his territory now, he has cut us apart, I am getting the hell out of here. That sniveling scout is dead and will not cause a threat..."

Willy had heard enough. He cleared his throat, and the two guards looked up at him, cursing when they realized he was right there. Before they could even move, he fired and sent them sprawling backward. There was a murmur among the Jolabwe, but Willy knew they couldn't see him. Rushing forward, Willy snatched the headset from the guard and put it up to his ear. "You son-of-a-bitch. You didn't have to kill Diego."

Gallagher's voice rose in pitch as he said, "He was of no more use to us."

Willy twisted the guard around, trying to reach his scanner to record Gallagher's message. "You coward. You and Chambers will go down for this. I will see to it by my own hand. You want a war; I will give you that war. Send all your troops down if they are that expendable to you. Send Vladimir, I would like to meet him again." Willy finally changed the scanner to record the conversation, but the line went dead.

The haze of hatred started to recede and he tossed down the headset before he realized that some of the Jolabwe were moving forward. The first Jolabwe was only a few yards away, and Willy fired with the pistol as he lunged backward. The Jolabwe's shot tore up a chunk of ground, and the Jolabwe hissed as it fell backward. The forest was alive with hissing and moving branches. Willy turned and ran low as shots filled the air. The whole line of Jolabwe was moving forward into the forest chasing Willy.

Suddenly Willy caught sight of a pair of eyes ahead of him. Before he knew it, a bolt streaked past his head and a Jolabwe behind him screeched. The air became full of a sudden volley from more Hingandu. As Willy turned around and unshouldered his rifle a second volley was fired. A few Jolabwe took shots before they all turned and ran. More Hingandu than Willy had realized were present, moved forward, starting the slow hunt. Willy fired once, striking a Jolabwe that had turned to fire, when suddenly Sydni was standing next to him, firing at another Jolabwe.

What had happened finally hit Willy. Gordo Diego was dead, along with eight other humans; the path they had taken was now sealed, and again he had no proof. "They'll make it look like I killed Diego," he said.

"I know," she replied. "We know you didn't, and so will Bucky."

"Will Tanya and Barkley believe me?"

Sydni shook her head and said, "I don't know. Do you think he could have gotten to any of them."

Willy looked at her, and she could see the sadness in his eyes, and she thought that even tears were forming. She had not seen him cry since the night Fred Donnelley had said Willy was not to see Phyllis anymore. "No. Tanya has no family left alive and is way too stubborn. Barkley was broken when we picked him. Life had taken away what he wanted. He may drink and gamble, but he won't give us up."

"Why did Diego?"

"I never knew he had a kid. It was not listed on his record. I did not know he had a serious girlfriend either or I would never have brought him on this expedition."

"It's not your fault," Sydni said, putting a hand on his shoulder.

"I know, and it is not like this job isn't without risk, but my God! He has a daughter out there, who will think her daddy was betrayed by a friend. She'll have no one there as she grows up." He looked at her again and said, "I will think of that on the day I kill Vladimir and Gallagher, and given the chance, the day I kill Chancellor Chambers."

"I'll be standing beside you."

They both paused as they heard another outburst of shooting from Jolabwe. Willy was staring off into the woods, where the Hingandu had disappeared, and he said, half aloud and half to himself, "I was going to let them all go. I was going to run back to Remington and let them all go back safely to the ship, but when they killed Diego, I snapped. Something cold grew in my belly and I snapped."

* * * *

"What happened to you?" Tanya asked when she saw Barkley lying in sick bay with a nurse applying salve to his cuts and a healing stimulator to his bruises. He was not wearing a shirt and had fading bruises.

"I ran into a Russian wall."

"Why didn't you call me? Oh, my God. What happened?"

"Lieutenant, respectfully, I will ask if you wait until we are done here to grill my patient," the nurse said.

Tanya held up her hands and said, "Yes, ma'am. May I wait here while you do?"

The nurse nodded and continued working on Barkley. Tanya moved off to a corner and leaned against the wall. It took the nurse twenty more minutes before she called the doctor, who checked Barkley with a hand held medical scanner. He looked over the results and cautioned Barkley about heavy work and activities, and said that he should report back every day for a week to stimulate his ribs and facial bones.

Finally he gingerly put his uniform shirt back on and started buttoning it as they walked out of sick bay. "Where the hell did Vladimir catch you that you couldn't respond?" Tanya asked.

"In my room. He came in last night, trying to get me to work for Gallagher. Trying to bribe me to turn on Willy and Sydni."

"Bribe you?"

Barkley's smile looked awkward with the healing cuts and bruises. "Yeah, they think because I gamble that I am in debt or something. Willy told me that if I ever got into debt, he would bail me out, but I am so far up on this cruise that it would take me the rest of this cruise to lose it all."

"So when did the beating start?"

"Well, he then threatened my wife, not realizing that she was dead, and my parents are dead, and I basically have no family except the scouting corps. That just made him mad and he threatened that if I told anyone about it he would kill me."

"We need to tell the Captain about this," Tanya said.

"No. Let him think I have submitted and won't say anything. I can't help Willy and Sydni if I am dead, and it won't hurt if he thinks I am just trying to get out of the way."

Tanya nodded and said, "Okay. He has not threatened me at all, but he would get similar results. You guys are my family. I have no other."

Barkley smiled and said, "Not to mention you are the most stubborn...." she glared at him and he paused looking for the right words. "Lieutenant I have ever met."

She grinned. "That's more like it."

"I guess he would get similar results from Gordo, too. He doesn't have anyone."

Tanya stopped dead in her tracks and said, "Damn!"

"What is it?" Barkley said, stopping after a few more steps.

"That's just it, Gordo does have someone. Don't you remember that night back at the beginning of the cruise when we were all sitting around drinking, and he said he had a girlfriend and a little girl back home?"

Barkley shook his head and said, "I don't remember, but that was a long time ago, and if I was drinking, who knows what I could remember."

Tanya was looking at her scanner. She tried to send a message to Gordo, but his scanner was switched off. "He's already left to go down. Lord, I hope Vladimir didn't talk to him before he left."

"Come on," Barkley said, urging her to keep walking. "Gordo give in to Vladimir? Give me a break. Besides, he told us in secret. So it is probably not on his record, they don't know if we don't tell them."

Tanya took a deep breath and let it back out as she started to walk along with Barkley. "You're right, of course. Look how jumpy they have me. Okay, but we need to talk to him when he gets back. He needs some warning."

"Until then, I could use some real food, and even though breakfast is almost over, maybe we can still catch the tail end."

* * * *

Gallagher was whiter than normal and he just sat there drumming his fingers on his desk since cutting off Willy's communication. Vladimir sat across from him waiting for the outburst or orders. Then Gallagher looked down and started punching in codes on his keyboard, saying, "First I call Chambers, then we ready an extraction crew. We need to at least bring back the bodies. While I inform Chambers, you go find that corporal we used last time. We need to splice this whole communication to make it sound like Willy Colton killed Gordo Diego and then attacked our crew. Get on that."

Vladimir stood up and said, "Right away, sir."

Vladimir was gone and the line was connecting through to Chancellor Chambers. Gallagher's heart was pounding so loud he could hardly hear, and his hands were shaking. Chambers face appeared and he said, "You've called me back quickly, Jasper. Tell me the good news." He paused and said, "You don't look so good."

"Sir, we executed your plan, just as you said to, but...but...." Gallagher stammered.

"But what, Jasper?"

"Willy Colton disarmed Gordo Diego, our team was assaulted, and we suffered one hundred percent casualties. He truly was a ghost out there. He did not show up on any of our sensors, and he cut through our team with amazing speed."

Chambers shook his head and looked down. "He is no ghost. He is a man. We have to find a way to take him out of the picture."

"Sir, what about not dealing with him? Just cut him off. We help the Jolabwe and we let them escalate the war as they want. We can support the war and just ignore the problem. The only way there will be a problem is if he gets onto the ship."

Chambers squinted and slowly began to nod. "You may be onto something there, or at least until a time when I can get Bucky Dollinger removed and then we could proceed a little faster." As he spoke, Chambers had looked away from the screen, but then he looked back so suddenly that it nearly made Gallagher jump. "Okay, we give it time, but we need to take care of this mess."

"Working on it, Chancellor. I am having the tapes altered to make it look like Willy Colton attacked Gordo Diego and then attacked my guards during a training exercise."

"Brilliant! Good work. Inform the Captain immediately that your guards were attacked while responding to the scouts' needs. Then you can have him help mount a response."

"I will do that right away, Chancellor."

"Call me in a few hours and let me know what is going on."

"Yes, sir."

The screen blinked out and Gallagher quickly punched in the code to the captain. After a minute the captain appeared from the bridge and said, "What is it, Gallagher?"

"There is a big problem, Captain. I need your help planetside. One of my squads was attacked, while responding to a call for help from one of the scouts."

Willy took a long ride along the mountains after warning the other Hingandu to leave the area quickly, as more ships would bring other off-worlders to search for their dead. He had seen many men and women die, he had killed other species and several rogue Special Forces who had rebelled during the Skalkanian Bush Skirmish, but never had he felt so responsible. Sergeant Diego had been his responsibility and he had left him without a weapon.

So Willy spent two hours flying low along the trees in the mountains, but none of it was as beautiful as it had been the other day. He wondered if it would ever be as beautiful again, knowing the blood that had been spilled on it, and that he might have just let his anger open the door to an escalation that he has been trying to avoid.

Finally he let Remington turn toward home and, once in the village, Remington just spiraled down, dropping Willy off in the courtyard. Today Willy had noticed that there were several people in the courtyard, standing just in the shade of the overhang; he had not wanted to see anyone, but he knew there was no way to avoid them, so he just let Remington continue his path. At the last second, he urged Remington toward the back of the courtyard to give him some room before anyone came forward and talked to him.

He dismounted and stretched, and then he unslung his rifle and ammo pouch and set them on the ground. Turning back to Remington, he started unharnessing him and rubbing down and scratching where the harness had been. After Remington pushed his muzzle into him and rubbed it around, Willy pointed skyward and said, "Home."

Lifting his head, Remington roared aloud and then flapped his wings and rose into the air. The flapping of wings faded, and Willy heard the pounding of feet. Willy spun just as Dekonal was within a few feet of him and he opened his arms and they hugged.

"Willy, thank God you are safe. I was so worried about you."

He pulled her closer, smoothing back her hair. "I am safe. I am here with you."

"Sydni told me about your friend, I am sorry."

Willy kissed her and then softly said, "Can we talk about it later, when we do not have company?"

She traced his cheek with her hand and said, "Of course." She gestured back toward the house and said, "Shortly after the news of the battle came back to us, they started showing up to speak with you."

Willy let go of her and bent down, picking up the harness, rifle and pouch. She offered to take something, so he let her carry his rifle. Among the faces he recognized was Quartainian. He said hello to everyone on his way inside, where the war council sat at the long dining table with Sydni, Quistqui, Conrad, and several others. Douka looked up from the conversation when

Willy walked in. The others looked toward him, and Dekonal softly said, "Let me take your things."

As Douka motioned for Willy to step forward, he let Dekonal take his other things from him. He stepped past a few other warriors and took the head seat at the table. "Douka, Klisk, Watkil, welcome to the Colton home."

Klisk and Watkil nodded, and Douka said, "Thank you, the hospitality of the Colton clan is excellent, and I am sorry to intrude at such a bad time, but I felt compelled to speak with you."

"You have brought many warriors with you."

"This is the full war council. The three of us still make the most difficult decisions, but each person serves their purpose and specialty."

Willy nodded and looked at Sydni, who looked as if she were holding back a tidal wave of grief over Diego's death. He wished he could give her strength, but he felt drained himself. He tried to smile, but that felt pathetic to him. Turning back to Douka, Willy said, "I will be blunt with you, Douka. My sister and I have suffered a great loss today. A very close friend was killed today on that battlefield, so I will ask you to get straight to the point."

"I understand. A survey of the area afterwards confirmed you had eleven kills, most of which were at close range."

Willy's tone was stone cold. "Ten kills, Douka. Ten." Douka tilted his head and looked at Watkil, who shrugged. "One of them was a very close friend, and I did not kill him."

Douka nodded with realization, and he could tell Willy was very upset. "Two of your kills were done with your knife and hands," Douka said. Willy nodded. "Our people are not used to fighting in the manner that you did today, and it is the council's wish that you and Sydni join the council as teachers, and be in charge of training some of our forces in this method."

Willy looked at Sydni and asked, "You explained guerrilla warfare?"

"More or less. Hit and run, silence when possible. Small raiding parties to work on parts of other larger war parties."

"And that is what they want?"

"I also kind of explained our scout jobs to him and how we would act in war-time. They want a longer discussion of how many groups we would need to effectively cover the area."

"What do you think?" Willy asked.

Sydni shrugged. "I am up to it if you are. They were impressed by your work today."

"Very much so," Quistqui said.

Willy looked at him and nodded. "Thanks." Then looking back at Sydni, he said, "I have no problem with it. It will mean a lot of work, but everyone I have met here has potential to work in a squad like this."

"Agreed."

They looked at each other for a minute, and then Sydni shifted her eyes to Douka and back in a quick movement. Willy knew that this was his cue to be the one to answer for them. He looked at Klisk, Watkil, and then Douka and nodded once. "We accept. We will be a part of your council and we will train all the warriors you want in this form of combat."

Douka looked relieved and smiled. Standing up, he said, "We thank you. You are already advisors now, this added duty is more than we should ask. I am deeply sorry at the loss of your friend, and I am sorry about the timing of our request. We shall leave you and your clan alone to deal with your sorrow. If you need anything, do not hesitate to call upon me. When you and Sydni are ready, tell Quistqui, who is a new member of the council, and we shall convene a meeting."

"We will, and we will not take too long. You can expect us to call within two days."

All of the war council filed out of the house slowly, except for Quistqui. When everyone else was gone, Willy looked at Quistqui, who said, "Willy, Sydni, I have never lost a friend in battle, so I will not say I know how you feel, but if you want someone to talk to, or to hunt with or ride with, please ask."

Clasping his shoulder, Willy said, "Thank you, Quistqui, I will."

"Thank you, Quistqui," Sydni said.

Quistqui got up quietly and left.

Willy looked at Conrad and then Sydni. He reached out his hand and held hers. "I am glad you came back when you did, brother. I do not know how long I could have held it all together." Her eyes brimmed with tears. "It didn't hit me until I came back here. I saw what they did to him. He would barely be identifiable."

"You shouldn't have gone over and looked."

She shrugged and softly said, "I had to. I felt like I had to."

Dekonal placed her hands on Willy's shoulders and kissed the top of his head.

Conrad said, "He was a good scout. Always jovial. Excuse me." Conrad pushed out his chair and headed toward the stairs.

Sydni nodded. "I will miss that laugh of his, and his jokes, and his smile...." Her voice trailed off and she stared down at her light hand in Willy's. His claws flexed involuntary.

A tear broke free and rolled down his cheek, and dropped to the table. His throat choked up as he tried to speak, but he managed to say, "I didn't know he had a little girl." He patted one of Dekonal's hands with his free hand and looked up at her. "He never told me."

"It is not your fault. He turned against you."

Willy shook his head and said, "No, he was turned into a pawn against me. All he tried to do was protect his family, I can understand that." He knew that he had to forgive Gordo, he knew Boris would have. Sometimes people made choices that were wrong, but that was all part of being Human or Hingandu.

Conrad came back in the room, carrying a wooden box, saying, "I was going to save this, for an appropriate time, like our wedding day, but today would seem to be more appropriate. Some may consider this wrong, but I can think of no better way to salute one of your fallen comrades."

Using a small knife, Conrad pried the lid off and pulled out a dusty bottle of brown liquor. He wiped away some dust and showed a label of Jack Daniels. "One gravity cart was filled with liquor and wine from my private stash. I figured that even though we were going to be stranded, there was no reason to just give up a fortune in real alcohol. This is an old bottle from the original distillery on Earth before it was destroyed. I heard that when a scout had fallen, tradition was that you drank to him."

Dekonal went into the kitchen and Sydni said, "Now Gordo would have appreciated that. He complained about the synth bourbon, but said he couldn't afford the real stuff, and any real stuff would have done."

Returning with three glasses and a rag, she tossed the rag to Conrad, who caught it and said, "Thank you."

Willy stared at the bottle and nodded. "Gordo would have flipped over that bottle." He wiped off his cheek.

"Do you drink this cold or warm?" Dekonal asked.

"Some ice," Willy said, pushing back his chair to stand up.

Dekonal stopped him and bent low, kissing his cheek. "You sit there. I will get it."

He remained seated. Conrad had wiped the bottle clean and opened it. He reached over and poured a small amount in each glass as Dekonal chipped ice from a block in the freezer. She came back with a small bowl of ice and put a couple of chunks in each glass.

Conrad and Dekonal sat down and each one picked up a glass. Dekonal had enjoyed their sayings that they used before they drank, they had used a word from their homeland; toast. It sounded funny to her.

They held their glasses up in the air and touched them together. "To Gordo Diego, may we never forget," Sydni said softly in English.

Speaking in Hingandu, Willy said, "To Gordo Diego, may his spirit live on in his daughter, and may he find peace, where, I promise, Gallagher and Chambers never will.

Chapter 17

After listening to the tapes that the Captain had played for her several times, which documented Willy's attack on the squad and Gordo, Tanya asked to be dismissed. The Captain, thinking she was upset at the death of her friend, let her go. Tanya was upset, but she would not allow herself to believe that Willy had attacked Gordo. They had been friends. What if Vladimir had gotten to Gordo before he went planetside? Then maybe Willy had killed him to save himself. All the way to sick bay she couldn't believe that Gordo was dead, maybe there had been a mistake, but it was his voice that she heard screaming, and Willy's voice threatening him.

Tanya had dated a young doctor assigned to the Orion, even though they didn't have much in common, they still met for dinner or lunch from time to time. So she went to his cabin first. His tall frame nearly filled the door, and his tee shirt and boxer shorts hung from his thin frame. "Lieutenant Williston," he said with a nod.

"Doctor Sanik, I am sorry if I woke you."

He smiled, which had been the first thing that had attracted her to him. "That depends, is it a business call or a personal call?"

Shrugging, she said, "From the way you are dressed, I wish it was a personal call, but today is business only."

"What can I do for you, Tanya."

"Nine bodies were brought up from planetside this morning, and I need access to the morgue to get a look."

"I was working when they came in, ghastly sight. I have worked many industrial and ship-related accidents. However, these men were deliberately killed, and I have never seen anything like it."

"One of them was a scout." She said so matter-of-factly that it surprised her.

"I am very sorry. I didn't know that. Look, come in, please and I will get dressed and take you down there."

"Thank you."

He yawned three times on their way down to the morgue. Once he had her inside, he showed her the vaults where they kept the bodies. There was a whole wall of such vaults. Dr. Sanik helped her pull each body out on a sliding tray, until they got to the one marked, "Sergeant Gordon Diego." She put her hand on his, saying, "Not that one. I would rather be alone when I look at him."

He looked down into her eyes and then nodded. "Okay, I will leave you here alone, but promise me if you need someone to talk to you will either come get me, or talk to someone else. You don't have to be alone to deal with this."

"I promise, Don."

He left her alone, and when he did, she went back to the first body and studied it. It was a male with his throat cut all the way to the bone. She had this technique ingrained in her since her first lesson as a scout: how to kill. The next two people were dead with a single shot to the head with a rifle bullet; Willy's favorite weapon. The next one was quite ghastly as his neck was twisted backwards at an angle Tanya knew any scout was capable of doing. The next two had single pistol blaster wounds to the chest, leaving gaping holes, which meant that the shots had to have been at a very close range. The last two were also dead from rifle fire with shots to the chest. Each kill was definitely a kill that was in the style that would say a scout had killed them; Tanya could not deny that.

She hesitated at the last door though. This was Gordo. Her hand trembled for a moment before she controlled herself. She was not examining bodies as Gordo's friend; she was trying to prove that there was a lie present. She was trying to prove that her commander was innocent of the death of a subordinate. Taking a deep breath, she opened the door and pulled out the cold tray.

Diego's body was barely identifiable, except for the top of his face and the tattoo of the Jolly Roger on his upper right arm. He was covered with rifle fire from a pulse rifle. She documented at least five wounds, covering the lower face, upper chest, abdomen, his left arm and left leg. She sighed and glanced at the other bodies laid out before her, starting to piece the real story together.

A nearby desk had a monitor, and Tanya powered it up and punched in the Captain's code. After a few minutes, Bucky appeared on the screen and said, "Lieutenant, how can I help you?"

"Captain, if you have a moment, could you come down to the morgue?"

"What the hell are you doing down there?"

"Sir, I am looking at the bodies, and I can prove something by the bodies alone."

Bucky looked away and then looked back. "What are you up to, Lieutenant?"

"Proof, Sir. Just like you asked for."

He looked away again and then said, "I will be right down."

The image of the captain blinked out and Tanya wanted a recording of the bodies for her own personal records; too many other pieces of evidence had disappeared already, she would just have to store it where Vladimir and Gallagher couldn't find it. She pulled out her scanner, sent a message to Barkley, and then spent the remaining time waiting for the captain scanning each body very carefully.

Bucky came through the door and nearly shouted, "This better be good, Lieutenant, and quick."

"Yes, Sir," she snapped with a salute.

She walked to the first guard's body and pointed out his wounds. She quickly worked her way down the line pointing out each wound, only pausing when she reached Gordo's body. She stepped aside and let Bucky see Gordo. "This is Sergeant Diego, Sir."

Bucky examined and noted the difference in the wounds and ferocity in which Gordo had been killed. "I see the difference, but they could say he was very angry with Sergeant Diego and went off."

Tanya started shaking her head slowly. "You know Willy almost as well as I do, sir, and there is one thing that is inherent in him, he doesn't lose his cool. Look at his other attacks, not to mention that there is a philosophy behind any scout's survival. Gordo himself had told Willy that there was a squad of guards and Jolabwe coming after him, for fear of being located quickly. If you fire once, they don't know your exact location. If you fire two, three or more shots, then they can find you quickly and one against eight is not good odds when they know where you are."

The silence in the room was uncomfortable for Tanya until Bucky smiled in relief. "Are you saying that they killed Diego, he killed them?"

She nodded. "Yes."

"Why would Ambassadorial Guards attack a scout?"

"Gallagher's order."

"Okay, say I believe you, we are back to proof."

"Sir, what I am about to tell you I must ask you to not use right now, for fear that it would cause another death."

Bucky wondered what kind of jewel she had, and wanted to know what she had learned, so he went along with it. "I will not use it until you deem it safe."

"I found Barkley this morning in sick bay. He had been beaten severely by Vladimir, in an attempt to persuade him to betray Willy and Sydni. He did not give in, so he was threatened that if he reported it, he would die. Barkley is not afraid of him. He wants them to think he is scared so he can continue to work toward our final goal of helping our commanders."

"Have his medical records been recorded?"

"Yes."

"Okay, I won't take action for now. Get in touch with both commander Coltons, get Willy's side of the story, pass on the information Sergeant Diego was supposed to," he paused for several seconds, and then he said, "pray that we can find our way out of this."

"Aye, aye, Sir."

Bucky turned to leave, but stopped when he got to the door. He turned back and said, "Does he have surviving family?"

"A daughter and girlfriend."

Bucky nodded. "I will write the best letter I can for now and see that his daughter gets full compensation. Lieutenant, I once again offer my condolences. If there is anything you need, ask."

"Thank you, Sir."

The room filled with a very eerie silence, and Tanya had to take several deep breaths to hold herself together. She kept telling herself that she was an officer, and she had to be the stolid one to tell Barkley the news.

Barkley loped in at his usual gait and he still smiled through his bruises, saying, "I have heard about subversive meetings, but in the meat room?" He glanced around and said, "Geez, what did you do, wipe out a squad?"

"Barkley, there was a major battle down on the planet surface today."

He leaned against the desk and nodded in the direction of the bodies, "Who are all of them?"

"Most of them are Ambassadorial Guards," she could tell Barkley was counting the bodies, and started walking toward them, but before he got far, Tanya caught him by the arm.

"Who is the extra one?" He shouted, knowing it was probably one of his three friends.

"Gordo." It stopped Barkley in his tracks.

"Gordo?" he asked in barely a whisper. "Why Gordo?" He turned back to the bodies and Tanya let him go. Barkley walked along the line of the dead, and stopped again when he saw the tattoo. "How?" he asked, standing over Gordo's body.

"Well, Gallagher has a tape that says Willy did this, first to Gordo and then to the others."

Barkley looked at Tanya and said, "Willy didn't do this. Willy couldn't have done this." He pointed to the other bodies and said, "Those, yes, but not this. Not with five shots."

"I know, and Captain Dollinger knows, but somehow Gallagher has manipulated communications to create a tape to the contrary."

Barkley smoothed back Diego's singed hair and softly said, "I am so sorry, buddy. I should have warned you. Maybe I could have stopped you from going down, maybe I..."

"No," Tanya said putting her arm around Barkley's shoulder. "Don't do it to yourself, Barkley. We couldn't have stopped Diego from doing anything he wanted to, and if keeping his family safe motivated him, maybe he would have slipped past us. We can't beat ourselves up, but we can keep working toward our goal, bringing down Gallagher and Chambers."

Using his sleeve, Barkley wiped the tears that were streaming down his face, but he couldn't stop the flood that had started. "You guys are my family, and now they have taken my only brother away."

"We'll get them. I promise you we will get them."

* * * *

The war council met at Willy and Sydni's house, filling up the dining room and spilling over into the kitchen. Dekonal had discreetly led Conrad outside to tend to some plants that they had planted for a small garden in the back of the courtyard near a couple of small trees. Douka called the meeting to order, and everyone was instantly silent. "Willy and Sydni, welcome to your first war council meeting. Klisk, Watkil, and I have discussed this type of battle you call guerrilla warfare, and we have come up with some questions." He looked at Sydni and she nodded. "How many warriors do you need for one group?"

"It depends how large you want the groups," Sydni said. "We have always had anywhere from five to eight warriors."

Klisk then asked, "How many groups?"

Sydni looked at Willy, who sat next to her and said, "What do you think, for a force as large as this village?"

Willy shrugged and said, "Anywhere from six to ten." He looked at Klisk and asked, "How many strong, brave, smart warriors can you give me as leaders?"

Douka and Klisk looked at Watkil, who looked around the room and spoke softly so only the other two elders could hear. As he talked, he counted off with his fingers. Soon both of the others were nodding and Watkil said, "With you and Sydni added, I have six that we could give you, each with five warriors that they can pick to follow them."

Sydni glanced at Willy, who was nodding in approval, and she said, "that will be a good number. Once you point out who the other leaders are, we can hold a meeting with them before they pick their warriors, but I have a question. Will you be able to find five warriors who will listen to my every command?"

Willy hadn't even thought of that, she was such an excellent leader that it had never crossed his mind. "Or me, for that matter," he added.

This time discussion washed through the whole crowd, until Douka hushed them. "Quistqui, Quartainian, you have closer ties to the warriors, what do you think they will say."

Quistqui, who had less seniority than Quartainian, looked at him and let him speak first. "I know several that saw both of you in battle, or have seen the results of your battle, and I don't think you will have any difficulties." Then he looked to Quistqui and asked, "What do you say?"

"I was the most skeptical about the two of you. I have talked to other warriors who respect what you have done. You should not have a problem."

She looked back to the elders and said, "That was my only question."

"I would like to add one thing," Willy said, raising his hand a little and gesturing with two fingers.

"Go ahead," Douka said.

"I want the leaders to know that practice will be long hours of hard work, and the same when we pick the other warriors, and that they should only ask for volunteers who are willing to give the time."

Douka nodded. "That is fair and wise for one so young." He smiled at Willy. "We will give each person the chance to say they do not want to become guerrilla warriors." After a short pause, he said, "Which of you would like to be the leader of the guerrilla warriors?"

Willy looked at Sydni and she was shaking her head. "You have a better command of the language; you make a better choice."

"You are as capable as I, I do not wish to overshadow you."

"Excuse me, Douka, Klisk, and Watkil, for I am about to speak in my native language if you don't mind." They all nodded in approval. She looked back at Willy and in English, she said, "Willy, never in my life have you made me feel like I have been in the shadows, in fact I always felt that you were.

Shine now that you have the chance. I am here with you and Conrad and I couldn't be happier. Be the leader and I will be able to work with you."

Willy smiled at her. He had never felt like he had lived in her shadow, he had lived in the shadow of the whole colony; she had been the sunlight. "Okay," he said in English. Then in Hingandu, he said, "I will lead the guerrilla warriors."

"Very well," Douka said. "Watkil."

Watkil looked down the long table and said, "We will first ask the following members to be a part of the guerrilla warriors. Willy, Sydni, Quartainian, Jasina, Quistqui, and one who is not a member of the war council, Ulik. What say you?"

Willy smiled and answered first, "I am in."

"Me too," Sydni said.

Quartainian nodded and said, "I will go freely."

From the kitchen, Jasina said, "I will." Willy and Sydni looked at her, she was standing with her arms crossed, wearing a long sleeveless shirt tied at the waist with a belt, and a pair of tight stretch pants that showed the muscles in her legs. She looked like she was in great shape. She smiled at them. Her skin was a light brown with thin, chocolate-colored stripes.

Willy and Sydni nodded to her, then looked at Quistqui, who was already smiling. "I will be honored to work with Willy and Sydni."

Douka stood up and said, "Is there anything else we need to talk about?" No one answered, and he continued, "That is all. This meeting is ended."

Several small conversations broke out immediately, and several people said goodbye and headed for the door. Douka thanked them for the use of their home for the meeting and said that Ulik would report to them by the second day after their mating ceremony.

The house cleared quickly, although the newly appointed guerrilla warrior leaders stayed behind. Willy and Sydni had them sit around the table and Willy said, "I do not want to get started without Ulik, but I want to welcome you to my home. I want you to know that as your leader, my door is always open to you. If you just want to talk, if you have a problem, or even if you want a hunting partner. I want you to be comfortable here. In case you don't know, tomorrow I am mating with Dekonal and Sydni is mating Conrad. We will start training the second day after the mating ceremony. Meet here in our courtyard just after the midday meal." He paused and looked at Sydni, asking, "Do you have anything to add?"

She said, "I just want to say what Willy said is true. You are always welcome in our home."

Conrad came in the back door, saw that they were still having a meeting and just walked to the far side of the kitchen and waited.

"Do you have any questions?" Willy asked.

"No," Quartainian said. "I do wish you a happy ceremony day, and congratulations."

"As do I," Jasina said. "Have a wonderful and beautiful day."

Both Willy and Sydni smiled. "Then we will see you in a few days," Willy said, standing up.

As Jasina and Quartainian left, Quistqui lingered behind. Sydni walked into the kitchen to see Conrad, and Willy walked Quistqui to the courtyard door and outside. They stopped just in the shade of the overhang, and Willy saw Dekonal kneeling in the small garden, working on her plants.

Quistqui cleared his throat and said, "I want to thank you for trusting me in a position under your leadership."

"They think you are a good choice, and I don't disagree with them. You are an excellent hunter and warrior."

"But after the way I acted when you first arrived and then when Sydni arrived. No one would have blamed you for not accepting me as a guerrilla warrior."

Willy smiled and patted Quistqui on the shoulder. "You are to be family after tomorrow and I will tell you this again, I understand what you were doing, now that you have accepted me, it is over."

"Thank you."

"I will see you tomorrow."

"A horde of Jolabwe warriors couldn't drag me away."

Inside, Conrad was sipping a glass of water, saying, "Sorry, I did not mean to interrupt your meeting."

"You didn't," Willy said. "This is your house too."

"I stayed outside as long as I could, but I started having an anxiety attack." He took a deep breath and sighed. "I'm okay, but I think I will stay in the rest of the day."

Sydni stepped closer and put her arms around his waist. He looked at her and smiled, and then they kissed. "It won't bother me if you stay in the rest of the day. In fact, I was thinking of staying in the rest of the day, too."

"On the day before our wedding?" he asked.

She raised her eyebrows and said, "Do you object?"

He looked away and acted as if he were thinking about it and said, "Well, it goes against my better judgment, but I guess I will not object."

* * * *

Tanya sat at a table stuck back in the corner of Six O'clock High, cradling a drink in her hands. Her dress white jacket was lying crumpled in a chair next to her with her cover on that. She did not feel like having any company, but she did not have any booze in her room and she more than needed a drink. The service had just been given for Gordo and although she did not want people to see her red eyes and runny nose, she didn't know where else to go.

The bar was by no means crowded, but the people there were making a fair amount of noise. Music started up at the music box flashing near the small dance floor. Barkley stood punching in the codes of the songs that Diego had always loved to listen to.

Barkley sat back down across from Tanya and sipped his drink. "He loved this song," Tanya said.

Nodding, Barkley said, "He certainly did."

There was a long pause, each of them drinking, but not certain what to say. A sudden hush ran through the bar, and when Tanya and Barkley realized it, they looked up to see Bucky standing at the bar. Someone finally got over the shock of seeing the captain there and yelled, "Captain on deck!" Everyone stood and saluted. The bartender handed him a glass and a bottle, and Bucky turned and walked over to Tanya and Barkley's table. Setting down the bottle, he saluted and said, "As you were." They eased up and he said, "I cannot stay long, as you know what kind of rumors would spread if I stayed and started drinking. However, I cannot let your loss go unnoticed as I believe that Gordo was the only innocent one who died in the melee."

Opening the bottle, he poured a fair amount in his glass and refilled theirs. Bucky picked up the glass and sniffed the liquor. All eyes were on him as he raised his glass. Bucky had been a flier until he was promoted out of the position, but every flyer took pride in the fact, and he was revered in Six O'clock High. "To one of those who will be missed on the flight deck, or off the wing. May he be ahead of us somewhere, making sure the way is clear and safe."

In unison, there was a resounding, "Here, here!" Everyone drank. Bucky slammed his empty glass on the table, followed quickly by Barkley and then Tanya. "I wish I could stay and drink with you, but I need to go now. The rest of this bottle is the captain's compliments."

"Thank you, Sir," Barkley said.

"Thank you, Sir," Tanya echoed.

"Somewhere in there have a drink for Sydni and Willy, too."

"Yes, Sir," they said together.

Bucky turned and said, "Ladies and gentlemen. Good day."

When the Captain had left the bar, murmurs ran through the crowd. Most were impressed even further with their captain that had come to have a drink to a fallen flyer.

Pouring more in their glasses, Barkley said, "You come up through basic and schools, having all these notions of what navy captains are like, and what officers are like, and then someone like Captain Dollinger comes along and blows all those stereotypes out of the water."

"Disappointed?" Tanya asked.

"No, not with any of the officers I deal with."

He held up his glass and said, "To Gordo."

"May we avenge his death."

They drank again, and as they poured another, Jackson Jeffries walked up to their table. They gave him an unenthusiastic nod and he returned it. "Can we help you, Commander?" Tanya asked.

"No, I just wanted to say, I have flown with many people, and I have sparred with many, and Sergeant Diego was an outstanding flyer and will be sorely missed by all squadrons."

Barkley looked up. "Thank you, Commander. That means a lot."

"Now with your scout staff depleted, feel free to call upon my squadron if you have any flying missions you need filled."

"Thank you," Tanya said.

Jackson left them and walked back to his place at the bar. Barkley took a deep breath and sighed. "I just feel like we have to do something. Something in the back of my head is nagging me and is trying to tell me that there is a way out of this."

"I know what you mean, but every time I get restless, I just picture those guards down there and know that they killed Gordo, but Willy made certain they paid dearly for it." Tanya paused, holding up her hand and said, "I know that those who ordered Gordo's death are still breathing, but in time, they too will get what's coming."

They drank as more songs played that reminded them of Diego. When the bottle was about half empty, and they were working their way through memories of Diego and laughing at stories of about him, there was a commotion nearby. Looking up they saw an unusual sight in Six O'clock High; five Ambassadorial Guards, who showed, by their unsteady gait and loud conversation, that they too had been drinking. Tanya's blood boiled at the sight of their insignia on their uniforms, but she tried to ignore them. She was there for Gordo, not them.

But when one of the guards spotted Tanya and Barkley, he shouted, "Look, it's some of those wuss scouts. Like the one that got C-squad killed."

Tanya's chair shot out behind her, hitting the wall as she stood up, and Barkley was on his feet a second after her. The room became silent. Tanya picked up the bottle and two glasses and walked over to the bar, where she softly said, "Will you hold these? I don't want any spilled."

The bartender nodded and placed the bottle and glasses down behind the bar. The same guard that had spoken then said, "Ooooooooo. What'cha gonna do, Lieutenant. Are you and the sergeant there gonna take on all five of us at once?"

Tanya looked around and then said to Barkley, "It hardly seems fair. It only took one scout to take out a whole squad, and here we only have five of them." She turned back to the guard that had spoken and said, "You certain that you don't want to go get a few more of your buddies?" The guards looked back and forth among them, and before they said anything in return, Tanya said, "You have thirty seconds to leave this bar. We are here remembering our friend, and you are not welcome."

"And what are you going to do if we don't leave?"

Tanya glanced at her watch and said, "Twenty-five seconds."

The guards spread out a little and bristled at her comments. Barkley stepped up next to her with the adrenaline clearing a little of the fuzziness that he had from the booze. He examined the guards, trying to figure out which one of them had any training, and which one of them was ready to fight.

The tension in the room was palpable, and Tanya just looked at her watch counting off the time. When the thirty seconds were up, she looked up and smiled. "You're still here. Don't say you weren't warned."

"Make us leave," the first one said, but before his mouth was even shut, Tanya kicked with lightning speed, catching him full in the face, sending him tumbling face first into the bar.

Tanya took a karate stance and said, "Pick up your friend and leave, or you will be thrown out."

The guards rushed. Tanya somersaulted between two of them. As they turned she kicked one in the chest, sending him crashing into their table and the wall. The second one grabbed at her, she came at him with a fury of swinging fists, striking him in the head, chest and abdomen.

Barkley stepped to his left, sweeping the first one's feet out from underneath him; he slid across the floor, and the second one swung at Barkley. Grabbing his wrist and using his momentum, Barkley turned the guard around and slammed his head onto a table where a few flyers had been sitting. Their drinks went flying. "Sorry, guys," Barkley said as he pulled the guard up and slammed him head first into the other guard who had gotten up. Their heads smacked with a resounding thump, and the one he was holding went limp as the other one staggered back into Tanya, who spun on him like a loosened tigress and caught him in the face with her open hand, sending him to the ground.

With all the guards down, Barkley held his arms across his ribs and said, "Oh, I shouldn't have done that with broken ribs."

Tanya helped him back to the table and righted a chair for him. The waiter, who had receded to the bar, walked out to help straighten the chairs, stopping when Barkley said, "I messed up their drinks, can you get them a round on me."

"Belay that," a Lieutenant said. "Sergeant, you two just gave us a great floor show, it was worth the drinks."

Wincing in pain, Barkley said, "No problem. We do matinees on the weekends."

A smattering of laughter went around, as Jackson snapped his fingers to a few of his men and motioned to have the guards removed. "We don't need that trash in here." Then turning to the bartender he said, "Why don't you call a medic team to respond to a minor altercation outside the bar? It would seem a few guards beat themselves up out there."

More laughter as Tanya righted her chair and retrieved their drinks. When things had settled back down and their drinks were back in front of them, she asked, "Did that help that nagging feeling any?"

Smiling, Barkley replied, "Quite a bit, actually. The nagging shifted to my ribs though."

"Your face still looks bad, good thing they didn't hit you there."

Barkley laughed, but that only hurt his ribs more. "I knew if the commanders left us alone long enough, we would start getting into trouble."

Tanya grinned and said, "Just think, this is only the beginning."

Lowering his voice, Barkley said, "I have an idea. Something we should look into doing, to help."

Tanya, leaning in closer, asked, "What is it?"

Barkley grinned, glanced around and said, "Same as what Willy and Sydni were doing, but we can hide it a little better. I was thinking about the way they hooked in. I can do it a little better."

"Permission granted," Tanya whispered, "but let's focus the rest of this evening on Gordo, tomorrow we can get back on track."

Barkley nodded and took a long gulp from his drink and said, "Orders are orders."

The afternoon was warm, but the breeze that gently waved the grass to and fro made it very comfortable. It was a perfect day to stand on the hill where Dekonal prayed, surrounded by close friends and family, to conduct a mating ceremony. Tyuk, the holy man, had been to visit the Colton Clan house several times after they had all decided to be mated, and he was confident that they were ready. He wore a gray coat and pants with a white shirt underneath, and Conrad remarked how much he looked like someone would dress on board the ship.

Willy and Conrad both were wearing black pants and white shirts they had brought down with them. Dekonal was in a silver and white dress that was designed like one she had worn on Willy's first morning in the village, that wrapped its way around her from neck to a long skirt. The silver picked up the flecks in Dekonal's eyes. Madak had fashioned one for Sydni using gold and white material.

The two couples stood facing Tyuk who smiled and looked around. "With this day, God is giving his blessing to this mating ceremony." He looked around at Chakkdon, Madak, and Doqui, then to Quistqui and Nurian and over to the grandparents of Dekonal and other family members. Douka, Gonnaktu and their families stood where the male's family normally would be. "It is truly unique that this gathering comes together today, and I am very happy to see those who have turned out to help us bless this union."

Conrad stood in agony, shifting from foot to foot with sweat on his forehead. Sydni squeezed his hand to reassure him, and prayed that he would last the whole ceremony. Willy and Dekonal had really wanted to have the ceremony on the hill where they had met, and they knew that Conrad could not last long on the hill, so they had explained to Tyuk that they needed a very short ceremony.

"God brings couples together not only to enrich their lives but to enrich the lives of the village. No longer will you be two separate people going about your day, but you will be one life, bound together by God for the rest of your lives." He looked at the two couples and said, "Please face each other."

Once they were all facing each other, Conrad became still. He stared into Sydni's eyes and the world ceased existing around him. He could have been anywhere in the universe as long as he was there, staring into her eyes. He mouthed the words, "I love you."

Sydni winked and mouthed back, "Me too."

"Willy, Conrad, do you swear to love, respect, and provide for Dekonal and Sydni, in the name of God and in his manner for all time?"

Willy was smiling, and Dekonal was a direct reflection of that. He did not notice all the people watching them, he just stared at Dekonal and listened to Tyuk's voice. He shifted both of Dekonal's hands to one of his and reached up and touched her face, tracing a stripe on her cheek, as he had done some many times before. Willy answered, "With all my heart, with all that I am, forever and ever."

Conrad heard Willy's answer and realized that he was supposed to answer. "I will," he said in Hingandu. Then in English, he added, "Always."

Dekonal's heart rose into her throat and her eyes brimmed with tears. She had seen this day in her visions, but never had she thought it could be as beautiful as this. She leaned her face into Willy's hand and closed her eyes as Tyuk said, "Dekonal, Sydni, do you swear to love, respect, and provide for Willy and Conrad, in the name of God and in his manner for all time?"

Dekonal echoed Willy's words by saying, "With all my heart, with all that I am, forever and ever."

Since Dekonal had repeated Willy's saying, Sydni decided to copy Conrad's by saying, "I will," in Hingandu and, "Always," in English.

"Then in God's vision, and here among the Hingandu people, let no person try and interfere with this mating." With his hand, he made a motion that looked like a question mark, and said, "You are now one, go forth and live as one."

Willy leaned in and kissed Dekonal as Conrad and Sydni kissed. Just as Willy and Dekonal's lips parted, she stared blankly ahead, as she had a vision. Willy waited; he had seen her do it before. As she came out of it, she smiled at Willy. "What is it?" he asked.

"I am pregnant with two babies."

Conrad and Sydni turned to congratulate Willy and Dekonal and Willy hugged Sydni, saying, "Twins."

The four of them congratulated each other and then others came forward. They lingered on the hill for a long time, laughing and talking. As a Brotu flew by, Willy remembered that even though it was his wedding day, there was still a lot of Jolabwe patrolling around searching for trouble. So Willy gently began to urge his new mate and sister and brother-in-law toward the crowd of Brotus that Tunnak was tending.

Traditionally, there was a post-ceremony party held at the clan house. So they held it at Willy and Sydni's house. Everyone invited brought the food, and Doqui roasted a large Saka and made a pot of his stew as main courses. The courtyard was full of people except near the heat of the roasting pit, and food filled the long dining table.

The occasion was more than Sydni had expected her wedding day in the Hingandu village would be. The same band that had played on the day they were accepted into the village was present to play after dinner, and as people started to filter out, room was cleared to dance. Darkness set and the lights were turned on out back. The fire was stoked into a bonfire. Willy and Dekonal danced into the night, laughing and holding each other; sometimes Sydni would coax Conrad to dance, and everyone left would gather in a big circle and clap to the beat as they danced.

Chakkdon, Madak, Quistqui, Nurian, Doqui, and a woman he had been dancing with were the last ones to leave, long after the band had stopped playing. Quistqui ran inside and picked up his pack, which he had brought over without them knowing. He came outside and handed it to Willy. "This is a present from me. After all that happened when you first arrived, I thought it was necessary."

Willy said, "I told you it was not necessary."

"Then it is a present to my new brother."

Willy smiled and opened the pack. Inside was a bundle, wrapped in a dark tanned hide. As he picked it out, he handed the pack to Quistqui. He unraveled the hide and there was a tomahawk with the Coppertroid crystal blade. It was wide on one side and tapered to a spike on the other.

Quistqui stepped up and said, "I made it myself, except for the blade. The shaft is from a bone in the Gaza-kan, which is stronger than any wood we know. It is wrapped with some of the hide from the Gyod, and the ornaments hanging down are polished scales from the Gaza-Kan. May it serve you well through your life."

"Thank you, Quist. I will carry it with me always."

Then Quistqui pulled out a sheath for it. "This should hook through your belt and you can carry it."

Willy was amazed and as he put the head of the tomahawk in the sheath he said, "Thank you. It is too kind."

With that, they said their good-byes and left the newlyweds alone for their first night. As they stepped inside, Sydni expected to find a mess, but before people had left, they cleaned up the mess of the party.

As they stood in the kitchen, Willy said, "We are now officially the Colton Clan." He elbowed Conrad in the ribs and said, "Thanks for not taking my sister into the Singh clan. We need all the clan members we can have."

Conrad laughed. "We have more than enough Singh clans out there. They can spare me."

Dekonal was arm-in-arm with Willy and was absent-mindedly rubbing his chest. "Are we still going to the ridge house?"

Sydni said, "Look, I hate to see you guys fly way up there tonight. It has been a long day and Conrad and I don't really mind sharing the house on the night of our mating ceremony."

Willy opened his mouth to speak and Conrad cut him off, "Really. We don't. We talked about it this morning and we have shared this house from the start and that does not make a difference on this night."

Looking at Dekonal, he said, "It is your call. If you wish to go we will go, if you want to stay here, we can."

Dekonal looked down and Sydni could tell as well as Willy that she was blushing. "I would like to go. I have not been up there for years, and the sunrise there is breathtaking, and…" She stopped and shook her head. "No, it is too silly."

"What?" Willy said, pulling her tighter.

She looked up into his eyes and sighed. "It is silly."

"I doubt it."

She paused again and smiled weakly at Sydni and Willy and said, "My mother told me about her ceremony night, and how beautiful it was, waking up out far from other people, protected by my father. I always dreamed that I would do that."

Willy pulled out his scanner and punched in buttons to call Remington down. "So we go. We are already packed, so there is no reason not to go."

"Really?" she asked.

"I told you it was up to you. I think it is a great idea and will make a wonderful memory."

Her smile gave him the best wedding gift he could have asked for. Then pulling away, she said, "I'll go get our things."

She was off and running. Willy smiled and looked at Sydni and Conrad. "I guess if you want to, you can have sex in the kitchen now."

Embarrassed, Conrad looked away, but Sydni winked and said, "Does that mean we can use the dining table?"

"Sydni!" Conrad said.

Willy laughed and said, "Certainly, just don't tell me about it, because then while I am eating dinner, I won't be able to get the picture out of my mind."

Sydni poked Conrad in the ribs, which made him jump. "I won't say anything, brother. Trust me." She pulled Conrad's enflamed face toward her and said, "Look lover, I don't know why you are embarrassed, you are the best lover I have ever had."

She kissed him, and Conrad said, "I was raised to be discreet. I can't help it."

Dekonal returned toting two packs, Willy's rifle, and Remington's harness in her other hand. Willy jumped to help her, taking the harness and packs. "We will see you guys day after tomorrow, sometime before our meeting."

Sydni hugged Willy and said, "Have a great time. Don't hurry back."

As he walked out the door, Willy was laughing.

CHAPTER 18

The technicians who had visited the Clan house wanted to meet with Willy, Sydni, and Conrad. They said it needed to be a secluded spot and described a pasture down along the ridge above the village. The day after their meeting with the guerrilla warrior leaders, they walked into the mountains, following the path that they had described. There was a group of Hingandu working at some makeshift portable tables. Their Brotu mingled not far away under some trees.

Conrad was taking long slow breaths to control his fear of the openness, while Willy and Sydni were in awe. The high pasture had signs of grazing animals passing through, but they could not see any of them now.

Azia, who had discussed the rifle with Willy immediately called him over and said, "I have been working on the weapon you had, and I think I have come up with something that you may like; I would like you to test it out."

She removed a cloth. There were three rifles with dark wooden stocks and with a reddish grain, and the barrel was a burnt gold color. Willy picked up the first one and looked at it. It was a carbon copy of his Remington rifle. "Have you fired this?" He asked.

"Yes," Azia said. "I am not very good with shooting this kind of weapon, though, and I want you to fire it. I also copied the thing you called a scope, but used what we use in our view finders."

Willy looked through the scope, and although it had a bit of a yellow tint to it, the clarity was superb and the zoom capability was even greater than his own. "This will change the light type so you can see better at night and then one so you can pick up on the heat of one's body."

Willy switched it past the night vision, knowing that it was too bright to see at this hour of the day, and then he hit the infrared and smiled. It was like an old friend, even weighing nearly the same. "You have outdone yourself, Azia."

"I had all the people who work on the weapons working a long time to copy it all, so I cannot take all the credit."

Willy handed that one to Sydni and picked up the second one, which was the same, except there was a magazine sticking out the bottom of the stock. "A magazine," he said to himself. "Very interesting."

"You described it to me and I thought you might like it. It holds three more projectiles than the other one."

He again nodded and handed it to Sydni when she set the other one down. As she was examining it, Willy picked up the last rifle. It was not a bolt action, and had a magazine that was much thinner. He looked at the barrel and realized that it too was smaller. Then he realized it was some sort of automatic or semi-automatic. He found the breech and pulled it open, examining the inner workings.

Azia touched the rifle and said, "This was the most exasperating of them all. I did not sleep for one night trying to figure this out. You described it and drew it, but I was having difficulties replicating it." She paused and said, "I had to make the projectile smaller to make it work. So the projectile is not as damaging, but certainly big enough to tackle even a mad Corunthu."

"Corunthu?" Willy and Sydni both asked.

She smiled and thought about it. Pointing up she said, "It is a very large creature, with much hair, and horns that start in the head but curve real low."

Sydni hit Willy on the arm, and in English she said, "That creature you showed me out on the plain with the trunks that looked much like an elephant."

Willy nodded. "Right, yes. That will be more than enough."

As Sydni looked over the last rifle, Azia pulled out a pack from underneath the table and started rummaging through it. "I have projectiles for both types, and I hope they do not disappoint you, because I made them a little differently than the ones you use."

Sydni set down the rifle and Azia handed them each a bullet that matched the size of the 7mm. The tip was a tiny chip of the Coppertroid crystal that was used on their weapons, otherwise it looked exactly the same.

She then handed them the same thing but cut in half to give them a view of it. "See, on impact, the chip will push back into the projectile, expanding it greatly, and the second core will hold it together and maintain its weight."

Then she handed each one another bullet. The large mushroom-shaped bullet was still quite heavy. "That is after I fired it."

Willy shook his head and said, "I don't know how you did it in such a short period of time. These are great."

"I had to do some extensive testing over the past couple of weeks to find the correct projectile. Some of them burned up in flight; some of them disintegrated on impact, causing very little damage. I believe I have figured out the correct ratio now."

She pulled out the smaller bullet and showed it to them. It was closer to a .243 round. Willy examined it and handed it to his sister. "What do you think?"

"I want to see what the penetration is, but they look excellent. Of course I prefer the rapid fire."

Willy nodded and said, "I knew you would say that."

"You are going to test fire them for me?" Azia asked.

"Only if you insist," Sydni said with a wink as she picked up the smaller rifle.

Azia made a sound that sounded more like an excited mouse as she turned around and started rummaging through her pack again. She pulled out three magazines and handed them to Sydni and then again with three magazines for Willy. Willy picked up the bolt action rifle with the housing for the magazines and slipped one in. It glided into position without any resistance and barely any noise. Then he pulled the bolt up and back, and it slid, seemingly frictionless and nearly silent. The bullet popped up and into position, and it slid easily into the barrel as he closed the bolt. Glancing sideways at Azia, he said, "If this shoots as well as it is put together, you are the greatest."

"Thank you," she said.

Sydni slid her magazine in as easily and then she pulled back the bolt and let go to see how loud it would sound, and it snapped back into position quietly. She looked at Willy and nodded. "I am as impressed as you already."

"Where is the target?" Willy asked looking around.

Azia pointed and Willy could see six white orbs three hundred meters away. Then he looked at Azia and said, "Remember we talked about the path of the projectile, and the rise and drop of the bullet?" She nodded. "Do you have that information?" he asked.

She returned to her pack and pulled out the clipboard and the sheets of paper she had used to take notes. She flipped through several pages and then she said, "Right here." Handing the clipboard to Willy, she said, "It is cut into segments of measure."

Their standard measure for longer distance was just over a meter long. Willy showed the chart to Sydni and then asked Azia, "This is for this projectile?" He wiggled the 7mm-sized magazine in his hand.

"Yes," She said. "And a few pages down you will find a chart for the smaller projectile."

"Look how flat that shoots," Sydni said. He flipped a few more pages down and showed the smaller projectiles, which was even flatter and faster. "These bullets are very efficient," Sydni added. "Shall we try them?"

"Definitely."

"You first."

Willy knelt on one knee and the other techs all moved around so they would be even with or behind him. He adjusted the scope and zoomed in on the target. He put the cross hairs on the center of the white orb, which he figured must be two meters in diameter. There was an X on the front of it and Willy zeroed in. He gently squeezed the trigger and the rifle fired. It kicked as hard as Willy's rifle, but it didn't sound nearly as loud. Downrange the bullet struck the left-most orb 5 centimeters low and three centimeters to the left. Willy jacked the shell out and quickly fired at the second orb and it struck the same place. He quickly repeated again on the third orb and again it hit in the same place. Standing up, Willy looked the rifle up and down, saying, "That is an incredible weapon."

Sydni took Willy's place and fired slowly at the first two orbs and then fired four shots into the last orb, sending large chunks of it flying into the air. "Nice shooting," Willy said, watching through his scope.

"Nice firing weapon. Not too much kick, or noise. Very nice."

"Thank you," Azia said. "Shall we go see what the damage looks like and how the projectiles performed?"

They walked down and examined the bullets and Sydni explained that they had aimed at the cross drawn on the orb, which was about two meters long, to see how much the projectile would drop. The last one Sydni had shot at was riddled and almost nothing was left. Azia split each orb that Willy had fired on and examined the damage the projectile did inside the orb. Willy examined and said, "That is an amazing amount of damage. Probably one and a half times what I get with my standard bullet."

When they split open Sydni's first one, the damage was almost as good as Willy's. "Do you believe that kind of damage?"

Azia dug out the projectile and handed it first to Willy. He examined it so Sydni could see it at the same time. It was mushroomed to almost twice its diameter. "It has retained a lot of weight, several pieces have splintered off to cause separate damage. Perfect. How did you make such a great copy with so little?"

"It is what I do. Besides you gave me such detailed information, it was only a week of trials. You are happy?"

"Very. How difficult is it for your workers to make these?" Sydni asked.

"Not at all. I was told that if I could help you, my group was to be at your service. The war council wants to see how this weapon works in a larger group." She paused and looked over one of the orbs and then said, "I may be speaking out of turn, but I think the war council hopes you decide to give such weapons to your new groups and that could be the test."

Willy slipped out the clip and tapped the top bullet with his finger, asking, "We would need many, many projectiles. More than you make bolts for the crossbows."

"They are easier to make," Azia said. "We do not need people to make them, there is a machine that makes it."

Willy did not understand when she said, machine, but he knew what it had to be. "For both sizes?" He asked. She nodded. "Well, Syd, what do you think?"

She held up the rifle she had fired. "Not as much kick, faster, less movement."

Willy furrowed his brow and then looked at Azia, "We need thirty-six of those." Willy pointed at the rifle Sydni was holding. "With ten magazines each."

"We can make them," Azia said. She glanced back to the tables, where the other Hingandu techs were waiting and said, "We should get back. As anxious as I was to show the new weapons to you, they want to show Conrad their new things."

"What should we do about these?" Willy asked, putting his hand on one of the split orbs.

"The rain will take care of them and they will go back to the ground."

They headed back, asking if they could keep the current rifles for practice and show the new guerrilla warriors. Azia told them they could have all of the prototypes and they would receive the new ones as soon as they were completed.

Back at the tables, the other techs were really anxious and jittery over their new toys to show Conrad. Sydni looked around and was trying to figure out where Conrad was, when she realized that he had walked over to the edge of the cliff and was leaning against a squat tree with a gnarled trunk. She was almost in shock as she walked up to him and put her hand on his shoulder. "Are you okay, lover?"

"I'm okay. I was just enjoying the view."

"You," Sydni laughed. "You are enjoying this." She swept her hand across the rolling foothills below.

"In a manner of speaking." He faced her and said, "It struck me while I was standing on that hill marrying you. I love you more than any words can express. Because of your love, I can conquer anything. We can conquer anything. This isn't open space, it is full of your love, and I can live with that."

Sydni had no words for it; she did not know how to respond, so she just grabbed him and kissed him. As soon as her lips weren't busy, she said, "You are an incredible man, Conrad Singh, and I would love to take you away and make love to you, but the techs want to speak to you about some new technology." She bit his bottom lip and whispered, "We can pick this up later."

"Promise?"

"Certainly."

They walked back over to the techs, who suddenly became still when Conrad approached. The lead engineer stepped forward and said, "We have been looking forward to this meeting. Since we last saw you, we have gotten permission to show you that which we hid from you." Pulling away a cloth, he said, "This is our examiner."

He picked it up and handed the examiner, which was almost twice as big as his own scanner with the screen taking up the upper half and a keypad on the bottom. As Conrad started pointing it around, he realized it was scanning for life forms. He did not understand the readout that flashed across the bottom of the screen, but he recognized basically what it was doing. Then the tech walked around and started showing him the different types of scans and what the readout was telling him.

"This covers all scans that we use, plus one that I don't quite figure," Conrad said, his voice rich with excitement. "How does it work with this?" Conrad pointed to his amulet.

"It has a harmonizer."

"Harmonizer," Conrad repeated and looked at Willy and Sydni, who shook their heads. "I don't understand that word."

The tech thought about it and looked at the other techs and then back to Conrad. "They work together at peace using the same setting and it stops off-worlders from seeing us and hides us."

"Tandem or harmony or equalizer maybe," Sydni said.

"Must be," Willy said.

Conrad nodded and said, "It would make sense." Then looking at the tech, he said, "I understand. Will you show me the inside and how the harmonizer works?"

Another tech smiled and pulled away a cloth revealing an examiner already taken apart. Conrad moved forward without saying a word, and when he found his voice, he said, "Can you show me?"

The next couple of hours passed quickly for Conrad as they showed him the inner workings of the examiner and harmonizer. They went over and over the information and explained in great detail the intricacies of the work. When they returned to the house, each with their new things from their day's adventure, Conrad apologized but went straight to his lab and started working, leaving the others to fix dinner.

* * * *

Willy was very happy that the morning had gone well with the new leaders that would be working under him, and quickly they seemed to be banding together to a tight group. This was his and Sydni's plan, to get them comfortable first and then pull in all the other warriors that they would need. He had introduced the idea of working with the rifles and the response had been overwhelmingly positive. The target practice had lasted all morning, breaking finally at lunch.

Doqui was waiting for Willy at lunch and asked if he would go hunting with him. It had been several days and they were in need of some fresh meat, so they set off to the east, looking for the spoor of some Saka Doqui had seen while riding in the morning. Willy noticed that Doqui was inattentive and kept looking at him, so he finally stopped and asked, "Doqui, you seem rather preoccupied today. Is there something on your mind?"

Doqui stood straight and asked, "Is it that obvious?"

"It is, my young friend. What is it?"

"I will be honest with you. I have heard much about the new group of warriors. I feel that I am qualified to be in such a group and I would consider it to be an honor."

Willy pursed his lips and tilted his head a little. Doqui had held himself together in battle and he was an outstanding hunter, but he was young, not to mention his wife's brother. "I will be equally honest with you, Doqui. I trust you as a hunter, and what I have seen of you in battle, you are capable and calm, but you are young."

The disappointment to Doqui was evident in his frown, and he almost bristled as he said, "I am old enough to join any war party and start my own family."

"Easy, Doqui, remember I am the new one here. I do not know everything."

"I know, but I have worked very hard to make certain my age has nothing to do with any decisions made about my life."

"Okay. Let me think about it. We are not choosing yet, and I will make certain that you are considered thoroughly for acceptance."

Doqui squinted and looked into Willy's eyes. Then he nodded. "That is all I ask for."

They continued the hunt and hunted until nearly evening, continually chasing down a small herd of Saka until Willy herded them toward the waiting Doqui, who took one down. After field dressing the Saka, they carried it back to the village and started prepping it. Doqui was working on skinning it when Chakdon walked through the back door to the courtyard. He had no agenda and was just seeing how his extended family was doing.

When it was convenient, Willy separated them and took Chakdon toward the house. Once they were out of earshot, Willy asked, "I may be totally out of line asking this of you, but I would rather make a simple mistake than a deadly mistake."

"What is wrong?" Chakdon asked.

"I do not know at what age a boy is a man and can make decisions on his own."

Glancing back at Doqui, Chakdon said, "If you are asking about Doqui, he is old enough to make his own decision. I would like to make some of them for him, but he is old enough that I can no longer. Good decisions or bad."

"Then you would not advise me?" Willy asked.

"No," Chakdon said, holding up his hands. "I could make a worse decision than you, because mine would be based on what I see, and where family is concerned, that is not good."

Willy nodded and said, "Then I will make my choice. Thank you."

"Doqui will make the right decision."

They prepared a fresh dinner that night, and invited Quistqui, Nurian, and Madak. The gathering lasted until late in the evening, and as Doqui was walking out through the courtyard to leave, Willy stopped him and said, "About what you asked me today, while we were hunting."

"Yes," he said, looking down, his voice filled with sadness.

"You will be my first choice. I want you in my group."

It took Doqui only a few seconds before he realized what Willy said. "Really?" He asked looking up. "I am to be a guerrilla warrior?"

"Yes."

Doqui's shout was not only indescribable, but several people heard it many blocks away. Before he turned away, he shouted, "You won't regret your decision, Willy. I promise."

Doqui took several steps and jumped up and vaulted over the wall, still shouting. As his excited shouts faded, Willy said, "I hope not."

* * * *

The ship seemed quieter at night. Although it was engulfed by the constant darkness of space, Bucky could imagine the captains of old, sailing the sea, using only the sun and the stars to guide their way. If he worked at it, he could imagine himself standing on the deck with a gentle breeze filling the sail and the ship gliding through smooth waters. He stood looking out the window of his office trying hard to imagine, but Admiral Oats' words rang clearly in his head; he wanted Willy and Sydni brought in to stand trial for their crimes. He had not wanted to hear any theories or speculation; he wanted hard cold facts and bodies to court marshal.

How could he bring in Willy and Sydni to stand trial when he felt they were not at fault for what was going on? How could he stand by and watch Gallagher reap the benefits at everyone else's expense? Bucky didn't know how to fight the power that backed Gallagher. Chambers had a long reach, but Bucky had the power locally. He would have to find ways to resist or delay. The truth could not be hidden for long, with so many digging for it.

His door chimed, but it was barely audible since he had the computer mute it. "Enter," he said and the door slid open. Turning to face the door, he saw Gallagher enter. His heart sank, but he figured at this hour of the night, no one else would show up.

"Captain Dollinger, I just received a communiqué from Chancellor Chambers that said you would now be seeking to arrest Commanders Willy and Sydni Colton. Is this true?"

Bucky cleared his throat and clasped his hands behind his back and said, "That, Ambassador, would be of a military matter and none of your business."

"I do understand that, and am always quite aware of it." He bowed a little, placing his hands together. "I just want it to go on the record that my resources will be available to you if they are needed."

"It is on the record, but I can guarantee you that the Orion does not need the help of your guards, they already have proven to be ineffective in that capacity."

Gallagher's face turned scarlet, but he did not lose composure. He knew that his dealings with the Captain had been too shaky already, and he had been warned to try and patch things over, in case Chambers' campaign to have the captain removed from his commission was not successful. "I am not happy about what happened with my squadron on the planet, Captain, but

I assure you, my guards are as capable of retrieving your scouts as any squad aboard this ship. It is not my place to argue military policy with you. I will remind you that I represent the UWC as well, and since this makes my job difficult, it is my problem too."

"Yes, Ambassador, I do understand, but they are my orders, not yours, and I will ask for your assistance if I need it. However, I have studied your problem between the Hingandu and the Jolabwe peoples, and I believe that this impending war you speak of is not the commander's fault, but an inherently planetary one."

"So now you wish to speak on planetary policy for the UWC?" Gallagher clasped his hands behind his back and continued, "Well, as you have told me to stay out of your command, I will say the same to you, Captain."

"Then at least now you understand how I feel about your constant interference."

"Constant interference..." Gallagher started, but quickly checked himself. "If you feel that I have given you constant interference in the past, Captain, I do apologize. I will certainly try to improve my conduct in the future. Good day."

Gallagher turned and walked back out of the office, leaving Bucky to pace back and forth, but he did not have long to stew in his anger, because his door chimed again. "Enter," he said in the gruffest tone he could muster.

The doors slid open, and when Tanya saw the look on the Captain's face, she snapped to attention, saluted and said, "Lieutenant Williston reporting, Sir."

Bucky eased up a little and said, "At ease, Lieutenant. What do you have to report?"

"It has been a while, Sir, but he called us in. It is Barkley's call, and I am letting him go unless you have other orders."

Bucky turned and stared out at the stars. "Come here, Lieutenant, I have to tell you something."

Tanya ran up next to Bucky and stood to his right. She waited for several minutes as they stared out at the moon covered by water. He glanced sideways at her and said, "The order has come down from admiralty to bring Willy and Sydni back. It is a direct order that I cannot disobey." He paused and said, "However, I can delay it, and give them a chance."

"What are my orders, Sir?"

"Same as they have been. Have Barkley go and meet him, relay what I have said, and that I am giving him a chance, but to steer clear of patrols and squads, because they will be so ordered to bring him back."

She sighed. "Yes, Sir."

"Can Barkley be trusted not to turn on Willy and Sydni?"

"Without a doubt."

Bucky's tone became gruff again. "How can you be certain?"

"They already beat the hell out of him trying."

"I remember. He will do."

"He leaves in a few hours. He gave us only a short notification this time."

"Go on, Lieutenant. Remind him that this may be your last contact."

"Aye, Aye, Sir. Thank you, Sir."

"And then tell him that I am sorry, and I will do what I can. Dismissed."

* * * *

The woods were devoid of the chatter usually made by birds and small creatures, leaving only the myriad of insects in a continuous symphony. Barkley knew that someone else was in the woods with him, but his scanner wasn't picking them up. He moved with the patience of a slug, belly-crawling along the ground through the thickest brush he could find. Then he saw Willy sitting just inside some evergreen trees, waiting patiently. Barkley walked through the last opening into the evergreens. Willy watched him, and Barkley couldn't shake the feeling that he was a small animal being eyed up by the predator. Barkley sat facing him and said, "Hey, Commander."

"Barkley."

"I am glad you called us. We needed to talk to you."

"Are you alone?"

"Yes, Sir. They beat me to a pulp trying to get me to turn on you. They bribed me, threatened me, but I have no weak spots. You guys are my family. I spent a morning in sick bay having them patch me up."

"Fair enough." Willy paused and said, "I didn't kill Diego."

"I know that, Sir. If I thought you had killed him I would never have showed up on the same planet. Tanya had her theory that Vladimir broke him and then when you escaped attempts to stop you, the guards turned on him and killed him."

"Good theory. It is very close to the truth."

"How many Hingandu do you have hidden out there, waiting to make certain that you are not attacked?"

"More than enough."

Sydni walked between two trees and crouched next to Willy, and said, "Barkley."

"Commander. I am glad you're here though, because Captn' gave me a message to pass on. Gallagher passed on a recording that had you killing

Gordo. We know it was false, so does Captn', but he can't prove it. Admiralty says that you have to be brought in. A direct order he says he cannot disobey. He will delay it as long as possible, and he will try and give you time, but if you see any troops, try and steer clear because they will be after you."

"Thanks for the warning," Willy said.

"Definitely," Sydni added.

"It is the least we could do. Look, he said this was the last time we could contact you without following his orders, but I do not feel bound by the UWC as much as I do by you two. Is there anything you need or want? I will come back down if you do."

Willy looked at Sydni and then to Barkley again. "I am telling you, Barkley, I am actually happy here."

"Me too. Doc is too, in his own way."

Barkley nodded. "I need to get a scan of a Hingandu for the captain, if it is possible. He needs it to try and make part of his case." He looked down at his hands, which were fiddling with a long blade of grass and said, "Is it true? Are they humans?"

"Just like me," Willy replied. "I don't know how they got here, but I have to believe that those engines I found have something to do with it."

Barkley nodded. "If they tell the public about this back home, it will cause a major uproar."

"True," Sydni agreed. "It could help the military with budgeting though, give them a reason to need a new fleet."

Willy growled. "Who knows how they will twist it, but that will not take place or change policy for a while. I am worried about the present problem of Gallagher stirring up the Jolabwe with promises of technology."

"I will tell you something, Commanders. I have set something in place, but I have spiced it up so it will not be as traceable."

"What?" Sydni asked.

"I have set up a system to tap into the ambassador's line again, and...."

"No," Willy nearly shouted.

"It is too dangerous, Barkley," Sydni said.

"Look, I took one of those bulky receivers they placed in there for you and I cut it down to one third the size and hid it. The antenna on my scanner is internal, and I swear no one will know about it until I have more than enough incriminating evidence to send on via the captain."

"Don't do it on our behalf, Sergeant," Willy said. "It is too late and not worth the consequences."

Barkley shook his head and squinted as he looked at them both. "You don't understand, Sir. They have taken away the only family I have had since I was a young man. They have tried to make me betray that family. They beat me until I swore I wouldn't tell anyone, and I can live with that. However, they killed the man that was a brother to me." A tear escaped Barkley's watery eyes. "My God, if I didn't have the want to totally squash Gallagher and expose his and Chambers' plot, I would slip into his office and kill him with my bare hands."

"Who beat you to a pulp?"

"Vladimir. He tried threatening me and I only laughed at him. There is no one out there that they could threaten me with. The news flash is, they already have. I spend all my time looking out for Tanya."

"I am sorry," Willy said, hanging his head. "We have let you down. All of you."

"No," Barkley said. "That is just it, you haven't let us down. You have fought the system and you are standing up for what is right and correct. If I thought you'd let me, and that I couldn't help you better from aboard ship, I would be down here living with you guys."

"We would love to have you," Sydni said. "But don't do it. You stand to go far in the Scouting Corps, don't blow that, for us."

"Okay, but don't think that I am not going to do everything I can to prove your innocence. Everything I had was taken away, you knew that when you signed me on, and now Gallagher and Chambers are taking it away again."

"We signed you on because we knew that you had great potential, you just needed a reason and some hope," Sydni said, shifting her weight.

"Thanks." Barkley smiled. "Given the chance I will kill both Gallagher and Vladimir, but don't worry, I will only do that if I absolutely can get away with it."

"There is a line for that, Barkley," Willy said. "If you do it, you will be fighting me for the honor. Although, the thought of Gallagher and Vladimir spending time at the Alpha One Penal Island facility would not bother me a bit."

That made Barkley laugh. "Granted." Barkley's eyes lit up and he said, "You guys can't leave us alone for long. Tanya and I already got into a fight in Six O'Clock High. A squad of Gallagher's guards stumbled onto us as we were mourning Diego's death, and they started taunting us. The Twenty-First just stepped back and watched as Tanya and I cut our way through them. Jeffries had them piled outside the doors and called the Marines saying that they were fighting amongst themselves." Barkley laughed. "It felt good to lash out, but I still wish it had been Gallagher."

"True. Look, I would love to sit here all day and catch up with you, but it is too compromising for both of us, especially now. I will ask if you can scan one of our friends and then we will have to separate."

"Gotch ya, Commander."

Willy shouted behind him in Hingandu, "Quartainian, will you come forward and be seen."

Barkley had started learning Hingandu, but he was still trying to master Jolabwe, so he was lost at what Willy had said. Soon a man that looked just like Willy, except for skin tone and stripes, walked in from where Sydni had come. He smiled and spoke to Willy, "Reporting."

Willy, still speaking in Hingandu, said, "This man needs a scan of you to prove something back where I come from. I ask this not as your leader, but as your friend. It is not an order."

Looking at him, Quartainian said, "Then how can I resist a friend. I have no problem with that."

"Do not let him see the amulet of protection as you hand it to me. I trust my friend, but if he does not have knowledge, then they can not hurt him to get it."

Quartainian nodded. He made it look natural when he turned around and walked several steps, removing his amulet and his pack, and then handed it all to Willy with his crossbow. "I am ready." Willy and Sydni backed far away so their amulets would not affect the scanner, and in a blink, Quartainian showed up on Barkley's scanner. "Damn," he said. "How does that happen?"

"Just call us ghosts," Sydni said.

"The others already are." After a few adjustments, Barkley shut down his scanner.

Willy quickly tossed Quartainian's stuff back to him. "Go, Quartainian. Take the others out to the Brotu and we shall follow quickly."

Quartainian turned and was quickly swallowed by the forest. Willy said, "The possibility of an attack exists now that our position has been compromised. We need to leave."

Barkley snapped to a salute and said, "Yes, Sir. Good luck, Sir."

"Thanks, Sergeant," Sydni said. "Be careful back aboard ship."

Willy turned to walk away, but he stopped and looked back at Barkley. "We still are your family. If things get too bad you could come here, but from here, there is no going back without solid proof. We won't contact you again to come down. Keep flying overhead if you have news and I will try and contact you."

"Yes, Sir. Take care, Sir."

Willy and Sydni melted into the woods. Barkley started running toward his ship. He had what he wanted; now he needed to report to the Captain.

CHAPTER 19

The Colton clan life grew quiet and content, and if it hadn't been for the constant marauding of the Jolabwe, they would have used the term peaceful. The major attacks against the Hingandu were in the next two villages to the north, but in the village where the Colton clan lived, the attacks were farther out and inconsistent. After a few weeks of working with the guerrilla warrior leaders, the process of picking squads started. Both Sydni and Willy had help in picking theirs from the other leaders. Each person chosen had the chance to decline the position, but no one declined. Quistqui never said anything about Doqui's training, but Willy had noticed him more than once watching his brother run through exercises and nodding and smiling. They practiced at different hours in different terrain for different periods of time. Sometimes their drills would last four or five days and sometimes they would last just through the morning.

Three representatives came and drilled with the squads to learn what Willy and Sydni knew to see if they could implement the same procedures in their villages. The rifles were made and they practiced with them daily. Willy and Sydni noted who were the best shots in each group and had each of the leaders taking note. Usually among a squad of scouts, each scout would define themselves a niche; snipers, close combat, trackers, and stealth were some of the most common that would help a leader choose where to deploy the squad in different situations.

After a couple months of strict preparation, ordered by the war council, the squads went through a series of mock battles, set up against the other war parties. Once both Willy and Sydni felt comfortable, they started patrolling along the outskirts of the forest, armed with their new rifles and scanners. They were immediately effective and repelled much larger groups of Jolabwe that sometimes outnumbered them five to one. The elders of the war council were very pleased to report such information to the council elders and to the full council.

As Willy and Sydni worked with the new scout squads, Dekonal's belly grew quickly over the first few months, then slowed down nearing full term. She was happy living in the Colton Clan and with her family's home next door, she received a lot of support during her pregnancy. They decided that since their courtyards shared a common fence, that they would link the two together by creating an archway with a swinging door.

Chakdon and Dekonal continued to work with the council, reporting what they saw, and sometimes Willy would wake up to hear Dekonal quietly sobbing. He would try to console her and ask what was wrong, but she would only say that she could feel great sadness coming. She did not know why or how, but it made her cry. So Willy would lie next to her, holding her in his arms and whispering to her.

In the full moon of the month that the Hingandu people referred to as the moon of the fire leaves, Willy was called home early from the field, where two of the squadrons were patrolling. Dekonal had gone into labor and was in the process of giving birth to his children. Two healers were brought in along with Madak, while Willy waited in the dining room with Conrad and Tyuk. Willy, the ever-patient hunter, could not keep from pacing back and forth.

Sydni had called in Jasina and Ulik to take over their patrols so she could be at home as well. Then, after a couple of hours of labor, and pacing the kitchen floor, Willy stopped in his tracks. Tears welled up in his eyes and his sister looked over at him. He heard the first faint cry of a baby. After that, the second baby was born in quick succession. Madak called Willy, Sydni, and Conrad upstairs so they could see. Wrapped in dark blue blankets, each of the children had been set upon their mother's chest where she held them. Willy knelt at her bedside and whispered, "Our children have come."

"Two boys, like their father. Look, no stripes and gold-flecked eyes."

"With all the beauty of their mother," Willy said and picked one up and unwrapped him just enough to see his arms and chest and then wrapped him up again.

"Sons to add to the Colton clan," Conrad said. "This is a proud day for the clan."

Willy smiled at him. Sydni moved forward to touch the tiny nose and coo over him. Handing off the bundle, Willy said, "Go ahead, Aunt Sydni, hold him."

Sydni didn't even wait for him to finish the sentence before she was taking the baby in her arms. "Oh, hey there, little guy. I'm your Aunt Sydni."

Willy turned back to Dekonal and kneeling down beside her, he smiled. He took her free hand and leaned close. "I love you, Dekonal. You are truly wonderful." He kissed her, and when he looked at her again, tears brimmed over her eyelids and rolled down her cheeks. He wiped them away with his hand and said, "What shall we name both of them?"

Shaking her head, Dekonal spoke in a voice somewhat raspy from screaming. "First you must do as I told you."

"I told you I am not a good singer. I do not have a clear voice."

"I love your voice, and it is tradition among my people. Hold your sons in the moonlight and sing from your heart, to let the world, the people, and our ancestors know that your sons are born. Let your voice carry over the village and into the woods, and if it is your honest voice, then fear not your skill at song. It will not matter."

"Then we will name our sons?" Willy asked.

Smiling and nodding, Dekonal repeated, "Then we will name our sons."

Standing up, Willy kissed her forehead and said, "For you and my sons alone, I will sing." He picked up his other son from Dekonal's arms and stared at the tiny face, for which he was now responsible. For a moment he looked at that face and wondered what his parents must have thought when he first arrived, so different, so strange. What had it meant to them? He looked at his sister, who was still cooing over his son, but now with Conrad's help.

They handed him the baby, and he held one in each arm. "I will now go and attempt to sing." Dekonal laughed. "If one of you laughs," he whispered, "I will show no mercy." Both Conrad and Sydni laughed.

Once Willy left, Dekonal said, "Sydni, Conrad, follow him. He does not realize that in the tradition, friends will help him sing his song once the people begin to hear it. You both know the song, you helped him memorize it. Go, and help him."

"Really?" Sydni asked.

"You want me to sing?" Conrad asked.

"To help your friend you have left your ship, your life, and your world. This is nothing compared to the sacrifices you have already made, not to mention the tradition in your new home."

Sydni slapped Conrad's stomach and said, "Come on." Before he could protest further, Sydni grabbed his hand and pulled him along. They went to the front door and waited for Willy to start. Sydni whispered, "You do remember the words."

A quick shrug and Conrad looked her in the eyes and said, "I have only come to fully grasp their language in the last couple of months. I will try to sing what I can."

Outside, alone in the street, Willy stood with his face to the moon, and he held his sons' faces to the moonlight. Then he looked at their faces and whispered, "I am your father, Willy. I will teach you to hunt and fish and fly Brotu. I will protect you and provide for you with the help of your mother and aunt and uncle." He cleared his voice and looked back up at the moon and began to sing. The start was shaky and weak, but when he looked down into their now open eyes, Willy's voice took on a whole new tone. Steadily his voice increased.

Conrad looked up at Sydni and whispered, "At least if he is off key and I am off key, we show a united front."

His statement earned him another slap, this time on his shoulder. Sydni opened the door very quietly and stepped outside. Conrad was right behind her. When Willy began to sing the second verse, both Sydni and Conrad joined in and instantly Willy's singing became stronger. Using his head, Willy motioned for them to come closer. By the end of the second verse, two more voices joined in. Madak had followed them out, and Dekonal's father stood in the street, light from his doorway lit the street around him. With another look at his sons' faces, Willy stopped feeling self-conscious about his singing and just sang louder. Soon more people stood in the street singing, including Quistqui, Nurian, Doqui, Douka, and soon it seemed as though the whole street was out singing, their unified voices growing stronger and stronger.

Dekonal listened from her bed, straining to hear her husband's faint voice, and she relaxed when she heard his voice grow stronger. Shortly after that, she heard Sydni and Conrad join in. She could hear their strange voices carrying the song to the world of her twins' birth, and she knew the people would never forget this birth. Her mother and her father both joined in the song and quickly others joined. Not wanting to be left out despite her raspy voice, Dekonal joined the song.

Willy softened his voice near the end and cocked his head. Faintly he could hear his wife singing the song from within the house. He knew that he would never forget this day. When the song finished, many people came forward to offer their congratulations, and Willy, the proud father, was all too willing to show off his sons.

It was after only a little while, though, that Willy announced, "I have left my wife too long without her new sons. Please feel free to stop by at any time to visit, but I must go."

Sydni took Conrad's arm and held it tight. She noted the smile on Willy's face, and knew that this was a day that he had thought he would never see.

His pride swelled over and was filling Sydni as well. Conrad patted her hand and said, "Aunt Sydni. That fits you well."

"Thank you. I think that Uncle Conrad is very sexy." She slapped his rear end and said, "Or should I say, Uncle Doc."

"Uncle Doc. Sounds like something your brother would call me." As they walked in the door, Conrad asked, "Does it make you want to start a family of our own?"

"Very much so." Sydni said latching the door. "Very much so. However, I don't see how I can justify it until this patchwork war is over or dealt with. I do not want to be bringing a life into this universe while I am trying to defend our new home."

Conrad smiled his knowing, confident smile and said, "It makes sense to me. I can wait as long as you, but I am selfish. I want you all to myself for just as long as I can."

Sydni kissed him and said, "Somehow God blessed me by sending you into my life. And every day that I wake up in your arms, I cannot thank Him enough."

Upstairs Willy knelt at Dekonal's bedside, where she now sat, propped up by pillows. "Your song was magnificent," she said, touching his face. "Your voice was strong and your words were clear. Thank you for singing."

He placed one child in Dekonal's arms and the other he held. "I will never be able to tell them apart," Willy said, "but we must name them soon."

"Yes. Are there any names you would like to give them?"

"I have not given much thought to it, but there was a man, who helped shape my life and he taught me very much. His name was Jean-Pierre. I would like to name one son that."

"Done. That means you are holding Jean-Pierre of the Colton Clan."

"Do you wish to name one a particular name?"

"Yes. My grandfather to me was a wonderful man, and taught me many lessons about my ability to see visions. I would like to name this son after him. Chakdall."

"Then our worlds come together and we name our children accordingly. Chakdall and Jean-Pierre of the Colton Clan."

* * * *

Quistqui crouched in a thicket of dense Cuzira berry bushes. He had been thinking of his nephews born just the night before when Jasina crouched next to him. "They are not Jolabwe," she whispered. "They are Humans. Just like Sydni. They are spread out, sixteen of them in a broken line, heading into the forest."

"We cannot let them go any further," Quistqui whispered back as he looked at his scanner, turning on the voice part as they all had been taught by Willy and Sydni. "We cannot let them go any further into the woods by any means."

Willy's voice emitted from Quistqui's scanner very faintly, as Quistqui had turned it down so the Humans would not hear it. "What's up, Quist?"

"Humans, Willy. Sixteen of them spread out just south of the valley and heading into the mountains."

"That's not good. How are they dressed?"

Quistqui held the scanner toward Jasina, who said, "They are wearing a one-piece uniform with green and brown patches. Their faces are painted green and brown and they are wearing funny hats that have wires running to their mouth and up in the air."

"Marines," Willy said half to himself. "Probably recon-one. Look, that is a nasty bunch, and all of them shoot well. I would prefer they don't get killed, but they cannot be allowed anywhere near the village."

"Yes, sir."

"You have the advantage of surprise, but keep a couple of your group in reserve to watch any of them that split off. They may try to get behind you. If you fall back, fall back toward the small falls to the south. I am coming with my group to at least back you up. There is an English word you can use which means to go away, it is 'Leave.' You can try it if you feel obligated, but don't feel obligated at the risk of injury."

"Yes, Willy. We understand," Quistqui said.

Willy signed off and so did Quistqui. Jasina and Quistqui moved back to their groups and discussed their plan with them. They each picked a sharpshooter to stay back, with orders to keep an eye on their scanners. Then they spread out in a line, where Quistqui would be in the middle and he would let himself be seen to draw attention. They decided to give the Marines one chance to retreat or they would attack. They all knew the path of falling back, and each knew the signal if their scanners buzzed three times.

Once everyone was in position, Quistqui readied his rifle and stood next to a tree where he would have easy cover if they looked hostile. He held his rifle at waist level, just out of their view, but where he could fire off some rapid cover fire.

One of the Marines caught sight of him and stopped and spoke into his microphone. Quistqui caught the Marine's eye and held his stare. The man talked more into his microphone, but did not move.

Pointing past the man, Quistqui said, "Leave."

The Marine looked astonished at the English word and spoke again into his microphone. Then he said loud enough for Quistqui to hear, "I am

Lieutenant Nathan O'Hare of the United World Council, and I am here looking for Commander Willy Colton and Commander Sydni Colton."

All Quistqui understood was Willy and Sydni. So in Hingandu, he said, "They are not here. Leave." He used the English word at the end.

As the Marine spoke again, Quistqui could see two more Marines move just within range of view, thinking they hadn't given their positions away. Quistqui didn't look at the one he saw coming in closer and closer, he just watched and waited. If that one made an aggressive move, both groups of guerrilla warriors would attack, not to mention that he was ready to defend himself.

The standoff continued, but Quistqui quickly realized that the others were moving in on him. Quistqui couldn't resist the smile that crossed his lips as he continued to stare at the Marine. Once again he pointed and said, "Leave."

The Marine started speaking again, but Quistqui didn't care, his full concentration was now on the two closer Marines. Even though he was looking directly at the Marine standing in the open, he was not paying attention to him.

Then, in a rush of leaves, the closest Marine, on Quistqui's right jumped up at him. Quistqui's first reaction had his rifle aimed at the Marine and firing point blank, knocking the Marine back. With one fluid movement, he shifted his rifle to the second closest Marine, who was about to fire. As he fired his rifle, he ducked down and jumped back. The forest erupted in a cacophony of gunfire, and the tree where Quistqui had been splintered and cracked. The volley of fire stopped quickly and Quistqui examined his scanner, seeing that four of the Marines were dead, two wounded, and the others were reorganizing.

Moving back, Quistqui took stock of his group and found one wounded with burns to his shoulders. Quistqui ordered him to take a position back with the other two so that he would be off the front line. They repositioned themselves and slowly moved back a little to make the Humans come forward. Their scanners showed them slowly moving forward again. Jasina took her group and worked on out-flanking them to one side. The next clash was one-sided. The Hingandu inflicted several casualties in a quick hit-and-run attack.

As Jasina and Quistqui repositioned their groups, they heard Brotu fly overhead. They fell back again, this time setting up in a new formation to keep the humans off guard. As the humans moved forward, Quistqui noted that two stayed back. When the next Hingandu fired, the two humans who had stayed back fired what Willy had called rockets, which caused three trees to keel over and killed one of Jasina's group and wounded another.

They dropped further back. As Jasina and Quistqui met again, Willy appeared from behind them. Willy whispered, "My group is setting up a line of defense, and so is Sydni's group. Send your wounded back to the falls. I will go with you to out-flank them and since they can't see us, we'll get them from behind."

As Quistqui and Jasina passed out quick orders, Willy checked his scanner. The Marines had many severely wounded that had dropped far back and were moving away with the help of the other wounded. Nine healthy Marines headed toward them slowly. Willy motioned for Quistqui to take his group to the right and cut behind them, while he went with Jasina's group to the left. They had set up several hand signals and he gave Quistqui one that meant silence if possible. Quistqui nodded and was ordering his group in the same way.

Willy let Jasina lead her crew around, each constantly checking their scanner. When they had cut around behind the Marines, they started moving in. Willy was the first to reach a Marine who had stayed back to launch rockets and he left the Marine unconscious and unarmed. The other Marines were not as lucky. A short, stifled scream alerted the last two that their buddies had been taken, and they started dropping back, just slipping through the line of Hingandu to escape.

The two Marines could have been stopped, or tracked down, had Willy chosen to stop them, he was closest, but he let them go; he wanted a couple to get away unscathed. He wanted someone who was not injured to be able to relay the whole story, from beginning to end. Once the Marines were in full retreat, Willy knew a landing craft would be heading down shortly to retrieve what was left of the two squads. The track record of the Marines also showed that they would be coming to extract the dead bodies as well.

Each Hingandu, who could, grabbed a Marine and started dragging them back toward the site of the initial clash. Once they dropped the bodies and stepped away, they knew that the Marines would pick them up on their scanner, so he ordered them to drop and run back into the woods.

Willy met with Quistqui and Jasina shortly afterward, when they rendezvoused with Sydni's group back at the small falls. "How did the fighting start?" Willy asked.

Then Quistqui explained the strategy he and Jasina used. Willy was relieved. Then they explained how they tried using the word Willy had taught them, but the Marines attacked anyway, so they attacked back. Jasina was upset at the loss of her fellow warrior, but they knew with increasing attacks came increasing deaths, and the toll on the Hingandu was starting to happen. They knew that before long, there would be more deaths, and the best they could do was fight well to honor their friends.

Overhead, they all heard a ship pass by, and Willy knew it was a transport ship. "Quistqui, you and I will stay with our groups to see that the Marines pick up their wounded and dead then leave. Then we will head out once they have left." Quistqui turned to leave when Willy stopped him. "Quist, the ones coming to pick up the others will have intense listening devices. No sounds. None."

"Understood."

Willy and Quistqui's groups were set up long before the Marines came for their wounded and dead. Another squad spread out as the Personnel Drop Ship swept in, landed, and started loading in the soldiers.

After the squad returned to the ship, it took off and sped into the sky. They waited for several minutes before they headed back toward the village. Willy was not happy about the loss of his first Hingandu warrior. He stood staring back into the woods, now quiet except for the insects and a single songbird. Men and women died in wartime, Willy knew that, but today someone had died because they were coming after him. The Marines had attacked which was a new twist and if the UWC was going to become aggressive to stop him, then it would become increasingly more dangerous. The war council needed to be aware of the new situation.

Chakdall and Jean-Pierre filled his head, and for a moment, he wondered if the warrior who died had a family. He turned and left, following the others back to the Brotu.

The only sound in the room was breathing, and Willy could separate his wife's breathes from his children's. He had just watched the mate of the man who died react to the news of his death. He had watched as the mate cradled a little girl to her chest and rocked as she cried. It had chilled him to his core. He had felt so alone and unattached before the Hingandu came into his life that he had never thought much about the results that such a death left behind.

Late afternoon sun streamed in an open window, illuminating the foot of the bed. Willy crouched in the doorway as Dekonal slept with a child nestled in each arm. They looked so peaceful that he did not want to wake them. He closed his eyes and said a prayer for the family of the warrior, hoping that he could bring peace back to this world. He smiled at the irony. They called him a warrior and a member to the war council, but all he wanted was peace.

Tanya stepped inside the Captain's quarters, which were as immaculate as ever, and she looked at him sitting behind his desk, his uniform in disarray and his face unshaven for several days. He nodded toward the bar and said, "Can I offer you a drink, Lieutenant?"

"No, thank you, Sir. I am going on duty. Barkley and I are pulling in ten satellites and launching new ones. Tech duty."

"There are other alternatives," Bucky said, sitting up a little.

"I don't want to go down after them, Sir. If Gallagher orders it, I will have to or be sent up on charges."

"The charges would never stick, Lieutenant."

"Not unless Chancellor Chambers wants them to."

Nodding, Bucky said, "True. I am all too much proof of that."

"We hear that even XO Cho has limited powers, taking most of her orders from Gallagher himself."

That perked Bucky up and he leaned forward. "Tell me. What else have you heard?"

"Well, that they sent down two recon squads of Marines after Commanders Colton, and only a few came back alive."

"They killed two squads of Recon Marines?"

"Well, if the story that is floating around is even partially true, there were a couple of squads of Willy in the woods. The Hingandu cut right through the Marines."

"Ghosts?"

"That's the story they're telling."

With a grin, Bucky smiled. "I wonder how they do that? But if someone is going to come up with it, it would be Conrad, Willy, and Sydni." A short bitter laugh came out and ended abruptly before he said, "If there were ever any three people I would pit against a ship of the UWC or even the UWC itself, it would be them."

"Yes, Sir. It looks like they are doing a good job at that." Tanya shifted her weight and then asked, "Any other orders?"

Again Bucky laughed. "No, Lieutenant, I am long past giving any orders. It is not my show anymore."

Tanya looked down at the deck. "Don't give up on them, Sir. We are all that stands between Gallagher and the Commanders."

"I would say we have long since been knocked down."

"Maybe, Sir, but I will fight for them until they eject my dead carcass out the same portal they sent Diego through." She looked up and Bucky could see the fire in her eyes. "If you can think of anything, please call me, Sir." Tanya turned on her heels and walked out of the Captain's quarters.

Bucky stared at the door long after it closed behind her, Tanya's words burning into his ears, and her eyes burned into his. He knew he had to snap out of his depression. There had to be something he could do.

* * * *

Barkley leaned over the desk that used to be Conrad's, looking at the blueprint that Andrea had lain out. She was pointing at the schematics and talking, "It is not that difficult a conversion, and it is a relatively small satellite. All you have to do is open that small hatch and set the frequency. Also, I have placed a miniature cloak on it, and the transponder is gone. They will never be able to track it, or even sense it for that matter."

"And you know he will be using that frequency, Major?"

Andrea looked up and said, "I would stake my commission on it. It was missing when he left. I did the inventory myself. They could set up their own system down there, never hooking into the ship, and the ship would know nothing about it either."

"And this is strong enough to transmit to Earth itself? We can literally tap into the media with it?"

Andrea smiled. She liked Barkley's cunning, not to mention his loyalty, which is what she had herself. She respected Conrad above all else, and she knew he would only have defected for a very good reason. "Sent and received. We can switch this, which will give us a view of the media's frenzy that may be started." She paused and looked at Barkley. "Do you have information, yet?"

Barkley shook his head. "Not yet. The Ambassador and Chancellor Chambers have said nothing incriminating, but they will, sooner or later. But if Commander Colton has a copy of his information, he could send it."

"This satellite is already aboard your ship?" Andrea asked with a smile.

Barkley turned his head, coughing. Then scratching his day-old stubble, he grinned. "I just want to turn the world on its ear. People like Chambers and Gallagher ruin lives and kill for their gain, and if I can wipe the platform out from under them, maybe we can get some justice."

"You have my support, Sergeant. I will help you in any way I can."

"I think that you have given me all that I could want. You are taking a great personal risk, Major."

"You are taking a bigger one."

Barkley grinned again. "I am a scout, ma'am. Willy and Sydni taught me to take risks and hang it all on the line. They would be doing it for me."

* * * *

"We have a good solid lead, Chancellor," Gallagher said, sweating and rubbing his hands together. "They are in the mountains, and they defended the outer lying valleys with a great ferocity." Pausing to wipe his forehead with a handkerchief, Gallagher studied Chambers' face. "We lost nearly two squads of Recon Marines in a skirmish with what was described as a strong force in which everyone resembled Commander Colton. They came from nowhere and hit and ran, appearing like ghosts to strike them down."

"Ghosts again!" Chambers shouted. "There are no ghosts, just skittish Marines."

"Yes, Sir," Gallagher said, his voice almost squeaking.

"Look, this is simple. They get ferocious, we send greater forces backed up by air support. Start flying over the area, they cannot hide forever."

"Yes, Sir."

"I want that insubordinate, treasonous, murderous Colton brought to justice." Chambers leaned close to the video lens and lowered his voice. "I want results, Gallagher. I want results, now."

"Yes, Mr. Chancellor."

"Give me another report in two days, Gallagher. Don't make me send out another ship with your replacement."

"I won't fail you...." Before Gallagher finished his statement, the vid screen went blank. Chambers was gone.

Still shaking from the threats, Gallagher slammed his fist down on his intercom button, and said, "Get me Captain Cho, immediately."

He flopped down in his over-stuffed chair and breathed deeply as he sopped up the sweat on his face with the already-soaking handkerchief, wondering how many people he would have to send down to die before they captured or killed both of the Colton Commanders. He knew he had to keep it up now, no matter what the cost. It was either their hides or his.

✶ ✶ ✶ ✶

A month had passed since the birth of Chakdall and Jean-Pierre, and the number of attacks by Jolabwe had increased, with an alarming increase of fly-overs by fighters from the Orion.

Conrad was scanning two missiles that he was helping Sydni and Willy place on Willy's ship. "This is it." he said. "I really think that these missiles will penetrate any kind of field that the Orion could put up."

Willy was fastening one of them down, within the missile release chamber under the wing. "They look impressive, Doc. If they work anywhere near as well as those bullets do, then they will be perfect."

Sydni stopped and cocked her head a little and asked, "Tell me, why we would want to fire at the Orion?"

"Say they find a Hingandu village, unlikely as it would seem, say they do. Say they send in ships to attack, but during our time down here, our techs reconfigure shields. This has grown to be my home, and the last thing I want to do is sit around and have it be too late to react if something happens. Hopefully we will never have to bother with them again."

Sydni closed the hatch where she had been working and nodded. "Fair enough."

Willy jumped from under the wing and stared up into the sky. He grabbed Conrad and pulled him close to the ship. "Fighters, low. Stay within the cloaking field. Willy looked at his scanner and said, "We have been out here a long time, but I want to make sure they are not watching us when we bolt for cover."

Quickly Sydni and Conrad heard the ships coming closer. Then the ships roared overhead, flying along the path back toward the village. Shortly thereafter Sydni said, "They're making a loop. Maybe they saw someone."

"God I hope not," Conrad said.

Willy started to say, "Maybe they are just doubling back over their path to see...."

He was cut short by the sound of explosions not far off. Faintly, Willy heard a scream. He tensed as the explosions continued to shake the ground. His frozen moment of disbelief turned to anger. As he sprinted for the tree line and the path, he automatically hit the auto-startup on his ship. Conrad and Sydni were following him close behind.

The ships circled and then made wider and wider circles, until they passed over him. He knew by the sound of fire mixed with the moans and cries of people that whoever they had hit were close.

Smoke curled into the air from a large field, where a stream slowly curved through. Several trees were burning slowly, and the stream was dumping into a large crater, of which there were several pocking the field. Bodies lay across the field. Willy stopped. Some moved with anguish as Willy had seen in wartime. Some did not move, and one crawled toward a bundle on the ground a few feet from her. The realization set in. This was not a war party; this was a gathering party made up of women and children. The woman he saw crawling was Dekonal.

As Sydni and Conrad made it to the edge next to Willy, he shouted and ran forward. Conrad, who had never before seen a war other than on video, stood in complete shock with his mouth hanging open. Sydni picked up her scanner and called a general announcement to the guerrilla warriors. In her accented Hingandu, she said, "Bring everyone possible, bring healers, bring

Brotu for the wounded and dead. Follow my signal to the northern path to the lake." She left her scanner on and rushed forward.

Willy slid next to Dekonal as she picked up Jean-Pierre. She looked over him as he cried. Her leg was bleeding and burned, but her eyes were fixed on Jean-Pierre. "Dekonal," Willy said, "Where is Chakdall?"

Dekonal looked around, and Willy could tell shock had already set in. "He was right here. We ran for the trees, but I fell. I dropped Jean-Pierre. He is crying." She snuggled Jean-Pierre close to her breast and stroked his face cooing to him.

"Where is Chakdall?" Willy asked in a soft voice.

She looked around and tears began streaming down her face. "Mother took him as we ran."

Willy looked at the bodies ahead of him as Sydni scanned Dekonal and Jean-Pierre. "Her wounds are not life threatening, and Jean-Pierre is unharmed."

Willy had not heard her; he just stood up and walked toward the craters ahead. Looking at the bodies. Several breathed and moved and cried. And then he saw her. Madak was trying to use her one good arm to drag herself toward a mud-and blood-soaked blanket. Willy knelt next to her and put his hand on her face, saying, "Rest, Madak, help is on the way. I will take care of Chakdall." Madak tried to talk, but all that would come out was an anguished cry. At Willy's touch, she stopped clawing at the ground.

Willy crawled forward and picked up the bundle. He didn't have to look inside the blanket to know, but he did it anyway. Chakdall looked quiet and content, but a little pale. Willy felt the blood from the blanket run down his hands and soak his sleeves, but he shifted Chakdall to one arm and cradled him as he traced the tiny outline of his face. Willy rocked back and forth, and tears began to roll down his face, blurring his vision. "No," he said half aloud. "God, let me be wrong."

Slowly he folded back the blanket and saw the gaping wound on his son's ribs. Sydni was standing beside him, and then she scanned Madak and held her hand. "Help is coming, Madak. Help is on the way."

Inching forward, Sydni knelt next to Willy and scanned Chakdall. His wounds were so extensive, even had they had access to the Orion, it was too late for Chakdall, he was dead. Willy was refolding the blanket and moaning. Sydni put her scanner on her side and put an arm around Willy, her face now streaming with tears.

"Willy," Dekonal said just loud enough for him to hear. "Where is Chakdall? He was right here."

Willy looked up and he looked at Sydni, shaking his head as if he were asking. Sydni just shook hers too. Deep inside Willy could feel a cold spot growing inside. A deep hatred was brewing and he felt it grow as he stood up and turned to face Dekonal. With his voice cracking, he was barely able to say, "I have him. He is right here."

With every step he took toward Dekonal, the cold place took hold and grew stronger. By the time he reached Dekonal he was numb. Willy knelt in front of her and she leaned forward to look at Chakdall. Her tears redoubled when she looked at the pale face, and she looked up into Willy's eyes, looking for hope, but could only see his distress. Willy closed his eyes and shook his head.

"No," Dekonal said, reaching out one arm for Chakdall. "I don't believe it. No. I won't believe it." Willy relinquished his hold on Chakdall, and he could feel his heart breaking with every horrifying beat. Dekonal started screaming, which in turn started Jean-Pierre. Willy put his arms around all three of them. He looked up as he heard the fighters pass nearby again, and at that instant his ship flew over the edge of the clearing.

He looked where he knew it would be and he looked at Sydni. "I am going after them, they cannot live," he said. "Conrad, record this. We must have a record of this brutality." Sydni opened her mouth to protest, but he was already running and keying in his commands to the ship. It appeared close to the ground and lowered itself. As he reached the side of it and grabbed the handholds, the cockpit slid open. Sydni watched him move with trained speed as he slid his helmet on, closed the cockpit, and secured his seat belt. He did not look over at them before he angled his ship up and fired the thursters. He left in a roar of flames and shot straight into the sky.

Willy jammed his scanner in its slot and keyed in his ship's access code. The screens and scanners came to life and his ship re-cloaked. He started a search. The three ships that had attacked Dekonal were just starting to head for the upper levels of the atmosphere.

He could hear chatter on the comm link, but he opened up all frequencies. He wanted to be in close when he attacked. He armed all of his weapons and plotted an intercept course with the ships. He still held the thrusters open. The intercept was 30 seconds away.

Locking on with his missiles, he held his fingers over the fire button and looped in behind them. Deep inside him he found a very cold spot, and from there he said, "You have shown death, now face death." He fired at the first ship.

The missile rocked the ship, and he could hear the pilot screaming. He locked in again as the ship trailed particles and smoke. He fired a second shot and quickly angled away from the others, so he would not be susceptible to any attack. The other two ships were banking and cutting erratically trying to get away from him, but Willy quickly turned in on the second one.

He heard the scramble call go out on the ship and someone was shouting at him from the bridge, but he did not hear them. Willy was focused. Using his lock on key, he set a missile and his lasers. As the second ship came into close range, he fired. With both weapons going, the pilot never had time to scream. The ship disintegrated into a fireball of burning fuel and was extinguished.

The last pilot was now kicking in the afterburners in a direct line to the Orion. As Willy gave chase, he remembered the two new missiles he had. He brought up his armament listing and activated one of the slots where he and Sydni had placed the missiles. He was gaining little by little on the last ship when he fired the missile. His ship's scanner could not detect it, but he watched closely as it approached the other ship.

"Go to hell!" Willy yelled just seconds before the missile hit and exploded the ship. Willy continued on toward the Orion and said, "Get Captain Dollinger on the line."

Alexandra Cho came online and said, "Captain Dollinger is no longer in charge of the Orion. This is Acting Captain Cho."

"I see," Willy growled. "So Chambers finally got through. That is why women and children are dying on the planet."

"Commander Colton, there has been no such offense. As I understand it, you and other individuals planetside attacked two squads of Marines."

"All fabrications, XO. Those individuals tried to communicate with the Marines and were attacked. Then those three fighters just leveled a field full of Hingandu." Willy's hand started to tremble and his voice became deeper. "They killed innocents, they killed my son." The Orion locked on his screen and he took the manual override and aimed his missile at the launch bay where the first readied squadron would launch from and he fired.

"Tell Gallagher to bring them on. Tell him to send all his forces down and I will kill them all. Tell him to send more ships, I will shoot them down, and every day I will bring a present up here until the Orion leaves this space or is a drifting hulk riddled with holes. You cannot see me. You cannot hear me. You cannot stop my bullets. You cannot stop my missiles, XO. I have become the ghost that you have heard about. I will wreak havoc among you, and in your sleep, I will come and destroy."

His missile hit seconds after he stopped talking and created a bright flash on the side of the hull. Cho started calling orders as bells and alarms were sounding on the bridge.

Willy's scanner blinked and he cut off all the channels and flipped on the voice channel of his scanner. "Willy, it is about time." Sydni said.

"I was busy."

"Are they dead?"

"Yes."

"You are needed here. We have evacuated almost everyone to the healing center in the village."

Willy looped his ship 180 degrees and headed back toward the planet. "I am coming home."

"Remington will be at the landing site waiting for you."

"Willy out."

He clicked off his scanner and wiped his eyes again, wondering why the cold spot did not go away now that the murderers were dead.

In the clearing where the ships were, Willy could see Quistqui on his Brotu holding the reigns to Remington. Once he shut down his ship, he climbed out, tossing down his helmet and picking up his scanner. He nodded at Quistqui, whose eyes were rimmed in red, but did not say a word. Remington nuzzled his leg and sniffed at the blood soaking his shirtsleeves, shirt and pants. He patted Remington's head as he climbed on; they rode home in silence.

Gallagher had been listening to the three ships as they had spotted the Hingandu and he heard them talking about killing what looked to be hostiles as per the ambassador's orders. Then he listened as the ships were attacked, and his hands grew cold when Willy started talking. He started sweating when Willy mentioned his name, and thought his knees had given way when the missile hit the ship. The alarms started to blare and the general announcement kicked in. "Hull Breach, Launch bay one. Evacuation procedures in effect for sub deck one."

Sitting at his desk, Gallagher punched a button on his control panel and said, "Get me Vladimir, stat." Knowing it was going to get bloody, he figured he might as well send in the one who wanted blood the most.

Willy had never been in the healing center, but he knew where it was. He rushed inside to a large waiting area connected to the long hallway. Doqui was among the many waiting in the outer area, and his face showed the strain of the injured and dying. "Where is Dekonal?" Willy asked.

"Fifth room on the left," Doqui said, pointing down the hall. He started to say something else, but Willy was already running.

There were several people in the room, including Chakdon who was crouching next to Dekonal and speaking softly. Sydni was in the doorway, watching and crying. Out of habit, she put her arms around Willy and he kissed her forehead. A healer and assistant looked at him briefly. "What is it?" Willy asked in a whisper.

Sydni choked down the lump in her throat and whispered, "They are trying to help her, but she will not give up the babies."

Willy stroked Sydni's hair back and said, "I will take care of it."

Leaving Sydni and walking past the healers, Willy put a hand on Chakdon's shoulder. "Father, I will have a moment please."

Chakdon nodded and stood up. Turning to the others, Willy said, "Please, may we have a moment? I will call you back in shortly." Reluctantly they all filed out of the room. Once they were gone, Willy softly said, "Lover, look at me."

Dekonal looked up and into Willy's eyes. Her face curled up in pain, but not from her wound that still dribbled blood, but from her heart. Willy's chin quivered and tears brimmed his eyes. "They want to take my boys away, Willy," she said.

"No, I won't let that happen," he said. A brief smile invaded her face and was gone in a wave of tears. "Your leg does need the attention of the healers."

"I know." she said. "But our boys need me."

Reaching up to her face, he traced the stripe along her cheek and said, "Of course they do, but how about if I hold them, while the healer looks at you? Our boys need you to be healthy." She looked down at their faces and nodded. The tears again spilled down over Willy's cheeks. "I need you to be healthy," he added.

"You will hold them?" she asked, looking up.

"Right here, where you are, and they can treat you."

"You promise?"

"I promise."

Willy took Jean-Pierre, who had fallen asleep, and cradled him in his right arm, and then reluctantly, Dekonal gave up Chakdall. Willy waited, as Dekonal forced herself to her feet and shuffled aside so he could sit. Willy just hung his head down as he cried, looking into the faces of his sons, and Dekonal placed a hand on his shoulder and kissed his forehead. "I love you," she said.

"I love you too," he said, looking back up. "Forever."

"What are we going to do?" Dekonal asked in a whisper.

"Whatever we have to, my love. Whatever we have to."

She leaned again, her wounded leg nearly buckling under her and kissed him. Then looking toward the door, she said, "I am ready."

The healer and assistant came rushing in, helping Dekonal to the bed, where they started working on her leg. Willy couldn't stop the tears and decided he didn't want to stop them. Looking up, he saw Sydni standing in the doorway. He saw the look of helplessness on her face, but he didn't know how to help her; he didn't know how to help himself. He bit his lip and shook his head.

From the bed, Dekonal said, "My love. Are the children still sleeping?"

"Yes, Dekonal. They are."

"Good, I think they are very tired." She paused and then said, "I was thinking, do you think we could take them and go up to the mountain hut where we spent our first night of our mated life?"

"That would be a splendid idea. As soon as your leg heals a little."

"Great." She sounded groggy and tired.

After a few minutes of silence, the healer said, "She will sleep for a while. We have stopped the bleeding and cleaned the wound. It does not seem to be a deep wound. We will be back in a few hours to change her bandage."

The assistant came over and said, "Shall I take the child, Willy?"

"No," Willy said in nearly a growl. "I promised her we would be here when she was ready."

"Yes, sir."

Sydni came in with fresh blankets and wet cloths. "I will help him," she said.

The healer and assistant left. "Shall we clean them up a little?" Sydni asked, crouching down and wiping the tears from his cheeks.

They spent nearly an hour cleaning up both Chakdall and Jean-Pierre, and re-clothing them in fresh blankets. When they had finished, Sydni made him take off the bloody shirt and wash himself as she held the babies. Once this was done, Willy sat back in the chair to wait for Dekonal to wake back up. Long after Sydni had left, and dispersed Willy's squad, Willy sat in the quiet room, straining to see his sons' faces in the dim light.

Dekonal woke to the hungry cry of Jean-Pierre, who had gone a long time without food. When she saw Willy sitting there, she smiled and said, "You are still here."

He walked over to her and gently gave her Jean-Pierre as she started feeding him. She looked at Willy, cradling and bouncing the other bundle. She started crying and patted the bedside. Willy walked around and nestled up next to her. She pressed her crying face into Willy's arm and then his chest as he put an arm around her. They sat that way all night, sometimes quietly talking, sometimes crying, but Willy never saw sleep that night and the cold place in him grew.

CHAPTER 20

The second day after the attack, well before dawn, the funeral party arrived, riding Brotu, at the Shrine of Halkala. All six squads of guerrilla warriors flanked Willy. Tyuk and Chakdon flew ahead. The healers did not want to release Dekonal from the healing center, but consented to let her ride to the top of the mountain for the second ceremony.

Tyuk took Chakdall, bundled as Dekonal always bundled him, from Willy. He turned and stood next to the rock formation and held him toward the heavens. Willy stood straight and tall, with all his warriors lined up behind him, and his father-in-law at one side and Sydni on the other. Tyuk offered up a prayer to God that one so little would not enter the spirit world alone and that He would guide his spirit into peace.

Turning to Willy, Tyuk handed him Chakdall and stepped aside. Willy looked up at the faint moon as it shone brightly between the thin layer of patchy clouds. He held Chakdall up toward the moon and then close to his body. Speaking in English, he said, "Just a month ago, this life came into being and blessed our lives. And therein I promised to provide and protect. I sang my song of thanks. Now I ask for peace. Peace for this child that never had a chance to know anything else and peace for the broken hearts he has left behind." Willy's voice cracked, and everyone present did not need to understand his words to understand his pain. "Give me the strength to carry on and protect his brother and mother and all others who could ever suffer such a fate."

Willy looked at the dark face, illuminated by only moonlight as he walked back to the others. Remington let out a half-roar, half-moan, which sparked several others to do the same, creating an eerie call in the early morning hours.

Soon after they were all riding again, back to the mountains, where the second ceremony would take place; where Dekonal would be waiting for one last glimpse of her son. There was a place along the ridge where the Brotu roamed where the Hingandu had several funeral pyres erected. Dekonal, Jean-Pierre, Conrad, and Nurian were waiting among several others as Willy and his companions arrived. As they landed, they urged their Brotu down along the ridge.

Willy stood next to Dekonal, who passed Jean-Pierre on to Sydni. Willy kissed Chakdall and gave him to Dekonal, who kissed him as well. Dekonal then hobbled forward and placed Chakdall in the center of the pyre and said, "Travel in the forests and mountains of peace with God."

She stepped back and took Willy's hand. The sky in the east had lightened and now a thin line of color had started. They all watched as the patchy clouds along the horizon caught fire with red and orange light that slowly spread the length of the horizon. Then the center grew intense with bright red and orange as the ball of fire rose, peeking from behind a cloud. The red raced across the clouds, then stretching from horizon to horizon; the whole sky was tinted in red, while behind the clouds in the east, the sky brightened with yellow and orange. As the whole sky was involved in the sunrise, Quistqui and Doqui stepped forward and each unsheathed their knives. They ran their knives along the logs causing the logs to catch fire, and the thick fuel that had been placed along them caught quickly.

As the sky burned itself out, leaving only the ashen clouds and the brightness in the east, everyone's eyes came back to the pyre, which was leaping with flames. As Dekonal began crying again, Willy held her. Long after the fire burned out, they were still standing there, and people began to file past them, offering condolences. Once all were gone except Chakdon, Sydni, Conrad, Quistqui, Nurian, and Doqui, Dekonal's legs gave way. Willy scooped her up in his arms and held her until the fire fell to embers and then ashes before he carried her back down to the healing center.

Once Dekonal was resting again, Willy walked into the hallway and leaned against the wall. He was exhausted, but every time he closed his eyes, he saw Chakdall's still form cradled in his arms. He looked up and down the hall and could just barely see Sydni sitting in the waiting area rocking Jean-Pierre in her arms. Chakdon walked out of the room across from him and sat next to Willy. "I have neglected to ask how Madak is doing," Willy said in barely more than a whisper.

"She will survive. The healers say that she will walk again with some work, but she lost her right arm just below the elbow. She is distraught."

"It has been tough on all of us," Willy said. "And she was in the middle of it."

"She was carrying Chakdall. She feels responsible."

Willy looked up. "What?" he asked. "Because she was carrying him?"

Chakdon nodded as Willy forced himself to his feet. "Where are you going?" Chakdon asked.

"To tell her otherwise. Others are responsible for these deaths, and some of them have already paid for it with their lives. She is not responsible."

"Willy," Chakdon said, as Willy turned away.

Stopping, Willy said, "Yes."

"When was the last time you slept?"

Willy didn't turn back he just kept on walking as he said, "I cannot remember. Seems like it was a lifetime ago."

Willy found Madak staring toward the window as the bright sunlight shone in the room. As he walked around the bed to face her, she blinked and then tears began to brim over. "I am so sorry, Willy." Her voice cracked and the lump that formed cut off her next words.

"No," Willy said kneeling at her bedside and brushing away the tears. "No, there was nothing you could have done differently."

"I could have left the baby with her and he would still be alive right now."

"We don't know that, Mother. We cannot think like that. He is gone and some of the people responsible for it are dead. They will never harm another person, ever."

Madak just shook her head and took Willy's hand with her left hand. "But I…."

"Shhhhhhh, rest. You need your rest. You need to heal fast, not only for yourself and Chakdon, but Dekonal is going to need your support. I have to go. If there is anything I can do, tell Doqui."

Chakdon walked in and came around next to Willy. He put a hand on Willy's shoulder and said, "Go, get some rest, Willy. We need you to be strong too."

Willy squeezed her hand and bent low to kiss her forehead. "Let peace into your heart, Madak."

Once Willy was gone, Madak's tears started again as Chakdon knelt at her bedside. "I saw his face," she said. "I saw his heart break and there was nothing I could do about it. As his world started crumbling, I could not even reach out to console him."

Chakdon kissed her hand and then said, "My wife. My love. My reason to get up every morning and come to bed every night, there was nothing that could be done. Now we will all have to help each other heal, and with God's help, and the love that fills our family, we will be whole again, someday."

Down the hall, in the waiting area, Willy leaned against the wall and watched Sydni, who was focused on Jean-Pierre. She looked up, and the smile faded from her face. "Do I look that bad?" Willy asked.

"Honestly, yes you do. You look like something the Brotu have been kicking around up there."

A weak smile crossed his face for an instant. "Good, I was beginning to think I only felt that way."

"Why don't you go home, take a shower, and sleep for a while."

"I don't want to be far from either of them."

"Then I will take him home with us. I will watch him. The healer said he gave Dekonal something so she would sleep for a long time."

"How is Conrad?"

Sydni smiled. "He had never seen nor smelled the end result of a battlefield, but he started helping and tending to the wounded and documenting with his scanner; but once it was all over and it hit him what had happened, he was quite ill." Standing up, Sydni stood next to her brother and placed a hand on his cheek. "You look like you are about to keel over, and you smell pretty ripe."

Glancing back down the hall, Willy said, "I will go get cleaned up, but I cannot promise sleep."

They walked home, and Willy looked at the increasingly cloudy sky, wondering if it would rain today. He thought rain would be good, maybe it could wash away the stench of the past couple of days, and the blood, and the craters, and the tears. Willy looked up along the mountain and could see another fire burning. He wondered if anyone had told him how many had died in the attack, but he couldn't remember. So much of the past two days had been a blur.

In the house, Willy insisted that he would tend to Jean-Pierre and put him down for a nap. Sydni watched as Willy stopped at his door and paused, steeling himself to go in and face all the things that Chakdall had now left behind. But, as if he knew his father needed it, Jean-Pierre cooed and gurgled. Willy looked down and smiled, and Sydni could see his shoulders relax a little. He went in and shut the door.

Inside, Willy focused on Jean-Pierre. "My little son. Shall we take a shower and get you cleaned off? I know Aunt Nurian and Aunt Sydni were taking care of you, but you are a little man, and need to take a shower."

Willy started the water in the bathroom and threw his own clothes in a corner. After adjusting the water to a temperature and pressure that would not harm Jean-Pierre, Willy stepped in the shower with him. Jean-Pierre loved the spray of the water. He smiled and laughed and gurgled and watched with his big, gold-flecked eyes as the water caught the light just right. "I have many things to show you, Jean-Pierre. So many things that I do not even know where to begin." After a while, he took Jean-Pierre out and dried him off and then put him in a fresh outfit. Jean-Pierre stretched and yawned, and Willy knew that he would sleep for a while. So he set Jean-Pierre in the tandem bassinet, weighted to keep rocking long after anyone stopped pushing, and as he pushed it with his hand, he was rewarded by another smile. Willy watched as Jean-Pierre's eyes grew heavy then finally he was asleep; what Willy had been avoiding looking at was the empty bassinet. After giving the bassinet another push, he walked back into the bathroom, turned the warm water up and took a long shower, mostly just standing under the water and letting it run down over him, washing away his tears.

* * * *

Vladimir had taken down a shuttle with three Marine leaders, an Ambassadorial Guard leader, and Sandra, Gallagher's translator. They met in the large meeting room, and Vladimir handed over a package, saying, "A small token of our appreciation for your assistance in these matters."

What the Marine leaders did not know was that the present was blueprints for them to make faster moving ground vehicles, based on their current technology. Gallagher, who was buying troops to throw into the forest after the Hingandu and the Coltons, had prearranged this.

Using Sandra, Vladimir discussed his plan for attack, criss-crossing the troops through the woods, keeping them near each other for backup and using the ships overhead to help as well. Vladimir kept an eye on not only Zartig, but also the warriors that would be going out with his troops, and he wanted to make certain that they understood Sandra. He had the leaders working with Sandra so they could learn some basic commands and phrases to help guide them all into battle.

They stayed through the night and drank and ate and talked, the Jolabwe trying to pick up some English and the Humans trying to pick up some Jolabwe.

After they went over the plan one more time in the morning, Vladimir sent them on their way to go meet their troops in the field as he took a shuttle back up to the Orion. He was trying to be a good leader and not go for the blood lust himself. He wanted his rank back, so he knew he had to behave. The coordination for the attack was taking place in the war room on the Orion, where he could see and hear everything coming in from the field.

As he sat in the over-stuffed chair, he grinned at Gallagher, who paced back and forth along the wall with the satellite image of the ground and their troops. He pushed a comm button and said, "Proceed to launching point and wait for my command."

* * * *

The walk home was slow, but Willy held Jean-Pierre in one arm while he supported Dekonal with the other. The rain had not started yet, but as the morning wore on, Willy figured it would start. It was not only the rain. He had the feeling something was about to happen, but he couldn't figure it out. So he concentrated on his family and getting them home. Inside, Willy found Conrad in the kitchen, tinkering on more missiles. After he welcomed Dekonal home, he went back to work.

Willy got Dekonal into bed, using pillows to prop her up, and gave her Jean-Pierre before he checked her dressing. Once she was settled, he laid down next to her, looking up at her. She reached over and rubbed his chest. "I was told you have not slept yet. Is that true?"

"Yes, my love."

"That is a long time to go without sleep."

"I know. I just can't help it."

She ran her fingers over his lips and he kissed her fingers. "Rest now. It is my turn and I will watch over you."

Willy smiled. "Thank you. I will try." He closed his eyes and concentrated on emptying his mind so he could sleep. He couldn't shut out the sounds, though, and it was the simple sounds that hurt the most. There were only two other breaths in the room beside his; two breaths where there had been three. He sighed. Dekonal rubbed his chest when he sighed, and she whispered, "It will be all right. You deserve to sleep now."

Willy tried, but his mind wouldn't stop racing, only to come back to Chakdall laying on the ground bundled up. He thought he might have even drifted off and dreamed it all, when he heard Dekonal take a sharp breath. He opened his eyes and looked at her. Her gaze was fixed forward and she was still, her lips barely parted. It was a vision, and he knew it to be the first since the attack. Not wanting to disturb her or distract her, he waited to move until it was over.

She blinked and looked down at Jean-Pierre, then over to Willy. "I thought you were sleeping," she whispered.

"No. What made you gasp?"

Her face looked sad and her lips were curved down into a frown. She shook her head and said, "Another attack. This time big." Willy leaped out of bed and ran for his scanner, sitting on a pile of his things. Dekonal continued, "There are many groups of them all over and in the air. This is a war, not an attack."

Willy turned on the scanner and reports were coming in. There was movement all over and his squads were already deployed. He caught someone saying that they had massed the rest of the village's forces for defense and sent riders to get help from the other villages. Willy looked up at his wife and son sitting on the bed and he felt tired. There was a battle, in which no one had called him to fight, and there was his broken family. He wondered where his duty was.

Dekonal looked into Willy's bloodshot eyes and could see the confusion in his stare as he paused. She saw that if she did not tell him to go, he would go crazy waiting for news of his warriors and sister, and if something happened to one of them, without him there, he would never forgive himself. She tried to see if she told him to go, if he would return, but the vision was not there. How could she bear it if she was to lose her mate as well? What would she do?

She whispered his name, as she envisioned him saving many lives, "Willy. Someone out there needs you. Go."

Focusing in on her, he hesitated. Then he pressed his button for Remington and was changing into his battle clothes. Before he left, he stopped next to her and said, "I love you. I will be back as soon as it is safe."

"Be careful."

"I will." He kissed her and then kissed Jean-Pierre and ran out the door, snatching his new rifle and harness.

As he went down the stairs, she said, "Come back to me alive."

Outside the back door, Willy almost ran into Nurian, who was walking up to their house. "Sorry," Willy said as he stopped.

Nurian just smiled. "Quistqui asked me to come over and look out for his sister. He said if there was a battle, you would find out, and be on your way."

Willy looked dumbfounded and he said, "Really? Quistqui knew I would be going."

Nurian turned to walk into the house, saying, "He said he swore you had visions too by the way you seemed to know things. He said he would bet a herd of Brotu that you would be going."

Willy smiled. "You have a smart mate, Nurian."

Remington was just landing and as Willy was harnessing him, Conrad stepped outside. "What is going on?" he asked.

"There is a major battle going down. I may need so many of those missiles that you couldn't possibly work long enough."

"Damn," Conrad said. "Why won't they give us a break?"

Willy sat on Remington and looked at Conrad, who for a moment looked like the weight of the house was on his shoulders. Willy winked at him and said, "They will. Once I find a way to expose Gallagher for what he is or sink enough of your missiles in the hull of the Orion to send it limping back home."

Before Conrad could reply, Willy took off in a flurry of flapping wings and was gone. Just as he passed out of sight, Nurian came running out, holding Willy's scanner. She looked at Conrad and said, "He forgot this."

Conrad took it and said, "I will hold onto it for him."

* * * *

Silence permeated the woods as Willy's group moved into position as per Sydni's orders. Willy's group joined up with Sydni's and she was in charge of all the guerrilla warriors. They had crawled down along a small rock ridge covered with Cuzira berry bushes to set up and ambush the large group of Humans and Jolabwe moving up out of the forest. In the distance, they heard a ship fly past, breaking the silence, but causing more tension. Everyone had heard how the ships swooped down and attacked without provocation. Now they were about to give them a reason to attack. Hatred burned bright for a moment within Doqui as he thought about his nephew, his sister, and his mother, but he could hear Willy's words. "Do not fight with hate in your heart, make it cold. Hate is hot and will make you mess up. When it is cold, it will help you kill."

Doqui scanned the lowland below through his scope and saw movement. They were making their way in. Sydni said not to fire until she did. She waited near the point of the lowlands towards where she hoped they would travel, then and she would have her squads spread out to close a trap on them.

The sound started and grew steadily, then little droplets made it through the upper canopy. It had started to rain. Doqui smiled. He loved the rain. He wondered if the Humans and the Jolabwe felt the same way.

Hidden down the same rock formation was Sydni. She was motionless, but keeping her eyes on the forward movement of the group heading towards them. She would never have led the Marines into such an easily defended area, but then again, there were no scouts with this group. She wondered if Tanya and Barkley were serving anywhere in this operation, and for a moment, she prayed that they were not.

The rain started falling and Sydni smiled. The Marines had had very little battle time as it was, and they had been cooped up in the ship for months. Any diverse conditions were going to work to the Hingandu's advantage, especially on their home turf. Sydni looked at her scanner and checked the readings again to make certain that as this group moved forward, she was not being out-flanked.

Finally, the closest Marine had moved within twenty yards of her, with others close behind, and she knew that she could not stall any longer. She didn't know if she could stomach killing humans, but they were the intruders here, and they were encroaching. Then the vision of the field where Chakdall had died passed before her. It was humans who had viciously attacked unarmed people and children. Seconds after that, Sydni fired, killing the first Marine of the battle. Two more dropped before any more of the Hingandu joined in. Their ambush ripped the Marines to shreds.

Little did they know, that far back in the fight, a Marine was calling in an air strike and bathing the rock formation with a laser so the attack fighters would be able to hone in on it. As the fire fight grew, with the pinned-down and wounded Marines trying to return fire on the well-hidden Hingandu, two attack craft banked and headed toward the rock formation, arming both missiles and pulse lasers.

The two fighters curved slowly around, taking a wide berth to avoid alerting the Hingandu and to get the right alignment for the attack. As they skimmed the treetops, the first ship opened its missile tubes.

Neither pilot had time to focus far ahead of them. They were following their sensors, letting the computer guide their course. Neither had seen the one man atop a Brotu, perched in the upper canopy of the trees. Willy was there and waiting as the ships neared the rock formation. His first shot went directly into the missile tubes, and the ship burst into a fireball as it passed overhead. His second, third, and fourth shots hit the nose cone and cockpit of the second ship. It held steady for a moment, and then cut sharply as the dead pilot leaned against the stick. It careened over Willy's head, crashing and exploding into the forest, just missing the Marines that had called it in. Willy let out a yell of victory, knowing that normal bullets never would have touched the ships, that only the modified Hingandu ones would.

Willy also knew Marine tactics, and he knew that somewhere just below him in the exchange of fire was a Marine with a laser targeting system and radio, calling in an air strike. Dropping from Remington into the upper canopy, Willy climbed down until he could just see the Marines below. After a quick search, he found who he was looking for. Willy's first shot shattered the laser-targeting device in the Marine's hands, and his second bullet struck the Marine as he shouted and looked up. Willy fired three more shots, killing three more Marines before he climbed back up to Remington. Standing in the stirrups, Willy surveyed the treetops and saw three more ships circling several miles away. A thin trail of smoke curled into the air.

He looked down for a moment and knew that the Hingandu squad below him could handle the fight themselves until any Human or Jolabwe reinforcements showed up, but he needed to knock down the ships so they couldn't hammer the on ground forces. With a tug of the reins and a mumbled word, "Go," they were flying along the treetops. Willy wondered if the focused flyers would see him coming if he wasn't on radar, but he knew he had to be close for an effective shot, so he had to risk it; lives were at stake.

As the din of weapons firing grew, Willy decided he had come close enough. He had Remington perch on a new tree, swaying down enough so the trees would better hide them. The ships made three passes, firing their weapons at the ground before they came in a direction that allowed Willy a shot.

They were coming in faster than the first two ships he had already shot down, so he wasn't certain if he would have time to take two down, but he aimed his rifle and waited. Willy could see the pilot in the cockpit and he fired two rapid shots, shattering the window and killing the pilot. As the ship plummeted forward, crashing into the trees only yards away, Willy fired on the second ship, wounding the pilot, who pulled back and rose quickly into the air. The third pilot acted quickly and veered away, racing directly over Willy, who thought for an instant he had been spotted, but the pilot only saw Willy just before he passed over. They made eye contact.

Instantly, Willy was pushing Remington's head down, shouting, "Go." Remington dove into the canopy right above the battle. The skies were not safe while that pilot was looking for him, but Willy soon thought his mistake might have been diving above the battlefield. Hingandu shouts rose as they saw a ship drop from the sky and then Willy, flying on Remington, entered the battle. This made the Marine and Jolabwe contingent look up, and they started firing at Willy. Willy was letting Remington guide his own way through the thick trees. Willy could see that the Hingandu were in a better position than the Marines, and that the ship had crashed right down among the Marines.

The leaves and branches around them erupted as if they were stuck into a shredding machine, and Willy felt Remington flinch, losing altitude a little and moaning. Terror struck through his heart as he looked back and forth for injuries and found a bleeding hole in Remington's right wing. He needed to get out of this situation. The ship raced past overhead, and Willy looked for a thicket on the ground. A stand of evergreen trees was ahead about one hundred yards. He angled that way, praying that Remington's wings would hold out.

Glancing behind him, he saw a group of Marines and Jolabwe break away and start to follow him. There would be a hell of a fight, Willy thought to himself, and he smiled. His next thought was that they should have sent more Marines.

As they touched down, Willy was jumping off Remington, his heart pounding. He gave hand signals that he had taught to Remington, who moved away from him, running on the ground. Willy crouched low to the ground and ran into the evergreens. The minute he looked out, he shook his head. Four Marines were at a full run, chasing him down, and behind them he could see as many Jolabwe, running as fast as they could.

Willy dropped three of the Marines and two of the Jolabwe before they took cover. As he moved out of the evergreens, crawling as fast as he could, the evergreens were shredded by fire from the remaining Marine and Jolabwe. Willy strapped the rifle across his back and drew out his knife and ax, knowing that his ammunition was limited and that he would need it for another chance at more ships.

The Marine was looking about wildly, and moved cautiously forward as the Jolabwe moved, closing in behind him. Willy would have to time it just right.

When he was within a few yards of the foursome, the ship Willy had shot, with the wounded the pilot, crashed to the ground, as if on cue, with an earth-shaking explosion, making all three of them look.

Willy jumped up, swinging his knife and ax. In a flash, the three were on the ground, and only the Marine was still breathing. Willy walked over and the Marine looked up at him, trying to move away and gurgling blood from his mouth as he tried to speak. For a moment, Willy saw a young man that he would have been fighting to protect; some mother's son. Then he heard a ship fly over and he could hear the explosions in the clearing where his son had died. He stripped the Marine of his weapons and left him to die.

The other Marines were dead. Willy took two rockets off of them and grinned; now he would be able to use one of their own weapons against the ship. He flicked on the sighting for the missile and he scanned the sky. The last ship was hovering over the battlefield and firing short bursts into the forest. Willy locked on the target and paused, waiting to see if he had a good shot lined up, and then he fired.

A high-pitched whistle rose above the din of the fighting as the missile streaked through the forest, climbing into the upper canopy, and bursting into the open air above the trees just underneath the ship. The pilots warning lights flared and warning signals buzzed seconds before the missile slammed into the belly of his ship. The ship exploded, hanging in the air for a moment, and then crashed to the ground in a giant fireball. A cheer rose among the Hingandu. Willy moved silently through the woods, gaining better access to the Human's flank. Taking his time, Willy camouflaged himself using grasses and small branches from some bushes, then he crawled closer to the Jolabwe and Human line.

Another group of Jolabwe was rushing forward when Willy opened fire from his position at the base of several bushes. The fire, and dropping Jolabwe, gained the attention of several Marines, who started stalking toward the Jolabwe, only to have Willy stop them too.

Willy crawled forward until he reached the Marines, and then he listened in on one of their comm hook-ups. A Marine was shouting into his mic over the sound of battle, "We need air support and we need it now. We are taking heavy damage."

A bridge officer answered the call, "No can do, all flights are grounded until we know what is dropping them out of the sky."

Willy smiled. His plan was working. Now with some relief from the air, he could concentrate on helping the ground troops. Dropping the pulse rifle he was using, he picked up a lesser-used pulse rifle. Glancing at the Marine's scanner, he sized up the force that was only several meters ahead.

The Marines and Jolabwe were taking heavy losses, but of course he could not see the Hingandu, so he did not know what their losses were. He moved forward until he could see more of the battlefield.

Positioning himself alongside a tree, he started targeting Marines and Jolabwe that he could drop before anyone discovered where he was. He started shooting his targets, and he hoped no one would notice that a sniper had gotten around them. He had taken out over half a dozen when the line of Marines started to move, and he thought he had been found out when a group of Hingandu pushed forward through the forest from where he had landed with Remington. It was a regular group of warriors, and their crossbow fire started tearing up the ranks of the Marines.

Two Hingandu stopped on either side of Willy and said, "You can get up. They have moved back." Willy stood up and looked at the two warriors. One continued, "Thanks, you gave us the opening we were looking for."

"Who is leading you?" Willy asked.

"We are acting with Quistqui's group in supporting them."

"Good. Tell Quistqui that Willy said not to fall into deep pursuit, but remain on good ground and remain cautious. This is not close to being over."

"I will tell him," one said, pulling his scanner off his belt.

Willy was impressed to see that not only his guerrilla warriors were carrying the scanners now. This would give them even more of an advantage over the Marines. "Broadcast a message to all Hingandu and tell them to secure any weapons and scanners of dead Hingandu, the humans and Jolabwe cannot be allowed to have them. It could hurt us."

"Yes."

Both Hingandu next to Willy looked toward the rest of their group as pulse rifle fire sounded nearby, and several Hingandu shot a downed Marine who had been lying in wait. The Hingandu with the scanner turned back to Willy and started to ask, "What would you..." His voice faded away, because Willy was no longer standing there.

Although still moving cautiously, Willy nearly ran back to where he had left Remington. A quick search found Remington waiting. An examination showed only the single bullet wound to the wing, which had not hit any bone and already had stopped bleeding. "Can you fly, boy?" he asked as he mounted. Remington's only response was a simple flit of his wings that lifted them off the ground, rising into the air. As they broke the upper level of the canopy, the rain was pounding fiercely, and Willy relished the cool water, wiping away the sweat and some of his camouflage.

Knowing now that the skies would be free of attack ships for a while, Willy directed Remington as high as he could fly and still see the terrain. He was looking for more smoke and more signs of battle. He flew past where Sydni and his group had been, and he caught a glimpse of Jolabwe retreating.

Then, about a half a mile from where Sydni's group had been, a tree shuddered and then fell crashing into the forest. As he neared, Willy could hear the sound of rifles and another rocket exploding. After one circle, just above the treetops, Willy flew away from the sounds of battle to find a landing place; he didn't want a repeat of his last attempt.

The landing was without incident, and once Willy had Remington hidden away, he started heading in the direction of the battle, reapplying some camouflage from his pack. Rain was now pounding down through the trees to the ground. Willy checked the charge on the pulse rifle and then started crawling along the ground, looking for more victims.

* * * *

There was a palpable tension in the village, and it was very quiet in the streets. Conrad had sat in the back of the courtyard until the rain had started, and then he moved up under the overhang. He had been fumbling with Willy's scanner since Nurian had handed it to him, trying to decide if he wanted to turn it on and listen for any news. His heart pounded in his chest as he thought about Sydni being out in the battle; he didn't know what he would do if she didn't make it out alive.

Shaking his head, he softly said, "Don't think about it. Don't think about it. They are going to be okay. They have to be." As much as he tried to convince himself, though, he couldn't get the thoughts out of his head.

Giving in, he flipped on Willy's scanner. After a second, the screen read: Scanner reinitializing…Action complete. This perplexed Conrad, wondering why the scanner would have initialized, and then he remembered that Willy had flown and placed his scanner into the ship for the first time since Conrad had brought it planetside. He started scanning the files, and then he realized just what had reinitialized. The files were the ones that Gallagher had used against him, had been stored in the ship, and had refreshed into his computer.

Conrad stood up as Gallagher's voice came to life on the scanner, and he nearly shouted, but he caught himself thinking of Dekonal, who was resting. Then, his second instinct was to turn on the speaker to call Sydni and Willy to give them the news, but the speaker came to life with a flurry of Hingandu. It took Conrad several seconds to sort out the information, and then he realized that now would not be a good time to inform Willy and Sydni. The news would have to wait. From the sound of things, the fighting was still pretty intense in some areas and quiet in others.

He listened, hoping beyond all hope to hear Sydni's voice. Then he heard it. She ordered her group to take cover along a path and remain quiet. Then she was silent. Conrad breathed a sigh of relief. His wife was still alive, and they now had the information they needed to stop Gallagher. He stretched, yawned, and for the first time in days, he smiled.

Chakdon walked into Dekonal's room and leaned against the doorjamb, waiting to see if she was awake. Nurian had been downstairs sleeping at the table, and Chakdon had sent her home to get some sleep. His face had drooped and although his skin was dark, there were even darker circles under his eyes. He yawned, thinking Dekonal was asleep, but she whispered, "You look tired, father."

"I am, but I will be okay."

"Go home, get some sleep. I will be fine."

Chakdon walked over to her, glancing in the crib at Jean-Pierre, who was sleeping. "I couldn't sleep. Men and women are dying out there, and the visions will not stop."

"I can see them too," Dekonal said. "I cannot see the outcome, though."

Sitting on the edge of her bed, Chakdon said, "I can only see that it will change our lives forever, but I cannot be certain how. It is not clear yet."

"I see Willy coming through this alive," Dekonal whispered, "but not for a day or two, and then he too will be changed."

"Chakdall's death has filled his heart with hatred. That will not be easily overcome."

Dekonal looked at her son, who stretched and yawned in his crib and then settled back down. "It will be easier than you think. Love will cure it. He only needs time."

"I hope you are right, Child."

She reached up and put her hand on his shoulder and said, "I have to be, Father. If there is one thing I absolutely know, without question, is that Willy has more room in his heart for love than he ever will for hate. He will come through this." Dekonal shifted in her bed, wincing in pain, but trying not to show it. "How is Mother?" she asked.

"Better every day," He replied. "Growing stronger, and beginning to accept her disability, although I will say, it will be some time before she is healed in her heart."

"I will make the trip over there in the morning with Jean-Pierre to visit her. I will show her that we will survive. We will get through this, together."

"The healing center is starting to receive the wounded from the battle already. I am certain she will enjoy your company, though."

"Why don't you go, father?"

"I sent Nurian home to sleep for a while. I will stay and look at my grandson and know that somewhere in the world there is some peace."

Jean-Pierre made some noise and both looked. He was waving his arms and gurgling. Chakdon picked him up and sat in the rocking chair next to the crib. Dekonal yawned and said, "You can stay as long as you wish."

"Thank you."

Dekonal closed her eyes, hoping to sleep as Chakdon started rocking back and forth, humming a song to his grandson. The rain kept a steady beat on the roof.

* * * *

The rain splattered against the screen of Sydni's scanner while she was trying to read it. Her long-range scan was showing nobody but Hingandu within half a mile from them. They had not seen any fighting since the sun had gone down. Willy's unit and hers had had only one casualty, while the support they had been sent from the village had taken several casualties. She wondered where Willy was. She had seen his work in the downing of the attack ships, and then in an attack on the troops she had first fought. Then there had been several sightings throughout the day as Willy criss-crossed the various battles. Since darkness had set in, she had heard of no more sightings.

She knew that there was still heavy resistance to the south, and firefights were still breaking out. Since the Hingandu could see the Humans and Jolabwe, they were winning most of the skirmishes in the dark. The groups to the north were within scanner range of a large contingency of Humans and Jolabwe, and were currently discussing a night attack. The general consensus was that it would dishearten both the Humans and Jolabwe and give the Hingandu an even greater edge.

Sydni had agreed with them. They were looking for Willy's approval, but he did not answer a call on his scanner. His lack of participation worried Sydni. She wondered why he hadn't contacted her about his group of warriors, but she only came to the conclusion that he had his reasons.

Her scanner buzzed in her hand, and she glanced down. On the very edge, at the half-mile point, two blips appeared and then two more. She keyed in the mic and coded it for the groups she was commanding. She took a deep breath and said, "Okay, wake everyone around you. A new group is moving in."

CHAPTER 21

Tanya and Barkley sat in the Captain's office waiting room, knowing that they had refused a direct order for the first time and probably the last time in their careers. Tanya looked at Barkley and said, "Did you set up all you needed to set up?"

Barkley nodded. "They just need to figure out that it is running and they can take care of it from down there."

Tanya paused and asked, "I know it is unusual for an officer to ask a sergeant, but are we doing the right thing?"

Barkley looked at the floor and breathed deeply. Without looking up, he asked, "In your heart of hearts, what do you say?"

"I say that I know those are humans, and that there is no way I want to kill any of them. I do not want to face either Willy or Sydni. This is war, and I do not want to be fighting them. Our friendship must overrule the UWC and the Ambassador."

With a smile, Barkley looked up and nodded. "You know, Tanya, I wouldn't have said it any differently. So we will face the consequences together. Come what may."

"Prison colony Alpha?"

"Come what may."

The door leading into the Captain's office opened, and Gallagher stormed past them, leaving only Acting Captain Cho standing in the doorway. Both Tanya and Barkley stood and saluted.

"Get in here," Cho said turning around and striding back into the office.

Tanya led the way with Barkley following closely, and they stood at attention where they always had when Captain Dollinger had ruled the bridge. Cho waited several seconds before she turned to them, then spoke in a level tone. "Disobeying a direct order is a serious offense." She moved directly in front of Barkley and said, "Sergeant Billings, your commanding officer has refused to go into battle. Did she make this decision for you?"

"No, ma'am. We came to the same conclusion."

Cho had been turning to face Tanya, but she stopped at his sentence. "So now we have sergeants concurring with their commanding officer? How is it that an enlisted man would be advising an officer?"

"Scouting is not just a usual duty call, ma'am. The scouting program takes in the consideration of all involved." He cleared his throat and said, "Not to mention the fact that she asked my opinion."

Cho nodded her head, but squinted as if she were trying to see into Barkley's mind. "She asked your opinion?" Turning then to Tanya, she asked, "So you have to ask for the opinion of a sergeant, Lieutenant?"

"Have to? No, Ma'am. Wanted to? Yes Ma'am. He is well informed, and among the scouts it is less about rank and more about trust."

"Is it?"

"Yes, Ma'am."

Cho broke away and paced for a moment, and on her second turn, she said, "So you both chose to stay aboard ship, ignoring the need of your fellow soldiers on the battlefield?"

"It puts us in a peculiar position, Ma'am," Tanya said. "You would be forcing us to go fight a battle against people who are family, and in a war that is wrong. Those are humans down there."

"Loyalty is a good thing, Lieutenant, but loyalty to an outlaw is not." She paused for a minute and then said, "You refused a direct order from a superior officer, which in this situation could be construed as treasonous."

"Respectfully, Ma'am, Vladimir is not my superior officer and neither is Ambassador Gallagher. It clearly states in the Scouting Charter for the UWC Orion that the commanding officer of the scouts is only subject to orders given by the captain or a rank officer above the position of captain."

Cho smiled and nodded her head slowly. "You are sharp, Lieutenant. Both Commanders Colton have taught you well, and that alone impresses me. You are very correct in your interpretation of the contract, however, there is something I can do about it." Cho stopped and stood straight and took a deep breath. "Lieutenant Williston and Sergeant Billings, I hereby order you to report to duty under the supervision of Ambassador Gallagher and Vladimir concerning missions to support ground troops during this battle."

"Respectfully, Captain Cho, I must decline on moral standing," Tanya said.

Turning violently to Barkley, Cho nearly shouted, "And you, Sergeant?"

"Respectfully, Captain, I must decline on the same grounds."

"Damn it!" Cho said turning away. "What is this navy coming to when a Lieutenant and a Sergeant are willing to disobey a direct order?"

"On moral grounds," Barkley added.

Cho turned on them again, this time her face was red and her voice was gaining volume. "That is bullshit, Sergeant! Because someone you worked with is down there does not give you moral grounds! So I will not ask you a second time!"

"Ma'am, our moral grounds do not rest on either Willy or Sydni. Our moral grounds are that we will not go fight in a war where we are killing other humans."

"Other humans...Lieutenant, they are not humans. They are hostile and have killed many Marines. We needed to strike back."

"In time, Ma'am, it will be shown that they are humans. I have seen them with my own eyes, and I will not attack them."

Cho looked back and forth between them, shaking her head. "They will court-martial you," she hissed.

"We know," Tanya said.

"Your careers will be over no matter what the outcome."

"That is a consequence we are willing to accept."

Cho walked over to the desk and pressed a button. "You study your regs well. On moral grounds, even weak moral grounds, I cannot brig you without incident, but you will be confined to quarters for the duration of this cruise, where you will be court-martialed upon the completion of the trip."

The outer doors opened and two Marine guards walked in. "Confine these two to quarters. They are not to leave with the exception of meals and exercise periods, and those will be taken with an armed escort." Neither Tanya nor Barkley responded and Cho breathed out. "Get them off my deck."

The Marines stepped aside and let Tanya and Barkley pass them on their way out. Cho watched them until the door shut and then she mumbled to herself, "What could make them stick to their guns so strongly? Why are they willing to destroy everything they have become?" She walked over to the starscreen where she had seen Bucky pace so many times. As she looked out at the stars, she wondered if she was making a mistake. Then, leaning her forehead against the screen, she sighed; she knew she wasn't really in charge either.

* * * *

Gallagher burst into the war room and waddled up to Vladimir, who was busy plotting on a board showing the battle ground. He was shouting orders into a mic and listening from a headset. Vladimir glanced up at Gallagher's entrance, but quickly was drawn back into the melee below.

Standing next to him, Gallagher tapped his toe incessantly until Vladimir turned to him, "What is it, Gallagher? I am very busy right now."

"We need to do something fast!"

"What would you have me do, Ambassador?"

"While I call to consult with the Chancellor, you are going planetside to personally oversee the assault."

"What? How do you expect me to coordinate the battle from planetside?"

"Turn that over temporarily to Colonel Watkins, he has more than enough experience. Take a team of my UWC Ambassadorial Guards with you and start making something happen."

"Make something happen?"

Gallagher swung around and started walking out the door. "Do it Vladimir! That is an order!"

Vladimir ripped the headset off and threw it across the room. "Colonel, the troops are yours. I will be planetside shortly; I will keep in constant contact. Inform me of all developments."

As the door shut behind Vladimir, Colonel Watkins stood up and a lieutenant retrieved the headset. "About damn time," he said looking over the board. "Leaving the troops in the hands of a freaking first lieutenant. What the hell was admiralty thinking? Lieutenant, get me a general line to the troops. I want them to know who has the command now."

"Yes, Sir," the lieutenant said running back to his station.

* * * *

Gallagher looked at the screen as Chambers appeared, saying, "What the hell is it now, Jasper?"

"Sir, we have problems."

"Problems? I don't want to hear about problems, damn it all! I want to hear about successes."

A sheen of sweat formed across Gallagher's brow and he started nervously drumming his fingers on his desk. "We started this war against a people we can't see. The war has been raging for two days and nights, going on the third day. We have thrown everything at them that we can and they keep pushing us back."

"How can this be? We are the technologically advanced race. We have attack ships, we have flown across the galaxy to get there, and you are telling me we cannot defeat them in a ground war? What about our attack ships?"

"Sir, they have figured out a way of bringing down our attack ships. They have taken about twenty and our fliers are grounded at this time."

"What the hell do they have that can bring down an attack ship?"

"We do not know. I have sent Vladimir down to personally oversee the operation."

Chambers put his hands through his hair and looked away from the camera. When he looked back, he had a seldom seen look of frustration, and Gallagher was suddenly happy that he was very far away from Chambers. "Look, Jasper, give it two more days. If you cannot have it resolved or at least have us winning by then, we'll use the ship's weapons and rip that forest apart. Then we will find them."

"The Orion's weapons? Sir, that is in direct violation of the UWC Constitution."

Chambers lowered his voice and said, "Jasper, I know the constitution. I am the UWC and the populaces of the worlds are idiots. They will never know about this. We are too deep in this to be stopped now. If we back down and allow either of the Coltons to survive, they could bury us. These idiots back here will keep reelecting me because they are stupid and do not know what really goes on in the universe. Wipe out that race, rape the land of their Coppertroid and no one will ever know."

Gallagher didn't know how to respond; his mouth was open and he just stared at Chambers. After another moment, Chambers added, "Two days, Jasper. Two days and I will call and check. Make it happen."

The screen went blank, and Gallagher sat there for a long time, staring at his screen in disbelief. As the realization of his orders set in, his hands started to shake and he headed for his supply of alcohol.

Dawn came in shades of gray and even darker shades of gray and green on the forest floor. The rain had come and gone for two days and nights, and as the third day of the war started, the rain was falling again. The number of Jolabwe and Marines seemed endless as they constantly entered the forest. The riders sent to the other villages returned with news that the war was isolated to Alar's village, and in response, they sent warriors. Many had died on both sides. Already the scavengers and insects were gathering, and the only thing keeping the stench down was the rain. Most of the Hingandu had been whisked away to the village for their families to mourn or the healers to mend.

When the ships returned to attack the ground forces, Willy found someone with a scanner and passed the word that they could be brought down in several ways. Hingandu scaled the trees and the ships started falling from the sky; once a dozen more were brought down, the ships disappeared again. Willy was sad at the loss his village was taking, but he was very pleased for their willingness to improvise and adapt to the fighting situation.

The fighting had taken turns and Willy constantly moved about the forest, finding where he could best hurt the Marines and Jolabwe. For two nights he inched along the forest, moving into enemy encampments and striking terror into their hearts as he would silently kill in their midst. Sometimes someone would scream, which would only strike even more terror. Willy was doing more damage solo than if he had been leading his group of guerrilla warriors, although he wished that he could have them doing the same amount of damage. For a moment he smiled and thought how he could use Tanya, Barkley, or Diego. His smile faded. He had prayed that he did not cross Tanya or Barkley in the middle of the night.

Willy yawned from his position in the hollow base of a tree where he had camouflaged himself. Numbness had set in. He knew he didn't have much time; he still hadn't slept yet. His medkit was exhausted of both caffeine and stimulant. During the night he stopped long enough to eat from a Gombo fruit tree. Soon he would have to sleep.

Then he smelled them. It was a fresh group of soldiers; they still smelled of the Orion. He lifted his head and singled out one scent, a scent he never thought he would smell on his planet's surface. It was Vladimir. Willy's body came to life with a new energy, and he quickly forgot all about the numbness and sleeplessness. Slowly, so as not to draw attention from anyone who might have been looking, Willy started to crawl toward the scent.

It took him the better part of two hours to come within range of the squad of Ambassadorial Guards, and there, right in the middle of them was Vladimir, speaking softly into a headset.

The forest around them was thick with evergreens on the far side and various brush and ancient trees on all other sides. Willy looked through his ammo bag. He had more than enough left since the evening before when he met up with a squad who had just been re-supplied; the place that made the projectiles was working around the clock to produce bullets, and now Willy's magazines were full and he had plenty extra. Willy started to judge his plan of attack, knowing that the response to firing at the group would produce a large amount of return fire. He was judging his plan of escape so he could hit and run.

Once he figured out where he would run, he started stretching so when the time came he would be able to react quickly. Then he found a hole in the brush that would suffice for his targeting needs and he lined up his shot. Hate was in Willy's heart as he aimed at Vladimir, but when he was set to fire, he took his finger off of the trigger. It was too easy to kill Vladimir that way; what Willy wanted for Vladimir was suffering and pain.

Willy's target changed, and he targeted the heavy weaponry person first, and knew his next three shots when he squeezed off the first round. Pandemonium struck the squad when one went down in their midst; Willy fired two more times before he rolled behind the base of a tree and the others in the squad began firing into the forest around him. Willy crawled along a little wash as they shredded the brush and snapped small trees where he had been, and as the shooting died off, Willy heard another fire fight break out not too far away.

As he came back into range of the squad, they were taking cover behind trees and a couple guards were close to the area where he had been lying. Vladimir was looking around wildly and speaking loudly into his mic. Willy smiled and targeted the three closest to him. Without hesitation, he dropped those three and was rolling away again, as the forest around him again was ripped apart. One of the remaining squad members rushed forward, firing into the woods and screaming. Willy waited until the soldier made it to where he had been when he fired, knocking the soldier backward.

Vladimir was shouting orders to the last of the squad, telling him to get up there and find the shooter, as Vladimir himself moved forward. Standing to get the angle he needed, Willy shot the weapon in Vladimir's hand, and then shot the last guard who was tentatively moving forward.

Stopping in his tracks, Vladimir looked around and said something into his mic as he still held a piece of his weapon in his left hand. Willy moved slowly but finally positioned himself where he could take a shot at Vladimir's scanner and disable his ability to speak with other troops. The firefight was still raging on nearby, and Vladimir was calling for help, until Willy shot the scanner off his belt.

Vladimir felt trapped, but deep down he knew who was shooting at him. He knew, as he was standing there, that Willy Colton was keeping just out of view, but constantly moving around him. Vladimir didn't try to pick up another weapon. He knew that Willy would shoot him the second he tried. So he tried another tactic.

"I know it is you, Colton. Any fool can see that. Why don't you come out and face me like a man?" Vladimir started to circle, to keep an eye out for Willy, and he continued, "Reinforcements are on the way, and I am going to escape, and you know what I am going to do? I am going to make certain that Chief Su dies in his hospital bed before he ever wakes up."

Willy, who had been circling, stopped. He turned and headed straight for Vladimir, who didn't see him until he was very close, due to the camouflage. Willy removed the branches and grasses from his uniform, but kept his rifle aimed at Vladimir.

"You are going to die, Vladimir. I should have killed you back on the Orion."

"You should have tried. You don't look well, Commander. Worse than your usually ugly face."

"I am more than capable of taking care of you, Vladimir."

"You think you are, only because I have let you have the edge before."

Willy's eyes were locked on Vladimir, and even through the camouflage on Vladimir's face, Willy could see the sheen of nervous sweat and the near panic in his eyes. "You want I should give you a scanner so you can call Gallagher?"

"Why would I want to call Gallagher?" Vladimir nearly spat out the name.

"Because he is the only reason you have lived this long outside a penal colony. For the ugly slob that he is, you have been wet-nursed by him the whole time."

Vladimir's voice climbed a pitch higher as he said, "Are we going to fight or are you going to shoot me?"

Willy pulled the trigger. Vladimir jumped nearly a foot, bringing his hands up in front of him, but Willy had dropped the barrel and shot down in the ground between Vladimir's feet. Willy laughed. "You son-of-a-bitch!" Vladimir growled as he looked at the divot in the ground.

Willy looked around and made certain that there were no weapons near Vladimir, then he set his rifle down and moved forward. Vladimir struck a defensive pose and shuffled forward. "I will enjoy this, Vladimir. As your life drains out of your body, beneath my fingers, I will rejoice." Willy moved forward as well.

"As I will rejoice when we crush these people and rape..."

Willy burst forward, spinning and kicking, striking Vladimir in his face and sending him stumbling backward. Vladimir grabbed his face and stood straight. He spat blood at his feet. "Touchy, touchy. That is unlike you, Commander." Vladimir inched forward as he spoke. "Usually, when you feel better, you keep your cool."

"I thought you were ready to fight," Willy said. "That's right, you really don't know how to fight."

Vladimir rushed forward, and Willy barely side-stepped the swinging fists, but managed to trip up Vladimir, sending him into some brambles that held him momentarily before he ripped himself free and turned back to Willy. "I am going to rip you apart, Colton. I will take you, then I will kill your sister, and then I will find your other boy and I will crush...."

Vladimir could send Willy into a blind rage for the many things he had done, but when Vladimir mentioned Jean-Pierre, Willy went berserk. In charging Vladimir, Willy was going straight for the kill striking blow after blow with his fists, and giving Vladimir several openings that he finally took advantage of, sending a combination to Willy's jaw that knocked him back.

As Willy tripped over a root, falling backward, Vladimir followed closely. Willy rolled back on his shoulders, and then shot his feet up at Vladimir's stomach, stopping him. Then a quick side kick to the knees brought Vladimir down, giving time for Willy to get up.

Willy struck out at Vladimir, not with his fist or foot, but with an open hand, and for the first time in his life, Willy struck a human being with his extended claws. He tore open four slashes in Vladimir's chest, just a few inches too low to catch the throat.

Blood streamed down Vladimir's jumpsuit as he backed up, screaming. Willy swung again, this time opening up two wounds the length of Vladimir's left forearm.

Vladimir caught Willy in the side with a kick followed by two quick jabs to the face. Willy grabbed Vladimir's arm, pivoting, and threw Vladimir into a tree just five feet away.

Before Vladimir could even move, Willy was there. He picked Vladimir up and slammed him into the tree again. Vladimir grabbed Willy by the hair and started pulling his head back, but Willy slammed his fist into Vladimir's throat; then as Vladimir lurched forward coughing, Willy head-butted him.

Willy held Vladimir up against the tree and started pounding on his head. With each blow, Willy spoke a word, "You.... will...never....hurt...anyone.... again. Not...me...not.... my...family...not...chief...Su...no...one."

Vladimir's face was already bruised and blood was pouring from his nose and mouth. Vladimir's head rolled about as if it had a life of its own and his eyes glassed over. Willy's hate had not abated, though. Vladimir's heart still pumped.

With one quick motion, Willy pulled Vladimir off the tree by the head and slammed Vladimir's face into his knee. Then for a moment, Willy could see Chakdall in his arms. He could see Dekonal sleeping with both her babies in her arms. He could see Madak and Chakdon dancing on their wedding day.

The crack of Vladimir's neck echoed through the forest, snapping the visions from Willy's head. He looked down and saw Vladimir's twisted head in his hands and he let go. Then he looked around. The forest was silent. Willy stepped away. He looked down at his bloody hands, and he fell to his knees, sobbing.

Sydni had watched from the time Willy threw Vladimir against the tree, but she did not say a word for a long time afterward. Her warriors had just driven back two squads of Jolabwe, when she had heard the shooting nearby. She ordered her warriors to stay behind. She keyed in her scanner and whispered to Conrad when he answered. "Get Dekonal on this line now, sweetheart."

"You're okay. What is going on?" Conrad whispered back.

"Shh, I will explain later. Just get her on and have her remain silent until she is spoken to."

The scanner went silent and Sydni walked slowly up to Willy, who hadn't heard Sydni approach until she was kneeling next to him. He looked up at her and said, "Vladimir is dead."

"I saw," she said, placing a hand on his shoulder. "He won't bother anyone again."

"No."

"How long has it been since you've slept?" she asked.

Willy shook his head. "I can't remember. It has been a long time."

"You need to go home and get some sleep."

"I can't leave you guys out here. My duty tells me I need to be here."

"You will be no good to anyone if you can't function, and your duty is at home right now. There are people there who need your help."

Willy looked at her as if to question her words. She held the scanner out to him and said, "Dekonal needs you."

"Willy?" Dekonal said.

Taking the scanner, Willy asked, "Dekonal?"

"Come home, Willy. Please come home. I need you and Jean-Pierre needs you."

Willy's shoulders slumped and Sydni started running her hand across his back. "Willy, you have done more for this war than any other person, but you need to stop. We can hold them off for now and when you get some sleep and feel better, we will be here, ready for your help again."

Holding the scanner up, Willy said, "I am coming home, Dekonal. I am coming home."

"I will be waiting," Dekonal said. "We will be waiting."

Conrad came on the line and said, "Sydni, we need to talk. I have discovered something."

"Okay, I will call you back as soon as Willy is on his way back."

"Please do," Conrad said.

Sydni wondered what was wrong with Conrad. She could hear something in his tone, but she wasn't certain what it was. "I promise."

When she turned off the scanner, she said, "Come on Willy. Let's get your gear and get you home."

✶ ✶ ✶ ✶

Willy walked in out of the rain, carrying his rifle, pack, and harness as Remington flew back up to the top of the cliff. Willy didn't see Conrad and Nurian sitting at the table, he just headed for the stairs. Each step felt like an eternity, and took all of his concentration. As he walked in his room and saw Dekonal leaning over the cradle, he dropped his equipment.

Dekonal ran over to him, not paying attention to his wet, muddy, and bloody clothes. As she hugged him, she began to cry. "I have missed you so much, my love."

"I love you," he whispered. "I have missed you too."

Dekonal started stripping off his wet clothes. "You need to go to bed. You need sleep."

Willy yawned and absent-mindedly started helping Dekonal as he stared at Jean-Pierre in the cradle, sleeping. Willy smiled.

Dekonal walked tenderly on her wounded leg, as she walked into the bathroom and came back with a towel and started drying Willy off. "Come to bed," she said, taking him by the hand.

He followed her and crawled under the covers on his side of the bed. Dekonal climbed in with him, and although he smelled of body odor, blood, and dirt, she wanted him to feel at peace. She wanted to make him feel like he was home. Willy was asleep before she had even settled in beside him.

✶ ✶ ✶ ✶

Sydni was looking over Conrad's shoulder as he worked on the computer he had set up in his room. She was drying her hair and was dressed only in a towel. "Okay, so we have the tapes of what Willy and I recorded, how can we send it out? With Bucky no longer in charge of the Orion, and Cho only acting on what she is told by Chambers, what do we do?"

"Look, right here," Conrad said, pointing to a grid on his screen. "We are getting a signal from a satellite."

"That's impossible," Sydni said, pausing and looking closer at the screen. "The frequency of this computer is not set for the UWC satellites, how could this be? Could they have figured it out and are trying to track us?"

"Possible. Andrea is smart and she could have set it up." Conrad started typing on the keyboard and as he did, he said, "I am going to mask all our other activities on this computer and just connect to it long enough to see what its intentions are, then I can disconnect if it starts hunting for us."

Dekonal walked in and said, "Hello, Sydni. I am relieved to see you home safely. Have they retreated?"

"No, but we have pushed them back and there is an uneasy cease-fire right now. Most of your warriors are still in the field, coming home in shifts to get some rest and some decent food."

"Any word from my brothers?" she asked, without looking into Sydni's eyes.

"Yes, just before I came back, I spoke with both of them. Quistqui was wounded, but it was not very serious. It was cleaned and he is still in the field. Doqui is healthy but tired. He is scheduled to come home on the next rotation."

"Look at this," Conrad said, his voice just barely a whisper. "Barkley and Andrea had to have set this up."

Conrad punched a few more keys and Barkley's voice filled the room. "Willy, Sydni, Conrad, if one of you receive this, it means that my plan worked. This satellite is set up to the computer you took with you, and it is set up to broadcast information directly to the media, the UWC, and on delay to the Orion, so you can broadcast without them trying to block any such transmissions. Another link is set up from the Ambassadorial link to the council, so if Gallagher has more conversations with Chancellor Chambers, they will be logged here. Tanya and I are under pressure to lead the fight against you, but we have refused, and I fear that soon we will be under arrest. Good luck and God speed."

The message was a loop and started playing again so Conrad turned it down. "Willy needs to hear this," Conrad said.

"I heard it," Willy said from the hallway as he held Jean-Pierre. "Damn that man, he is quite tenacious."

"You're awake," Dekonal said, turning and hugging Willy.

"Yes. I feel much better." He kissed her. "But unless Barkley came up with any more evidence, we are still out of luck."

Conrad swung around in the chair, and his white teeth were exposed in a broad grin. "That's what you have missed by being out of contact. When you left your scanner here, I turned it on to check on the battle. I saw that it had reinitialized when you last flew. Your ship's computer had stored what you had in it before, and we have your evidence again."

"I don't believe it," Willy said, moving forward.

"Believe it," Sydni said. "And look," she said pointing at the computer screen. "It looks like there is information cued up."

Conrad swung back around to the computer and typed in some more information. A split screen appeared with Chambers on one side and Gallagher on the other. The first two messages were vague enough about the battle, but the third one was devastating. When Chambers talked about how dumb the people were, Willy laughed, but the second Chambers discussed using the ship's weapons against ground troops, his laugh was gone. Sydni looked to her brother in disbelief.

"We must send these messages now," Willy nearly shouted. "Or it will be too late for much of the forest. We cannot allow the ship to fire at us."

Conrad replied, "It will not take me long to input from your scanner. Is there something you wish to preface the message with?"

Willy and Sydni exchanged glances, and Willy said, "I think we should put something down, Conrad, some sort of preface explanation. Nothing too long, because I believe the conversations will speak for themselves."

Conrad nodded and said, "Okay. Give me a few minutes and I will have it ready, but I think you should preface it. You have been with this from the beginning."

"I have to get changed," Sydni said, putting her hands on Conrad's shoulders. "I am going back out as soon as you send this. We must keep repelling the Orion's forces, but be prepared to pull back before they fire their weapons."

"Me too," Willy said.

"Must you go back already?" Dekonal asked.

Willy looked at Jean-Pierre and slowly nodded. "That will be crucial. We need that order to be stopped, but if it is not stopped in time, the warriors will need much direction to get out of there in time."

"Okay, I have sent these files to the main computer," Conrad said. "It won't be long now."

Once Willy and Sydni were changed, they were again standing in the room. Willy was checking over his rifle while Sydni checked hers as well. Dekonal was standing in the hall behind them with Jean-Pierre gurgling and cooing. Willy, without looking up, said, "Did you add the scanning of the attack?"

Conrad nodded and said, "Yes. It is there in great detail."

Willy's voice grew as deep as a growl when he said, "I hope they rush the UWC Chancellor's office and burn that bastard alive."

Sydni patted his shoulder and said, "They will, Willy. One way or another, they will."

"Okay," Conrad said, turning around, holding up Willy's scanner. "We are ready for your performance."

"What should I say?" Willy asked, looking between Sydni and Conrad.

Sydni took Willy's rifle and leaned against him, shoulder to shoulder. "Brother, I think if you say what comes to your mind, it will be stronger than anything we could think of."

"We need a neutral background. They should know nothing more than they have to for now."

They moved into the hallway, and Willy stood facing them, stopping long enough to lean over and kiss Jean-Pierre. Then he nodded and said, "I guess I am as ready as I will ever be."

Conrad flipped on the scanner, took a deep breath, and looking up at Willy, he nodded.

Sydni looked at her brother, standing up, facing the worlds, about to be broadcast throughout the known universe, and how powerful he looked; once he had shed the cloak he used to wear around the Orion, he had shed it for good. The smile she held in her heart showed through her eyes.

"I am William Colton, formerly a Commander in the UWC assigned to the UWC ship Orion as co-chief of scouts. For years I have lived among you, under a cloak, and my case is still taught today in biology classes. My cloak is off now; you need to see who I am. As a conspiracy unlike any in the history of the UWC came to my attention, I was forced to go into exile and Captain Bucky Dollinger has been forced to step down because he would not send forces after me. I am living among a peaceful community that, due to the greed of Chancellor Chambers, is now under siege. People have been killed..." Willy's voice trailed off and he looked down. "Innocent people have been attacked and killed." Looking up, Willy's eyes were glassy and he fought for control. "As I speak, a war is raging in the forest on this planet, and since the UWC forces are being pushed back, Chancellor Chambers is giving the order that the Orion's weapons be used against the forest where these people reside." Willy leaned forward. "Stop him. Don't let him hurt these people any longer. They are not just another race on some far planet that does not deserve your attention. They are humans who were somehow, in some way, placed on this planet many, many generations ago."

Willy motioned for Dekonal to step over next to him. She did without hesitation. "Read the scan of these two people. See for yourself. Stop Chambers from killing more people. Stop them from killing a piece of us. Look at the evidence that has been sent, and you tell me what you think. Do what is in your heart."

After running a scan of Dekonal and Jean-Pierre, Conrad stopped the scanner and wiped a tear from his cheek. "If that doesn't stop it, nothing else can."

"Send it and pray, Conrad," Willy said. Turning to Dekonal, he said, "Sing and pray that we are not too late to stop those weapons, or it may be too late for anyone in the forest."

CHAPTER 22

"I cannot and will not do any such thing!" Acting Captain Cho shouted from her console on the bridge, slamming her fist down. "What you ask is beyond every regulation set forth by the UWC itself."

"Captain Cho," Gallagher said in a voice that oozed with his best diplomacy, "you do not understand the unique position this battle has placed us in. Please, let us go to your office where we can speak directly without the crew watching."

"I understand that soldiers are dying and there is no air support, but that does not give me the right, or anyone the right, to order the use of the ship's weapons against a planet. I want this discussion to not only be public, but above board. I want the crew to hear my position."

"You are making a very big mistake, Captain Cho. I will only warn you once."

"I wouldn't fire this ship's weapons on ground forces unless the Chief Commander of the UWC forces called me and told me that it was permitted. So you just shut the hell up and get off my bridge, you slime bag." Gallagher opened his mouth to interject again, but Cho pointed at him and yelled, "Security to the bridge on the double."

"I am leaving, Captain, but you will be sorry," Gallagher yelled back as he made it to the doors to exit the bridge. The doors shut behind him as he was still saying that she would be sorry.

Once the doors were shut, the bridge exploded in a cheer. The officers and enlisted men both were cheering their acting captain's speech to the ambassador, but Cho snapped. "Belay that!" Everyone was silenced immediately. "I will have none of that. This is serious. Our soldiers are dying down there and there is not a damn thing I can do, but I will not tolerate you cheering about anything."

Spinning around she stalked across the bridge to her chair and sat down. "Lieutenant Mutasi, get me fleet, stat!"

"Yes, Ma'am."

Captain Cho was surprised at the short time it took Lieutenant Mutasi to get fleet on the line, and she went to the Captain's office to take the call. She walked to her desk and then pressed a record button, so her conversation would be recorded. When she was ready, she said, "Acting Captain Cho."

There was a brief pause and Admiral Oats filled the screen. Cho saluted and the salute was returned. "What is it, Captain Cho?"

"Sir, I know you gave me a direct order to follow the Ambassador's orders, but he has gone too far. He has gone way too far."

"Easy, Captain. Explain what he has done."

"Sir, he just came to me asking me to turn the Orion's weapons on the ground and start annihilating the forest. He has neither a set target nor any place in particular. He just wants me to destroy the forest, hoping to kill the Hingandu and find their home."

Oats looked away and then back. "Hold on, Captain, I have another priority call. I will be right back."

The UWC Naval Symbol appeared and muted music began to play. Cho tapped her foot, but did not change her expression. She had heard of many stories where a commanding officer would come back on line and the officer waiting would be caught complaining about how long he was taking. Although she knew the reason for her call was extremely important, she would not show any impatience.

After five minutes, Oats came back, and Cho could have sworn that he looked quite pale. He just stared at her until she asked, "Sir, what is it?"

"Word has just come down to me, Captain. Do as the Ambassador asked."

"What?" Cho nearly shouted, which for the first time since he had come back online had Oats actually looking at her. "Sir, that is directly against the High Command's orders. It is against the UWC charter. Not even on your authority can I commit such an action."

"It is not on my orders, Captain. The orders have come down from the UWC and the Fleet Command. Do what you are told, or you will be court-martialed for treason."

Cho felt as if someone had kicked her in the stomach, and her breath left her with a hiss. For the first time in her career, she stammered, "S-s-si-sir. You are ordering me to go along with their plan? That could kill thousands of innocents or more. We could be destroying a whole race, species of animal or plant."

"Captain Cho, we have Marines dying down there. What do you propose to do about that?"

"Pull them out, Sir, and end this war. I must ask for you to remind me why we are fighting this war."

"Don't start with me, Captain. I am giving you a direct order. Use the Orion's weapons on the ground, as per the request of Ambassador Gallagher."

"Sir, we are taking orders from the ambassador?"

"Damn you, Cho! Respond to your orders or I will have you removed and someone who will respond shall be in your place."

Another kick. Her mouth was dry and she could hear her heart pounding in her ears. She snapped to attention and saluted. "Orders understood, Sir."

"Carry them out, Captain, or you will be facing me."

"I said orders were understood, Admiral. What more would you have me do?"

"Your job, Captain. Your job. Oats out."

The screen faded to stars and Cho said, "I pray that I can find some way of stopping this before the damage we do is irreversible." She slumped into the chair and turned off the recording she had been making of the conversation. She hoped that someday she could turn on Chambers, Oats, and Gallagher and fry all of them for this atrocity.

She pressed her comm button on her desk and said, "Sergeant Combs. Get Bucky Dollinger to my office on the double."

"Aye, aye, Ma'am."

She knew if anyone could find a way around this, Bucky would be the one. Bucky knew the ship better than anyone, he would figure it out. She prayed he would.

Willy had finished harnessing Remington, and he was working on Sydni's Brotu when Dekonal walked out into the courtyard and slowly limped her way across to him. He cinched down the last strap and turned to face her. She reached out her hands to him. He took them and pulled her closer. He was just inches from her. Her scent filled his nostrils and he sighed. "You are so beautiful. I wish I could stay here with you."

Dekonal went up on her tiptoes, kissed his forehead and whispered, "You will be. Soon we will have time to be happy. I can see that now. Not long and we will have the peace you have been seeking."

He kissed her and leaned his head against hers. "I wish I could see that which you see. I wish I had as much faith in what you see."

Squeezing his hands, she replied, "All you have to do is believe and it will carry you through the rest of the battle."

"You do that," he said in barely more than a sigh. "You bring me through all of this. I will do what it takes to come home."

They kissed until Sydni walked out, trailing Conrad, who slowed down as he saw Willy and Dekonal kissing. Turning back to Conrad, Sydni strapped her rifle across her shoulder and attacked his lips with a fury of kisses. He lifted her off the ground as they kissed, and she moaned. When he set her down, she ran her fingers through his hair and said, "I promise I will be home again soon."

"I will miss you." He said. "I spend half of the night and day praying for your safe return."

"Keep praying," she whispered in his ear. "It makes me feel warm and safe knowing that you are back here praying."

"Okay. Be careful out there."

"I will." She kissed him quickly and then turned away to leave. Dekonal was stepping away from Willy as Sydni mounted her Brotu. "What do you say, brother?"

Willy mounted Remington and said, "I say we go get our people the hell out of that forest and pull back before they fire off that damn fool weapon."

With a quick pull of reins, they both rose into the air on the flapping wings of their Brotu. In moments, they disappeared over the house. Sydni kept alongside Willy. They had not discussed where they were heading, but the logical place for the Orion to fire the weapons first would be where the Marines encountered the most resistance and work their way back to the mountains. As Willy scanned the forest below, his heart sank at the thought of the forest being destroyed. Things were bad enough with the lives that had been lost.

Sydni was scanning for their troops and found them along lines facing off with the Marines and Jolabwe. She held her scanner out to Willy and pointed. Willy agreed with her as to where they should set down. The sun was warm, and as they dropped through the still-wet leaves, the coolness of the shade was remarkable. Several people glanced up as they drifted down on flapping wings, landing just behind the lines. Ulik and Jasina walked up as they were dismounting.

"What has been going on?" Willy asked.

"Nothing," Ulik said. "A few skirmishes, but that is all. We have noted that many of their reserve forces have moved back a ways."

Willy and Sydni both looked at their scanners and nodded. "Do you think they are preparing?" Sydni asked.

"Yes, I believe they are," Willy said. "We need to get everyone up and down the line out of the area."

"If they think we have pulled back, though, they will adjust their aim back further," Sydni said.

"True," Willy replied. "So we need a diversion. Something that makes them think that we are fighting or moving forward so they will keep it trained on this area."

"One squad of guerrilla warriors could do it," Jasina said.

"I agree," Ulik added.

Sydni and Willy looked at each other. "Where is my squad?" Willy asked.

Ulik pointed and said, "By the pool at the little falls."

"Okay, Ulik, you stay here and move everyone back past the stream. Jasina, you go down to the next group and move them back as well. I will take care of everyone below the stream and take my squad into the zone to keep them guessing as to where we are. Sydni, you fly down farther and get the rest of the warriors moved back."

"How will you know when they are going to fire the weapon?" Sydni asked.

"We will have to get close. Before they fire that thing, the Marines and Jolabwe should pull back."

"What if you are wrong?"

Willy had started to run by the time she asked the question, and he shouted back over his shoulder, "Pray that I am not."

Sydni was mounted on her Brotu and lifting off the ground as Ulik shouted an order and called into his scanner. Jasina had taken her cue from Willy and already had disappeared around a tree.

Willy made the ridge and saw the pool below. Remington had followed him and he made a motion that sent Remington running toward the interior of the forest. Willy ran down a game path worn into the brush, and, at the base of the ridge, he turned toward the pool and was greeted by Doqui. Within moments, his squad was around him, eager for orders.

"The humans have a weapon that can destroy much of the forest. We need everyone to move back beyond the creek. However, if they believe that we have moved back, I believe that they will just fire the weapon back further into the forest, so we need to make them think we have not moved." Willy looked at the eager faces ready to serve and he hesitated. "I will only ask for volunteers. I will be heading to the enemy line to make them think that we are still here, nearby and fighting them."

In turn, each member of his squad said they would go too. Then Willy pulled out his scanner and set a broadcast message. "Everyone pull back beyond the stream and pool. Repeat, everyone pull back beyond the stream and pool immediately."

Then after a quick scan of the enemy position, Willy turned off the scanner and hooked it to his belt. He pulled his rifle off his back and checked his magazine. Many Hingandu were now moving past, and heading toward the stream. Willy's squad followed his actions and started checking their weapons.

"Two-person teams, we need everyone accounted for. The double vibration from your scanner means pull back and pull back fast, no matter what. That means do not stop running until you are past the stream."

Everyone in his squad started nodding in agreement. Willy pointed out the two person teams and the direction they were to take. He looked at Doqui and smiled. As he turned and ran, Doqui was right behind him and moved quickly alongside.

The access tube seemed small, but it had been many years since Bucky had crawled through the access tubes of a starcruiser. His muscles ached and his shoulders were knotted, but the smile on his face was unmistakable. Cho had called for him, and they had a very long and private conversation. Although he knew he could count on several members aboard the ship to help him, there were only two that he would have asked to do the mission, and they were under arrest and awaiting court-martial. Because he knew the schematics and layout of the ship he had decided since his career was already blown by his choices, that he would not subject others to the same fate.

He reached the weapons array and quickly found the access panel he needed. It was not only simple enough if one knew what to look for, but it would take a repair crew hours to identify what had happened and then several more hours to fix the damage. Laughing, he knew it would look like an overload due to months of inactivity.

He used the ladder to prop himself up and then he opened the access panel. Tracing several wires and optic clusters, he finally found the ones he was looking for. Within minutes he had crossed several cables which would still allow the main weapon to fire once and then short out.

The sound of the ship changed a little, and then its orientation changed. Bucky could tell whenever the ship changed course or speed. He had lived most his life shipside and he was in tune with his ship. After closing the panel, he started climbing back down the tube. Orders would be given soon that would fire the weapon, and he needed to be far away by then. However, the smile on his face would linger for a long time. He just hoped Willy and Sydni would not get caught in the blast.

* * * *

Silence permeated the forest, except for the faint electronic hum, which warned both Willy and Doqui that the Marines were nearby. Willy knew that they would send energy pack generators down to the front lines to keep the supply for their weapons. He did not understand why they would give away their position so easily, but Sydni reminded him that the noise was imperceptible to her ears.

They crawled the last few feet until they saw the first Marine, who looked towards the sound of the battle. Someone in his squad had already started. Willy paused as he looked at the Marine in his scope, knowing that he was some mother's son, also aware that if they did not push this assault, many Hingandu could be wiped out in a heartbeat. More sounds of Marines returning fire started nearby, and Willy squeezed the trigger. Doqui fired seconds later, and the camp in front of them exploded with the sounds of shouts and curses.

Doqui shadowed Willy and they started wreaking havoc among the Marine encampment, which quickly brought a heavy response. A two-man pulse cannon started leveling a portion of the forest, tearing at tree trunks and ripping apart the underbrush.

Moving with the quickness of a Saka, Doqui jumped over Willy and ran hunched over to an ancient split trunk tree. He aimed through the V-shape and fired five quick shots, which resulted in a resounding explosion and a blinding flash of light. Many Marines were now calling out for medics and back up.

Rolling twice, Willy made it to the same tree as Doqui and fired behind him as two Marines started to out-flank them. Tapping Doqui's leg, Will signaled that they should try and out-flank the marines instead, to make them really guess where the assault was coming from. A blast rattled the trees and Willy guessed a rocket had been fired at the next group down the line.

Leading the way, Doqui half-crawled, half-ran and then belly-crawled until they could see several makeshift shelters, and a dozen soldiers running around. Willy and Sydni had given the command that no soldier wearing a Red Cross symbol was to be harmed unless that soldier was attacking them. Three medics were tending to the wounded. As Doqui started firing at the Marines hunkered down to shoot at the oncoming force, Willy changed the mode on his scope to search for the regenerator. He saw the heat signature from the machine, and he fired four rounds into it, until a quick lightning display sent several Marines running from their shelter.

It was quicker than Willy would have believed could be done, but the Marines started to pull back, and in seconds the soldiers began firing blindly into the woods as they were carrying their fallen buddies.

Willy's scanner buzzed at his side. He checked it and the message from Conrad read: "Picking up massive energy reading from Orion....run."

As he punched in the code for retreat, he grabbed Doqui by the shoulder and started running. Willy said a quick prayer that they were in time.

Doqui matched Willy's stride, which was as fast as Willy could run. To Willy, the run out seemed to take hours, but even when the pool came into view, he still could not feel a sense of relief.

The small hairs on the back of his neck tingled as they stood on end, and Willy knew that the gun had fired. He grabbed Doqui again and dove for the pool.

Orion's weapon struck the Hingandu forest with the force of an earthquake. A small rock tumbled from the formation at the Shrine of Halkala. During a brief respite from the battle, Sansanal had gone far out on the plain stalking a flock of large birds that flew as the searing light filled the sky and then shook the ground. At his desk, Conrad bowed his head and unconsciously shook it as he prayed for his new found family. Dekonal watched, as she held Jean-Pierre, who woke suddenly, startled and crying as if from a bad dream. Alone on the cliff, Gonnaktu sang to soothe the uneasy heard of Brotu and far out in the woods he could see the smoke rising. Remington shook his head at the blast and roared in response. From her hut, in her village, Borsha felt the tremor and wondered what new horror had been unleashed on their world. Sitting in a chair, holding Madak's hand from alongside her bed, Chakdon rested his head on the bed and said, "It is over."

The bridge of the Orion was filled with smoke, and Cho stood in front of her chair, demanding, "What the hell happened, Lieutenant?"

Lieutenant Constantino had been the weapons person on duty when the fateful shot had been fired. The resulting short-circuit from Bucky's mission into the access tubes had fried the weapons control panel on the bridge and left his hands black. Constantino looked at Cho and said, "I do not understand, Captain. Everything was in order, there should have been no problem."

Cho pressed a button on the panel next to her chair and said, "Engineering, this is Captain Cho. Send a team up to repair the weapons console and find out what went wrong when we fired that monstrosity."

"Aye, aye, Captain," the chief's gruff voice came over on the speaker, just as it would have for Bucky.

Looking around, Cho said, "Well, can anyone tell me what we did, or did everyone's system fry as well?"

Everyone turned back to their stations, and the ensign sitting at the scanning desk said, "Direct hit, Ma'am. Right where we were aiming."

From the comm, a lieutenant said, "Marines report that the fire was laid down directly over where they had encountered a fierce attack."

"That's better," Cho said, sitting back down. "Constantino, go get your hands checked out at the sick bay and report back quickly." Looking at the commander sitting next her, Cho added, "And will someone clear this room of smoke." Seconds later the ventilation fans kicked on and she took a deep breath of fresh, recycled air. Silently she thanked Bucky.

* * * *

The blast from the Orion's main weapon left a crater in the ground several hundred yards in diameter, and had knocked down trees many yards past that. Willy felt the blast and within a second the shock wave hit. He stayed underwater as long as he could, but his lungs screamed for air. When he came up, the air smelled of charred trees and brush, and the distinct odor of energy residue. His eyes burned from the same effect.

Doqui stood up, dripping wet, staring down at the crater, which was at least two hundred feet deep at the center. Steam rose from the side of the crater where the blast had hit an underground stream, but quickly a trickle of water headed for the base of the crater. A tree fell several yards away, burning, and tumbled into the crater, pulling a large chunk of the bank of the stream with it, starting a run-off into the crater.

"Let's get out of here," Willy said. "The Marines will be investigating soon, I don't want them to see us."

Doqui looked at him and then back at the crater. He had never seen such destruction before, but he managed to say, "I know, we will have plenty of time later, we must go."

He and Doqui waded through the chest-high water to the other side and walked among giant trees that were now pushed over. Willy pulled his scanner off his belt and opened a channel. "This is Willy. Doqui and I are safe. Give me a roll call."

The squad ran through their names, but the last two who he had sent in the position next to them did not respond. Willy made it to the cover of the brush and tree line and started heading toward the other groups. As he did, he ordered the others to head in his direction. He did not like the way it sounded.

They had not gone very far when his scanner picked up the faint life signs of his two men, and Doqui quickly spotted them among the fallen trees. They ran to them and Willy ordered, "Call in two groups of healers with Brotu."

Joknual was lying next to a fallen tree with a large cut across his head and a wounded shoulder, while Bunth was half-crushed by a tree and his life signs were fading fast. His face was twisted up and smeared with mud, but when he saw Willy, he smiled. A trickle of blood ran out of his nose and ears. His voice came in short wisps of breath. "You said leave no one behind." Bunth's hand still clung to Joknual's sleeve. "He needs help."

"Don't talk," Doqui said, kneeling next to him and taking his hand. Doqui called into his scanner for healers and looked back to Bunth. "We'll get you out of here."

Willy had tossed down his rifle and was chopping out large hunks of the green tree with each stroke of his ax. "Hang on, Bunth. I am not giving up on you."

The rest of the squad showed up. As two of them carried Joknual to a flat spot and laid him down, the other two began hacking at the tree as well. "Doqui, cover us. Scan that far ridge and if you see any life form, waste them."

Doqui squeezed Bunth's hand and was gone, finding a tree to hide behind so he too would not be a target.

As Willy cut through his portion of the tree, it shifted and Bunth moaned. "Sorry."

The sound of Brotu filled the air as two medical teams landed. They rushed to Joknual first. As Willy's team cut through the rest of the tree and lifted it away, two of them ran over. Willy knelt next to Bunth as the healers worked on him and said, "You're looking good now, Bunth. Don't give these guys a hard time, let them take care of you."

As they loaded him onto a stretcher made to be strapped between two Brotu, Bunth asked, "Joknual, is he alive?"

"Yes," Willy said, taking Bunth's hand as they carried him to the Brotu. "You saved his life."

Bunth tried to speak, but only a gurgle of blood came forth, and Willy thought he saw tears in his eyes. The healers were efficient, and quickly had both of his squad members in the air, heading toward the village.

"Fall back, into the tree line," Willy said after he picked up his rifle and scanned the far side of the crater. Doqui ran past him, and Willy turned and followed.

Once again in the tree line, Willy called into his scanner, "Report, how does it look?"

"Everyone was cleared out," Sydni said. "There are a few broken bones due to falling trees but nothing serious along the blast area. Two of your team disappeared off my scanner though."

"Yes, they are now on their way to the village. What about the Marines?"

"They moved back along the same line as the group you were fighting, but nothing since."

"Why haven't they fired again?"

Willy could picture Sydni shrugging her shoulders as she said, "I don't know. They have had more than enough time."

"Maybe someone intervened," Willy said, unable to suppress a smile as he pictured Tanya and Barkley rigging the main gun to short circuit.

"You don't think...." Sydni let her voice trail off.

"I don't know," Willy said. "We need to be ready for another blast. Let's move everyone back further and why don't you come here to the crater. You should see this."

"I am on my way."

* * * *

Conrad held his breath during the tense time of the blast then he heard the voices of Sydni and Willy. He sighed and realized for the first time that Dekonal was standing behind him with Jean-Pierre crying. Glancing at her he nodded and said, "At least we know they survived that one."

Rocking Jean-Pierre, Dekonal asked, "How long until they can fire the next one?"

"Any time. Only moments are needed."

Dekonal looked toward the window as if she could see the next one coming from where she stood and whispered, "The damage is bad?"

Conrad looked at her. In the moment she saw his eyes, she could see his answer, but he spoke anyway, "Very bad."

They waited. Time passed, and although Jean-Pierre stopped crying, he remained awake, fighting his drooping eyes and the severe onset of yawns as though he were afraid to sleep again. The day wore on without another blast. Conrad was almost asleep in his chair when the line started blinking. After staring at it, he keyed in a series of commands and the screen came alive in a four-way split. Sound issued from one picture to the next. "...Immediate session was called at the UWC, at three in the morning upon the receipt of the recordings from the UWC Orion..."

The screen shifted and a new voice came on, "Several sources say top military liaisons have been called in and that the Chief of the Navy, Fleet Admiral Ngo has left the Hawaii Naval Complex and is in route to meet with the UWC. While Chancellor..."

Another screen shift brought another voice, "...has been held up in the compound since the first reports came in. His press secretary, Donna Roland has made a brief statement that the charges are unjustified and that the tapes are fake."

Conrad was recording everything, but he forwarded on the same screens to both Willy and Sydni's scanners as he turned the volume down and glanced at Dekonal, who was now alert with the strange voices on the screen. "What does that mean?"

"Our message got through," Conrad whispered. "Our message got through and is causing a commotion among the leaders of my old world."

"Is that good?"

"Dekonal, it is the best thing that could have happened for us. It may be why they have not fired the weapon at us again. It may have saved our lives."

Willy's picture appeared and they could hear his voice telling their story. "Look, sweetheart," Dekonal said to Jean-Pierre. "Father is talking to his world." A smile traced across Conrad's lips and he quickly looked away, prompting Dekonal to ask, "What is amusing about what I said?"

"I think Willy would disagree with you about your statement. Many months ago Willy stopped thinking of that place as his world." Conrad pointed at the computer screen, which was now showing footage of the Orion as it passed Saturn on its maiden voyage. "This is his world and will always be his world."

Dekonal smiled. "I believe you are correct," she said. "How about you?"

Conrad nodded. "Yes. Not as quickly as he has, but yes."

"His speech to his old world, do you think it will stop the war?"

"I believe it will. The people of our worlds are much like the people of your village, and none of them want to have this happen again."

Sydni filled the computer screen and the volume rose as she said, "Conrad, record and send the image I am about to send through my scanner."

"Anything you say, love."

He keyed in the command and she started to scan the crater. Conrad swallowed hard as Dekonal behind him gasped. "It is devastating," Dekonal breathed out in horror.

"Quite," Conrad said. Once he had recorded enough to make a good show back home and had the correct information on the type of damage and energy used, Conrad stopped taping. "Got it, Sydni. I will send it on."

"We caused quite a stir, haven't we?"

"I'll say."

"I will talk to you more, soon. I need to get out of here."

"Bye."

Her image shifted and blinked out and the screen reformatted with the media broadcasts. Conrad typed a message stating that the latest damage was in and that the Orion had fired its main weapon on the ground forces on the planet. He sent the scan and message and sat back to wait.

A message came back to the computer, and thinking it was Willy or Sydni, Conrad answered it. "Hello," he said eagerly, shocked to see an unfamiliar human face. "Who are you?"

"Sir, I am Robert Laramie with the Galaxy News Network."

"GNN?" Conrad asked, only half aloud.

"Yes, and it took me a while, but I have traced the transmissions we have received about the plight of the Orion. Did you send those messages?"

Conrad stared at the face on the screen that was on the far side of the galaxy. For a moment he looked into those blue eyes so far away and he wondered what Willy would suggest. He suppressed a smile. He had not made it to the rank of Admiral in the UWC Academy of Sciences without knowing what to say. Command decisions were there to be made, so he made one. "Yes, I sent the transmission."

"How did you manage to bypass the Orion?"

"Mr. Laramie, people are dying down here, and I am not going to start answering technical questions. There are bigger things going on."

Annoyed, Conrad leaned forward to cut off the transmission, but Laramie pleaded, "Sir, please, I apologize for my insensitivity." Conrad stopped his forward movement and still stared at the reporter. "Sir, can you tell me your name?"

"I am Conrad Singh, formerly CSO of the UWC Orion."

"Doctor Singh?" Laramie questioned.

"My old title does not have much meaning where I am now."

"Where are you?"

"I am planetside, living among the people that are being attacked by the order of Chancellor Chambers and his puppet, Ambassador Gallagher."

Laramie paused, then asked, "So you are saying that this has all been orchestrated by the Chancellor."

"You have obviously seen the same transmissions that I have."

"A new press release is stating that Commander William Colton and Commander Sydni Colton are charged with murder, treason, and desertion. What do you say to that?"

"The facts were twisted to implicate them, and then they were backed into a corner, since they knew the danger that Gallagher and Chambers posed to the people of this planet."

"Danger? Can you clarify that?"

"Gallagher and Chambers want something from this planet, only part of which is Coppertroid fuel. They want to physically remove these people from their homeland to start a mining station. We found out that they were planning to trade technology to another race on the planet if they would start a war to help drive them out."

"That is outrageous."

"Yes. Listen to their conversations. They killed one of Commander Colton's scouts and tried to blame him. The only people that were killed by either of the Commanders were people in battle situations."

"The accusations against them are false?"

"Resoundingly. Chambers has been manipulating things here for a long time and I would suspect he has more at stake in this planet than just his Chancellorship. Even now, the captaincy of the Orion is a puppet show with Gallagher running it on this end and Chambers running it on the other."

"So Captain Dollinger is working with them?"

"No, he has been relieved of duty, and his XO has taken charge. I have to clear this channel, Mr. Laramie."

"Dr. Singh, please just a couple more questions...." Conrad cut the connection and then quickly blocked the channel, deciding to wait until Willy and Sydni were in the house to answer any more. What he had given the reporter should edge the media along in the right direction. Soon after he had cut off the GNN reporter, the scan of the crater was plastered all over the media channels.

Chapter 23

Cho walked quickly across the deck of the bridge and slipped into the opening doors of the Captain's office. Fleet Admiral Ngo was waiting and filled the giant screen in the office. Her stark white hair was pulled back in a bun, and her face was creased deeply along her forehead, eyes and mouth. Her dark skin looked tough to Cho, but then she thought it might just be the fact that the one person in charge of the UWC Navy was calling her. She knew those dark brown eyes were examining her as she snapped crisply to attention and saluted. "Acting Captain Cho, reporting, Ma'am."

"What the hell is going on there, Cho? Where the hell is Bucky?"

"He has been under house arrest, Ma'am, he has spent much of his time in his quarters."

"You had him confined to quarters?" Ngo shouted. Her face was reddening quickly.

"No, Ma'am. I have him under guard as per Admiral Oats' orders."

"Oats," Ngo hissed looking away from the screen. "Get him to the bridge stat, Cho. I want to have a long conversation with both of you." Cho turned to put her on hold, and Ngo said, "Don't put me on hold until he gets there Cho, I want to speak with you A.S.A.P."

"Yes, Ma'am," she said again.

She called a general announcement, knowing it would be the quickest way to get Bucky to the bridge. "Captain Dollinger, report to the bridge. I repeat Captain Dollinger report to the bridge, stat. This is an emergency."

After taking a deep breath and straightening her blouse and coat, she took Ngo off hold and said, "He should be on his way, Ma'am."

"How much of this is true, Cho? Don't pull any punches, this is a direct order."

"How much of what is true, Ma'am?"

"Don't mock me, Cho or I will bust you down to ensign and assign you to scrubbing my head!"

"Respectfully, Ma'am, I have an idea as to what you are talking about, but I don't understand how you found out."

"You have not seen the transmissions?"

"No."

Ngo looked away again and then nodded. "Of course. There must be a delay going to you so you wouldn't block the transmissions. Smart, very smart. Hold on." Ngo stepped away from the video screen for a minute, and if it were possible, she seemed to be scowling even more when she returned to the screen.

Cho looked toward her door as Bucky ran in, leaving the guard at the door. Cho motioned for the guard to remain outside. The second Bucky saw Ngo on the screen he screamed, "Yes!" Then quickly he stood at attention and saluted. "Captain Bucky Dollinger reporting for duty, Ma'am."

"Captain, your ship is a mess. What was that outburst for?"

Bucky could not contain his smile, and he said, "Ma'am, if you are online with us, then obviously someone got through and let either you or the world know what was going on out here."

"Did you report through command?"

"Yes, Ma'am. I suspect somewhere between here and your desk I was undercut. I would not bow to the ambassador's orders to pursue Willy and Sydni Colton planetside with troops and the next thing I know I was sitting in my room."

An alarm went off and Cho ran around the desk to see what it was. "Incoming transmission from a frequency we are not using, Sir," Cho said, happy to have Bucky back in his office.

"That is probably the message that was sent to the media throughout the three UWC worlds. Watch it."

Bucky joined Cho as she started the message. Willy appeared and they listened closely. Ngo examined them closely to see their reactions, and as Gallagher and Chambers talked, Bucky said, "Son-of-a-bitch, I knew they were up to something."

Then the pictures came up, of the massacre in the clearing, and Bucky dropped into his chair, and bowed his head, shaking it slowly. There were pictures of the dead, ripped apart by what they all recognized as weapons from an attack ship. There was a wounded woman nearly ripped in half, and a mother crying, holding her baby in a blood-soaked blanket and rocking back and forth. Bucky, who had considered himself a hard-ass all his life and had seen the ravages of war, cried at the sight. The words of Willy echoed in his ears. "You killed my son." The color drained from Bucky and he couldn't stand to look at any more.

Then the scan of the crater came up and Cho's knees nearly buckled and she felt as though her heart stopped. She never would have ordered such an attack. She never would have done it, if Oats had not ordered her. The transmission ended and she looked for the source. It was an unregistered satellite.

"What do you have to say about all this?" Ngo asked in a manner that reminded Bucky of Chief Yamamora. "Why the hell did you fire the ship's weapon at the planet?"

Cho looked up and said, "I refused. I have witnesses who saw me refuse, but Admiral Oats then ordered it, saying that he would replace me if I did not..." she paused. "Ma'am, with your permission, I have a recording of the Admiral's conversation with me."

Ngo's eyes went wide. Looking away from the screen again, she said, "That would be interesting, wouldn't it." Looking back to the screen, she said, "Permission granted, Commander."

It only took seconds and Cho was playing the recording of her conversation with Oats for Admiral Ngo. When the recording stopped playing, Oats could be heard in the background shouting that it was a fake. Ngo looked away again and said, "Take him away! Place him in the brig, he's under arrest for treason." The shouts faded. Then she looked back into the office off the bridge of the Orion. "Okay, Bucky, this is on the record. Start at the beginning and tell me everything you know."

Bucky looked up for the first time and then sat straight in his chair. "It is a long story, Admiral, I suggest that you get comfortable." So Bucky told his tale, from the time of the Coppertroid discovery through the day when Oats placed him under house arrest. Admiral Ngo listened intently and did not interrupt as Bucky spoke. As he neared the end of his story, Bucky started pacing back and forth in front of the desk. His voice was barely more than a whisper when he told about Willy killing the pilots after the death of his baby. Finally he stopped and looked at Ngo. "I should have found a way to stop this," he said softly. "So many deaths. So many innocent deaths."

Ngo cleared her throat and said, "Bucky, you reported through channels, and those channels broke down. It would seem from your story that Chambers had some sort of information over Oats that made him do what he wanted. I have several investigations going on at this time."

"That doesn't help the fact that maybe had I been adamant about it to the point of insubordination this could have come to your attention."

"Looking back you can see such paths of action, but you have been a line officer most of your life, Bucky, I cannot see you disobeying direct orders. Now, Commander Cho, fill me in on this war. Who ordered it?"

"Gallagher, Ma'am."

"Ambassador Gallagher?"

"I was ordered, by Admiral Oats, to take my cues and receive my orders through Gallagher. I argued over that order, but I was told that this was a special assignment sent down through command. That is why I copied the second conversation."

"What did they say the war was about?"

"After the incident where sergeant Diego, a scout, and a squad of UWC Ambassadorial Guards were killed, they said that Commander Colton was using the Hingandu to attack squads of Marines and Jolabwe. After hearing the Captain and seeing the evidence, I believe that the initial reports may be suspect."

"Are our troops still battling planetside?" Ngo asked.

"We had pulled back to safely fire the weapon," Cho said.

Slightly shaking her head again, Ngo asked, "How many times did you fire the main weapon?"

"Once," Cho said.

"Only once?"

Cho looked at Bucky, who stood straight and answered, "We conspired to give the planet some more time, and to give us some more time as well. I sabotaged the main gun so it would short out and not be able to fire for several hours. We knew the war was wrong, and especially with the use of the main weapon."

Ngo nodded and smiled. "Your ingenuity will be duly noted. Due to the circumstances, my flagship is being prepared and re-staffed for immediate deployment to rendezvous with your ship. I am reporting back to the UWC, which has been in session since the transmission first came in. I have assembled two attack forces and I am recommending that we arrest Chancellor Chambers and his staff for treason, murder, conspiracy, coercion, and a list of other charges. I will be departing as soon as Chambers is under arrest." Ngo looked away and then back, "I have some things I need you to do for me in the meantime, Bucky."

"Yes, Ma'am."

"First, Bucky Dollinger, I am restoring you to your captaincy of the UWC Orion with all duties and responsibilities. Cho, I am sorry to give you a taste of captain and then remove it, but you are back to XO."

Cho grinned and saluted, "It is a pleasure to say; aye, aye, Ma'am."

"On my orders, you are under martial law and have all authorities in that sector until I arrive. First, arrest that son-of-a-bitch Gallagher and make him rot in the brig. Second, pull all troops off the planet and try and make contact with William Colton or Sydni Colton to arrange a treaty."

Bucky shook his head and said, "That might not be easy, Admiral. We have put both of them through a lot, and using a phrase from the Scouting Corps it would seem that they both have: *gone native*."

"They are still officers in the UWC Navy, Captain, and that does not disappear nonchalantly. Find a way and contact them. I am giving you total autonomy to do what you can to restore things and assess the situation. We need to cover ourselves. The damage has been done; let's see if we can fix some things now."

"Yes, Ma'am."

"Good, now I must go. I will call you with an update of my progress."

"We will be standing by, Ma'am."

"Ngo out." The screen shifted to the Seal of the UWC Navy and then disappeared. The screen went blank.

Facing Cho, Bucky said, "Commander Cho, I am ready to resume my duties as captain of the Orion."

Cho saluted him and said, "Command is yours, Captain."

Returning the salute, Bucky said, "Thank you, XO."

"Let's get Ambassador Gallagher up to the bridge, and then let's get a whole squad of Marines up here."

"Sir," Cho interrupted. "I have something I would like to do first." He nodded and then followed her to the door to the bridge. She opened the door and stepped onto the bridge saying, "Captain on deck!"

Everyone stood and saluted. Bucky returned the salute and said, "As you were. You will be the first to hear, I am now in command as per Admiral Ngo."

The crew on the bridge clapped and cheered at the news, with Commander Cho leading the way. "XO, if you would, please call a squad of Marines to the bridge and then summon Ambassador Gallagher." Spinning as he had so many times before, he faced the Lieutenant in charge of the comm and said, "Lieutenant Mutasi, get me whoever is in charge of the war room, stat."

"Aye, aye, Captain."

Bucky sat in his chair and said, "Yeoman, run to my cabin and pull out a blue uniform and jacket. Then run by the barber and ask him to report to my office when he can."

Bucky looked at the young man, who would probably enter the academy when the cruise concluded. He was waiting for Bucky to give him the usual nod to tell him he could go. The smile on his face was unmistakable, he was happy the captain was back and sitting on the bridge. Bucky nodded.

"Captain," Mutasi said from the comm. "I have Colonel Watkins on the line."

Bucky pressed the comm button on the panel next to his chair and said, "Colonel Watkins, this is Captain Dollinger. I am once again in command of the ship and I have complete authority. Bring 'em home. Do not delay, bring our troops home quickly. If one more soldier dies, heads will roll."

"Yes, Sir, Captain. Welcome back to the bridge."

"Thank you, Colonel. A little later I will come down there. I want statistics on what has been going on."

"I will have them ready, Sir."

"Dollinger out."

Cho was standing next to Bucky's chair and when he clicked off the comm, she said, "Sir, the Marines and Ambassador Gallagher are in route."

Taking a deep breath, Bucky sat back in his chair and relaxed. "Where are Lieutenant Williston and Sergeant Billings?"

"In their quarters, Sir. They refused a direct order on grounds of morality."

"I guess they were right, weren't they? I will personally go release them once Gallagher is in custody."

"They would appreciate that, Sir."

* * * *

Willy was half-asleep, leaning against the tree, relishing the silence and thanking God that he had made it out in time; it had been a close call. His squad, what was left of it, was within a few yards napping as well, when Quistqui ran over to him. "Willy," he said, kneeling down. "They're pulling back, and not just a little. I followed them down to the plains and the large birds you fly are dropping down and picking them up."

Sitting up, Willy said, "How long ago?"

"I ran straight here, informing Sydni on the way."

Willy took his scanner and summoned Remington, who was bedded down not far away. When Remington was standing next to him, he looked at Quistqui's scanner and said, "all the humans and Jolabwe?"

"Yes. All along the forest they are leaving."

"Okay, I am going to ride to the edge of the forest. Take my warriors and yours and meet me there."

Quistqui nodded, and as Willy mounted Remington, he opened a channel to Sydni. When Sydni replied, he said, "Hey, they're pulling out, and fast. I am on my way to investigate, want to meet me there?"

"Meet me," she said. "I am already in flight."

Willy laughed and urged Remington to take off. "On my way," he said before turning off his scanner.

As he broke through the upper canopy, the sun immediately warmed him, and he smiled. He could hear the sound of engines and he could see the vapor trails of the troop carriers flying in and staying far away from the forest. A majority of the weight that was on his chest started to lift.

Willy was feeling confident enough that he didn't even drop down through the canopy, he just flew into the area where the plain and the forest mixed and dropped down low. Using his scanner, he quickly located Sydni, sitting on her Brotu next to a large clump of trees. "They really are going," she said without looking at him.

"It looks that way," Willy replied. "Do you think our recording sent to the media had anything to do with it?"

"It was a strong piece with some heart-wrenching scans that would break the heart of any mother, not to mention your heart-felt plea at the beginning. Chambers' enemies will eat him alive with that hijacked call."

"We were just too late. We had the right idea all along, we were just too late."

"Yes, but look at the destruction they would have caused had we not acted when we did."

"Of course you are correct, sister."

"You should pay attention to me sometimes, bro."

Willy looked at Sydni and said, "You know, Syd, I never thanked you."

"For what?"

"Finding me."

"Finding you. What do you mean?"

"When I came back out to fight, I was in a blind rage, going and killing where I could and any way I could. There was a haze about me that I barely recognized who I was. But when I killed Vladimir and you were standing there, you brought me back in. I think I would have just continued to kill."

"You were exhausted and suffering a deep grief. I would have been the same way."

"I would have found you," Willy said.

"I know you would have, maybe even quicker than I found you."

"Thanks."

"You're welcome."

A squad of attack jets flew closer than any others, but were just paralleling the forest and showing no signs of aggression. "I think we should talk to the War Council about this. What do you think?"

"It would be a sound path to take. They need to be apprised of the situation." Sydni reached out for Willy's hand and as he took hers, she said, "I think we did it, Willy. Deep down I feel like this pullout is it. We are finally free to live our lives the way we want to."

"I can't go back," Willy said. "My life is here now."

"I know," Sydni whispered. "I feel the same way too, but I will have to discuss it with my husband. Our decisions were made under the assumption that there would be no going back. If this is truly an end to the war, maybe we will have freedom among Humans again."

Willy nodded and squeezed her hand. "Time will tell."

They let go of each other's hands and continued to watch the vapor trails. After a little while, Sydni looked over at him and said, "You know, we trained our warriors very well."

Without looking, Willy said, "I know, they can sneak up on almost anyone."

The ragged group of warriors walked out of the forest in varying places and times. Most of them looked tired and were slouching a little. Some of them had torn clothes and some were bloody from wounds they had received during the battle. Willy glanced at them and thought what he could do with a whole army of such warriors. He thought there was nothing they couldn't accomplish. He was as proud of them as he was of his scouting squad. For a moment he prayed that Tanya and Barkley were safe and alive.

Gallagher walked onto the bridge and looked at Cho, who was standing by the captain's chair and said, "Well, have you fixed the damn weapons, Captain?"

Cho smiled, which stopped Gallagher in mid-step. "Yes, Ambassador. As a matter of fact, we have fixed many things since you were up here ranting and raving. For starters, the weapons are in working order."

"Then give the order to fire," Gallagher nearly shouted as his face flushed.

"I am unable to give that order."

"What the hell? Are you refusing? Admiral Oats gave you direct orders, and as long as you are captain..."

Bucky's deep, commanding voice interrupted Gallagher, "Commander Cho is the XO on this ship, Ambassador." Gallagher's knees buckled, but he managed to remain standing. "Admiral Oats is no longer giving me orders, Admiral Ngo is giving orders." Bucky smiled, showing his gleaming white teeth in contrast to his stubble-covered face and longer than normal hair. "My first order is to have your ass thrown into my brig, where you are to be held until Admiral Ngo gets here with word of your future."

Gallagher's flushed face drained to white and he gasped for breath. "Y-you...can't. Chancellor Chambers won't..."

"I fancy the sight of you arriving to a penal colony. My suggestion would be to send you to a hard labor camp, where they send murderers." Bucky walked closer as he spoke. "They will know that you are a child killer, Gallagher. They will come to know that you killed many children." Leaning closer, Bucky asked in a whisper, "Do you know what they do to child killers in the penal colony? I hear it is not pleasant."

"You can't do this. You do not have authority over me!" Gallagher's shouts were an attempt to muster his own courage.

Bucky was unable to control himself for one brief moment; he lashed out and hit Gallagher square in the face, sending him sprawling backward across the deck. "That was for Willy's child. Admiral Ngo called for martial law out here, Gallagher, and that makes me the law." Bucky stood straight and adjusted his rumpled, dirty uniform and said, "Ambassador Gallagher, you are formally charged with murder, conspiracy, and treason. You are to be held in the brig until such a committee can be convened to consider what action is to be taken." Looking up, Bucky said, "Guard."

Bob walked out of the Captain's office trailing a full squad of guards carrying stun sticks. "Major, shackle this man and take him to the brig. If he even speaks out of turn, you have the authority to stun him and drag him there."

"Yes, sir." Bob's squad of guards knew what to do. Gallagher looked in horror at the cold, set faces of the Marines as they shackled him.

"Gallagher, where is Vladimir?"

It took several seconds for the question to sink in, but Gallagher finally said, "He went planetside to fight and I have not heard from him since."

"Good," Bucky said. "I would like you to post guards as the ships return with the troops, and when Vladimir returns, arrest him and anyone with him."

"A pleasure, Sir."

Looking at a Lieutenant, Bob said, "Proceed to the brig."

"Yes, Sir," the Lieutenant said.

Bucky walked down to the deck where most of the officers were bunked. He knew that as a scout, even Sergeant Billings shared a bunk down there.

Bucky had the guards posted call the scouts into the hall. As Tanya and Barkley stepped into the hall, one of the guards shouted, "Captain on deck!"

Out of habit, both Tanya and Barkley stood, saluted and looked. Bucky returned the salute and grinned. "Captain!" Tanya shouted.

"What happened?" Barkley said as they both rushed forward to greet Bucky.

"It is over. Your status is stricken from the record, you are back on active duty, and it is all over. Somehow, some way, Willy, Sydni, and Conrad rigged a satellite to broadcast information to the media back in the three worlds, which started an uproar. Admiral Oats is under arrest, Gallagher is under arrest, and I don't think Chambers will be free for long. The troops are on their way shipside and I have been ordered to strike a peace with the Hingandu people and reestablish communication with Willy and Sydni."

Both of the scouts breathed a sigh of relief. Bucky added, "Care to be assigned to the Captain again?"

Tanya stood straight and saluted, "Lieutenant Williston and the scouting squad reporting for duty, Sir."

"Get cleaned up. When you two are ready, come to the bridge and we will see what we can do."

* * * *

The fire in the council lodge burned bright, and the war council was present with the addition of Alar, who sat away from the others just to listen. Willy was pacing back and forth and had just finished his story of the Humans and Jolabwe pulling out. Douka threw a large branch on the fire and said, "So do you think this means an end to the war?"

Willy stopped long enough to look at him and then continued pacing. "I don't know, Douka. This is what I believe, but until I make contact with them, we will not be certain."

"What would you say our course of action should be?"

"I am of the belief that we pull our warriors back to rest, heal, and eat well. We can be prepared if they try again."

"And what of the weapon that destroys the land?"

"If they wanted to fire it again, they could have many times by now, destroying most of the forest. If I look at the facts then I believe that the war is over."

Douka nodded and looked into the faces of the other council members. "What do the others say to this?"

Shifting his legs, Watkil said, “Willy has not lead us down the wrong path yet, and I believe he and Sydni know more about Humans than we do. I say we take his recommendation.”

“I also agree,” said Klisk.

“Are there any who disagree?” Douka asked. He glanced at the faces again, and even paused at Alar, who simply nodded. “Then make it so. Bring the warriors in; send the others back to their villages with the knowledge that we may need them again soon. Leave patrols at the edge of the woods mounted on Brotu, and rotate them so everyone has much time in their own homes.”

The fire crackled in the silence. Then everyone started to disperse. Willy crouched opposite the fire from Douka, who had made no move to leave. As he stared into the fire, Douka asked, “Do you have something on your mind?”

“You mean besides the death of every Hingandu involved in this war?”

Shadows from the fire played across the deep creases in Douka’s face as he shook his head. “Willy of the Colton Clan, life is uncertain, and every moment should be savored and cherished. From all you have told me, maybe it is you who was to be our salvation, and you who stopped the Humans from destroying our whole world. Your heart is heavy. Much death has laid itself at your feet, but it was not your doing. Those that walk into the Hut of the Past will not believe that either.”

Willy sighed. “I am glad that you, Douka, see the good in me, for sometimes I think it is difficult to find. I will check at the Healing Center on two of my warriors, and then I will go back to the plains and keep watch for Humans or Jolabwe.”

Willy stood up to leave, but Douka spoke loudly. “No, Willy. I will not have that. You go see your warriors, so deep in their hearts they know that you care, then you go home to your family to start healing the wound this war has left on yours.” Willy moved to argue, but Douka slammed his staff down on the ground making a loud thump and said, “Do not disagree with me. You have fought long and hard for the Hingandu, as all Hingandu should for their people, but others have lost little compared to your family. Today you go rest and smile and laugh with your wife and son. Their hearts are heavy too and they need your guidance now more than we do.”

Bowing slightly, Willy said, “As you wish, Douka. I will send others to guard the forest.”

Outside the council hut, rays of brilliant sunshine intermingled with patches of darkness as a cloud passed over the sun. People were milling around, and Sydni, who was leaning against a nearby hut, said, “I have dispatched riders to patrol the edge of the plains and others to send the rest home.”

"Thank you. I have been ordered to go home after I check with the Healing Center."

"I will go with you, and then I too will return home."

They walked along in silence, and as they neared the Healing Center, they could see the mass of people waiting outside for news of their loved ones. Willy knew many, but many were just more faces that he did not recognize. However, walking up with Sydni at his side, people just seemed to step out of their way. At the door, the young apprentice healer recognized Willy and Sydni and asked if he could help.

"Bunth and Joknual were probably the last two warriors brought in here. Very serious. Do you know of their status?"

"I will be right back."

The healer disappeared down the hallway. They waited patiently at the door, looking at the mass of wounded within that overflowed into the hallways. The healer returned and said, "I am sorry to tell you, they have done all they could, but the man crushed by the tree did not make it, however, the other man is expected to fully recover."

Willy had known that Bunth would not make it, but he had hoped. The crushing injuries from the tree were just too much for his body to handle, yet the man he had drug out of the woods, saving him from the blast, would survive. Sydni put her hand on his shoulder and softly said, "Let's go home, Willy. Let's go home."

They walked quietly through the streets, nodding or saying hello to people they knew as they passed, but the overall feeling throughout the village was somber. It was a long walk home for Willy and Sydni. Their house was a comfort, and Dekonal met Willy just inside the front door. Without a word, he engulfed her in a hug and held her as Sydni walked upstairs.

Conrad was standing with one foot on his chair, his elbow on his knee, and the computer was quietly repeating a message. Sydni dropped her pack in the doorway and set her rifle against it. She was standing next to Conrad as he turned to face her, and then she moved up against him as he put an arm around her.

She listened to the message. "Willy and Sydni Colton, this is Captain Bucky Dollinger of the UWC Orion. Things have changed. I am in command and your scans and copies of conversations have turned the tables. Contact me; we need to talk." The message began repeating itself.

Conrad could feel Sydni sigh and almost sag against him. "Is it true?" she asked in a whisper.

Rubbing her arm, he said, "I believe it to be true, love. I have been waiting to hear from you and Willy before we respond." He kissed her forehead and asked, "Is it true that the Marines are pulling back?"

"Yes," she said, nodding. "They are probably almost all gone."

"Maybe it is over," he said almost absent-mindedly.

Willy walked down the hall carrying Dekonal and stopped long enough to listen to the recording. They looked at Willy and when the loop started again he shook his head. "I think we all need some time away from it all. Turn it off and ignore it."

Sydni gave him a questioning glance that he had seen all his life, and he answered before she could ask. "Douka told me that my family needed me and we needed time to heal. Bucky has been and maybe again shall be my friend, but right now the Colton Clan needs time to be whole again."

He looked into their eyes until Conrad looked down at Sydni and said, "He is a wise man, that Douka. I can't say that a little time to tend to family needs would hurt things."

"Agreed," Sydni whispered.

"I will talk with you soon," Willy said, "and we can figure out what to do." He carried Dekonal into their room and shut the door.

Reaching over to the keyboard, Conrad turned off the looping message. "Come on, my love. I say we take their lead and ignore that message. I have not been able to sleep in days." He pulled her closer and kissed her. Shifting, he continued to kiss her until he scooped her up in his arms.

As he started heading to their bedroom, Sydni talked past his lips on hers, saying, "Maybe you are right."

* * * *

Moonlight broke the darkness of the room, lighting a patch on the bed and floor. The world was quiet again since Jean-Pierre was quelled by the soft singing of his father from the other room. Sydni had never thought of her brother as having a pretty voice, but the song, full of love for his son, convinced her. She knew Conrad was awake, by the sound of his breathing and the lazy movements of his hand against her bare shoulder.

As a whisper of a breeze shifted the curtains at the window, Sydni whispered, "Conrad, I have to ask you a question."

"What?" he whispered in return.

"If the war is over and they call to reinstate us to duty, what do you want to do?"

"Be with you."

Sydni smiled and rubbed his stomach. "And I with you, sweetheart, and I with you. But where? Back aboard the Orion? Down here on the planet? Where?"

"You know, had you asked me months ago, I would have insisted on living aboard the Orion. Over time I have grown to love this place. Our home." He paused after he said it. "I have made friends, and we probably have more friends than I had shipside. Most important of all, I no longer have the fear of open spaces as I once had."

"You would stay here?" Sydni whispered half as a question and half out of surprise.

"If you want to go shipside if we can, I will go. If you want to stay here, I will stay. I have learned that I can be happy anywhere."

"We need to make the choice." She took his hand and kissed the back of it. "I do not want to make the choice alone. I want us to make a choice that will make us both happy."

Sliding out from under her, Conrad twisted to his side where he could see her face. She turned a little to face him, propping her head up on her hand. Conrad reached out and slid a lock of hair out of her face and said, "What will make you happy? Can you, after what you have seen, go back and live under the UWC rule or shipside?" He looked down, and she knew there was something more he wanted to say, so she waited. "Maybe I am a coward, and running away made me not want to face them anymore, but I don't know that I can go back."

"No," Sydni said. "That does not make you a coward. You did what you believed in, and that does not make you a coward, but a brave man. Leaving the ship was not running away."

Conrad breathed deeply and smiled. Sydni ran her fingers through the graying hair on the side of his head that was accented by the shifting moonlight. "I think I have found a freedom here that I never have known before. I have found out how to live alone and in open spaces. But most importantly, I have found a family here. I guess deep down, I want to stay, but have been afraid to admit it."

Sydni's heart jumped at his words and there was no way she could suppress her smile. Leaning forward, she nearly growled, "You don't know how happy you just made me." Then spontaneously burst into laughter before she could cover her mouth and suppress it.

"What was that for?"

She got up and faced him, resting on her knees and sitting back on her heels. "Don't you see? We were accepted into this tribe of people months ago and we considered ourselves Hingandu. That is who we are. I already know Willy will never go back. He may never again step foot aboard a star cruiser class ship." She started to speak, yawned instead and smiled again. "Tomorrow I shall tell my brother that my Hingandu mate and I plan to stay planetside."

Conrad laughed, but not as loudly as Sydni had. "Next must I learn to hunt?"

Sydni felt giddy and she giggled at the thought of Conrad hunting. "You must not do anything other than be Conrad Singh to make me happy."

Sitting up, Conrad grabbed her waist and kissed her. "Do you forget," he said, smacking his chest. "I am Conrad of the Colton Clan."

Sydni pealed out in laughter again and then said, "Look, Conrad of the Colton Clan. Your wife needs some water. So you sit back and relax. I will be right back."

Conrad sat back, propping himself up against the wall. "I will patiently await your return."

Sydni was chuckling as she stood up and walked to the wardrobe-closet and grabbed a kimono-like robe that was given to her on her wedding day by Dekonal. She wrapped herself in it and tied the sash before she headed downstairs.

The house was open and the warm breeze flowed through the house as if it were breathing. Sydni herself, although exhausted, was at the same time exhilarated. She paused in the kitchen as she heard a faint voice coming in with the breeze. She stepped up to the back door and looked out. In the center of the courtyard, where there was a grassy patch, Willy sat with Jean-Pierre. Jean-Pierre struggled to keep his balance as he sat up and waved his arms. His tiny laugh moved through the air with his father's voice. Willy was singing again.

Sydni didn't know how long she stood staring out at them playing, but her already full heart spilled over and tears trickled down her face. She had overheard Willy's conversation with Douka, and Willy was following the sage advice. The door opened and closed silently as Sydni went outside and headed toward Willy and Jean-Pierre.

She knelt next to Willy and his song faded away. "I didn't hear you go outside," Sydni whispered.

Jean-Pierre interjected with a gurgle and a laugh.

"I heard you and Conrad laughing, though," Willy said smiling at her. "It was beautiful. As leader of this clan, it makes me very happy to have laughter in our house."

"I might as well tell you this now, brother. We have decided where we want to live if the UWC wants to take us back and restore our responsibilities."

Willy's smile disappeared more at his sister's tone than her words. "Where?" he asked, his voice reverting to his deep somber tone.

"My Hingandu husband and I want to stay right here, where we belong. Our family, friends, and home are all here. We will stay regardless."

Reaching out, Willy hugged his sister and held her for a long time. When he released her, she asked, "What are you doing outside at this hour?"

Motioning toward Jean-Pierre, Willy said, "He was restless, and after I soothed him, he wouldn't go back to sleep."

"Like father like son?" Sydni questioned.

"It would seem so."

"Well, I will leave you two out here to play. Just don't go into the woods without letting us know."

The comment about Willy's childhood was obvious, and he looked at her and smiled. "I hope I give him all the right reasons to want to stay." He reached over and picked up Jean-Pierre, who had stretched out his arms. His next sentence was barely a whisper, "Could you imagine what they would have been like together?"

Sydni heard him and forced herself to stop the tears welling up in her eyes. "I can. They would have been like us."

* * * *

Willy and Sydni brought the war council to their home and translated the message for them, asking what they should do. When they were told that they knew best, Willy answered, "We are Hingandu now, those are not our people. We did not want to make a decision for all the people by ourselves." Douka had smiled at the answer. The council decided to speak with them, but only after they could discuss it with a full council meeting of the Hingandu. Conrad was authorized to send a quick typed message that read: "The Hingandu people will speak to you when the council decides on what to say. Willy, Sydni, and Conrad are alive."

The repeating message stopped when Conrad sent out their reply. Bucky stood at the comm desk on the bridge, trying for an hour to raise Willy, Sydni or Conrad, but all he did was make his voice hoarse. They were not listening. A council meeting had been set to take place in several days, when they could gather the required leaders.

After sending the message to the ship, Conrad had made a comment that back on Earth it was the day before Thanksgiving. Sydni had always loved Thanksgiving, so Willy suggested that they have a large family gathering at their table to celebrate and the idea was set.

That afternoon Willy, Sydni, and Doqui set out to hunt while Dekonal, Nurian, and Conrad started cooking in the kitchen to prepare some other foods. Quistqui was out with his squad patrolling the border, but he would be able to be free for the meal on the following day.

Doqui and Sydni had each taken a Saka just before dusk. They carried them back to the village in the darkness, singing a hunting song Doqui was trying to teach them, but they laughed more than sang.

The meal was prepared and on the table at midday. Willy took the seat on the far end of the table from the kitchen while Dekonal sat on the end closest to the kitchen. Madak came in with the assistance of Doqui and Chakdon. Quistqui and Nurian were also present, and Curtia, the woman that Doqui liked came as well, bringing a bowl of red Gombo fruit.

Steam rose from the warm food as Dekonal and Nurian sat down, and Willy stood up and looked around the table. Quistqui was bouncing Jean-Pierre on his knee, and everyone looked up at Willy. "I want to thank you for being here today. Although we are now Hingandu, there are some traditions from my home that Sydni, Conrad, and I would like to hold onto. This day would normally be known as a day of giving thanks to God." He paused and looked around the room again. "This day, I have more reasons than ever to give thanks. I think most of my reasons are evident; my new family and my extended family. After all that has happened, I am thankful that we can all be sitting here this day to share a meal. I am thankful that this war is over and we can start living and enjoying life." Motioning toward the food, he laughed and said, "Now I will shut up before the food starts getting cold so we can eat."

Laughter filled the room, and Willy was especially happy to hear Madak laughing. Her wounds were far from healed, but she had insisted on coming. Her dress was pinned up so her bandaged-covered stump was showing. Willy could see the pain in her eyes mixed with the joy of seeing her family around her. Every once in a while during dinner she would look at Jean-Pierre, who went from family member to family member, and her eyes would well up. He knew she would always feel responsible, even though the responsible parties had paid or would pay eventually.

After the meal, Doqui went to the back door and picked up his pack. He brought in a package wrapped in the hide of a Muntaka. Willy opened it up and found three pouches made of Muntaka hide attached to straps. The pouches were adorned with a small-embroidered bird on either side. "Curtia made the pouches. I stopped at the funeral pyre after Chakdall's death and each pouch contains a portion of ashes. I thought that you, Dekonal, and Jean-Pierre would want this reminder."

Doqui glanced back and forth between Willy and Dekonal. Willy reached out and grabbed the back of Doqui's neck, saying, "I knew that you were a good hunter when I accepted you as a guerrilla warrior, and you have proven yourself more than most men with more experience. I knew you had a good heart from the day I met you, but you are wise beyond your years, I shall cherish this forever."

Dekonal looked at the pouches, and then, as Willy let go of him, she kissed his cheek and hugged him. Willy looked at Curtia and said, "Your kindness is remarkable and I will remember you always."

Curtia blushed and looked down. "Thank you," she said.

"Yes," Dekonal said, still holding Doqui. "Thank you, Curtia. They are beautiful, and you, you little sneak." Tears streamed down Dekonal's face. "In my time of pain, you found a way to brighten my heart. Thank you."

"Okay, okay," Doqui said. He kissed his sister's cheek and patted Willy's shoulder. "I was happy I could do it."

Chakdon took Jean-Pierre from Nurian and carried him over to Madak. "Come see your grandmother, boy." He sat next to Madak and said, "Here, my love, he wants to be held by his grandmother."

"No," she said shaking her head. "I cannot."

"You can and you should."

Moving her stump, she just whispered, "I cannot. I should not."

Willy moved away from the chatter of Dekonal, Nurian, and Curtia and moved over to the opposite side of the Madak. He crouched down and lightly touched her hand. She looked into his eyes, and hers were on the brink of tears. "Madak. You have been more of a mother to me in my short time here, than I ever felt my mother was, although I know she tried. I cannot live with your pain. I know that deep down, you believe that what happened to Chakdall is your fault. We have spoken about this before." Taking her hand in his, he continued, "You have so much love to give, and Jean-Pierre will need twice as much love. You can give him more with one arm than most people can with two."

Turning and shifting in her seat, Madak nodded and reached for Jean-Pierre. Chakdon gently lifted Jean-Pierre into her arm. She cooed at him, kissed him, and slowly began to rock him.

Willy stood up, glancing at Chakkdon, who mouthed, "Thank you." Willy nodded.

The day wore on with the group moving outside into the warm afternoon. Not too long after they moved outside, Madak was taken home and put to bed so she could rest. Chakdon stayed with her, but Doqui returned to the group.

After a round of leftovers, Doqui and Curtia left for a walk, and Quistqui and Nurian were next to leave. After a while, Willy and Sydni were left outside alone looking up at the stars. They could see the Orion moving across the sky and Willy asked, "Do you think you will miss it?"

"A little. If you had asked me months ago, I would have never believed that I could be so happy settled down, married, and living planetside without any UWC facilities."

Willy laughed. "Had you asked me, I would never have thought this was the type of life I would lead either."

"What do we do about sending Mom and Dad a Christmas card?"

They both laughed out loud for a long time, until their sides ached, unknowing that inside, upstairs, Conrad, Dekonal and Jean-Pierre were listening to them laugh. Even across the courtyard, Chakdon was smiling at the faint sound.

Looking at Sydni, Willy said, "Maybe this discovery will give them some kind of peace. Maybe they will be able to rest, finally."

Sydni looked at him and then away, saying, "No."

"What?"

"Maybe they would come here someday."

Willy smiled at the thought. He wished his parents could finally accept him. Maybe they would someday. Maybe all the media exposure would help. "Dad will hate the media. They won't leave him alone."

Sydni smiled and reached over and squeezed his arm. "As long as everyone leaves us alone now."

"They will; the UWC will not let anyone near this place now. Not after all that has happened."

* * * *

Early in the morning, before anyone else was awake, Dekonal woke Willy up and said, "Yesterday was your day of giving thanks. Let a new tradition begin, of our day of giving thanks."

Willy harnessed Remington, who he had called into the courtyard as Dekonal dressed Jean-Pierre. Then she packed some fruit and leftovers for breakfast. Before long they were airborne, watching the dawn begin. The sun was shining in streaks across the sky and landing in patches on the trees and in the rolling hills.

Shortly after arriving, Dekonal stood in her usual place to pray; Willy was at her side, holding Jean-Pierre. Dekonal started to sing, and part way into her song, Willy joined her, their voices mixing in harmony.

Printed in the United States
136499LV00004B/2/P

9 780595 469048